OF EARTH AND SKY

SKY

E.M. PETERSON

CHAPTER ONE: NIKKI

O nly this Conjuring Master could take the fun out of Matter Intention. Grell has surveyed the sixteen amateur conjuring league recruits for at least two minutes, and has yet to give any sign she finds our existence remotely interesting.

Orella looms beyond the dilapidated wooden bleachers flanking the training ground's east end. The top of Archbridge catches the morning sun, as the fog lifting off the city's slate rooftops promises one of the first hot days of spring. Sweat trickles down the back of my neck.

"I see a lot of green as spring buds, would-be arena combatants here," Grell says. She's in her sixties, and gives the impression of delivering orders even in normal conversation. "That's fine. But I've been at this long enough to know that most people who come through here aren't fit to enter the arena as so much as spectators. Only those already possessing talent with Matter will succeed. That's the steel, the raw material. And I'm going to hammer the hell out of you to turn that steel into a fine blade."

I don't recognize any of the nervous faces around me. These are not graduates of Orella Academy, the prestigious private school I attended, where future leaders of Terraltum learn to rule through the five magical schools of Intention and the art of politics.

One of the boys, with a rough-spun tunic and muddy boots—sure marks of someone from the Long Bank slums—whispers something to the girl next to him. She fails to suppress a laugh.

"You find my imagery funny, boy?" Grell snaps.

"A little," the Long Bank boy says. "I feel like we'd be fine without this three-act tough military commander show. We're just here to learn conjuring."

"Your name, what is it?"

"Stevven."

"Of course it is," Grell says. "If there ever was a face that earned the name Stevven, it's yours. Well, Stevven, you should know that if I come across as a military commander, I do so honestly. I fought with the Natantis army as Principal Conjurer in Barrun's War, leading a hit squad of conjuring disruptors. Two groups served the disruptor function in the war, conjurers and platoons of Kelluvan werebeasts. We were equally effective."

"That's not exactly a favorable comparison," I blurt, unable to stop the reflexive response to someone who was on the wrong side of the war. Grell eyes me darkly. Stevven's smirk suggests I've now martyred myself in his place.

"The war was long ago," Grell says. "There were many actions taken, on all sides, that have been the source of regret and atonement." Why can't I keep my Laputa-loyal mouth shut? Day one of my life as a conjurer, and I've already ticked off the one person with the most direct control over my fate.

"Apologies, I didn't mean to cast doubt on your motives. War requires a great deal that would be unthinkable during peacetime."

Grell studies my face.

"You're a conjurer, Nikki Laputa?" Whispers ripple through the group as Grell motions for me to step forward.

She continues, "Then I presume you're familiar with the rules of a one-on-one duel?"

"I'm assuming you mean to incapacitation, not death?"

"Precisely. As a demonstration, I want you to face me in a friendly duel. I think it will be instructive."

If this is the punishment she's devised, then I'm not about to back away.

"Shall we begin?" I say.

Grell stands with feet apart, and invites me to make the first move.

I pull my focus in through my breath. A presence waits to be born on the muddy surface of the training ground. It's as if it's always existed. All it needs is a tiny push into being. A little Intention.

I shout, thrust my hands forward, and a hulking beast appears in the space between us. My conjured chimera is a mass of black fur and rippling muscle, cat-like in form but the size of a tram car. Grell stares at the creature impassively as it snarls, preparing to spring at her. It's a bigger creature than I'm able to conjure easily, and I hope she doesn't notice that its edges lack definition.

Grell's conjuring is like a conductor leading a symphony. Three gentle, precise motions of one hand, and all hell breaks loose in orchestrated rhythm.

A half dozen oblong objects materialize under my chimera's paws, knocking it off balance.

A creature with the body of a monkey and arms ending in spinning metal points sits atop my cat's head, preparing to drive them into its skull.

And three tall figures with ghostly bodies surround me. Their faces yawn with chasms made of all teeth and no eyes, as a stench I can only describe as horror itself fills the field.

My chimera forgotten, I crumble to my knees, overcome with dread at what Grell has conjured. All my Intention has been sucked out of me.

It's over in three seconds. My beast stumbles to the ground with the point of the monkey chimera's arm in its brain, and I cower beneath a shroud of terror, which now gives off a piercing scream.

As quickly as they started, the conjurations are gone, and the only sound is the wind on the grass.

Grell pulls me roughly to my feet, her expression stern, though not unkind.

"You have some skill in the School of Matter," she says. "You might even have the raw materials. But remember, effective conjuring is not about overwhelming your opponent with pure power. Effective conjuring is about striking with deadly precision."

I try to compose myself as I bend to wipe the mud from my knees, but I'm shivering like I've been out in a cold rain. I try to shake loose the horror of Grell's illusions, but their screams and smell stick with me, even when I manage to rid my mind of their teeth-filled faces.

With a moment to think, I realize that Grell's demonstration went beyond power or rhythm. She effectively employed all three sub-schools of Matter: chimeral, physical, and illusory. There's a reason she's Conjuring Master.

Lessons with Grell are thankfully about more than beating up on her students. When we pair up for exercises, Stevven comes right up to me.

"That was a hell of a beast you whipped up," he says. "A little small by my standards, but not bad for an Orella Academy brat. Partners?"

"Sure, as long as you're okay with repeatedly getting your ass kicked."

He has a swagger in his shoulders that I find both amusing and sort of charming.

"That's actually the main thing I look for in a partner."

"Sounds like the start of a lasting and mutually beneficial arrangement."

"I hope you know I'm not gonna go easy on you."

"Believe me," I say, "I'm having a panic attack just picturing your conjuring prowess. I've actually gone ahead and preemptively pissed my pants to be on the safe side."

"Glad we're on the same page then," Stevven says, shaking my hand.

Most of the practice exercises consist of reacting to our partner. One quick chimera or illusion, one quick counter move. Switch people and repeat. Stevven conjures a bird that shrieks toward me, I conjure a net of vines to ensnare it. He conjures burrowing moles, I conjure a gelatinous blob that fills the hole and drowns the poor creatures.

Stevven and I are evidently the most advanced. These conjurers come from all over—a couple from the countryside where the usual options are farming or crewing one of the massive barges carrying goods up the Rhydwel, a few squandering a middle-class Orellian inheritance, and several like Stevven, from the Long Bank slums. All have come with dreams like mine, and most will have those dreams crushed. Intention is a fickle force, especially when

5

it comes to creating temporary life. All of your focus needs to be in the moment, which becomes harder and harder the longer you do it. It doesn't help that Grell stalks behind us, barking insults: "If you did that on the battlefield you'd be turned into a human pancake," "I understand this is difficult for you, but your lack of effort is an insult to me and everyone who's ever conjured." My personal favorite is: "Did you conjure that thing, or dig it out of the back room of Big Tom's Emporium of Useless Creations?" I have no idea who in the name of Earth and Sky Big Tom is, but I do now know exactly the kind of person I want to be when I'm Grell's age.

"I think we had an okay first day," Grell says at the end of practice, when I'm so drained I can barely stay on my feet. "Take a second to notice the air. Do you feel the Intention we've brought to this place?" My attention floats far away, but I do feel it, that unmistakable hum that follows acts of magic. "On the contestants' stand in the Conjuring Arena, this never dissipates. The conjuring that has gone before you leaves traces in the space, ghosts of greatness, of failure, of victory and defeat. You are here to live up to that legacy. Only those who can do so will be allowed to continue, for the arena is a sacred place. I will not allow it to be profaned with the Intention of the unworthy."

As she dismisses us, she keeps two conjurers behind. We all know what this means, and the rest of us hurry away, allowing them to face their humiliation in private.

Most of us take the tram back into the city together, but I sit at the opposite end of the car. I have three precious hours to rest before my night shift at the Sky Engines.

Just when I'm almost able to drift off, though, Stevven scoots into the seat next to me. He has a rakish smile on his face, which I wonder if he's ever without.

"Nikki Laputa," he begins. I almost respond *oh no* aloud. "I'm curious, what do you have to do to fall so far out of the matriarch and patriarch of House Laputa's favor to end up slumming it with wannabe conjurers like us?"

"Don't worry," I reply, "the only reason I've fallen out of their favor is the slumming."

"Rebellious. A chance to annoy your parents."

"It's almost comical how wrong you are. But why are you doing this? You've got Long Bank written all over you, this is hardly steady work."

Though the smile remains, I can tell he's completely serious. "I have four siblings, no mother, and a father who shows up whenever he feels like it. I also happen to be blessed with substantial skill in Matter, as you saw. With a little luck we could leave Long Bank behind for good."

"You also happen to have a boatload of modesty too, don't forget that."

"Modesty is a luxury you can't afford where I'm from," he says. "I'll let you and the other 'Great Families' keep your fake humility. It's nothing more than a mask for your hunger for power."

"Most people are hungry for power," I say. "Some people just luck into more of it than others. Luck doesn't care whether they asked for it or not."

Stevven eyes me shrewdly. "You didn't answer my original question."

"How far I've fallen?"

"My real question. Why you're here."

The glide of the tram pulling out of Terminus Station turns the first cramped houses of Long Bank into a blur around us. This is a question I've never had a good answer for, despite how much I've sacrificed to be here. The answer sounds as insufficient when I say it as it always does. That doesn't make it any less true.

"I'm here because I couldn't imagine doing anything else."

CHAPTER TWO: JAMIE

We pick up the jojum trail close to a mile out. It runs past a stand of pines and over a bed of thick moss. Paolo crouches over the faint trail, which is little more than a glimmer between dead leaves and new ferns, and immediately strikes me as other-worldly.

"Looks to be a whole tribe of them, by the wear pattern," Paolo says.

We follow the trail as it winds deeper into the woods, taking a circuitous route around the bases of trees, disappearing in areas of lighter ground cover, but obviously moving west overall.

"Jojum are incredibly rule-oriented creatures," Paolo says. "According to their laws they can only pass on the south side of trees older than eighty-seven."

"Eighty-seven?"

"In their number system, that's the ultimate triangular number. Don't ask me to do jojum math. Our minds can't grasp even their basic arithmetic." And I already struggle with Algebra.

I can always feel the change that comes with arriving in our magical pocket of forest even before my foot hits the last step getting off the bus. The backpack filled with Physics and Colonial American History textbooks lightens, and the air of the bus, thick with the smell of middle- and high-schoolers in varying stages of deodorant adoption, melts away. At the end of my gravel driveway the world of school—of what most would consider normal life—is already far behind.

Tracking the jojum is easy enough, if I take my time. My trilopex, Wesley, has rejoined us after finding some early spring berries. He ambles along the trail, rolling over it at points, finding endless amusement in how the jojum's dust turns his usually gray-blue fur into a miniature lightshow.

I almost mistook you for a jojum, you're sparkling so much, I think to Wesley.

I've been called worse, his thoughts reply. *If I recall correctly, this morning Paolo referred to me as your "pet."*

The slander.

One day that bearded galoot is going to push me too far. Wesley stares down Paolo who, unconcerned, has stopped to investigate a pattern in the bark on one of the evergreens. Paolo fills whatever space he's in with a bouncing energy and his stocky frame, and has a tendency to poke the easiest button, which is in this case Wesley's disproportionately sized ego. Wesley's no bigger than a mouse, though he lacks a tail and usually stands on his hind legs unless he's using all six of his legs to run.

It's April, and in the shadiest parts of the forest the last of the snow has finally melted, leaving a half-decomposed bed of leaves and pine needles smelling of autumn and winter at once.

I attune myself to the emotions in the forest around me. A woodpecker happily smashes his beak against a tree. His thoughts *clack* in rhythm to the strikes. They're gentle, content in the way only the thoughts of animals functioning instinctually can be. The squirrels in the branches above him are slightly more complex, one complaining to the other of a fellow squirrel who doesn't fight fair, the other lamenting forgetting where she stashed one of her stores of nuts.

I point out different plants and fungi as we pass them. There are ordinary ones like skunk cabbage, mayapple, hen-of-the-woods, wild violet, and pokeweed. Then there are less ordinary ones. I rattle off *turpentina* and *hypatia carnivora* before being stumped by *witchflower*.

"*Witchflower* is difficult to see," Paolo explains. "Someone without Intention might stumble over it or even pass right through it."

"Pass through it?"

"Some people think the only things that are real are the things they can see. In a sense—and only in some cases, mind you—they're right."

As we near a clearing, Paolo steps in front again. He points ahead, and I see twenty or so pale shapes in the brush. They're fragile creatures, humanoid, but with elongated limbs. About three inches tall at most. They wear flowing gray robes, and most shoulder wooden spears. The single-file line has stopped as the tallest jojum consults a map.

"Bah, Cornelius always mucks up the route. Who decided to promote that scrawny waif to head scout?"

"Bet it had nothing to do with his father being chief," a female jojum says behind him.

The leader's laugh sounds roughly like a cat coughing up a particularly resilient hairball.

"Nepotism does have its perks. If I were the boy's father, I'd sooner set him on squirrel duty than promote him."

"I'm sure he'd find a way to get eaten."

"Friends," Paolo says. Twenty heads turn as one. Nervous calls of "human" fly through the ranks. "We greet you in peace. May your limbs grow long and your ears straight."

"We welcome you in peace," the leader says, breaking out of the line to approach Paolo and rubbing his pointy ears. "May your wings never sprout."

"I don't think there's any danger there," Paolo replies with a chuckle. He mimics the leader's gesture, rubbing his substantial ears. "I am Paolo Swift, and this is my adopted son, Jamie Monroe." My stomach always twists when he introduces me like this. Adopted. As in, not his real son. But I maintain the presence of mind to rub my ears in the direction of the lead jojum, hoping it's appropriately formal.

"Pleased to make your acquaintance, Master Swift. I am Reginald Aquarius IV, Captain of Chief Archibald Libra XIII. You and your..." he scrutinizes me, as if not thoroughly convinced of my presence "... boy are known to us."

"I hope the tribe of Archibald Libra XIII has a positive impression?"

Reginald's eyes continue to blaze at me. They're shockingly blue, and his pale skin only makes them seem to glow brighter. Wesley takes a protective step between me and Reginald.

"We do not reserve positive feelings for humans, as a rule, but your actions as peacekeeper during our war with tribe Pisces have not been forgotten. That debt has still not been repaid, if my reckoning is correct."

"Diplomacy benefits everyone."

Reginald's eyes don't leave me. "Indeed. Does the boy speak?"

"Only when necessary," I say. "You learn a lot more by listening."

Satisfied, Reginald moves on to other business.

"Master Swift, we were actually going to dispatch a messenger to you from our new village site. Three nights ago, a werebeast killed one of our scouts."

"A werebeast?" Concern darkens Paolo's features.

"They've come back, apparently. And to a protected region too."

The air in front of me grows clammy with the anxiety of the tribe. I am not honed to their individual emotions the way I might be with less intelligent animals, but their collective angst laps over me without me having to search for it.

"Thank you for bringing this to my attention," Paolo says. The change in demeanor is immediate. "I will consult with my contact and determine how to proceed. Can I assist your tribe in any way?"

"The jojum do not take aid from humans." He pounds on his chest twice, and his comrades do the same. "But your generosity has been noted." He seems bitter to acknowledge that fact. What an odd, proud creature.

"We will leave you to your travels," Paolo says. "May the light never leave you."

Reginald bows his head. "May your shadow always fall on soft ground."

We watch as the tiny creatures hurry off into the brush.

Paolo turns to me. The sun is still an hour from setting, but all light has rushed out of the day.

"Are all jojum this strange?" I say to break the silence.

"Yes." Paolo chews on the inside of his cheek. "Strange, xenophobic, spiteful, and a little rude by our standards. But there is a certain nobility in their refusal to live by any rule beside their own."

"I could feel the fear coming off them." I can still feel it hanging like a cold afternoon shadow over the clearing.

"They have a lot to fear."

"A werebeast?" I ask.

"Not your run-of-the-mill magical creature. Werebeasts are rarely born. They must be created. Come on, we should return home."

I follow, apprehension growing inside me.

"Who would do that?" I say.

"You should know that not all forces out there are as benign as the ones in our forest. There are all sorts of banished Skyfolk here on the surface. But the amount of power such dark Organic and Pure Intention requires shouldn't be available to anyone down here."

"Does this mean you're leaving?"

If he leaves on urgent business, he won't let me have anything to do with it. Even when he has visitors—strange men and women who seem to materialize out of nowhere and meet over strong coffee or brandy in our living room—he keeps me at arm's length, insisting the meetings are no more relevant to me than it would be if he were a stockbroker or a graphic designer.

"Maybe. Probably, yes."

"Can I come with you this time?"

We're at the edge of our clearing, the low side porch of the house visible through the branches. A few weeks from now, the buds will become true leaves. I'm so used to it that I don't always notice, but now my eyes catch on the way Paolo's presence seems to flow continuously into the woods around him. He gives the impression of being able to disappear at any moment amid the trees. His Organic Intention is not something I've ever been able to replicate.

"You know you can't," he says. "This is my job, the reason I'm down here in the first place, and I'll need to move quickly. It isn't the sort of thing where I can teach you as I go along, as much as I'd like to. It could be nothing, and you've got school to worry about."

I nod, but I know from the way his smile flickers that it's not nothing.

"Besides, you've still got some training left to do," Paolo says.

"I spent the whole trip out there tapped into animals' emotions," I say.

"That's easy for you. Come on, just half an hour. Dig a little deeper."

I sigh. Wesley darts over to Paolo, as if to visually drive home the point that he's on Paolo's side.

"Fine." I let them go back to the house without me, taking up my usual spot against the trunk of the tallest tree within view of the house.

I breathe in and out, eyes closed. I sense the squirrels skittering above me, the insects in the grass under my hands. My power is in the Mind school of Intention, so it's not unusual that I can feel the emotions around me. I can even feel the residue of Paolo's worry and Wesley's desire for a nap as they make their way across the yard. Paolo has done his best to tell me what Intention is, but I know it's hard for him to put into words. Growing up on Terraltum, he was steeped in magic from an early age, so everything about it is second nature. I've never so much as seen the floating continent.

Paolo did manage to teach me about what makes me unusual, though. Most people will specialize in two of the five schools. You might have someone who can conjure powerful creatures as they do in the Matter school, or understand the workings of Intention-powered machines like acolytes of the Pure school. Or you might be like Paolo with his understanding of Organic, and ability to manipulate the elements with Elemental. But unlike most people from Terraltum, I can't manage anything other than Mind Intention. Paolo has tried to teach me skills from the other schools, so much so that we used to fight about it. But no matter what, I can't conjure the smallest creature, or make the smallest spark to start a fire.

I'm so distracted by the jojum's warning that it takes me close to twenty minutes to lock back into the emotional web of the forest. This is beyond reading individual emotions, which I usually have to bounce between. If I can relax my Intention and spread it wide, I can reach a state where I take in all the forest's emotions at once. It's a tapestry of wanting and instinctive movement, of daily rhythms and their interruptions. I let myself bleed into it, becoming part of that emotional flow.

When I finally snap out of it, it is getting dark, and it has been far more than thirty minutes.

I don't know if it's because of the effort of my training, or the lingering sense of dread, but that night my dreams are more watery than usual, lacking their usual stability and logic:

I am a coiled spring. I am a rubber band stretched too far. I am a temper already pushed to the brink. But I am also calm, projecting none of my internal anxiety. The hand on my shoulder reminds me I am not alone. And that I couldn't be alone if I wanted to.

The voice behind me speaks with depth and surety: "The day is almost here."

CHAPTER THREE: NIKKI

Night has long since fallen over the Eastbridge Docks as I make my way to my first shift at the Sky Engines. Rutted avenues wide enough for Intention-powered wagons now lie empty, dust settling in drifts against walls, buckets, and stray hydraulic lifts. The last boats finishing their journey up the Rhydwel have already had their contents emptied into rows upon rows of warehouses. My footsteps are an intruding echo against gray warehouse walls.

Through a gap in the uniform buildings I can see to the other side of Orella, where light blooms from my family's estate on the twisted spire of Hornhill. Where I should be.

Anxiety creeps through me, not just about the uncertain task ahead, or even a stray mugger stepping out from behind a grain barrel with a knife or a blast of Elemental Intention, but at the thought that I am so clearly out of my depth, displaced half a city away from the one I grew up in.

Get it together, Nikki. You chose this, and the Winged Ones know backing down isn't in your repertoire.

The only sign that this warehouse is any different from those around it is a pair of rusting automatons guarding the entrance, who eye me silently as I enter. A young guard mans the front desk.

It has the word *Security* scrawled unconvincingly across its wood front in fading black letters. Seeing me breaks the guard out of his obvious boredom, and he scrambles to sign me in on a decaying guest register, mumbling something about getting me permanent credentials. He says he hopes they'll be to my liking, given my prestigious heritage. I can't tell if this is an insult or not.

Lining the long hallway past the security guard are portraits of well-dressed, bearded men. The plaques beneath identify them as previous Enginemasters. As I move down the hallway and the portraits become more recent, I notice the men's clothes becoming less and less fine, epaulets that could've belonged to an admiral transitioning to leather shoulder pads, and eventually disappearing into formal but threadbare jackets. The sound of the engines, which had been a faint hum in the entry room, grows into a distinct chugging and clanging, until I open the door at the end of the hall and am engulfed in a cacophony.

I waver at the threshold, taking in the hall's expanse. A dozen passages weave off in all directions, while a central metal stairway opens onto a platform at least fifty feet in the air. Through the opening above, I see a contraption of pipes and gears in constant motion. The gears whir away, while steam hisses from pipes that snake into the walls and ceiling like scaffolding.

A man with graying hair and a belly paunch steps out of the rattling mess above me. He wears clothing that has been out of style for at least thirty years, a faded green vest over a yellowing, formerly white shirt, baggy brown pants tucked into high boots, and a pocket watch chain snaking into his vest pocket. Thick spectacles keep slipping along his ample nose as he walks down the steps. Every few steps, he stops and pushes them back up with his palm, adding to the already thick sheen of grease on the lenses.

"You must be Nikki Laputa. Welcome." He shakes my hand before I reach out, jiggling my arm awkwardly.

"Yes, pleased to meet you."

"I am Willem, the Enginemaster. I hear good things about your abilities. We're lucky to have a member of one of the great houses."

"The Sky Engines are as important an assignment as they come. I'm honored to be here." The words sound overly formal coming out of my mouth, and I watch as Willem tries to determine if they're genuine.

"Well it's good to have you," Willem says, waving for me to follow him up the stairs.

We pass a small young man a few years older than me, who is cranking a massive screw with a wrench. He pats the boy meaningfully on the shoulder.

"We usually get less impressive people."

The young man shoots a dirty glance in our direction, and I'm surprised to find that it falls on me rather than on the Enginemaster who has just insulted him. He's clearly recognized me, and thinks I have no business here. Not that I necessarily disagree.

"I hope I won't disappoint," I say.

"I know you're not here for the Sky Engines," he says, surprising me with a glint of intelligence in his droopy eyes. "But if you work hard, I don't care if you spend the rest of your time conjuring or bareknuckle brawling in Long Bank."

How does he know about my conjuring training?

"I'm just here to work, sir. And I've never been much of a boxer."

Willem chuckles through difficult breaths. As we reach the central platform, I see into the guts of the engine for the first time. Willem approaches the railing, paying no heed to the violent metallic battle going on below. I keep a couple feet behind the barrier, trying not to imagine being sucked into the grinding gears.

"It's not so bad up here, once you get used to it," Willem says. "Most of the machines are too complicated to control by hand, so it's mainly Intention that gets the job done. What are your schools?"

"Matter-Pure, last I checked."

"Ah, you may be the only MP we've got. Not much use for Matter around here, but Pure will serve you well. EP or PE would probably be the best suited."

"I'm guessing Elemental would need to be mineral-focused to be any good?"

"Right. The gears. Unless the machines catch on fire, then fire or water-focused can be somewhat helpful for avoiding incineration."

My worried expression seems to delight him.

"We are going to have a great deal of fun here, aren't we?" he says.

Willem spends most of the day showing me around the engines. The tour leads through dozens of smaller engine rooms hidden in passages branching off the main one.

"Each of the auxiliary engines can work independently, but not for long. They take some of the strain off the main engine, so it's important to keep them in working order. But in truth, if the main engine fails, we may as well jump off Terraltum ourselves and save the Council the formality of throwing us off. It takes skill and precision to manage the handoff between the auxiliary engines, and we would have to keep doing that every hour until the main engine gets back up and running."

"So don't kill the main engine. Got it."

Willem stands at the railing of one of the smaller engines. He points out the different elements: Intention condensers, tubes that siphon off the extra energy, and gears that, even in these smaller engines, are as wide as I am tall. Willem's stomach protrudes over the edge as he points to each component.

"If anything's going to act up it'll be the condenser. That's why in the newer engines there'll be a walkway straight out to it."

"And if the engines fail? I know we're not talking about Terraltum plummeting to the surface or something."

Willem seems annoyed even at the suggestion. "Of course not! But the least of it is that they could explode, wiping out this entire section of the city."

"It's mostly warehouses around here anyway."

"You and I are both around here too."

"A minor detail."

"But the more pressing concern is that the engines maintain our invisibility and keep Earthworlders from knowing of our existence."

"I always thought that was sort of built in to Terraltum. What good does floating up here do if our world is visible to the Earthworlders?"

"It is not 'built in,'" Willem says, face becoming increasingly red. "It is only the labor of past Enginemasters—as well as apprentices like yourself—that have kept the Sky Engines running and our world invisible."

I try to tell him that I did in fact know that, but Willem is off on a rant too quickly for me to get a word in.

"The educational system isn't what it used to be, is it? Even children of the great houses learn so little about their own world. Although I suppose being from one of the great houses does give one a certain amount of license not to pay attention in school."

He turns and walks out of the dim engine room. We follow a corridor lit at precise intervals by torches, away from the loudest noise.

That was an entirely inappropriate thing to say, even if I am only an apprentice. I imagine how my parents would handle the situation—my mother would likely remind Willem of my status in one precise phrase, while my father would clap him on the shoulder, growling a laugh that was anything but humorous. I opt for my own approach instead.

"Yes, school is such a bore when one has the burden of a future ruling Terraltum on one's mind," I say in the loftiest caricature of Orellian privilege. "It makes one wonder why we even bother going to school at all, when we could just pay someone to attend for us."

Willem's grateful laughter rings through the hallway as we turn into a cramped, dusty office. Papers covered with complex diagrams and calculations litter the table along the wall. Puffs of dust rise from the carpet.

"Please fill me in on how it works, sir," I say.

"It's not much more complicated than what I described. As you alluded to earlier, it is a common and regrettable misconception that the engines allow us to float above the clouds. Our ability to stay in the air is thankfully due entirely to the fundamental element that makes up the base layer of Terraltum, the same element that allows us to unlock Intention."

"Sky."

"Right you are." Willem's voice becomes muffled as the top half of his body disappears inside a cabinet in the corner. He emerges holding a pair of leather gloves and a thick leather smock.

"Fear not, Miss Laputa. You have not been charged with holding up your world. To tell the truth, we don't exactly know everything that the engines are responsible for. There are areas beneath the auxiliary machines that don't appear to have any relevance at all to invisibility. Complicated mechanisms, many of them so small you'd have to shut them down entirely to discern their purpose. But no Enginemaster will risk that, given how interconnected the entire system is."

"Sounds straightforward."

"Don't worry, maintaining the main engine is hard enough. Without years of training, even the most capable person can drive it into a spiral resulting in violent self-destruction."

I don't have an immediate response to this.

"Now, let's look at some schematics."

When I arrive home, exhausted and with thoughts only of sleep, my parents are awake and waiting for me in our stateroom. The first string of admonitions from my mother starts immediately, but my father still has said nothing after ten minutes. He hasn't even really made eye contact with me as he stands facing the mantelpiece, eyes resting on our family's crest. In the woodcut image, a jagged bolt of lightning intertwines with stalks of grass to form a clamshell shape. It's a symbol of Earth and Sky, which commonly signifies holding things together. Something tells me my father is trying his best to emulate it.

"It would be one thing if you didn't request it," my mother says. I'm sitting on the leather couch, trying to appear relaxed. "We could play it off as a political slight, or contest the assignment. But you can't very well contest an assignment you chose."

"You always say the Sky Engines are important," I say. "Shouldn't you be proud that your very own daughter is keeping them running?"

"It's trade work," my mother says. "Noble as it may be, your safety relies on our political power, which you aren't maintaining there. Besides, we all know that's not the reason you chose the position. Who would request the night shift out of a sheer sense of duty?"

It was too much to ask for them not to realize why I'd made the request. They've known it's my dream to compete in the Conjuring Arena. They must've figured out my plan to train during the day and work the Sky Engines at night. That's the compromise I've made—at sixteen and as an Academy graduate, I'm required to take an apprenticeship, but conjuring doesn't qualify, being more of a "frivolous pursuit" than an "actual job."

How childish my brilliant plan looks under their scrutiny.

"Nikki, this is serious. When all is said and done, you and Rian are the only legacy our family has. The war, our work in the government, none of that matters without you."

"So that means I can't choose the direction of my life?"

"Of course you can." She pauses, glancing over her shoulder for backup. My father isn't ready yet, though. That scares me the most. "We've always said you should do what makes you happy."

"As long as that fits within the Laputa-approved list of jobs."

"Everyone has responsibilities. Do you think a family living on Long Bank has any choice but to take whatever job will allow them to feed their children? That's the way the world works. We all have to make sacrifices."

I'm finding it harder to meet her eyes. The rug, pale yellow and inlaid with a diamond parquet pattern, is beginning to fray at the edges.

"That shouldn't be the way the world works," I say.

"Are you listening to yourself, Nikki? How can you come away from the upbringing we've fought to give you and act so immature?"

"There's nothing more immature than blindly following what people tell you to do."

"The only reason people—your *family*—tell you what to do is because they care about you, about your future."

"Do you care about my future, or do you care about your precious legacy? Pick one."

I've pushed my mother too far. I inherited a lot from her, including a scorching temper.

"Remedia," my father says before things go too far over the edge. His hands find her arm. He sits next to me, inviting my mother, who begrudgingly sits on his other side.

"Father," I say, "I'm glad your political dealings include concern for your daughter today, I know your schedule must be terribly busy."

He doesn't take the bait. He never does. I know this is part of why he's such an effective politician, but it makes being his daughter a royal chore.

"Nikki, I understand why you did what you did," he says. "I know how much your conjuring means to you. We both do."

"If you understood it, we wouldn't be having this ridiculous conversation."

"I worry that we may have understated the extent of the problem."

"Oh good."

"Listen to your father, Nikki," my mother says.

"We've been on the Council of Families since before you were born, back when we were still in hiding at Swift Hall," my father continues. "In that time a great deal has changed, and nothing has changed. There have been times when tensions ran high and periods of relative calm. But I can say with surety that there has never been a more dangerous time to be a Laputa."

There are ornate chairs along one wall of this stateroom that I'm sure have never been used. For most people, family drama unfolds in cramped kitchens or living rooms, or even in the public square.

"Looks pretty damn safe to me," I say.

My mother and father exchange a glance and I know they're communicating with more than their expressions. They share a rare form of Intention available to only the closest partners: a mindfold, a joint space that exists on a plane between them. It's a skill they picked up by necessity when they fought side-by-side against the Kelluvas in Barrun's War. Now every day they sit at the same table as the Kelluvas, deciding what bills will come before the legislature, and I know they must rely on their mindfold nearly as much.

"You always say the war is long behind us," I press. "Was that a lie?"

"Yes and no," my father says. "Outright war is unlikely with our current political system. That was part of the reason both Laputas and Kelluvas were brought onto the Council after the war. But there have been rumblings from the surface."

My mother jumps in. "By rumblings, your father means that we have reason to believe the Kelluvas will soon make a move to assert their power there."

"The surface has never been important," I say. "Terraltum is all that matters."

"There have been rumors of dark magical creatures on the surface," my father says. "Deathcrows, werebeasts, and others far worse than that. The Earthworlders have no Intention. They can't defend themselves against a threat they can't even comprehend. If we don't act, the Kelluvas will take control of the surface."

"Then stop them."

"We're doing everything we can," my mother says. "But no matter what happens, we need to make sure our family is positioned as strongly as possible. How will you do that if you're off at the Sky Engines and in the Conjuring Arena?"

"I don't want to be part of this."

"You can't choose the family you're born into," my father says. "You can't choose your responsibilities."

I get up, and to their credit my parents don't follow. "I know I can't choose my family. But for the first time in my life, I've made a choice. And I'm sticking to it."

As the door slams behind me, I feel a pulse of adrenaline. I haven't heard the end of this. I don't believe my family would lie to me about the threat the Kelluvas pose, but I can't turn down this opportunity for the sake of politics. Politics can't be synonymous with life, even for a Laputa.

CHAPTER FOUR: NIKKI

I f I were to describe the work at the Sky Engines in one word, it would be *sweaty*. By the end of my second week, I've learned more than I ever wanted to about how to clean gears while they're running, how to remove blockages from cooling pipes, and apply oil from a safe distance. In the process I've earned myself an impressive array of scrapes, minor burns, and near misses. But there's a certain satisfaction to knowing I can keep such an important machine working, even haphazardly.

"Where are mother and father?" I ask my brother Rian as we sit down to dinner at the table in our parlor. I'm still wearing my grubby coveralls. Dinner is a Seven Loaf—one of our chef's specialties—seven layers of flat, flaky dough, alternating with a beef sauce that's been reduced for seven days until it's as sweet and tender as the caramelized onions that provide its primary flavor. By tradition the reduction contains seven different spices, though I'm not sure which of these causes the bubbles to change from light brown to purple in color when the sauce is ready.

"At the guild offices, finishing the settlement with the workers." Rian is three years older and a foot taller than I am. He got my mother's thin frame, and though his gangly limbs used to make him look like a young horse learning to walk, he's grown into them.

I got my father's stocky build but not his height. I hoped having both would make me a more imposing figure in the arena, but now I think I'm just vaguely dumpy.

"Ah yes, the workers who 'agreed' to a small settlement, and no increase in wages," I say with a scoff.

"It's fair compensation, and much more than they'd get out of another family."

"Weird how fair can depend on which side of the transaction you're on."

Rian rolls his eyes.

"At least our parents aren't here to tell me how I've betrayed the family," I say.

"No one has said those exact words." He breaks off a corner of the loaf and munches on it. "Though I can't deny they were heavily implied."

"Come on, don't you start."

"You won't hear anything from me. It's not like I care about your job somehow besmirching our family's reputation."

"You apparently don't care about being caught using words like 'besmirching' either."

"Right. That's not the kind of besmirchment I'm worried about."

I kick him under the table. He drops his fork, depositing a spray of crumbs and sauce beside his plate.

"How ladylike," Rian says.

"You're the one getting food everywhere. Not very ladylike of you, either."

"So you're serious about this conjuring thing?"

"I know it sounds stupid, but I can't not take this shot."

Rian studies me. I'm still expecting a lecture. He's always been the one who thrived on following my parents' path. The Conjuring Arena is certainly not that path.

What he says instead is, "You're a lot braver than I am, Nikki. You're definitely stupider too, but you can't really have one without the other."

"I have a feeling that's about as much of an endorsement as I'm going to get."

"Afraid so. By the way, if our parents ask, I gave you a stern speech on responsibility and how fulfilling a career within the government is—which is true, it is fulfilling, though I don't expect you to believe that."

"It was a very convincing speech, but despite your masterful oratory skills, you were unable to convince your hard-headed sister of the obvious error of her ways, and she remains attached to her dubious career path."

"Let's go with 'well-reasoned and thorough argument' instead of 'masterful oratory skills'—that makes it sound like I worked hard on it."

"Deal."

A scuffing sound comes from the door to the receiving room and our eight-year-old twin cousins, Simon and Piper, hurtle into the room, unannounced as usual. They dive at me and my brother.

"Did your mother let you loose again?" I say, the oxygen crushed out of my lungs by Simon's hug.

"We ran away," he replies.

"We've decided to become outlaws," Piper adds. After considering for a moment, she adds, "We're living on the lam."

I focus and picture a lamb. Intention vibrates through my muscles, and I can feel a new presence in the room. When I release it, a two-inch lamb appears on the table in front of me.

The twins clap with joy. Piper extends a hand and the tiny creature stumbles onto her palm.

"You'd better hope it's a bigger lamb than that if you're going to live on it," Rian says. The twins cackle delightedly.

"A story?" Simon says.

"Yes, a story!" Piper tickles the lamb on the head. The creature nuzzles her finger.

I exchange a glance with Rian. He shrugs and I know he's thinking we'll never hear the end of it if we don't oblige.

"Fine," I say. "Rian, a story about a sheep, perhaps?"

"Not a sheep, a lamb," Piper says.

"Fine, a lamb." Rian adds a luster of drama to his voice. "There once was a lamb who walked on two legs." I have the lamb jump down to the table and kick my plate to the side, creating a stage. He stands on his hind legs. "His best friend was a goat with long horns." I place a goat on the table beside my awkward lamb. The goat starts chewing on my napkin.

Rian weaves a silly story about the two friends, and I follow his voice with their actions. As we go along, I conjure more creatures, throwing in trees for scenery and props as necessary. I try to work out my illusion muscles in addition to relying on chimera, though a couple illusions aren't as sharp as I'd like. Wherever possible I add my own comic touches—not difficult in a story about a goat and a lamb who can barely walk in a straight line. The lamb keeps falling over, but even in his final fight with the evil wizard

Ganymede—who conjures tiny flashes of smoke to surround the wooly protagonists—his stumbling veers him out of harm's way.

The delight on the twins' faces is all the excuse I need, and I know Rian, who spends most of his day deep in complex calculations in the Chancellor's budget office, welcomes the opportunity to let his creativity flow.

Once Ganymede has been defeated, neatly stuffed inside a wooden barrel with only his head poking out, we send the twins off. I allow them to keep the tiny gray wizard and the two heroes. They scurry down the hallway, rolling the barrel in front of them despite Ganymede's protests. I keep the chimeras filled with enough Intention to remain material on the grounds of my family's estate. Once they cross the border onto the dirt road leading back toward the city, the tiny animals and wizard drift away, leaving only a shimmer of lasting energy behind.

"The barrel again?" I say.

"Sometimes the classic solutions are the best solutions."

"At what point are they old enough for the hero to chop off Ganymede's head? I've been working on my blood spattering effects."

"Let's wait until they're ten at least," Rian says. "Let them believe problems can be solved without bloodshed."

"Imaginary bloodshed," I snap back. I can make my conjured creatures incapable of feeling pain, if I choose, though it's extra work. I always do my best to limit what my creations must endure. This response always feels like a bit of a hedge, though. Scholars have studied conjuring for as long as there has been a Matter school of Intention, and they have never settled definitively on where conjured beings actually come from. A vocal minority of academics believes that conjurations occupy a dimension adjacent to our own, and that the act of conjuring calls them temporarily into our own dimension. But I fall more into the majority camp, who believe conjurations are a part of the creator's being, projecting into the world in physical form. If one dies, a part of me dies too. That's the real reason Ganymede's head has remained on his shoulders for as long as it has.

CHAPTER FIVE: JAMIE

The computer lab at my school consists of three rows of ancient desktops that, if they don't actually take floppy disks, are at the very least floppy disk adjacent. We all bring our own laptops anyway, so the desktops serve mainly as scenery. As usual the arguing starts before the entire coding club has arrived.

"Let's just put all the entries on an array and pop them off when we need them," Serra is saying. "We're overcomplicating this way too much."

Brantley, as usual, embraces his compulsion to assert his Masculine Perspective all over everyone. "Sorry Serra, that's not the way to go. We're gonna lose serious runtime indexing the array over and over again. Simpler doesn't always mean better."

"I'm with Serra," I say.

"What a surprise," Brantley says. "You do know that just because you agree with her doesn't mean she's going to date you, right?"

The low light of the lab doesn't do enough to hide the deep shade of crimson Serra's face has become. I wish I had a witty response, but my brain has suddenly turned to embarrassed static.

"You guys suckkkkk," says Ian, the fourth and final member of the club, who's hanging his "I work with computers" messenger bag over the chair. "I'm all for minimizing runtime, but I don't think it's going to make a huge difference at the end of the day. We've already wasted our runtime with the amount of time we've spent arguing about it."

"Very true," I manage. "Array it is?"

"Array it is," Serra says, although eye contact is proving an elusive prospect for both of us. In the midst of the embarrassed energy, an intruder enters.

"Is this coding club?" asks the tall girl in the doorway. She has bright pink hair on one side of her head, pitch black hair on the other, and sports a pair of wired headphones around her neck that pump electronic music with instruments seemingly composed mainly of construction equipment. "Sorry I'm late. I didn't even know we had a computer lab. This is some OG Silicon Valley shit."

She introduces herself as Tess—spelled with two dollar signs at the end, she says, though we can't tell if she's joking or not.

"I've been with the startup club, so I'm just looking for other people to code with," Tess says. "We decided to sell our prototype, and there were disagreements about who should be compensated in what capacity. There were differing opinions about whether product managers who don't code actually 'did anything.'" She puts this phrase in air quotes. "Long story short, our school no longer has a startup club."

I don't contribute much to the conversation as we explain our project, a system for our library to track book and electronic resource usage, with the end goal of deciding whether the space could be better used for something else besides books. Tess immediately makes it apparent that she knows more than any of us about any programming language that's mentioned, and as we explain each feature, she gives immediate suggestions about how to improve it.

Though I could feel personally attacked as she demolishes ideas I'd spent weeks coming up with, instead I find myself watching how the emotions of the room have changed. It's often not this clear, but now I can almost see the vortex of energy around Tess, the way the others automatically pour attention and respect her way. It scares me, both for how obvious it is that if she wanted to, she could make the rest of the group do pretty much whatever she wanted, and because I'm not entirely sure she's creating it unintentionally. I've always hesitated to pull the strings of others' emotions, but I've often felt that a less morally inhibited person could give them a yank if they wanted.

After about an hour, in which we make greater progress than we have in the past two weeks, the conversation turns away from programming.

"So, Jamie, any plans for the weekend?"

"No, nothing much."

"Good to have a down weekend every once in a while, I guess," she says. "I got invited to a college party, but I don't know if I'm gonna go."

"For real?" Brantley says. "Who with?"

"Doesn't matter," Tess says. "There's a ninety-seven percent chance it'll be lame."

"I don't know if I've ever been invited to a college party," Serra says. It's technically a lie. None of us have ever been invited to a college party, or even a high school party, and we all know it.

"Really?" Tess says. "But you have at least gone to high school parties, right?"

Blank stares.

"You've got to be kidding me. Why not?"

"No one invites us," I say. "That's the main reason."

Tess' expression suggests she's just discovered a new, fascinatingly inferior species of mammal.

"That's wild," she says. "Good to know real nerds exist, I guess."

And like that, the vortex is gone. All the attention shifts to diffuse anger and insecurity—including my own. It settles foggily over the room. I half expect one of the others to say the obligatory "Well, this is awkward," but no one does.

I breathe a sigh of relief. She's not someone who can bend others' emotions. She's just a charismatic asshole.

When we get out, Tess heads to her pink and black Camaro and peels out of the lot. After Brantley departs in his much more sensible Civic, and Ian's brother pulls up in his Jeep, Serra and I are the last two, both stuck a year shy of a learner's permit. The campus has a calm this time of day, when most students and teachers have gone home, but a few extra-curricularly involved stragglers are putting off the prospect of a night of homework a little longer. The school's brick façade seems softer now that the only people here are here by choice, teachers and students alike.

It's the perfect backdrop for two awkward members of the coding club who I'm pretty sure both sort of like each other to have an uncomfortable wait for their rides home—the bus we take two days a week having long since departed with the normal kids aboard.

"Tess is quite something," Serra says. She still hasn't made eye contact. She sits on the flat end of one of the railings along the front steps. I've looped my fingers into the straps of my backpack, too self-conscious of how nerdy this looks to do anything else.

"This may be an unpopular opinion, but—ah—not a fan," I say.

"She's a really good coder," Serra says. "Like, really good."

"I don't really care how good she is."

"We can learn from someone like that, even if she's sort of a jerk."

"So you agree she's a jerk?" I say.

"Yeah, but even jerks can have a good side. We'll have to try to look around the jerkiness."

I truly envy Serra's ability to put a positive slant on people. I don't know if not being able to is a defect of mine, or merely a by-product of how sensitive I am to the emotions in any given room.

"I guess you're right," I say.

"I usually am." Serra gives me a shy smile. We've been friends for years, but the earlier awkwardness hasn't yet receded. "Do you think she's really going to a college party?"

"I do." I feign outrage and say, "I'll bet she even gets drunk there too! These kids are out of control."

I'm happy any time I can get a laugh out of Serra. But joking like this does feel like putting on a fake youthful glove that doesn't quite fit. Neither of us have been involved in "typical" young people shenanigans. I'm too weird and she's too shy, and in either case neither of us is cool enough for anyone to offer us booze. Oh well, I'm sure sobriety is a secret blessing.

There's a short silence before Serra says, "I hope my dad gets here soon. My guild has a raid scheduled later. I'd hate to let everyone down." Serra is heavily involved in a fantasy MMORPG called League of Hearthfire. Maybe it's odd, but I've always found it hard to get into fake online worlds about magic when real magic waits a few steps outside my door. Not that I can tell Serra that.

"Can't let the guild down," I respond, distracted as I see Paolo's pickup pull into the parking lot. "Good luck."

"Bye, Jamie." She waves and I open the door to see Paolo's concerned face. I throw my book bag on the floor and prepare for him to tell me that he's leaving.

CHAPTER SIX: NIKKI

My feet slap the cobblestones in Market Square. I weave between customers, past vendors selling fortifying teas and cheap magical rings promising to cure a variety of embarrassing maladies. There are always a few of Orella's less sane variety out and about in the middle of the day, and besides an earnest aileth who tries to convince me I'm his stepmother, I spot a couple of bald-headed people of varying races with thick ropes draped over their arms, indicating their involvement in a fringe religious group that worships Leonis Wingless, the fallen Winged One. I breeze past them, and see a conjurer reenacting a naval battle in the fountain at the center of the square. If this were a lazy summer afternoon, I would help him construct the battle, enjoying the melding of our abilities, and the greater number of boats we could bring into the fight. But I have an errand to run, and the engines are short-staffed today.

Four of the foremen at the engines came down with a sudden fever, and another was already out after cutting herself re-aligning one of the auxiliary engines. Just the day for Willem to remember he needs me to fetch a tincture from the herbalist on the other side of Orella. Today is a rare day shift for me. We have our first conjuring match this weekend against last year's amateur recruits, so we've been given a couple days off to rest in preparation. If I'd known that working during the day would mean running pointless errands for Willem, I might have foregone the extra sleep.

My path leads directly past the Conjuring Arena. I force myself to stay on task, even as the sounds of the crowd roaring and conjured beasts clashing pulls at me.

The odor of a thousand different ingredients clogs the air in the herbalist's shop. I close the wooden door behind me.

Arnic Leodell's stern features crease when he sees me, his dark beard adding to his face's severity as he watches me enter from his post behind the counter.

"What can I do for you, Miss Laputa?"

"Willem the Enginemaster sent me on his behalf. He requires a tincture for his back."

"Ah, yes, Willem did mention his back has been bothering him," Arnic says. "I believe I have some of the recipe I've given him in the past."

He disappears between drying plants hanging from the ceiling. I haven't heard of half the herbs in the shop. They're scattered in jars and on pegs all around the counter, and over tables along each wall. I pick up a glass jar holding a few dozen tiny feet. If they weren't so small, I'd almost think they were human.

"Jojum feet," Arnic says, appearing beside me and almost making me drop the glass in surprise. "Jojum are remarkable creatures."

"What are these used for?" I ask.

"We've found that it serves as a rather effective tonic for those suffering from Intention Sickness. A nasty malady, and an expensive remedy."

"But there aren't any jojum on Terraltum."

"We have to send someone to the surface to harvest. Like I said, an expensive remedy. The permits alone..." He shakes his head and pulls the jar out of my hands, replacing it carefully on the counter. He holds out a small glass bottle. "But your master won't be needing anything of that sort today. A simple muscle relaxant to ease the pain should do the trick."

I take the bottle, pay with the *duckets* Willem gave me, and hurry out the door.

I try to shake the image of the tiny feet out of my head as I walk back toward the Engines. Even if I had Intention Sickness, I don't think I could consume anything so human.

This time I'm not running when I reach the Conjuring Arena. I've made good time so far, good enough to convince myself that I can peek in. Willem will never know if I only stay for a couple minutes, aching back or not.

A ring of stone buildings encircles the wide sweep of the wooden stadium. Shops with concessions, venues to place bets, and taverns for those with less interest in the actual arena competitions. I enter through one of the betting halls, a Laputa-owned establishment and one of the more reputable spots. I could go to my house's box—the houses all own boxes for the sake of tradition, but rarely actually attend—but I might be spotted there. Besides, I'd rather go where the real conjuring fans watch.

I climb up a staircase in the back of the betting hall, where several older men and women scramble to place last-minute bets. My legs ache, but that's pretty much normal for my entire body these days. The stairs open into the arena's stands at each level, with a ticket office guarding each entrance. I keep climbing, not stopping at the openings on the lower grandstand levels, and only stepping out into the fresh air once I'm at the top level and have bought the cheapest ticket from the office there.

I join the mob of people observing from ten stories up. The arena contestants stand on platforms on opposite sides of the circular field. Up here, where there are no seats and onlookers jockey for viewing position along the wooden railings at the balcony's edge, is the best place to watch a match.

I squeeze in beside a young man whose eyes are locked on the competition. The conjurer on the near platform has summoned a massive bear-shaped chimera, which has a humanoid chimera riding in a saddle on its back. These aren't conjurers I know. I would have loved to see Tezzy Maltus, the champion three years running, though attending one of his matches generally requires buying tickets weeks in advance. We make a good chunk of gold selling seats in our box for his matches.

"What event is this?" I ask the young man.

"Pure battle," he says without taking his eyes off the action.

The conjurer on the far side has a set of four springy, rabbit-shaped creatures.

"They're too fast for it," I note as I watch the rabbits dart in between the bear's legs, taking every opportunity to aim powerful kicks at its joints.

The young man grunts his agreement. The humanoid on the bear's back lashes out wildly with a spear. As it swings, one rabbit jumps onto the spear, runs along it, and plants a kick on the humanoid's temple.

The humanoid manages to shake the rabbits off, but in its distraction, it misses what the rest of the audience has seen. A pre-emptive gasp rises as the sand beneath the bear's feet first rises, and then drops six feet.

Though Elemental Intention is banned in the arena, this combatant has employed a tried-and-true legal method using Matter: conjuring a large physical object beneath the ground and then letting it disappear from existence, allowing physics to do the rest.

The bear crashes into the pit, throwing its rider in a spray of sand. The crowd roars, sensing a swing in the battle. I'm almost surprised when the humanoid finds its feet, but the rabbits are instantly on it, kicking its legs with ferocity that I now see includes sharp points on their feet. The humanoid's conjurer throws a half dozen sharp spinning disks into the surrounding air, hoping to establish a defense.

The rabbits pause, as if unsure. But no one opts for a small chimera strategy if they're unwilling to sacrifice them. One rabbit launches itself into a deadly disk, shredding itself but pushing the disk into the humanoid's leg. It stumbles, and that stumble is all the rest of the rabbits need to leap onto its back and begin bludgeoning its skull.

The near conjurer sways, too tired to vent his frustration. They must've been at it for a while. The bear has crawled out of the pit and roars toward the rabbits, but it ends up spinning in a circle, too slow to catch the creatures.

Taking advantage, the far conjurer summons a large metal ball in the air thirty feet above the bear, then releases it. The near conjurer yells for the bear to move. Too late. The ball falls, crushing the beast, and the crowd erupts.

Bear and rider disappear as their conjurer's will breaks. He reaches for the red stone resting in a groove on the railing at the front of his platform. He holds the stone at shoulder level, then lets it fall to the field below. The crowd roars louder. The defeated conjurer sinks to his knees, exhausted. The victor raises her arms over her head. Her rabbits do a choreographed victory dance in the center of the arena, as firework illusions erupt above their heads. They pick up the fallen red stone and bring it to the base of the platform, fighting over which will be the one to deliver it to their conjurer. She summons a tiny bat to collect it. As she lifts it into the morning air, the crowd begins to chant.

A few numbers on the standings board along the façade to my left change to reflect the result. This isn't even a match with championship significance. The Conjuring Arena is this intoxicating every day. The thought of being part of this sends an ecstatic chill up my spine.

In the next instant, the clock above the standings pulls me out of it. I squeeze through the crowd, riding the railings most of the way down the steps out of the arena.

I barely notice the flow of Market Square around me. I keep the tincture tucked safely in my palm. The tram is almost empty at this time of day, and I find an express to Eastbridge Docks, and the work I've been neglecting.

Something is wrong. I can tell as soon as I enter. The clatter of the Engines is louder than usual, the rhythm less consistent. I hear shouting as I run down the hall. When I emerge in the central engine room, Willem is hobbling about, holding his back and barking orders. Hot steam shoots everywhere.

"There you are," he shouts when he sees me. "Did you have to fly to the surface to harvest the ingredients yourself?"

"Sorry, sir," I say, running up the stairs. "What's happening?"

"The main engine is fine, but it's not running at its full capacity. Maybe a leak in one of the cooling tubes."

"But the auxiliary engines should be handling the extra load."

"Yes, but the auxiliary engines aren't running at capacity either. Run down to engine seven and eight, that might be the source. We need to get this patched right away."

Great day to be understaffed. I run down the hall to the auxiliary engines.

I poke my head in at engine seven. Its steady hum tells me it's running well, but I check the intake valve anyway, and make sure the offset pans aren't overflowing.

Black smoke billows out of the clanking gear mechanism of engine eight. I cough away the smoke, and bring the top of my shirt up to cover my mouth. Based on the sound, it's a problem near the outbound Intention flow. There, raw currents of Intention funnel out of the machine and down a tube into the main engine.

They should, anyway. But here one of the condensers has broken and its domed top is stuck in the pipe. The condensers are made of Intention-repellant glass so they can concentrate the flow of Intention and push it out more efficiently. It's created a pocket of energy that can't exit through the outflow. The air around the outbound tube crackles with unstable Intention. I need to clear the condenser debris so the Intention can flow out before the engine gets torn to pieces.

Part of my training in the Pure School involved dispelling Intention, but those patches were tiny in comparison. This much might explode if I try, or could strike me and kill me instantly. No, I have to physically remove the broken condenser.

I lean against the railing overlooking the machine. It's one of the smaller engines, but still the size of my dining room. Intention sparks through my hair, standing it on end. A narrow platform runs along the near wall and up to the outbound pipe, but it's too small for me to stand on, especially with that concentration of energy.

I apologize in advance to the creature I'm about to create. This will not be pleasant.

I focus all my energy into my palms, feeling the flow of creative potential, twisting the yet absent mass into the right shape. A two-foot-tall goblin appears on the platform beside me. Hopefully the maxim that smaller chimera are hardier will prove true. He grasps a pickaxe in one clawed hand, and looks at me like I'm a jerk for creating him. Understandable.

Bending down to stroke his scaly head, I point to the blockage. He understands, the intuitive understanding between a creature and its creator. He swings to the platform against the wall by the outflow. As he enters the heart of the Intention field, his shape starts to shimmer. He yelps in pain as his arms twist into wings, and the pickaxe nearly falls out of claws that had been hands. I focus all my Intention on keeping him alive. My power wavers against the instability of the room. The chimera continues forward. His steps slow as his legs change shape. His nose has become a beak. He lets out a piercing shriek. But he's at the condenser, and swinging the pickaxe. The first blow chips the glass. It's taking him enormous effort simply to exist in the energy field. A second swing sends cracks along the condenser.

The goblin jerks forward, catching his hand on the railing to avoid falling into the engine. His pickaxe flies into the gears and vanishes. I cry out. The Intention field now completely blocks me from helping him.

My goblin chimera reels away from the railing. He bends his knees, takes two quick steps forward, and leaps off the platform, grabbing the condenser as he falls. For a moment he hangs from the glass, perfectly still. He cackles madly as the condenser rips out of the tube, and both goblin and glass fall into the spinning gears.

The pooled Intention rushes through the cleared pipe with a crackling *whoosh*, and I am alone on the platform. All is quiet. There is no clatter of shifting gears, no hum of machinery. I'm too exhausted to register whether this is a good or bad thing. The outward flow of Intention pulled most of my own with it.

Silence lengthens.

Shouts sound in the corridor behind me, but I can't even turn my head to identify them. Then I hear the machines coming back to life. Willem storms into the room, followed by two of his apprentices.

"What have you done?" he says, his voice a furious whisper.

"One of the condensers," I say, each word taking all my effort. "Intention buildup."

"You flooded the main engine. Luckily the fail-safes were working otherwise you could have destroyed the entire system."

"But I cleared the blockage. The machine is working now."

"You don't understand, girl. You just stopped the engines entirely. For almost a minute, our world was completely visible."

CHAPTER SEVEN: JAMIE

"It shouldn't be for too long," Paolo says. It's been three days since our encounter with the jojum, and with each hour more anxious energy pours off him. I do my best to dissipate it by keeping a window open and literally pushing it outside. The birds in the willow tree are grumpier than ever.

"There's a book in my library downstairs. I don't have time to find it now, but it's blue with eight gold rings on the cover. It may contain some information on werebeasts."

"I understand," I lie. Paolo rubs the lapis lazuli fragment of stone on the necklace he wears. I have never seen him without it, and in the last few days Paolo's hands have strayed to it more and more often.

"You deserve to know more than I have had time to tell you," Paolo says. "But if we're lucky, this will all amount to nothing, and everything will go back to normal."

He mutters something to himself, and moves to the hallway closet. He pulls out his old olive-colored jacket and a pair of boots crusted with a layer of mud.

"I have some urgent business now. An associate of mine has accepted my request for a meeting, and hopefully I can get more information out of him. Look for the book, and feel free to explore any of my books if you think they'll help. Just be careful of wading too deeply into any of them." He leans over and kisses me on the forehead. "You can't believe everything you read. Keep Wesley by your side and listen to his advice. He is surprisingly wise for someone so furry. And one more thing." His hand is firm on my shoulder, and urgency riles his voice. "The bus and school are one thing, but don't, under any circumstances, leave the house on your own."

Then he is gone, and the door shuts me in. Paolo's gray pickup sprays gravel as it speeds away. I pat Wesley's tiny head. *We're in this together, my friend*, he says.

"Thanks for having my back."

Always.

Though I try not to spend too much energy on them, my dreams from the night before stay with me, adding another layer of worry. I don't usually remember my dreams, but this one instantiates itself in my waking life with the force of memory.

I waited at the top of a skyscraper. Though a drop of hundreds of feet lay mere feet away, I was unafraid. Just restless, impatient. Like the air of an ER waiting room as loved ones wait for a doctor to appear.

"You're sure this is right?" whispered the girl beside me.

"Yes." I had double- and triple-checked the location. The helicopter landing pad beside us stood empty. "Be patient."

I clung to the assurance in those words, hoping they would relieve my own impatience.

Below us, the city moved. Honking cars and the traffic on the expressway were nothing more than ghostly wails this high up, and the lights flickered dully through the haze of smog.

Hours passed, and still we waited.

The waiting built up inside me, wrapping whatever tensile instrument was already strung there even tighter.

And then, between clouds, a light.

It streaked downward with the speed of a rocket launched from an unseen flying craft. Its teardrop shape trailed white flame. We stepped back as it roared, faster than any object I had ever seen, directly for us. We pressed against the five-foot wall around the roof's perimeter, feeling the pull of wind behind us.

Then it crashed into the landing pad. Silence followed the tremendous roar.

We stepped forward, fascination mixing with foreboding.

The dream stuttered then, like a software program failing to render an unfamiliar file.

But as we stepped forward, between the rebar and cement rubble that was all that was left of the landing pad, a figure unfurled itself. The figure projected pure immensity. A silver cloak covered its body and head. Even standing above the landing pad, I was directly level with the top of its head when it reached its full height. It did not speak. It only nodded in our direction, and within that nod was a wave of command.

With it, the dream cut out, as if unplugged.

I try to push the images from my mind as I open the basement door. If there's one thing that can chase away a nightmare, it's Paolo's books. I've been allowed in his library, but there was an unspoken rule that I wasn't to explore it when he wasn't there. I needed a guide if I was going to wander through the books' magical contents.

My favorites are about magical animals, and I've spent hours delving into guides to the flora and fauna of Terraltum. I love learning about the fifteen-foot electric eels that swim in the river

Rhydwel, and the eyeless Bog Crawlers that live in the swamps of the Western Reach and entangle their prey in three-hundred clawed feet before absorbing them into their spiny bodies.

It comes as a bit of a surprise to me, actually, that I haven't read about werebeasts before. Paolo's interests span Terraltum biology and history, but he rarely discusses or reads books on recent history or politics. Most of the historical volumes stop near the beginning of Barrun's War. There's enough to learn about the deeper history, about the War of the Sky, or back to a time that has become myth, when the Winged Ones cast one of their own out of their order for attempting to take over Terraltum. Or even further back, when all the magical beings on Earth banded together to raise Terraltum into the sky.

As I make my way down into the basement, lights flicker on in dozens of sconces along the brick walls. Paolo's absence gives room for my curiosity to run free. I approach the closest light and peer inside. A golden flame dances inside, but when I hold my hand over it, there is no heat.

Most of the volumes are scholarly in nature, with academic titles like: *Beasts of Land and Sea: An Investigation of Flight-Capable Aquatic Mammalia*, or *Expert Alchemical Recipes, a Beginner's Guide.* My attention catches on an old volume called *The Great Houses of Terraltum.* Three squares arranged in a row emboss its brown cover. Inside the squares are the names: Kelluva, Natantis, and Laputa. Smaller boxes form a lower row, but the names are too small and covered in dust to read.

"I guess I should look for the book Paolo asked me to find," I say to Wesley.

It would seem wise, given the circumstances. He runs down my leg and leaps onto one of the shelves, inspecting each book in turn.

After close to an hour, I've pulled half a dozen titles off the shelf to read later, but we still haven't found the one we're looking for. I collapse in Paolo's chair and stretch my stiff neck. Wesley slumps on the desk, beside a golden statue of Atlas holding the world. I've never sat at this desk, since it was where Paolo did all his reading and writing while I read books on the carpeted floor.

There's something strange about the statue. The world he holds is not a sphere, but is instead an oblong, puffy cloud. Spires of a city overflow from the top of the cloud. I clear away the papers around the statue's base, which I can now see forms half of a sphere. Familiar continents stretch beneath Atlas' feet and bent knee, and I realize that he's not holding up the world. He is standing on the world, holding up a city made of clouds. I rest my hand on the statue, on the cool sinews of Atlas' muscles. Am I going crazy, or do they tense with my touch?

The statue twitches. I pull my hand back.

Atlas nods his rigid head at me. Startled, Wesley scampers away, his six legs overturning papers. I stare into the golden hollows where the statue's eyes would be. He stares back, then jerks his head at the mass on his back. When I don't move, he jerks it again, impatiently. Is a miniature statue of Atlas getting annoyed at me? I rest my hand on the tiny city. It gives slightly on one side, and I fear breaking it, but Atlas nods for me to continue. The cloud swivels on Atlas' shoulders as I twist.

I'm thrown back into the chair as the entire room vibrates. Atlas gives me an eyeless wink as the bookshelves disappear into the floor, revealing a cavernous space beyond.

I sit at the edge of a cave more than twice the size of my entire house. Wesley squeaks at my feet. Bat wings thrum in the stalactites. Water trickles on rock.

It takes a minute for my brain to reboot before I can make it out of the chair and step into the cool air.

And Paolo says he doesn't know where our mold problem comes from.

A central walkway leads over a shallow river. Its stones suck the warmth from the air. My footsteps echo coldly. Twenty yards forward, the walkway becomes a tile floor cut between rows of stalagmites. Massive vases line the floor, their sides covered in swirling patterns. It has the feel of the receiving hall of a royal family from a more sinister age. I stop at a large suit of armor covered in a thick layer of cobwebs. Brushing them off reveals that the armor is coated with gold. A skillful inlay of flowers decorates the breastplate, with a design similar to the vases—I catch a bolt of lightning, and thick blades of grass rising to meet them. The helm ends in four jagged points. Is all this stuff Paolo's? At the far end of the cavern, I find a wooden stand. On it rests a blue circle, propped up on a metal tripod. It's a similar material to Paolo's necklace, crafted into a perfect circle a half-inch thick.

The jewel's color changes into what at first looks like a random refracting pattern. But out of the randomness come clear shapes—first crystal ocean waters, then tall mountain peaks capped with snow.

"What is this place?" I say.

Wesley doesn't answer my question, but says, *That is a Seeing Glass made from a shard of Sky. They are incredibly rare.*

A small waterfall sloshes down behind the stand, the water flowing from a narrow crack high in the wall. For a second I think that the water is falling fast enough to generate a current of air, but then I see the path that circles the pool at the waterfall's base, and disappears behind the shimmering water.

Warm mist rises from the water. As I approach, a gap opens between the water and the back wall, revealing that there is in fact no wall behind, only an opening, perfectly round and about six feet in diameter.

I guess we keep following, I think to Wesley. Like I could stop now. He shrugs. No one can make a shrug more indicting than a trilopex can—I think it's because they don't technically have shoulders, so it takes a movement of the entire torso.

We slide behind the falling water. I splash through puddles on the floor of the tunnel, which leads steeply upwards. I can still see, although there's no visible source of light.

At the top, an opening leads into the white of day. A blue glow coats the entire opening. I run my hands through it, but there's nothing perceptibly solid there. The backs of my eyes ache with the piercing light. I step forward out of the warmth of the cave into a harsh rush of cold.

Well this doesn't seem geographically possible.

With two steps forward out of a shallow cave, I stand on a high mountain ridge, my feet in a bank of snow. The tunnel behind me looks the same as it did from the other side. I shiver, my sweatshirt not enough for the chill air. Far below, between racing clouds, a river runs through a narrow green valley. More mountains jut upward beyond, their peaks capped with white. Cliffs converge to form pristine bowls of snow. My eyes follow the bend of the river.

Something's deeply wrong here. Even more wrong than walking a hundred feet up out of my basement and ending up in a snowy mountain range. The river does not keep flowing or end in a lake. It simply stops, as if the world has ended at that point.

Dizziness forces me onto my butt in the snow. I only vaguely register the cold biting at my legs.

After what appears to be the edge of the world, several miles down, another landscape entirely stretches to a second horizon. Earth. I am on a separate continent floating in the clouds. I am on Terraltum. I feel very small.

My whole life I lived above a portal to another world. I knew Paolo had some secrets. I knew he wanted to keep me from knowing anything about my mother and father, so much so that he refused even to show me pictures. I knew there was a reason he would rarely talk about his past. But wow, Paolo, this is a whopper.

"I think we should go back," I say. The dizziness hasn't subsided.

Wesley doesn't respond, but emotional energy pulses off him.

"Wes, are you alright?"

"This is the closest I've been to home in as long as I can remember," he says. He rarely speaks of his home in the enormous trilopex city below the capital. It obviously costs him a debt of longing every time he does.

My sneakers do little against the snow, but I step forward, toward the edge where a sheer cliff drops off, around massive boulders that have an almost man-made quality in their symmetry.

Once past them I can see further, past the valley below and over a wide forest, interrupted occasionally by patches of clear-cut brown. A wide river runs at the furthest point I can see. On it floats what must be, to be visible at this distance, an insanely massive barge.

"Did you know there was a portal to Terraltum in our basement?"

"I had suspicions," Wesley says. "Think about the stream of people who've come through the house over the years."

I always thought these Skyfolk possessed some power that let them come and go as they pleased. As batshit as it sounds, a portal to Terraltum is mundanely logical.

"Are there a lot of portals? I'm no expert but..."

"They were all supposed to have been destroyed after Barrun's War as part of the peace compromise. It seems someone hasn't been playing by the rules."

"Why? Why have an undocumented portal to Paolo's home?"

"I don't know," he says. "But obviously Paolo is wrapped more deeply in Terraltum politics than he let on."

The wind sends a rippling chill through my stomach and chest. Shock has kept me from feeling the cold temperature, but now it asserts itself in full force. I won't be able to stay much longer.

"Wes, I don't know the way to your home from here, but would you go back now if you could?"

The time has not yet come for me to return, he says, his words resonating in the deep way they do when he speaks directly into my mind. *Besides, imagine the suspicion an Earthworld boy wandering around Terraltum would cause. You're not exactly known for your chameleon-like ability to fit in.*

Tell that to the kids at school, I reply. *I'm known for being very not-weird and for having many friends who aren't even computer geeks.*

Apologies, I did not mean to cast aspersions.

Cast away, my friend.

The moment of levity has allowed Wesley to rein in his emotions. His usual reserve returns.

"Let's go, I'm getting cold." I tramp through the snow toward the portal, trying to convince myself that my world hasn't fundamentally shifted in these past few minutes.

The cave and the portal inside are exactly as we left them, stable passages that betray none of their profound importance.

Wesley's comment about Paolo's involvement with Terraltum sticks with me. I scan back through my memories of the odd visitors, most of whom I saw only in brief glimpses. My curiosity outweighed my respect for Paolo's wishes on only one occasion.

It must've been five or six years ago, so I would've been nine or ten. I came home from school to find Paolo standing in the hall between the kitchen and the living room with a woman. She was tall and stern, with posture that suggested a military background. She wore a pinstriped suit under a long, open winter jacket. Her dress shoes were wet, which I noted because it hadn't rained in weeks.

"Jamie, this is Molly," Paolo said, breaking off mid-sentence from whatever he'd been saying.

"You're getting tall," she said, bending down to shake my hand.

"Nice to meet you." Her hand vibrated with electric energy. She smiled kindly, but in the set of her mouth I could see pure, otherworldly power.

Paolo directed me to the kitchen as he usually did.

"It's a mac and cheese night, I'm afraid," he said, as if delivering soul-crushing news. "There's a box on the counter. Can you handle it?"

"I think so. I'm a talented chef, you know."

Paolo exchanged a smile with Molly. "I'm fully aware. Just make sure to grab a vegetable too."

"Aye-aye, cap'n." I retreated into the kitchen as Paolo and Molly disappeared behind the living room door.

After a box of mac and cheese and a whole red pepper, which I ate raw and uncut like some kind of demented apple, I'd satisfied my hunger but not my curiosity. Paolo and Molly had still not emerged. I started my homework at the kitchen counter, but my brain couldn't bring itself to focus on turning fractions into decimals. I shouldn't. Paolo said his business was his business. When I needed to know something, he'd tell me.

I gathered my schoolwork into my backpack and crept toward the living room door. If Paolo came out suddenly, I could pretend I was going upstairs to my room. I navigated over the least creaky floorboards until I was a pace from the doorway.

"... of the wider ramifications," Paolo was saying. "You're as valuable an asset as any operating on the surface. Without you, it'll take years to get our foothold back in Washington."

"That's the whole thing," Molly said. Her voice had the annoyed tinge of someone who'd long since tired of repeating herself. "I'm an *asset*, I stopped being a person to them a long time ago."

"You know that's not true. Remedia and Ebben care about you as much as anyone."

"When I took these concerns to her, Remedia Laputa told me the greatest gain comes out of the greatest hardship. What in the name of Earth and Sky does that even mean? Really easy for her to say when she lives in an estate on a hill with two annoyingly precious kids and a husband who would do anything for her, including whipping votes in the legislature for her social policies that he couldn't care less about."

Silence followed. A faint hint of sadness had joined Molly's frustration.

"Ebben Laputa is a good man," Molly said, her voice quiet. I had to lean closer to the door to hear. "I know it hurts you to hear that his intentions are anything less than unimpeachable, and I'm not suggesting that. When it comes down to it, Paolo, the truth is that I'm tired. I've been playing this long game of the Laputas since the war. Half the time I don't even know why I'm lobbying for what I'm lobbying for, and Washington is even more soul-draining than Orella. It's the family system wearing a name called democracy and with a true lineage of oligarchy, and that will never change. The paychecks rolling into my bank account just remind me that I'm one of the cogs that allows this awful machine to run. I can't even bear to look at my statements every month."

"But you *are* accomplishing something," Paolo said, a familiar tenderness in his words. "You're serving a crucial function. You're on the right side of this. You don't have to touch the money. Hell, give it to a charity for banished Skyfolk, cash it out and throw it to the wind in the middle of Fifth Avenue—it doesn't matter. All that matters is that when this is all over, the Kelluvas remain out of power."

"I don't think I can be part of it anymore."

"Molly, the Kelluvas are not the only force we must stop."

I could almost hear Molly shaking her head. "I'm not going to use your untested theories as justification for throwing away the rest of my life. You have no proof whatsoever."

"I know Almus," Paolo said. "It's impossible to speak with him as often as I do and not understand that he's not doing it for family. He's a zealot, Molly."

"If I hear one more word about the Wingless, I'm never speaking with you again. Is that understood? You're looking for a way to fool yourself into thinking this fight means something, when all it is is petty bickering between families. Trust me, Paolo, it's no more complicated than that."

"Alright," Paolo said, though I could tell it was killing him to let the matter drop.

My legs had become numb. I prepared to start up the stairs, fearing that I'd stayed too long. The last thing I heard Paolo say filled my veins with ice, both because of the words themselves and the graveness with which he said them.

"If you leave, you have to disappear completely. You were in those caves with me, you know the horrors they're capable of. This war will suck you back in eventually, and if you're not ready, it will do the same thing to you it's done to thousands of others."

I didn't hear Molly's response as I started up the stairs, but I knew I'd been a party to something I shouldn't have.

I return to Paolo's cave, then leave through the library, closing the concealed door behind me. I take a few of Paolo's books, but I close and lock the cellar door. If I leave the door locked, maybe I can pretend that life will carry on as it always has.

You should know that not all forces out there are as benign as the ones in our forest, Paolo had said. I don't want anything to do with those forces.

I still haven't found the blue book, but I can't make myself search anymore. The room in the back of our house is part greenhouse, part living room, with tall plants growing all the way up to the round glass ceiling. A couch and table sit in the middle of the room. I sink into the familiar folds of the couch, pulling a blanket over me. I turn on the old TV, hoping the noise will drown out my thoughts.

I sit through a news story about a rash of vandalized potted plants, an uplifting human-interest story about a lost dog returning to its owner, and several shamelessly punny weather updates. I almost turn it off during a corporate embezzlement story about a company called K-Corp. The newscaster is a bit vague on what the company actually does (telecommunications? Satellites?), but the smug face of the new CEO is striking for being covered in what appear to be the scars of old burns, and how aloof he is for someone who's just been given a prestigious position.

The next story is more interesting.

"We turn to conspiracy news, now, with a story out of Brighton, England. Half a dozen residents of this small coastal town are reporting seeing a UFO floating off the coast yesterday. Clark Jones, a reporter for the Associated Press, was on the scene to interview some of these would-be alien spotters."

The scene changes to waves lapping the pebbly shores of Brighton under a gray sky. A heavily parkaed reporter walks along the beach with remarkable difficulty.

"I am walking along the shore here in Brighton, not a mile from the famous Brighton Palace Pier. It is in this very spot that yesterday several picnicking residents of this coastal town looked out at the ocean and saw more than they bargained for."

The camera pans to a view of the sea, every bit as gray, ordinary, and not UFO-filled as the sky above it. The newscast cuts to a curly-haired, stocky woman in midsentence.

"...and that's when we turned to the sea and saw what at first we took as a storm cloud. But like I said, there was no weather yesterday, just the usual clouds, it being spring and all, and there was something off about it."

"What makes you think this was anything more than a stray cloud?" the reporter asks, jabbing the microphone in the woman's face.

"It weren't like any cloud I'd ever seen. For starters it was more solid-like, not at all what you'd expect out of your ordinary cloud."

A man speaks this time: "It weren't no cloud, I'll tell you that. Maureen says it was like a cloud, but Maureen's never been one to describe things the best way. I say it was more like a floating ship or craft, only instead of being made out of metal, it was made out of rock or something."

"Did it do anything?" the reporter says, clearly enjoying himself. "Did it swoop down, play angelic music, anything like that?"

The woman speaks again: "Don't be daft, this wasn't some flying saucer or some such. This was much, much bigger, and much, much realer."

"There you have it," the reporter says, back on the shore with his prominent parka. "Bigger, and realer, than any flying saucer. Did it abduct anyone? Did it disappear beneath the waves like an extraterrestrial Atlantis? We may never know."

I mute the TV and sit up. Wesley, who fell asleep during the corporate scandal story, has been watching with amusement.

"I don't know about you, Wes, but I'm feeling somewhat daft myself."

CHAPTER EIGHT: NIKKI

My parents' name and—less importantly—my age allowed me to spend the night in my own room rather than a cell. Our carriage journey down the hill ended at the Council Dome in Chancellor's Square. Every corner of this place speaks of refined power, of a government in command of itself and its subjects. Whichever previous Chancellor designed the square took the name seriously. A hundred years ago, a dozen contrarian mathematicians measured the dimensions in an effort to disprove the precision of its architects. They couldn't find any indication that the space was anything other than a perfect square, and several tenured professorships were lost in the ensuing mudslinging.

At each corner, a twenty-foot automaton sits dormant. The only indication that the metal beasts have any life in them is the shifting gaze of their watchful eyes. I've never seen them activated, but the Intention-powered machines add to the air of solemn authority.

The square's architect scattered fountains throughout the space, each depicting a great ruler or warrior, their postures suggesting that they're controlling the water through Intention, whether the pure physicality of Elemental, the conjuring of Matter, or the vine-heavy depictions of Organic. The people walking among the fountains range from harried government officials rushing to their next meeting, to tourists taking in the grandeur of the square and causing traffic jams by congregating at inconvenient points. An armed escort wards off the mob trying to catch a glimpse of me before the trial.

At one end of the square are the Chancellor's apartments, a massive brick building with wide, even windows, their shades drawn against curious eyes. On the other end rises the cold shape of the Council Dome, where all official council business—and a fair amount of unofficial but nonetheless vital state deal-making—occurs. The imposing structure covers the entire side of the square, the dome constructed of pure granite, a faceless container for the most important matters of our world.

Today, those matters include deciding my fate.

Chancellor Bella Natantis sits in an ornate oak chair at the far end of the hall, on a raised dais that forms a semi-circle around the central floor. I sit in front of it, alone in a hard wooden chair, with Willem and a dozen Sky Engine apprentices off to one side. Bella's Chief Magistrates flank her on either side, while further down sits Holmund Kelluva, the patriarch of the Kelluva family, and his son Benjamin. Across from them sit my mother and father, their faces the stern masks of judicial business. I may be their daughter, but today they'll be part of the process to decide my fate. They always complement each other so perfectly, my mother short, pale, built like a willow tree, and my father tall, athletically built, and with a rich brown complexion. Several officials of minor houses peer down from the gallery, as well as a member of the *Terraltum Free Press* with a large notepad. At a certain point the guards gave up keeping the rubberneckers outside, and the gallery overhead is one step removed from a mob.

The Chancellor's stern face takes in her surroundings with the calmness of someone familiar with every contour of the room, but her eyes are not unkind.

"Good morning, esteemed members of the great houses of Terraltum," Chancellor Natantis says. Her voice commands the room. It's easy to forget that when she succeeded her mother, she was the youngest Chancellor in recorded history. Before that, Yura Kelluva sat in that chair, only being replaced as a stipulation of the peace treaties that ended Barrun's War. By the way Holmund glares at her, it's clear he would rather that stipulation had not been honored, war or not.

"We are gathered today to discuss the events of yesterday afternoon," Bella continues, "in which a system failure in the Sky Engines caused the brief exposure of our civilization. What the ramifications of these actions will be, it is impossible to know. What we can grasp, however, are the facts." She meets the gaze of each member of the tribunal in turn, locking eyes particularly with Holmund Kelluva. His long black hair is slicked back against his scalp. He returns her gaze with as much boredom as he can muster. "Facts are all that should guide one's judgments in a case such as this. We must leave family loyalties outside this room."

As scared as I am, I keep coming back to the thought that I am supposed to be at my first conjuring match tomorrow. All I want is for this to be over so I can return to what I care about. The Council can give me whatever punishment they want, as long as I can compete.

"The facts are these. There was an issue with the Sky Engines, and while attempting to resolve the issue, an apprentice caused a temporary shutdown of the system. This apprentice, Nikki Laputa, sits before us. I call Willem, Enginemaster, to describe the nature of this mistake."

Willem stands and steps to the podium to my left. The acrid stench of the tincture I brought him yesterday is on his breath. He speaks haltingly.

"The apprentice was asked to investigate a failure with auxiliary engine eight. When she identified the problem, rather than contacting a superior member of the division, she acted on her own, risking destroying the entire engine system by releasing a flow of pure Intention into the main engine."

"May I ask how exactly this happened?" Holmund says.

Bella stretches one hand toward me. I stand without realizing I'm doing so, blood flushing my face. Fear almost causes my voice to crack. I take two deep breaths, but don't feel any calmer.

"Upon arriving at the auxiliary engine, I recognized that a broken condenser was blocking the outbound Intention flow," I say, knowing most people in the room have absolutely no idea what I'm talking about. "This created an Intention field that threatened the integrity of the engine. I cleared the blockage to prevent the engine from failing completely."

"And therefore risked the integrity of the entire system!" Willem snaps.

"Let her speak, Willem," Bella says.

Willem fumes at the podium, but holds his tongue.

"I would ask Ms. Laputa," Bella continues, "how exactly she cleared this blockage."

"I summoned a chimera. I knew I couldn't dispel the Intention field or risk stepping into it, so I conjured a chimera who removed the condenser from the pipe."

Holmund Kelluva and his son exchange a sneer. "You mean to say that you maintained a chimera through an Intention field powerful enough to shut down the main Sky Engine? Not even the best arena conjurer has that sort of skill in Matter."

I would've enjoyed Bella's smile under different circumstances. Harsh whispers sound in the gallery behind me.

"I can vouch for my daughter's conjuring ability," my father says, standing. "She was an early-emerging Natural in Matter."

"Thank you, Ebben," Bella says. "We are not here to debate Ms. Laputa's conjuring talents, although I'm sure they are impressive. Her testimony stands as fact until proven otherwise. Patriarch Kelluva, your incredulity has been noted. Shall we move on?"

"Fine, continue," Holmund says. He and my father sit on opposite sides of the room, staring each other down as if in preparation to do battle.

"Willem, what protocol should your apprentice have followed in alleviating the problem in engine eight?" Bella asks.

"The worst possible outcome when there's an Intention buildup in an auxiliary engine is for that Intention to flow to the main engine all at once," he says. "The only course of action an apprentice should take in such a situation is to first dispel the Intention field, and then clear the blockage. Clearing the blockage first risks destroying the entire engine."

Holmund pours false outrage into his voice. "Such an outcome would result in the permanent exposure of our world. Surely such an offense—"

His voice nearly drowns in the ruckus from the gallery. They have been becoming steadily rowdier, and with Willem's latest statement they smell blood. I can't help turning my head to glance at them, and do a double take when I catch a familiar face in the crowd. Grell sits totally immobile, immune to the swell of people around her. Her expression is unreadable. I can't believe she came.

"Patriarch Kelluva, your continual interruptions are a distraction from the facts at hand," Bella snaps. Energy crackles between her and Holmund. "Continue."

"Unfortunately, I concur with Patriarch Kelluva," Willem says. "If the apprentice was unable to dispel the Intention field herself, she should have sought help. She acted rashly, choosing to prove her own abilities over protecting the well-being of the engines."

"I only did what I could to prevent the engine from failing!" Is the old goat serious?

"Willem, in your estimation, what dangers would a failure in the auxiliary engine have carried?" Bella asks.

This isn't fair. These smug bureaucrats are prepared to punish me because I did something on my own, using my own skills rather than asking for help.

"A complete auxiliary engine failure would have been unfortunate, but not catastrophic. We could have resolved the issue in the main engine in due time. The apprentice did the worst possible thing she could have done."

I hate him. I hate how strongly he thinks that I failed, and I hate that he won't even use my name.

"Permission to speak, Chancellor," my mother says.

"Permission granted, Matriarch Laputa. Speak your mind, Remedia."

"Thank you, Chancellor. I believe we have been privy to a sufficient recounting of the facts. My daughter did what she thought was right, but youth does not always know when its abilities are overmatched. House Laputa stands willing to accept the tribunal's decision, but would ask for lenience, in the name of youth and youth's good intentions."

"She merely wishes for preferential treatment for her daughter," Holmund shouts. "I can tell you now that if my son were in Ms. Laputa's position, we would judge him as harshly as we would a complete stranger."

Bella turns to the Kelluvan patriarch. The complete disgust on her face suggests her dignified control had been requiring more effort than it appeared.

"What is wrong with you, Holmund?" Bella says. A bad breach of decorum, both for its directness and for not using his proper title. "You speak with the words of a child whose schoolyard enemy risks punishment from his teacher. I know as well as you that when your own brother sat here, you pleaded to spare him despite all the facts, all the evidence, showing that he had animated hundreds of werecreatures during Barrun's War. Those were war crimes. This is nothing in comparison."

If the gallery was loud before, it is frenzied now, their jeers not directed at either side in particular. They just love to see the mud flying.

"There was no evidence!"

"Your calls to limit the emotions of others while allowing your own to run free are at best hypocritical, and at worst risk the very integrity of our judicial system," she says.

"Be very careful, Chancellor, you are bordering on insulting my name," Holmund hisses.

"Are you threatening the Chancellor?" Bella says, calm returning to her voice. The Kelluva's response has let her off the hook.

Benjamin Kelluva stands. He is only seventeen, a year older than me, but already has his father's grim features, and wears his hair slicked back in the same severe fashion.

"I would like to speak, if the tribunal is willing to listen," he says.

Bella seems to be doing her best not to roll her eyes. "You are a member of this tribunal. You have a right to speak. Though my aunt's absence has been noted."

"I hope you will excuse my youth," Benjamin says, his voice lacking the power of his father's, yet with a smoothness no doubt acquired during his clerkship with Terraltum's High Court. "Matriarch Kelluva is not well and trusts me completely to act in her stead."

"I know we are all praying to the Winged Ones that Orchid has a speedy recovery, and can return to her post before too long. Speak your mind, Mr. Kelluva."

"I would ask that we move to pass judgment on this case. Ms. Laputa has clearly violated her core responsibility to protect the integrity of the mechanism that shields us from the Earthworlders. We have heard all the relevant facts, as far as I can observe them. I concur with Matriarch Laputa. Now is the time for a decision."

This Kelluva is far more dangerous than the other. Holmund is powerful, but he lacks emotional maturity. His son already has the polish to press his political agenda. Agreeing with my mother makes him appear amenable to reasoned discussion, while his condemnation of me stakes a clear position. Holmund is like a rough chunk of granite. Benjamin is like a diamond sharpened into a fine blade. One smashes indiscriminately, the other slices with precision.

My guilt was never really in question. Hollowness builds in my chest, and I fight to keep tears out of my eyes.

"Thank you for your input, Mr. Kelluva," Bella says. "If the tribunal will follow me..."

The members of the tribunal file out the door behind her, into the meeting room where a private vote will decide my fate. I'm still exhausted from my ordeal at the engines, compounded by my sleepless lifestyle over the past few weeks. This decision will decide the course of the rest of my life. Willem steps toward me and puts a hand on my shoulder. I shake it off, but his whispered voice is almost pleading.

"I'm sorry, Nikki," he says. "You were a bright apprentice, but there are forces at work here that you can't understand, forces that can only be held in check if I remain in charge of the Engines. I did what I must."

"I hope you fall into your precious engines and they grind you into pieces," I spit.

"Know that I am sorry. I never wished for this. In the future if there is any way I can help you..."

"Get away from me."

He retreats to his seat. I bite my lip and stare into the grain of the wooden floor. Voices murmur in the gallery. We've put on a good show for them so far, and I'm sure the finale won't disappoint.

The door to the inner chamber opens, and the members of the tribunal file out. That was quick. My mother and father walk down the stairs at the side of the dais, and stand behind me, playing the part of government official and concerned parent simultaneously.

As Bella takes her seat, she meets my eyes. "By vote of the tribunal of the three families, we find Nikki Laputa guilty of disabling the Sky Engines through negligence. Her sentence is Earthworld banishment for a term not exceeding three years. Due to the unintentional nature of her crime, she will be provided with a Piece of Sky. Ms. Laputa will depart Terraltum within forty-eight hours."

Hands rest on each of my shoulders, but fear overcomes even my mother's soothing touch. Three years. Three years without my mother or father. Three years without Rian. He couldn't bring himself to come to the trial, and now I know why. This sentence would've broken his heart.

Jeers of delight, boos, and shouts of every kind fly down onto me. The noise fades into the background as I hide my face in my hands. There will be no conjuring match for me tomorrow, or any other day. My dreams evaporate into the unfeeling, dignified architecture of the council chambers, as it slowly sinks in that I've lost my home as well.

CHAPTER NINE: JAMIE

I t's been three days, and Paolo hasn't returned. I tried calling him almost hourly, but his phone goes to voicemail each time. On Monday morning, I woke up at five o'clock and lay awake, deciding whether to go to school. I'd been too stressed out to do any of my homework and, Paolo's warnings aside, I ultimately let my lack of preparation stand as the reason for staying home. I manage to find Paolo's blue book with the eight rings. He'd stuffed it inside one of his top desk drawers, probably trying to make it easier to find. The entry on werebeasts is short:

Werebeasts are rarely born in the wild, and are only likely to do so when non-magical creatures are born in areas with high levels of malevolent Intention. Most often they are created using a difficult combination of Pure and Elemental Intention, the precise practice of which has been banned on Terraltum (See entries: Were-Wars, pp. 517-544, and Dark Intention Acts, pp. 121-122). Werebeasts can be trained in their early growth stage, and are best suited for pursuing a single target until that target is destroyed. Contrary to popular literature on the subject, werebeasts suffer no adverse effects when exposed to sunlight, and their existence has nothing to do with the appearance of the full moon—a common Earthworld myth that possibly emerged because of the preferences of those practicing Dark Intention to perform their rituals under the ominous presence of the full moon. However, given their vastly superior nighttime eyesight, many werebeasts will hunt at night to maintain the greatest advantage over their targets. They typically kill by severing the spinal cord at the base of the neck, and shaking their prey until death, though some have been reported to toy with their prey, inflicting as much pain as possible before killing and eating them.

Oh good. Now every corner of the house seems to hold a werebeast or other demonic magical presence.

The third night, shadows begin to creep in from the corners of my dreams. Presences try to assert themselves, but they're hazy. I know these shapes, though I can't name them.

"We have to go after them," a female voice says behind me.

"What do you want me to do? Any suggestions at all on a direction?" I'm furious. I can't tell if it's caused by fear or not, but the rage is real.

He just ... melted. Disappeared into the shadows at the edge of the clearing like an apparition. That after materializing equally as suddenly, already unleashing a furious assault. The rock behind us still bears the marks.

"I think we hit him," she says.

"Not hard. Not enough to slow him down."

"You're worried about disappointing 'father,'" she says, voice dripping with condescension.

"There's someone else we should avoid disappointing," I say, too angry to take the bait.

Her expression retains its mischievous glint. She may be a killer, but she has not yet come to terms with what we've unleashed.

From where I'm crouched, I survey the edge of the clearing. Dusk fills the wood with shadows, but if my read of our opponent's Organic is correct, we're unlikely to see an outline other than a shifting tree or a swaying fern. Anger builds. I pull in the energy of the area around me, and let it out in a curse that shakes the air.

I wrench awake. The rest of the night, sleep seems far away. I get up well before dawn and slip out of the house.

If Paolo isn't coming back soon, I have to find some answers. I step out into the shadows of the front yard, Wesley on my shoulder. He's kept me sane, reassuring me that the house is still safe, that Paolo would never knowingly put me in danger.

Out in the forest I am more at ease. These familiar pines couldn't possibly hide a snarling werebeast. Birds flit overhead, and I find no sense of alarm as I tap into their emotions. They're more concerned with building their nests and raising their young.

I return to where we found the jojum. The trail has mostly disappeared into the underbrush, but if I concentrate I can find some definite signs of their presence—the shimmer of dust, a bush with a square cut out of it, tiny pieces of charcoal from their fires. I follow their circuitous trail for close to two hours, with Wesley helping me when I lose the way.

There's a rustling in the branches above me. A jojum swings down out of the trees.

"I thought I recognized a human scent," says the jojum scout. "This is not the first time our paths have crossed, human."

"It is a pleasure to meet again," I say, rubbing my ears in an attempt at politeness, even as I forget the traditional jojum greeting.

"I'm sure," she says, hefting her long spear and appraising me as if deciding where it would do the most damage. "You've been tracking our party for some time. May I enquire whether you intend to slaughter and eat us? Or if you just intend to cut off our feet to use in a magical remedy?"

"None of the above. I know you're on a long journey, but I need to know if you have any information on Paolo's whereabouts. He's gone missing."

"Is there a reason that you have come to us with this?"

"I don't know where else to go. You're the only magical beings I know of."

"No surprise when an Earthworlder thinks that every magical being knows every other one. You must think we have weekly magical meetings."

"I meant no disrespect."

She balances gently on a branch, testing herself as she walks across. "I don't care what you meant. Because of our debt to Paolo, we will help you. Look for an emissary at your residence at sundown."

"Thank you."

"Your thanks is unimportant. You are a non-actor here. Your request will cause one of our warriors to neglect both his duties and the rules we follow by custom. After this, Paolo can consider any debt owed from the peace negotiations repaid in full, and expect no more special treatment from the jojum folk."

"I understand."

"Very well. Do not return to hassle us. I will not speak before brandishing my spear next time."

She bounces away.

All day I watch out the windows for signs of the jojum emissary. Around sundown I convince myself they're not coming, and start brainstorming increasingly more desperate ways of finding Paolo. But right as the sun hits the horizon, a flash streaks across the lawn and a jojum materializes. He's large for his species, and even from the height of my second story window I can see that he wears what appears to be a suit.

He pauses at the base of the porch steps, and reaches out a tentative hand. He flinches and pulls it back. A piercing whistle sounds throughout the house. I scramble out of bed, and hurry down to meet him.

"I was not told there would be such a strong enchantment surrounding your residence," he says, his voice impossibly deep.

"I'm sorry, I had no idea there was an enchantment." I walk down the steps and kneel next to him.

"No apology needed. I should have expected powerful Intention from Paolo." He extends a small hand for me to shake. I take it gently, energy humming through the grip.

"May I ask what kind of ... ah ... Intention is around the house, mister ... ah ..."

He laughs heartily. "I go by Telmud Cassius Jacoby. Cass works too."

"Jamie."

"There's a strong measure of protection around this home. I doubt any magical being who was not bidden could enter unscathed. It's a rather strong piece of Intention, both Elemental and Organic, one that mere skill alone could not create."

He sniffs, as if smelling the magic. "Although beyond the alterations made to both the house itself and the very land beneath it, if I guess rightly it is strengthened by the presence of a protected being in the house. Very interesting."

I have never thought of Paolo as someone with powerful magical abilities. But this creature speaks with reverence.

Cass says, "I see that you are relatively new to understanding Intention. I have heard stories about what happened in Barrun's War, and the part Paolo played. What I am referring to, though, is the pure devotion to someone other than oneself that this level of Intention suggests."

"Devotion?"

"Intention requires heart as well as mind." Cass smiles, then pauses, eyes on the house. "I have come to give you news, and warning."

"Did you find Paolo?"

"Not in the flesh. I spoke with a rather grouchy aileth who had talked to him two days ago, and he told me the last time Paolo was seen was with Hermus the potion maker."

"Where can I find this person?"

Cass hands me a piece of paper with an address written on it. The silver writing curls smoothly to the edges of the paper.

"Now for the warning. Hermus' interests are his own and he is certainly not to be trusted. He was banished for selling mislabeled tinctures that killed almost a dozen people, and has expressed regret only that he didn't get away with it. Recently, Hermus has been known to associate with the Kelluvas. Out of fear or loyalty, it's hard to know."

"Should I be scared too?"

"When people are afraid, they behave in dangerous ways. Hermus will do whatever he can to protect himself." The jojum straightens his suit, looking for all the world like a miniature businessman who's realized he's late to a meeting. "I wish I could help you further, but I must return to the duties of my tribe. I also must tell you, with regret, that you may ask no more favors of the jojum folk. We hold our debt to Paolo paid, and can offer no further assistance." Cass pauses, a frown on his delicate features. "You have the light of Intention around you. I hope it will aid you on your journey. May your shadow always fall on soft ground, friend."

Before I can answer, there is a flash, a ripple in the grass, and Cass is gone.

An address. It's enough to go on for now. Before I go inside to pack a bag, I let my eyes take in my house, filled with its fond memories of my early life. I never knew powerful Intention shielded me here, that when I felt warm and safe inside it was because Paolo had cast a protective barrier.

I walk up the porch steps and inside, the warning in Cass' voice gnawing at me.

CHAPTER TEN: NIKKI

"How much do you know about Barrun's War?" my mother says as we make our way down to the airfield, toward my banishment. One last gaudy but still claustrophobic carriage ride with my parents.

"Hell of a time for a history lesson, mom," I say. I'm looking out the window, watching the slope of Archbridge descend into Market Square on the south side of the river. The Rhydwel is a shimmering blue today. My eyes fall for the briefest second on the Conjuring Arena before it's swallowed by the buildings around it. I wonder when I'll see it next.

"This is important," my mother says. "That war was the beginning of our rivalry with the Kelluvas. The scars of it are everywhere."

Including in my father's eyes. He looks away, and says, "we believe a new conflict may be beginning. One that could be just as bloody."

"I'm getting banished. Doesn't seem like I'll have much to do with it."

"Your banishment has presented an opportunity, as unfortunate as it is," my father says. "We believe the Kelluvas may have been behind the Sky Engines failing."

By the Winged Ones. I feel targeted, and am reminded of my parents' warnings when I first started at the engines, of the need to retain Laputa power so I wouldn't be vulnerable. "So they're behind me getting banished?"

"We don't think so," my mother says. "Poisoning several of the apprentices and sabotaging one of the engines is well within their power, but making sure you would get blamed for stopping the engines seems unlikely."

"Why stop the engines?" I ask.

"The simplest explanation is that they wanted to rally anti-surface sentiment," my father says. "The Kelluvas are making a play down on the surface through their proxy, Almus Kelluva, the one who was banished after Barrun's War. While one part of his plan involves cultivating a werebeast army, this is merely a supplement to his main force. The most devastating forces are a group of teenagers we've been calling Changelings."

"Teenagers. Come on, this is ridiculous. I'd fight another snotty kid over a werebeast any day."

"The Changelings were not born," my mother says. "They were created by the Kelluvas and other powerful surface magic with a single goal in mind: becoming the most powerful wielders of Intention on the surface." She reaches over and touches the lapis lazuli fragment that now hangs from a necklace on my chest. The Piece of Sky I was given as part of the terms of my banishment. "Skyfolk absorb the Intention of the Sky around us. It's why we have access to magic while Earthworlders don't. But when we're away from it, our powers are greatly diminished. A Piece of Sky allows us to channel some Intention while on the surface, but we can't ever access our full power—there's simply not enough Sky to do so. We're dependent."

"But the Changelings have no such dependency," my father says, picking up the thread. "They have complete access to Intention, regardless of their proximity to Sky. In fact, it's been speculated that due to the process that created them, they may develop far greater Intention on the surface than all but the most powerful Intention-wielders on Terraltum."

That pulls me up short. I've been nervous about what being on the surface would do to my conjuring abilities. It seems unfair that these Changelings should possess so much Intention while mine is about to be diminished.

"You mentioned my banishment being an 'opportunity.' Thanks for that phrasing which, incidentally, is going to haunt me for my entire banishment."

It's a small blessing that being banished has given me full license to be a total brat without my parents scolding me. We're skirting Chancellor's Square now, on our way to Fenhall Square, where we'll turn south toward the airfield. A few curious aileth stop to watch our carriage pass, as if they know the shame that is riding inside.

"We have a mission for you," my mother says. "A mission for the family. There's a chance that if you complete it, it will undercut the Kelluvas so thoroughly that your banishment will no longer be tenable, and you'll be able to come home."

Well, they certainly have my attention *now*.

"We've been working on bringing as many of these Changelings to the Laputan side as we can," my mother says. "Employing our surface agents, we've managed to bring two into our grasp, and we think a third will soon be on our side as well. Seven are, sadly, a lost cause. There's one still in play, one who just happens to have been raised by one of your father's dearest friends."

They exchange a smile, one that tells me without question that it's no accident.

"Unfortunately, my friend Paolo is known to be intractable," my father says.

"Paolo?" I splutter. "The guy who sold you out to the Kelluvas at the end of the war?"

"He sold us out at our bidding," my father says. "He's been a double-agent pretending to work for the Kelluvas ever since. It's how we managed to have him installed as the boy's—Jamie's—guardian. This part of the plan worked to perfection, but Paolo's love for Jamie is proving to be a problem. He's been insistent that Jamie not be involved in the conflict, despite the fact that he was created for this very purpose. Every agent we've sent has been rebuffed."

"So I'm supposed to, what, beat Paolo into submission?" I ask.

"Whatever it takes," my mother says. "He has to see that Jamie will be drawn into this fight whether Paolo likes it or not. He's incredibly stubborn, not unlike his childhood friend—" a pointed look at my father, who almost smiles "—and his friend's daughter. Luckily you have two advantages over any other agent we could send. First, you have a personal connection as our daughter. Second, you are by far the smartest, most capable, and most persuasive person I know."

By the time I have the chance to process this level of praise, we're at the airfield. It's a broad strip of flat stone, Intention-powered craft parked in ordered rows for almost as far as I can see. They range in size from massive hovercopters—which are capable of traveling from here to the Western Reach in just a couple minutes, and can be loaded up with a military payload capable of devastating a city—to the two-person crafts favored by those who have to come and go on missions to the surface. They're teardrop-shaped, with a primary compartment in front and a long tail in back that can turn and vibrate to serve as a rudder. They also become invisible as soon as they launch off Terraltum.

We have to stop at security, where they check my Piece of Sky and travel papers. We have to say goodbye here, because only travelers and pilots are authorized to enter the airfield. Our goodbye is brief, tearful, and uncomfortable under the watchful eye of six armed guards.

The trip to the surface is uneventful. I'm too numb to process the vertigo of launching off the edge of my world, the way the clouds break below us to reveal the sprawl of the surface. The surface is unfathomably huge. There are wide pockets of uninhabited space on Terraltum, but down here they seem to spread forever, wide fields breaking into green mountains interrupted only occasionally by the thin strip of a highway, or clusters of buildings forming a town.

I turn my parents' mission over and over in my mind. It's all so new, so disorienting. But if there's even a chance of returning to Terraltum early, of picking up my conjuring career where it left off, I have to take it.

The airship pilot doesn't speak, except to point out the colony where we're headed once it comes into view. From the air, it's the saddest collection of ramshackle buildings I've ever seen. I guess it makes sense, given that it's effectively a penal colony for banished Skyfolk. There's no rule that says we have to stay there, but most do, both finding it more comfortable to be around our own kind and easier to stay hidden. The only thing that guarantees further punishment is forcing an Obscurer to have to step in and wipe a bunch of Earthworld memories by revealing anything about Terraltum or Intention.

If the colony is sad from the air, it's downright depressing once we land. The airship pilots drops me off and takes off again immediately, as if physically repulsed by the mere proximity to so many banished Skyfolk. I make my way through the narrow streets, passing groups of aileth who look strung out on some illicit substance, some of whom have obviously had their wings removed as punishment for whatever crime got them banished here. Most of the banished are human, and these are probably the most threatening. Within a couple minutes I've already had to sprint away from a man with a gray face who starts threatening me with a ball of fire growing between his palms.

I'm supposed to meet two beings who will help me on my mission. An aileth and a gnomin. These are the companions my parents, in their infinite, ineffable, indefinable wisdom have provided. I'm a bit early, though, so I throw caution to the wind and wander the town.

There's no order or structure to this town. Food vendors pop up on random corners, and there doesn't seem to be any central business district. In fact, most businesses seem to be run out of people's homes, or consist of a single table beside the road with scrap goods on it. Dust rises from the streets. It's spring and the sun isn't particularly hot, but there's something stifling about this place.

I find myself gravitating toward a rumble of noise at the far end of the colony. As I approach, the noise intensifies, with probably fifty or sixty voices yelling at once, the sound coming from what looks like some kind of pavilion. The pavilion is open to the elements at the sides but has a low roof surrounding the vaguely circular structure. I should be hesitant to approach this place, but I'd know that sound anywhere.

It's the sound of people watching a conjuring match.

I've just stumbled across a conjuring arena in a colony of banished Skyfolk on the surface.

I climb the back side of the pavilion—there's no thought of needing a ticket for this match—and find myself among a crowd of scary-looking humans, ailethier, gnomin, and even a few jojum sitting in their own miniature stands. The battle area is maybe a third of the size of the one on Orella, and is mostly sandy dirt with interspersed patches of grass. It is immediately clear that this is a different kind of conjuring match. The close quarters necessitate quick thinking and a more urgent brand of conjuring, while the spectators are so close to the action that they are yelling practically in the conjurers' ears. The other difference is that, rather than trying to accomplish an objective, the conjured creatures appear to be attacking the opposing conjurers directly.

A young man who can't be more than a few years older than me is at one end of this fight, his skinny frame buffeted by blows from a monster composed entirely of eight or ten connected fists.

He rolls away as an octopus bursts forth from his fingers, crushing its tentacles brutally around each hand. His opponent, a massive man with tattoos curling around his bald head, does something I've never seen in a conjuring match before: he punches the octopus *with his own fists* to try to get it off his creature.

This is desperate, dangerous, all-or-nothing conjuring. And I'm enthralled.

The skinny man eventually concedes after being thrown across the ring for a third time. His opponent helps him to his feet. I note a strange camaraderie between these men who were just a second before trying to beat each other to a pulp. For a second I think the young man looks a bit like Stevven, but the resemblance is only passing. I miss that annoying, braggadocios guy. If things had been different, I think we would've been good friends and teammates.

A new possibility has obviously presented itself. My dream of being a champion conjurer might not have to die. I could fight here, win here, become one of the best in this place where there is clearly a ton of talent. Then once my banishment is up, I could return to Terraltum, using my new skills in the more civilized version of conjuring in Orella. I almost feel my eyes well with tears as I consider this path before me.

But my parents' words hang over me. The urgency was obvious in the mission they gave me. Whatever threat the Kelluvas are trying to unleash, it must be of the existential variety. When it was between a career as a politician or as a conjurer, the choice was obvious. But when the choice is between living my dream and preventing our enemies from wreaking devastation, I know what I have to do.

I turn away, leaving the noise of the crowd behind me, and go to meet an aileth and a gnomin.

Ora the aileth bears a constant expression of disapproval on her obnoxiously beautiful face. Instead of being delicate, like most aileth wings on Terraltum, her wings are covered in a web of serpentine tattoos. The gnomin, Amby, has apparently recently learned the concept of walking and talking simultaneously. He is slightly taller than Ora, at about five feet, and has a large paunch that appears to be balding (it sticks out from under an awkwardly short Earthworld T-shirt), as the coarse brown hair on the rest of his body makes a desperate escape from his soft, fleshy tummy. He also sports a massive under-bite that, on a less strange creature, might be endearing.

"We're almost there," I say. We've been following a winding country road for several miles, stopping occasionally for Amby to rest his legs. I wonder how Stevven and the rest fared in our first match. That would've been yesterday. They probably got trounced without me.

"I think I saw an ant pass us," Ora says, flying effortlessly.

"Sorry if the pace isn't to your liking, but last I checked, you had to do what I say."

Ora flares her symmetrical nostrils.

"Being Earthbound has been the single greatest insult in my life," she says.

"Well, you should've thought of that before you decided to use your aileth magic to con innocent people."

Ora rolls her eyes. "The people I conned weren't innocent. Grand Juncture is full of gamblers who are only too willing to lose their money."

"Doesn't make it okay."

"Believe me, the trial made that abundantly clear." Ora exhales derisively. "Why is Terraltum bureaucracy always so much more concerned with the letter of the law than what's actually for the best?"

Though it does seem harsh that Ora was banished to the surface for something as basic as fraud, it doesn't take a genius to guess that there were probably prior offenses involved. Many prior offenses.

"You're getting off easy," I say. "Once we complete this little mission, my family will present a formal letter of recommendation for your return to Terraltum, and you'll be free to go back to tricking humans into falling in love with you or whatever it is you do with your free time."

Though not officially codified, it's become tradition for banished non-humans—ailethier, gnomin, even the massive but mostly gentle Tardigras water bears—to use service to one of the great houses as a backdoor to returning home.

"'Bring the boy to safety and ensure he is protected until his powers develop.' Sounds awfully open-ended to me," Ora says.

"Don't be so literal. As long as I have your spirit of cooperation, I'm sure I'll be lenient."

Ora's wings actually turn a shade of red as she fumes.

"Ms. Laputa, I do apologize if my speed is a problem for you," Amby says, inadvertently preventing physical violence. "You could leave me behind, if you wish."

"No, Amby, don't worry about it. It won't be long."

Trees overhang the road, forming a tunnel of newly sprouted green. Only a few cars have passed. When we hear them coming, Ora turns herself transparent while Amby sneaks off into the underbrush. The cars are almost magical in the way they glide along the road, stirring up gravel and dust in plumes behind them, nothing like the picture from my Earthworld Studies classes.

We reach a gravel path leading off into the forest, with a partially obscured house at the end of it. The blue crystal Piece of Sky on my chest quivers as I step onto the path, sensing the magical energy nearby. I clutch the fragment, reassured knowing a small part of my home is with me.

The house is large, though nothing like the estate I grew up in. It's composed entirely of angles, with odd sections jutting out at random intervals, and windows not always oriented in parallel to the ground.

"Is it just me, or does this house look accidental?" Ora asks.

"Ora, take a look in the windows. Amby, you go around back."

"What about you, Ms. Laputa?" Amby asks. From his intent expression I can tell he's very invested in this plan.

"I'm going to ring the doorbell."

I wait a few seconds for the others to get into position, and then approach the front porch. I try to step as quietly as possible. Ora is translucent again, buzzing around the upstairs windows, which reflect the blue of the sky. I think through the pitch I will make to Paolo.

There is in fact no doorbell, so I rap my knuckles on the door. I knock again. Through the pane of glass in the top of the door, I can make out a long hallway. Coats hang on a rack inside, and a long runner unfurls itself along the wood floor. Nothing stirs.

When my second knock goes unanswered, I conjure a tiny chimera to pick the lock. I give her strong hands covered with metal-spiked gloves, and make her small enough to fit inside the keyhole. It takes me a few extra seconds. Down here on the surface my Intention feels hard to hold onto, slippery somehow. My Piece of Sky is clearly not enough to channel all of my Intention down here.

"Ms. Laputa!" calls Amby, running as fast as his short legs allow around the edge of the house. "I think something got here before us."

I let the chimera dissolve as I step down off the porch. Amby's face is concerned, although it's hard to tell whether that's just how it looks normally.

I follow the gnomin to the back of the house. We're not the first unwelcome visitors. The back door hangs ajar, with the area around the lock splintered and surrounded by...

"Are those claw marks?"

"I will go ahead," Amby says. "There may be danger."

As silly as the little gnomin looks, his presence does faintly reassure me.

Amby pushes the door open with a creak, and then recoils.

"What's wrong?"

"There's an enchantment. I think it's non-human oriented. If I go in it will cause me terrible pain."

"Wouldn't whatever came before have hit the same enchantment?"

"If it wasn't human, yes. Although usually the worse the creature, the more pain they can tolerate."

My stomach lurches.

"Do you think it's still here?"

Amby breathes deeply through his nose.

"I don't think so. It hasn't been gone long, though."

"I'll go alone, then."

"Be careful."

Whatever came before us had no interest in going unnoticed. Dishes are scattered across the floor from where the kitchen cabinets have been torn open. In the living room, the bright yellow couch is missing an arm. The door leading to the basement stands open, hanging on half a hinge.

I creep up the stairs. I trust Amby's gnomish nose, if only because of its absurd proportions. But every corner and shadow still holds an imagined Fantasma, a shade waiting to leap out.

At the top of the stairs, the landing wraps around a wooden banister. Two rooms abut the landing on that side, while another, probably the master bedroom, is on the other. I don't bother searching the bathroom in between them, and instead go straight for the first of the two smaller rooms.

Whatever creature made the mess downstairs didn't touch this room. The bed is made tidily with a brown blanket. The rest of the room is clean, almost to the point of emptiness, with no other furniture besides a hand-made pine dresser and a bookshelf stuffed with encyclopedias. I back out of the room and make for the other.

The creature knew exactly which room to come to. The bed lies on its side on the ground, with the mattress demolished. A child's dresser has been upended and clawed from behind. Slashes carve through pictures on the wall. I stop to study the wall ornaments, past the ferocious claw marks to images of rolling hills shrouded in fog, a jagged cliff falling away into the sea, and a man in some kind of uniform holding a stick in mid-swing.

The room bears few clues about its former occupant's location. A couple reference books about magical creatures lie open on the bedside table, beside a half-drunk glass of water that is somehow undisturbed.

A clatter comes from the window, and I spin around, heart hammering. But it's just Ora letting herself in. She's either unaffected by the enchantment, or simply able to ignore it.

"This place is a mess," she says. "An aileth's parent would never let their child keep their room this filthy."

"Are you a parent?"

Ora looks aghast. She points to three faint vertical lines tattooed on her forehead. "No, child. I was born into the ruling order of ailethier, as you can see by my mark. We aren't permitted to have children."

"Sounds like an awfully limiting system."

"More limiting than the 'great' human families of Terraltum?"

"You know how hard I had to work to get the name Laputa? Being born is no small feat."

I step forward toward the open books. They're both at entries about werebeasts.

"Look at this," I say, handing one over.

Ora studies it, reading the whole page in a few seconds. Her brow wrinkles, pulling the three lines of the mark further apart.

"Maybe it's not a mystery what tore this place up," Ora says, handing the book back to me.

"How did he know what was coming for him?"

"He was able to leave, evidently. Werebeasts tend to leave impressive blood paintings where they make their kills."

"Come down here!" calls Amby from outside.

We head down the stairs, out through the kitchen onto the side porch. I take the book with me.

"You found something?" I say.

"Once I had Jamie's scent, I picked up a trail leading away from the house. He got away."

"Good, then we follow the trail."

"There are two trails on top of each other. The first is Jamie's. The second belongs to the creature that destroyed the house."

The image of the werebeast on the encyclopedia page stares up at me, the gaping mouth a mess of sharp teeth and stringy saliva. I hold the Piece of Sky on my chest and ask the Winged Ones to watch over me and the Earthworld boy.

CHAPTER ELEVEN: JAMIE

Even if I had a learner's permit, without a car it would be about as useful as a return ticket from the lost continent of Mu. I trek the two and a half miles into town, in time to catch a bus headed to Beverley. The whole time, Paolo's warnings not to leave the house echo through my head. He's not exactly leaving me a choice, though.

The bus ride is close to two hours. I try to keep my attention on the task ahead, rather than letting my mind wander to what might have happened to Paolo, now that the secret world he kept from me suddenly decided it wanted him back. A quiet main drag runs through the center of Beverley, shops on either side. Most of the shops lack customers, even though it's the middle of the day.

The address Cass gave me is on a street intersecting the main road. I count down the numbers until I stop in front of a tiny teashop. I'm embarrassed to admit I was sort of expecting a potion shop. The last few days have been so weird.

Pungent, humid air fills the shop with the thick odor of a dozen types of tea. A middle-aged man stands at the counter, pouring steaming water into a teapot. His baggy eyes find me as I enter.

"Can I get you something, young man?" he asks. His voice has an unmistakable edge of suspicion. Maybe he thinks I'm a coffee drinker.

"I'm looking for someone named Hermus," I say.

The man studies me, putting the teapot down on the counter.

"No one by that name here. Sorry."

For a second I consider stepping back outside and checking again to make sure I have the right address, but Wesley nudges me forward.

"Are you sure?" I ask, trying to project confidence. "I was given this address and told to ask for Hermus."

"Kid, I just make tea. If that's not what you're here for, I'll need you to get out of my shop."

I think he's lying, I say to Wesley.

Uh, obviously, Wesley replies.

"Sir, do you know anyone named Paolo? He was here not too long ago."

"I don't know a Paolo." His hands tighten on the cup he's holding.

I sit down at one of the tables closest to the counter. The man pointedly turns his back to me and fiddles with a knob on the water heater.

"Can I have a green tea, please?" I ask. "I don't usually do caffeine, but you make tea sound so appealing."

"Jasmine okay?"

"Whatever's cheapest and greenest."

The man sets his hands to work, scooping the leaves into a strainer. I extend a few tentative, sensing strands of Intention into the room. I recognize his nervousness, but I need more. Vague threads of emotion fill the air, as difficult to grasp as the steam that now rises from the kettle.

"It's not all that convincing that there would be enough customers to keep this kind of shop going in a town this small," I say.

Bristling frustration reaches me. Good.

"You'd be surprised," he says.

I'm close, the threads are there. All I need to do is tap into them.

"Always thought of tea as more of an urban thing, at least in America. Like hipster coffee shops and craft beer."

"There's a brewery down the road."

So suddenly I can't explain exactly how it happens, his emotions snap into place. They're so clear I don't even have to try to read them. I've got him.

"Is it also a front for one of the Skyfolk?" I say.

The man's face falls, and the cup he was holding a second before imitates it, falling and smashing on the floor.

"You're not one of them, are you?"

"One of who?" I ask. "Sorry, whom."

He grunts. His fear is so clear, so unbridled, so unhidden. It's a two-way connection, I realize, not merely something to be read, but something I can influence. I've never done it with a human before, but I try to project into his mind. Not words, exactly, but a sense that his fear of me is unwarranted, and will lessen if he helps me.

For a brief moment, the man's face remains unchanged, and I can't find his emotions anymore. I wish I knew what I was doing.

"You'd better come upstairs." With two flicks of his finger, the sign on the shop door on the other side of the room flips from open to closed, and the lock clicks shut. He leads me to the back of his shop, where a rickety staircase climbs to the apartment above.

I consider saying, "What about my tea?" but this is no time for wiseassery. The thoughts that escape the wall of Intention around this man's mind are frightened, not aggressive.

The apartment at the top of the stairs is probably dirty enough to be considered for superfund cleanup site status. Soiled dishes stacked in the sink overflow onto the counter, and a stiff scent of week-old vegetables clings to the stuffy air. In the next room an intricate setup of glass vials and jars is filled with the colored liquids of an in-progress experiment.

He points me towards a brown couch that was definitely a different color originally.

"I'll stand. I don't want to take up too much of your time."

"Suit yourself." The man sinks into the gray chair next to me, picking at the foam protruding from the arm. "I'm Hermus."

"I'm Jamie. Good to meet you. You've seen Paolo?"

"Yes, yes, he was here a few days ago. He was in a hurry, as usual. Rather pushy, actually."

"And what was he here about?" I ask.

"Don't think he'd like me telling you."

"How's he ever gonna find out?"

Hermus makes an uncomfortable expression. Something pops on the lab table in the other room.

"Paolo and I have been in contact a few times," he says. "We've both worked for the Kelluvas on and off. Paolo wanted to get in touch with Almus, the patriarch's brother, the banished one. Word is he's cooking up his own plans on the surface."

My mind flashes back to Paolo's visitors, to his warnings about the Kelluvas' power, but the pieces don't quite fall into place. "And where did he go to get in touch with Almus?"

"A spot not far from here. But that was days ago. They won't be there now. Look, I got no love for the Kelluvas, but I don't want them knowing I helped you."

"You're not telling me anything about their plans. You're telling me where my guardian is. Nothing more."

Hermus' eyes gleam at the word "guardian."

"The place is called The Crux. It's not three miles from here, just past the border into Caton. It's a sort of ... hub for magical activity in the area."

He doesn't specify what type of activity he means exactly. I pull a folding paper map out of my pocket, prompting an unpleasant laugh from Hermus.

"I thought kids like you used cellphones."

"It doesn't sound like Google Maps would do the job on this one. Can you mark the exact spot?"

He scrutinizes the map.

"Let me check it on one of mine," Hermus says. "Earthworld maps are hard to read."

He reaches behind the books on his bookshelf and pulls out a crumpled sheet of paper. The map on it contains dozens of markings I don't recognize. He circles a spot on his own map in light pencil, then compares the lines of roads and rivers to my map. After some consideration, he locates the corresponding point.

"There's no guarantee you'll find anything at The Crux. In fact, if I were you, I'd hope you didn't."

"Anything else you can tell us?"

The potion maker looks suddenly flustered. I realize his eyes aren't on me, exactly, but past me, out to the street. His anxiety, at a low hum since I stepped into the shop, suddenly thunders.

I glance out the window, but there's nothing. It can't be far past noon. The houses on the other side of the street wait lazily. My stomach growls.

"You don't know what the Kelluvas would do to me if they knew I talked to you," Hermus says. "Leave now. If you find anything at The Crux, it isn't my fault."

He shoos me toward the door.

"Well, thanks for your help." I'm at the stairs, and he continues to wave me away.

"My shop is closed. Please find another place to drink tea."

His nervous energy propels me as much as his physical presence. I consider trying one more time to persuade him to give me more information, but I already have what I need.

The door at the top of the stairs shuts loudly. A lock clicks. Then another.

We exit the teashop, returning to the warm sun on the street. Hermus' face pokes out through the curtained window on the second floor, watching as we cross.

The Crux. Exactly the kind of magical place I'd want Paolo to show me. But why do I still feel so afraid? Wesley bristles.

Something wrong? I ask.

Not sure. Doesn't smell like human towns are supposed to.

Let's get moving then.

I follow the map out of the center of town, and soon we are on a country road under budding trees. If not for the pit in my stomach, I would stop and enjoy the greenery. The new spring is promising that life is beautiful and full of hope after the short dreary days of winter.

As time winds on, the afternoon darkens, and clouds begin to form. Animals crash through last year's leaves, some of the sounds loud enough to raise a twinge of fear in my stomach. But I know the noise even a squirrel can make in dry leaves.

When rain begins to spray down, Wesley crawls in my backpack to keep dry, and I wish I could do the same. My sweatshirt is soaked within a minute, and my hair mats on my forehead.

Just as I'm getting used to the prospect of being soaked for good, the regional bus pulls up.

"You going to Caton, kid?" the bus driver calls.

"Nope just up the road a mile or so."

"Well, that's a mile you could be out of the rain. Hop on, the ride's on me."

That short stretch is enough time to remember how nice it is to be warm, and by the time I get off, I half consider going all the way to Caton and finding a hotel. My departure point is based on a rough estimate from the map, so it's a few more wet minutes before a dirt track appears several yards off the road. I plunge in.

Branches obstruct the path every few feet, and thick, muddy ruts carve through at odd intervals. Most of the trail is packed hard enough that mud only coats the bottoms of my sneakers. I keep a brisk pace, the squishing of my stride sounding against the soft tap-tap-tap of rain on the budding leaves. Movement keeps me warm. Somewhat.

As I continue on the trail, anticipation builds. Accompanying it is a strange feeling, like a soft humming in my limbs. At first I wonder if there's something wrong with me, if I'm dehydrated, or potassium-deficient, or have some other mundane ailment. But another unfamiliar sensation goes along with it: I can hear the voices of the woods more clearly, as if they're projecting themselves through unseen speakers. A squirrel near me is annoyed at both the rain and me, while a cardinal thanks his equivalent of a god for the shelter of a thick pine branch.

Even stranger, I hear a voice I've never heard before, a voice that doesn't speak in the frantic language of animal survival. A voice that speaks in creaks and groans. I can't understand it, but its vantage on the world is long and distant. My presence makes no difference, even as it doesn't go unnoticed. I am simultaneously watched and ignored. Its source strikes me suddenly. I'm listening to the voices of the trees. I've never heard these voices before, and they frighten me.

My pace quickens. I don't like this place, or how it amplifies my powers. The voices of the trees reach deafening levels, and I can't tell whether the ferns are speaking or merely swishing in the wind. I'm listening to an opera sung in a language I was never meant to hear.

Just when I despair of reaching my destination before the trees drive me insane, I emerge into a clearing. A tall rock cliff in the clearing appears at first glance to be made of granite, but its texture is off. No rock I've ever seen is that smooth, and when I move toward it the surface shimmers in rippling patterns. A wide semi-circle of similar stone extends from its base. Scores of blue markings run through it, cutting an intricate web of rivulets across the otherwise smooth surface.

A current of energy comes off the rock. When my foot touches it, vibrations ripple through me. Warmth breezes over me, and it takes a few paces before I realize that it's because, although the rain hasn't stopped, no water reaches me here. Drops don't bounce off an invisible barrier, or pour over the area like a waterfall. They simply cease.

Wesley climbs back onto my shoulder. He stays silent, as if out of respect.

As I continue toward it, I notice that the rock face is not altogether clean. Uneven marks score its surface. I run a hand over one of the marks, beginning to suspect it's a scorch mark. The rock vibrates, and I pull away.

In the grass to one side of the flat stone someone made a small campfire, long out now. The logs are barely burnt. A few ends are still brown. I find a shred of olive cloth by the fire. My heart sinks in recognition before my mental processing catches up. I know the article of clothing this fragment belongs to. It's from the jacket Paolo was wearing the day he left.

My imagination tries to conjure images of a battle between Paolo and an evil sorcerer, maybe Pure Intention flung in all directions, but it doesn't come. Paolo never struck me as one to engage in that sort of thing.

I continue searching the area, fear and frustration growing. Besides the pieces of cloth, I find no further clues. Paolo was here, but something violent happened and his coat was torn. That's all I have.

I look up the rock face, and realize that a small pathway leads, step-like, up the side. I start to climb, though my legs are already sore from my hike.

I scramble up, slipping twice before reaching the top step. I come out on a thin walkway overlooking The Crux. The walkway ends in a sheer wall at the other end of the rock face, while off to the side a gap in the stone ends in darkness, a small cave with only the first few yards visible in the fading light.

I turn my phone's flashlight on. The inside of the cave is remarkably smooth and completely empty. Soft moss grows on the floor. Rain patters outside. I hadn't considered where I would sleep tonight. I sit down on the moss at the back of the cave, leaning my back against the smooth wall. The rock gives off its own heat. The Crux below was unsettling, powerful in a way I didn't understand. But this cave comforts me. Out over the treetops, the sun is starting to set. It can't be much later than seven o'clock, but deep tiredness descends into my limbs.

What do you think? I say to Wesley, who has already curled up in a ball on the moss, his gray-blue fur shimmering as water falls off it.

I think it is as dry a place as any, he replies.

I was thinking more safety-wise.

Whoever was here before us is long gone. I think we will be undisturbed.

I stretch out flat on the moss, my thoughts falling easily away.

In front of me is a suburban house. It's on one of those quiet streets in the less well-off parts of town—an old truck rots and rusts in the front yard next door, and the ill-kept lawns are little more than strips between the squat homes.

The rear entrance is covered, but I prefer to be the one going in the front. Two of my brothers beside me, I climb the porch steps. A hum of Intention comes from the door, but the enchantment is weak.

I blow the door off its hinges.

Lithe movements take me through the wreckage of an entrance hall, and I hear rushing feet coming from the back of the house. I pour Organic Intention into my legs and glide into the kitchen in the back of the house in three steps. A pan flies at my head, and the protective shield I cast only softens the blow. I stagger into a defensive stance, blocking a burst of Pure Intention from the foe, who is crouching behind the kitchen table and launching everything he has at me. I create a wide shield, and soon his balls of Intention carom around the room, shattering chairs, knocking pictures off the refrigerator, smashing windows.

The barrage ceases when one attack strikes the man, sending him onto his back.

I stand over him. He struggles amid wooden splinters to rise at least into a sitting position. There is no fear on his face, though.

"You guys aren't the most respectful guests, are you?" The gray stubble on his jaw forms a hard line.

"Where is the girl?" I say. "Where's Callie?"

"Not here."

"Then where?" I put a foot on the man's chest, but keep my guard up just in case. He laughs unpleasantly.

"Somewhere you can't get her. Not that she'd have gone with you anyway."

"I'm not really used to taking no for an answer."

"Probably why you're such a prick, eh?"

I keep my anger behind a wall of calm.

"Since you're here, you may as well be useful," I say, eyeing the glowing blue shard on his chest. "Don't worry, your power will become joined with something far greater after you're dead."

As my hand closes around the man's Piece of Sky, a multilayered sensation, one closest to ecstatic guilt, builds inside me. As it builds, the edges of the room begin to fade out. The walls become empty space, the stove a simple square box of metal, even the kitchen table fading first into a rough geometric pattern and then into nothingness. Acceptance falls like a veil over the man's face, and then he too fades away.

CHAPTER TWELVE: NIKKI

F ollowing the boy's scent proves harder than I anticipated. He walked into town, but at that point got onto a bus—Ora fills me in on the word—and we are forced to ride the bus, getting out at each stop to see if Amby can pick up the scent. A few times it rolls off while Amby is still sniffing.

My parents supplied me with plenty of Earth money, which is called dollars, odd smelling paper bills with a regular shape that feels strange in my hands. On Terraltum, paper money is reserved for only the smallest denominations, while money of greater value comes in larger and larger coins, allowing you to tell by how heavy they are how much any given piece is worth.

In order for my two magical companions to go unnoticed, Ora folds her wings into her back, which, although uncomfortable, makes her look almost human. Even the minds of Earthworlders, so eager to rationalize whatever they see into the world they know, would trip over Amby's unmistakably gnomish appearance, so while we are within eyesight I summon an illusory haze around Amby. It distorts light and causes his appearance to appear, while not fully human, at least indistinct enough for most to look past him. The constant Matter Intention this requires would be barely noticeable on Terraltum, but down here it begins to drain me immediately.

We finally pick up the scent in the center of town. Rain has poured steadily for the past two hours, and Amby has to stop several times to find the weakening scent. Whenever he loses it, Ora flusters him with increasingly snide remarks about the famous noses of gnomin.

We arrive at a small teashop, obviously closed at this hour.

"His trail leads both in and out," Amby says.

"Maybe he wanted a cup of tea. Let's follow the trace he left after leaving the shop."

"Wait, do you feel that?" says Ora. She extends her wings and hovers a foot off the ground.

"No, what is it?"

"I can't tell exactly."

"I can smell it too," Amby says.

Both seem more concerned than I've seen them yet.

"It's the same thing I smelled in the house," Amby says after a moment. "It's rancid."

My untrained nose can't smell anything, but I take the gnomin's word for it.

"Where does the beast's scent lead?"

Ora's tone suggests she's no great admirer of human intelligence. "You want to follow it? You know we're talking about a potentially seven-foot-tall creature with eight-inch claws, razor-sharp teeth, and a brain that's had all areas not involved in killing and/or dismembering removed to allow it to focus more fully on said killing and/or dismembering."

"Are all ailethier this wimpy?" Roasting Ora might be the only thing separating me from my own fear, but it still feels good.

"They're all this intelligent."

"And this mean," Amby adds under his breath.

"Last I checked, you have to do what I say," I snap. "Where does the creature's scent lead?"

Amby sniffs, then leads us into the alley next to the shop. The alley is empty except for a dumpster. Fire escapes lead up the sides of the buildings on either side. Amby starts climbing the ladder on the side of the teashop. His footsteps are heavy on the rusty metal, but it looks like it can hold his weight. I follow him up, and Ora flies beside us.

At the second floor we reach a window—or rather, the remains of a window. The glass has been shattered, and deep grooves cut through the frame. Amby brushes some glass off the windowsill, gives me a scared glance, and climbs inside the building. I follow, with Ora close behind.

I nearly gag on the smell. I can't tell if it's the creature, the spilled potion ingredients on the floor, the dirty plates around the apartment, or some combination of all three that creates the overpowering odor.

There are the same signs of a brute force throughout the apartment as those in Jamie's house: a table overturned, the refrigerator smashed in, and a couch with deep claw marks on it. Papers are scattered around the apartment. Amby walks forward cautiously. A broken window lets in a chill breeze. Amby stops by it and sniffs. His expression quickly changes to relief.

"The creature went out this way," he says.

Relief quickly leaves his face when his eyes fall on the opposite corner. I put a hand to my mouth when I realize what he's looking at.

A dead body lies in the corner of the room.

With the damage that's been done to it, body is perhaps a generous term.

The man in the corner hasn't been dead long. His blood is not yet dry. Slash marks cover his torso and left arm, and his right has almost been severed at the elbow. Most of his blood has flowed out through deep holes in his throat, while both head and face have been brutally slashed several times. He was an older man, although it's hard to tell much else from what remains of his face.

Beneath the slashes on his throat, I search for a Piece of Sky. I don't find one. If his crimes were severe enough, he wouldn't have been granted one when he was banished to the surface, but what about the potions? Those would more than likely require the power of a Piece of Sky to focus his Organic Intention.

I kneel beside him, averting my eyes but directing all my Intention toward the man. He died in pain. I take his distress in, doing my best to dispel it. I don't know how much I can do for what remains of his consciousness, but I do what I can.

Ora and Amby stand on either side of me, their faces grave.

"Are you so eager to go after the beast now?" Ora asks.

"We need to find the boy," I say, "before the same thing happens to him."

Amby chokes back a gnomish sob.

"The boy was here," he says in a quiet voice. "Not as recently as the beast, but he was here."

"He must've spoken with this man. Let's look quickly. Time is running out." And I don't know how much longer I can spend in this place.

We spend a few minutes sifting through the apartment, even skimming over the papers on the floor. Most are potion recipes. At first we ignore these, but as I sort through them I notice that an inordinate number reference Intention stabilizers. Each recipe is slightly different, with notes scribbled in the margins, as if he'd been running dozens of tests.

"Why would a banished potion maker spend so much time making recipes for magical stabilizers?" I ask aloud, not expecting a response. "The only people I've ever heard of using that are workers in the Meluin Caves, who have to transport Sky."

My hand finds one of the papers that's fallen under a folding metal chair by the coffee table. It's a map, creased with the folds of many years, but lying open on the floor. I stretch it gingerly in front of me, afraid to rip it. Despite the tears in the paper, I see a spot marked with several circles in light pencil.

We stare at the circle, drawn around a spot called "The Crux."

"It could be a coincidence," Ora says.

"Or it couldn't be," I say.

"Or it couldn't be. I do know that place. It's one of the few places nearby where you can find a concentration of Intention. One of the old waypoints, placed by the guardians of the surface back before even the Sky Engines."

It's nearly impossible to imagine a time when the secrecy of my world didn't matter. And here I am, banished to the surface for exposing us for one minute.

This decision could decide whether the boy lives or dies. There are a thousand other reasons why the man might have circled this location, and there's nothing to say he marked it recently.

I don't want to make this decision. I imagine my trainer Grell, leading a battalion of conjuring disruptors during Barrun's War. She made life or death decisions every day. I wish I could ask her what to do. I'm tempted to follow this clue, but I know we can't be wrong. If we go to The Crux and he isn't there, it'll take hours to find the trail again. We don't have hours.

"We follow the boy's scent. At least we know more than we did before. Let's go." I stuff the map into my pocket.

Out on the fire escape, I breathe deeply, welcoming the fresh air. Before long, we are back on the boy's scent, taking the narrow road out of town.

We move more quickly than before. Amby doesn't complain, even though I see him wincing occasionally. About a mile down the winding country road, which is still slick with rain, the scent trail stops. As hard as he tries, Amby can't pick it up again.

"Dammit."

"I'm sorry," Amby says. "The werebeast didn't pass this way, if that's any consolation." The two trails had been following side by side for some distance, but the creature branched off some time ago.

"This may sound like a stupid question," I say, "but can were-beasts, you know, talk?"

"They're not noted for their conversational skills," Ora says, "but they can speak simple words and understand human speech well enough."

My thoughts race to a terrible possibility. Maybe the beast wasn't following Jamie's scent. Maybe it already knew where he was going.

"We can go back and pick up the creature's trail," Amby offers.

"There's not enough time." Seeing Amby's hurt expression, I say, "but it was a good suggestion."

Ora rolls her eyes.

There's only one option. "Ora, can you take us to the place on the map?"

"Yes, although there's thick woods between here and there."

"Then we need to get airborne."

I collect the dispersed threads of Intention, focusing my energy first on the Piece of Sky on my chest, then in the center of my mind. I push out other thoughts, all doubts, fears, and sadness. There is no room for them. There is only room for Matter. I envision a winged beast. I have conjured this same creature many times before, so many times that he has told me his name. He is Hediad, my windsteed.

Hediad appears in a flash before me. I think of him as a windsteed, though physically he doesn't resemble a horse. His skin is a chalky blue, covered in coarse white hairs that are almost invisible in the moonlight. Webs of veins run through his thick, leathery wings. At the end of each wing curls a tri-pointed claw. A faint crease along the bend of his back makes a good spot for a rider to sit. I approach his head and run a hand along his rough snout.

"Good to see you, old friend," I say. He snorts in acknowledgement, playfully nudging my hand away.

"That thing is incredibly ugly," Ora says, arms crossed. "Don't you have control over what you conjure?" In a flash of motion,

Hediad shoots out a wing, launching Ora five feet in the air. She flutters her own wings to catch herself.

"He's the best flier I've ever conjured. Or would you prefer I conjure some delicate show creature whose wings will snap in half as soon as you get in the air? I assure you I could make such a creature if I cared to."

"Could be a little nicer," Ora grumbles, settling back to the ground at a safe distance from Hediad, who locks one orange eye on her. His other eye winks at me.

Hediad's thoughts flow directly to me. I don't possess the Mind Intention to read most creatures' thoughts, but Hediad is one of my chimeras. He is, in a way, me. I feel the strength of knowing he could lift off at any second or rend an enemy with his jaws. I also feel the confusion of a newly conjured chimera, the inevitable result of coming into being so suddenly, which never goes away no matter how often I conjure him.

He remembers the past times he's existed, a fact I didn't realize until recently when he started swooping in the same rhythm I had used when I played a game with him in his previous existence.

It doesn't do to dwell on the implications of creating such transient life.

Somewhat drained after the first effort, I put myself to a second. This time, despite the fatigue of having conjured Hediad, the Intention comes more quickly, having already been gathered into a productive place in my mind. Hediad's sister, Droellaf, appears beside him. She is slightly bigger than her brother, and inherited my temper and tendency not to do as she's told. I find these features slightly annoying. I let Ora and Amby ride on her back, while I climb onto Hediad's.

Both of my companions are clearly uncomfortable with the first lurch upwards, but soon I am too lost in the exhilaration of flight to care. We rise over the treetops, and Ora points off into the greenery. Hediad surges ahead of his sister, who likes to let him think he can outpace her. With a sudden surge—and a cry of fear from Amby—Droellaf propels forward, past her brother.

I laugh and take Hediad higher, breaking us out of the race to admire the vastness of forest unfolding beneath us. Every now and again a small town or farm drives a gap in the budding trees, creating what could be divots on a flat lawn of grass. Though we haven't come far, I can already tell where we're headed. A slight pull comes from the magical area, an insistent tug on the Piece of Sky around my neck.

I pull up beside Ora and Amby.

"I take it you haven't spent much time in the air?" I yell over the currents of wind. The creatures flap their wings in powerful, even strokes.

"Gnomin live underground," Amby says, "partially to avoid this sort of thing."

"You'll love it in no time!" I shout as I pull Hediad into a tight downward spiral, brushing the tops of the trees with his claws as we pull up. For a minute all the pain of my banishment, all the anxiety of my journey, fades away. The wind blows my hair into a bushy mess that will take hours to fix, and dries my eyes out. Even with the wind, I couldn't be cold, as the heat of exhilaration burns in my chest.

As we near our destination, I make out a small clearing where a short cliff juts out of the forest. I steer Hediad into a slowly descending circle. With practiced silence, the two creatures glide down, landing flat on a wide stone at the base of the rock face.

Movement above immediately catches my attention. A cave looms atop the rock wall, and a large shadow climbs up the rock, scraping long claws against the mouth of the cave as it seeks a handhold. Ora has seen it too. I remember the lifeless body of the potion maker and fill with dread.

CHAPTER THIRTEEN: JAMIE

I awake to the sound of claws on the outside of the cave. The entrance to my shelter is still dark, but a presence is visible against it. I scrabble to my knees as I identify the shape. A large head, wolf-like and shaggy. Long arms end in claws that scrape against the rock and churn the moss, moving unsteadily as it climbs into the cave. From the fangs that glint in the faint light you would expect the creature to make loud slobbery noises, but it's utterly quiet. Save for the sound of its claws.

Terror. There is no second entrance to the cave, no way out except past the beast. I stand, my legs shaking. The creature already knows I'm here. It has come for me.

It finds its footing, and with a lurch its heaping shoulders enter the cave. Its sloping back bends forward in a crooked, deformed shape, as if it couldn't decide which way it wanted to grow.

Every part of me cries out to run, to hide. But I am alone, and the creature fills the entire mouth of the cave.

There is nowhere to run.

I am going to die. I can only hope it will be quick.

I do the only thing I can think of. I reach out to the creature, thrusting my Intention toward its mind.

It senses what I'm doing. Startled, it takes a step back, nearly slipping on the loose moss by the entrance. I cry out as my mind floods with its emotions. Dark. Primitive. Riddled with fear, anger, and pain. It knows exactly how despicable its existence is, that its only purpose is to destroy, to rend, to cleave.

The creature fights me. The link undulates like a rope between us, and I can feel him trying to shake it out of my grasp. I hold on as tight as I can, locking my eyes onto his.

The connection strengthens. I encounter not the current creature, but the shadow of what it used to be. Somewhere deep in its ancestral memory is the running Great Wolf, one of the massive animals that rule the western mountains of Terraltum. They are noble creatures, who value family and loyalty above all else.

This memory makes the existence of the creature before me all the more awful. The werebeast knows it will never be like its noble ancestors. It knows it's evil. This knowledge strikes me deep within my heart, and I find myself overcome with sadness. To live and know that one lives for no purpose besides evil. The inexorable weight of this existence almost crushes me.

The link breaks and I sink to my knees. I weep, not in fear of the beast's terrible claws, which now move toward me more urgently, but for its pain. And killing me will only deepen this pain.

There was nothing Paolo could've done to prepare me for this. I can't tap into that mind again.

A weight settles on my shoulder. Wesley runs a gentle paw against my neck.

I am with you, he says.

Promise me you'll escape, I reply. *Go while it's busy with me.*

I stand with you until the end, but that hasn't come yet. You have to reach out again.

The beast's hot breath fills the cave. Two more steps forward and I am almost within range of those long arms. It has slowed again, savoring my fear before it strikes the final blow.

I can't.

You have to. Give me some of it.

It disturbs me to do this. I never want anyone to experience pain, especially not someone I love as much as Wesley. But I know it's the only choice. I take some of the creature's anguish from myself, and form a connection with Wesley. Instantly I feel better. Wesley squeaks as the emotions flood him. I don't let him take all of it, only enough for me to try again.

I press the remaining fear to the side and return to the stream of emotion. My enemy's purpose is more resolute than before. The creature has felt my presence in its mind and is not pleased with what I've learned. The defensive shield it puts up makes my job even harder, but Wesley has cleared enough space. I tap every reserve of energy within my body and direct it into the flow of emotion, standing as I do.

The creature pulls up short again. All the same emotions are there, but this time they don't overtake me. This time I can see them at a safe distance, as if I stand beside a raging mountain river rather than being swept away by its current. Wesley strains to provide me with this buffer, continuing to drain the flow, and I know he's being hit with the full force of the creature's despair and anger.

I begin to mold the Intention, smoothing the singular purpose of destroying me from a sharp necessity to a dull desire. But confronting that issue head-on will not be enough. I bring that ancestral memory to the surface and ask the creature whether it could not instead be the being it truly wants to be.

It's a hard sell. This creature has spent its entire life believing in its own evil, lamenting it, but never believing it had a choice.

The creature freezes, stricken. Wesley has his eyes closed as he rocks back and forth.

Suddenly, I am not in the cave. A massive cavern stretches before me. It's illuminated, though I can't tell from where. I take halting steps forward, the sound echoing hollowly. A flat stone stands at the cavern's center. I approach it in a dreamy haze. A small creature lies uneasily on the stone. I stop twenty paces away, unsure.

My first guess would be that the creature was some kind of rodent, a feral underground dweller that lives a life without light. But the face is too long, the jaw too sharp. Pointed ears and gray matted fur. A wolf pup.

The pup is small, helpless, and strikingly hideous, its back bent at an angle, its jaw sneering, its limbs splayed in every direction. Its eyes catch mine, and I realize they're the same eyes that pierced me in the cave a moment ago.

I am face to face with a version of the very werebeast that is about to kill me. But we are no longer on the plane of my reality.

What now? Would killing the pup kill the beast? Is it that simple?

I step forward. My shadow falls over the stone, and the pup stumbles upright, so helpless, so pitiful. It whines and backs away from me. Another step and I'm right above it.

It wouldn't be difficult. I could probably snap its thin neck with one hand. Ordinarily the thought would never have crossed my mind, but I think about the slobbering fangs of the beast, the long claws that any moment could cut me in two.

That doesn't make the thought easier. The pup scratches nervously at the stone, sending an echo that dies almost instantly. Stalactites hang overhead. The drip-drip-drip of water cuts through the silence.

I don't know how long I have. Whatever I do, I need to do it quickly.

I extend a trembling hand. My fingers have not yet decided what they'll do. As my hand approaches, I take in the coarseness of the fur, the patches where chafing skin shows. I'm an inch away, but the pup doesn't run. It knows it's at my mercy. I wonder if this is how the werebeast feels when it sees me.

When my fingers touch the creature's fur, a stab of pain shoots through me. The cavern grows until it consumes the entire world. Then it shrinks to the size of the head of a needle, and nothing else enters my mind.

CHAPTER FOURTEEN: NIKKI

The werebeast roars before I make contact with it. Even in the cave's dimness, I see the creature rear its head back, almost striking the roof of the cave, and a small human shape dropping lifelessly to the floor.

I launch off Hediad's back, smashing into the beast shoulder-first at a ridiculous velocity.

Taken by surprise and seemingly already disoriented, the beast stumbles against the wall. I had softened my collision somewhat by creating a Pure Intention shield around my shoulder, but I still land awkwardly. By the time I have righted myself, the creature has as well. Hediad watches helplessly from outside, too large to come to my aid.

I don't bother being afraid. Even as tired as I am from the persistent drain of my earlier conjuring, the force of my Intention is still present.

The werebeast swings a claw at me, but it meets only another defensive wall, the bread and butter of the Pure School. Its howls pierce my ears. I back further into the cave, closer to the prone shape of a small boy. Two shades spring from my fingertips. The masses of vapor swirl around the creature's head. It bites at them, but its teeth pierce nothing but air. The sound of its frustration shakes the walls.

A shape scurries past the beast from outside, and I recognize Amby's squat frame.

Amby bends to pick up the boy.

Having given up on the shades, the creature charges forward once more. Amby has the boy across one shoulder, but his steps falter.

"Amby, run!" I shout through the effort of another conjuring, this one physical. A steel chain shoots from the floor and clasps itself around the creature's ankle. Amby sprints toward the door. The beast lunges at him, groaning against the chains. Amby's nearly at the opening when the chain snaps. A claw strikes out, digging a deep gash in Amby's shoulder as he and the boy disappear over the edge with a cry.

Now I'm alone with the beast in the narrow space. And he is pissed.

I try to form a chimera large enough to fight this brutal creature, but my Intention weakens. The strength of The Crux allowed me to perform the conjurations I had, but I still have to maintain Droellaf and Hediad outside. And I'm still not on Terraltum, the real source of my power.

The werebeast roars, trying to bring down the walls of the cave with its voice. Instead of a large chimera, I conjure dozens of smaller ones. They scurry around the beast, scratching at its paws and climbing onto its back to distract it.

The beast pays no attention. I have gotten between it and its prey, and it has decided I will serve as a substitute. It charges.

A shape fills the doorway. In the moment before jaws close on me, I am struck by its majestic poise. Ora's wings stretch to their full width, suspending her in the opening. She throws her hand forward. Blinding light fills the cave. I dart to the side as the beast hurtles past me. It crashes full force against the wall.

I run toward Ora, the roars of the beast behind me. Without a thought, I leap from the cliff.

Hediad waits for me. I land on his back as gracefully as I can in the dark. His sister holds strong under the weight of Amby and the boy nearby. As Hediad swoops past with me on his back, she follows us into the air.

The werebeast screams. I can see over my shoulder that it has already scrabbled down the cliff-face, and is taking long, loping strides into the forest. As long as I can keep us in the air, we're safe. I try to shake the fatigue from my head.

Hediad's labored breathing shakes his entire body. I don't have to actively concentrate to keep him in existence, but the initial act of Intention that created him still has to be held as a trace in my mind. This trace contains all the energy of the original action, only in a concentrated form. An unconscious part of me keeps this attention from dispersing. Whatever that trace is, it's not permanent, and continually drains me.

I focus on Hediad's breathing, trying to match my own to it. Once I quicken to his rapid pace, I dig my fingers deep into the white hairs that cover his hide until I touch his skin. I close my eyes, focusing on the link between us. Slowly I begin to steady my own breathing, allowing the air to flow through me in a relaxed, natural rhythm, relaying my calm through both our mental connection and the touch of our skin. Hediad's breaths slow as well. Confidence returns to his wing strokes.

We're out of danger for the moment, although I'm still exhausted. I hug Hediad tightly.

To our right, Droellaf carries Amby, who has set the boy down in front of him on the steed's back. Ora flies behind, binding Amby's shoulder with makeshift bandages salvaged from the ripped shreds of his shirt. Ora holds her own weight in the air, knowing how vulnerable our windsteeds are.

Her wings flap awkwardly to keep her aloft, but the image of her at the mouth of the cave still burns in my mind's eye. With all their scheming and sarcasm, it's easy to forget that ailethier are descendants of the Winged Ones, the beings who used to visit my world every hundred years, bringing with them a bountiful harvest and years of peace before flying off—to where, no one has ever known. The legends say that ailethier come from the union of Winged Ones and humans, and the majesty of their ancestors still lingers in them. In the secular world of Terraltum, the Winged Ones are as close as we have to gods. They have not come for nearly five hundred years, but I know I have experienced a shade of their presence tonight.

"I'm going to be expecting a great deal of appreciation for that," Ora says, flying over to me once Amby's bandage is secure.

"Believe me, you have it," I say, alarmed at how weak my voice sounds. "All the favors of House Laputa are yours."

Ora snorts. "You're not exactly in a giving out favors sort of position, sorry to say."

"Then ... Thank you for saving my life?"

"That'll have to do for now," she says, her voice the laughter of a morning drizzle on a mountainside. She points toward the shape in front of Amby. "Not much of a hero we've rescued."

The boy's skin is much lighter than mine, nearly paper white. Light brown hair lies limp across his large ears. My mother told me he's my age, but he appears to be at least two years younger. Could this boy really be a Changeling, a being created for his great power?

Based on the map my mother gave me before I left, it shouldn't take more than a few hours to reach our destination.

A tiny movement on Droellaf's back catches my attention. Amby is so startled he nearly falls off, throwing up his hands to defend himself. A trilopex stands defiantly on four of his legs on the boy's back, with his front two legs—the ones with the claws—raised to fight. I can't keep the laugh that springs to my mouth inside. Ora cackles. I double over, laughter rocking me so powerfully that I almost lose hold of the paper. I steer Hediad closer to his sister.

"Amby, are you alright?" I shout over the rushing wind.

"How do you mean, exactly?" He keeps his eyes on the trilopex, who is posturing dramatically.

Ora swoops over him. "Almost killed by a rodent!"

I level Hediad out and meet Amby's wounded eyes, letting my laughter subside.

"I mean your shoulder, Amby."

"I'll mend," Amby says. "My heart's still racing, though."

The trilopex squeaks angrily. Amby jumps again.

"This is not a creature of the surface." I study the trilopex closer, and am instantly struck by the intelligence in its eyes. "We mean you and your human no harm, friend."

"I call no one friend until I know their name," the trilopex says. "You may have saved us, but now you carry us off against our will."

"We bring you only to safety. My name is Nikki of House Laputa. We were sent to take you out of harm's way."

He bows. "A pleasure to meet a Laputa. I must confess it has been some time since I spoke with a member of your great family. My name is Wesley."

"Rats shouldn't talk," Ora mumbles, flying past us. "Isn't natural." I glare at her.

"The pleasure is mine, Wesley," I say. "This is Amby. He's in my service for the time being."

"How do you do, gnomin?" Wesley asks, reaching out a claw for Amby to shake.

"Well, thank you," Amby says. I don't bother introducing Ora.

Not that there's time anyway, as a gray shrieking missile careens toward us, crashing into Hediad's rump and sending him spinning.

I hold on for my life as another shape pelts toward me, this one striking Hediad's side before disappearing below us. Hediad fights to steady himself. I've lost all control. It's up to Hediad to keep us aloft.

A third shape swoops at Ora, but she dodges it. She stares after it, her sharp eyes scanning the new threat. Three gray-black creatures circle below us.

"Deathcrows," Ora chokes out. Deathcrows. They should be in the mountains of the Western Reach, not here on the surface.

I will life into my two steeds. The three deathcrows create a vortex as they rise again. Ora flicks a hand, and one is beaten back by a pulse of wind, but the other two continue toward us. I reach into my reserves and conjure a dozen chirping birds, which pester the crows.

The second this buys gives me long enough to take in the deathcrows. They're a jumble of harsh gray lines, with feathers so jagged I can't tell where they end and the saws of their beaks begin. Each has a wingspan of at least six feet. The birds' eyes stare cold and yellow.

I push Hediad hard, harder than I know he can take. Droellaf keeps pace beside him, while Ora lags slightly behind. The crows' cries are filled with malice and cruel delight.

Hediad and I dodge to one side, letting one hurtle past. The other rushes at Amby, who fends it off with a swing of his arm. My little birds disappear as I break my concentration.

The deathcrows are fast, but they are most dangerous in short spurts. In top condition, Hediad can keep a consistent pace for almost fifty miles that they couldn't match. He is not in top condition, though, and the birds circle back.

"You got anything, Ora?" I shout.

She sighs dramatically.

"I suppose I can try something. It's a little ... crude, though."

"Whatever it is, it beats the hell out of getting pecked out of the air!"

"So ungrateful," she says. She stops suddenly, falling behind us. The deathcrows are on her in an instant. She feints to one side, darts to the other, and wraps her slender arms around one of their necks, landing on its back. The creature isn't strong enough to hold her weight. It plummets, thrashing wildly, trying to throw her off. But Ora's grip is firm. The other crows chase after them. In another moment they are indistinct, writhing shapes behind us.

I continue to push the steeds hard, although I ease off as much as I think is safe. Amby gazes back, his eyes full of guilt.

"Ora will be alright," I say. "She's a lot stronger than she looks."

"She isn't very nice to me, but she may've just saved our lives," Amby says.

"Guess that counts as being nice, in its way."

A couple minutes pass. The wind has already turned my ears numb. Ordinarily being this cold would keep me awake, but all I can think about is my warm bed, the blanket my grandmother made for me when I was little, the fabric that stretched around me like caressing arms.

The sky is pale. Clouds drift across it. I wonder where above me Terraltum is, whether my eyes stare right through it, or whether it's on the other side of the world. Not that it matters, it may as well be the moon for all I can do to reach it.

I look over at the boy. He has slept through all of the commotion. At first I thought he had fainted from fright, but surely that wouldn't bury him in sleep this deep. I've only seen that kind of fatigue come from Intention Sickness—the malady that comes from spending all of your Intention. But no, that's absurd. This Earthworld boy doesn't even have a Piece of Sky with him. I shiver, not wanting to believe my parents were right about what he is.

Amby strokes the hair out of the boy's eyes, and rests a protective hand on his thin back. He keeps checking over his shoulder. I'm too tired even to turn my head. After almost ten minutes, Amby speaks again.

"Look." He points far into the distance. I force myself to follow his gesture. Three dark shapes catch the first light of the coming dawn.

We're in a deadly, long-distance race. Our destination lies no more than three miles away, but with every passing moment, the shapes grow larger behind us. Where is Ora?

You can do this, I think to Hediad. His only response is labored breathing as he keeps beating his broad wings. Pure will, the foundation of the Matter School, keeps him alive.

A mile passes below us. The birds may not be designed for this kind of distance, but they gain on us nonetheless. I can't push Hediad any faster. My own strength wanes. Amby has turned around on Droellaf's back, readying himself to fight.

"There!" I shout, as I see the marker I've been watching for, a high plateau that stands out against the rolling hills around it. "Around the other side."

Wings pound. I lean forward, spreading my weight across Hediad's back, curling my hands deep into his feathers. As we near the plateau, the wing beats stop and we begin to slow. We can hear the crows' terrible cries now. Our steeds no longer have the strength to beat their wings. We'll have to coast from here. I start a wide bank turn around the plateau.

One last conjuring, I decide, as we turn the corner and the deathcrows come within twenty yards of us. Pouring my last drop of energy into it, I fling my arms skyward. A dozen pieces of glass appear in the air, casting light in every direction. Confusion overtakes our pursuers momentarily as they pull up, unable to comprehend the illusion.

I don't have time to think about whether this means we've escaped. Instead, I see the ground coming up to meet me. My exhausted mind realizes far too late that Hediad is no longer beneath me, and that the ground does not look at all soft.

CHAPTER FIFTEEN: JAMIE

*T*he only indication I have that I'm alive is what I can see, but what I can see doesn't make much sense. I stare into a fire, halfway out of a thought I can't remember. It's like backwards déjà vu, where instead of happening twice, the thought never happened at all. I absentmindedly raise and lower the level of the flames, making them lap a few inches from my boot-clad feet, then drop to nothing. I try to ignore the bestial squeals of pain from behind me. Failure equals pain. It's a simple equation I learned long ago. That doesn't make it easier to block out the sounds of suffering.

I'm disturbed by something else, a presence in my thoughts, though it's too nebulous to put a finger on. Better to leave it be and continue to distract myself with the flames.

A whine turns into a bark. The second bark is cut short, and followed by a heavy thump. A door opens on the other side of the clearing. The figure has to bend almost double to fit through the door, even of the largest shed. It doesn't pause before coming toward me. Its size, its bulk, all make it seem as if it should shake the earth as it walks. But it moves at a glide, no sound coming even from its rippling silver cloak.

I stand. I am compelled to stand. And it stands above me, twenty feet from head to foot and wider than I am tall. My eyes must remain on the ground.

I WOULD SPEAK WITH YOU.

The voice is age borne upon a sound wave. It is all the cycles of Earth and Sky, of rising and falling. It is death.

YOU MAY LOOK AT ME.

As I lift my gaze I make out two massive eyes, pure black, but ringed with pale, glowing blue around the edges. They bore into me, alight with blue fire.

I awake with throbbing pain throughout my body. The pain is without context, ethereal, emerging only out of blackness.

I feel like I fell out of a tree. I know exactly what that feels like from the times I "came down the quick way," as Paolo called it.

On second thought, this is a lot worse than that, and it doesn't help that I know when I open my eyes, Paolo won't be there.

I open my eyes. He isn't there.

I'm on my back on a hard mattress. A candle burns slowly into a pool on the slate table by my bed. Water trickles. My eyes scan the walls, noting the roots that protrude from the hard-packed earth, but I cannot find a visible source of the sound. A thick rug the color of the walls covers the slate floor.

I see no sign of Wesley.

I sit. My legs, beneath soft white sheets, are only clothed in boxers. I stand, steadying myself against the bedpost, which appears to be made from the entire trunk of a young tree, bark and all.

My head spins. My mouth has the sharp taste and fuzzy sensation I would get after sleeping over at a friend's house and forgetting my toothbrush. A rough wooden door provides the only entrance, the cracks beneath it the only source of light aside from the candle. I take a step forward, easing my weight off the bedpost.

I have just enough time to feel the thick weave of the rug between my bare toes before my head spins and I fall in a heap. The bruises on my elbows and knees assert their presence loudly. I lie on my back for a long minute, waiting for the pain to subside or take me away.

Last I remember, I was about to be eaten by a giant werebeast. No, that's not quite right. Last I remember, I was inside the werebeast's mind.

The door whips open on rusty hinges. In the doorway, a lamp illuminating the hallway behind her, stands a girl. She is about my height, though with wider shoulders. Her black hair has been chopped off halfway down her neck and tossed lazily to one side. Fierce eyes catch me with an intense gaze. She gives off a vibe of owning whatever room she walks into.

"I thought you couldn't look any scrawnier when I found you," she says. "Guess I was wrong."

I scramble to cover myself with the sheet, climbing up onto the bed.

"Don't hurt yourself." She makes for a wooden wardrobe to the left of the door. She pulls out a few brown articles of clothing and tosses them to me.

I flail ridiculously, and the clothes smack me across the face. The girl snorts. She wears a similar outfit of rough-spun brown pants and shirt.

The girl turns the room's only chair toward me, sitting but politely averting her eyes as I struggle into the clothes. Despite their rugged appearance, they're soft against my skin.

"Well, that was rather the ordeal," she says when they're more or less on. "Good thing it was only two pieces of clothing, otherwise you might've passed out from the exertion."

She isn't very nice, I decide. Her eyes scan me and find me lacking.

"It's all set now," I say. "Thankfully I'm still conscious."

She smiles, happy I have a sense of humor if nothing else.

"My name is Nikki," she says. "I'm from House Laputa, not that that will mean anything to you."

"I'm loosely acquainted. You're from Terraltum?"

"I grew up there."

Behind the confidence, unhidden pain ripples off her.

"Tell me, Jamie, why are you so special?"

"Excuse me?"

"I risked a lot to find you. I fought off a werebeast and three deathcrows. My friend nearly gave her life allowing us to escape. Why were you all this trouble?"

My heart sinks. I can't think of a single reason, other than that I prefer being alive.

"I don't know. I can't see any reason why that thing would be after me either."

"That thing meaning the werebeast?"

I nod.

"Nasty creature," Nikki spits. "There's nothing but hate in them. They should all be destroyed, along with the sorcerers who made them in the first place."

"I don't know. It seemed like it didn't like the fact that it wanted to kill. It would rather have been kinder, but hate is all it knew."

Nikki laughs out loud. She leans forward.

"You may be the first person ever to come face-to-face with a werebeast and come out feeling sorry for the thing. When I found you, you had fainted from fear and were waiting to be eaten."

"I didn't faint. Well, not exactly. I made some sort of connection with the creature. One minute I was in front of it and the next..."

I trail off. Nikki watches me intently.

"And the next, it was like I was somewhere else, some big cave, and the werebeast was there, only he was a puppy. I tried to get close to him, but then..." I gesture in a thoroughly unhelpful manner. I wait for Nikki to laugh at me again, but her face is more serious than before.

"You're an Earthworlder. How could you—with no training in the Mind School—I mean—it doesn't seem..."

"What?"

"I've never seen it personally." Her voice is calm, but I see the gears turning behind her eyes. Are they green? Gray? "I don't mess with Mind Intention. Much too invasive for my taste."

"I told you, the connection just happened."

"Just happened? By the sound of it, you entered the werebeast's inner mind sphere. You're lucky to be alive for more reasons than one." Nikki stands and waves me up. "Come on, Master Root has been waiting to see you."

"But the pup," I say as I stand, wobbling only slightly. "Why was there a wolf pup in the creature's inner mind sphere?"

Nikki spins, her expression angry.

"You saw the inner projection of the creature's self, the true image of what it thinks it is. That's available to no one except the creature itself—save for someone willing to carry out Mind Intention of the most intrusive kind."

"I didn't know. The connection sort of came to—"

I cut myself off at Nikki's expression. The creature's inner projection. That terrifying creature sees itself as a defenseless, cowering pup.

A defenseless, cowering pup that fully intended to rip my head off, and could've done so easily.

Nikki keeps a dozen paces in front of me, forcing my sore legs to struggle along the bare earth of the passage outside my room. Torches cast light at even intervals along the walls. There is no wood, oil, or electricity. The torches simply burn. Every so often a passageway shoots off to one side, but we're clearly in a central corridor and Nikki ignores them.

"What is this place?"

"It has a name in the old tongue of those who dwell beneath the surface, although I can't pronounce it." I notice how the way she articulates her words gives them a sharp, powerful cadence. "Intruders like us simply call it Homestead."

"Are we..."

"Underground, yes. Far enough that it's best not to think about it."

"Do you live here?"

"I got here the same time you did. I'm just less of a bewildered puppy."

Nikki quickens her pace. I do my best to keep up, making my steps as little like a puppy as possible.

After several minutes the quality of the air changes, and the corridor climbs suddenly upward, becoming steps carved into the floor. At the top I bend over, putting my weight on my knees and breathing heavily. But the sight before us distracts me even from my wheezing.

The cavern we've entered is too large to be properly measured, with high ceilings that disappear into the darkness. Hulking columns of solid stone curl upwards, covered in blue moss that emits a faint glow. Grooves run along the walls, and it takes me a second to recognize that stairways have been carved directly into the walls, climbing without railings in crisscross patterns that intersect torch-lit passages. Round windows look out from high over the main cavern.

What I see before me is old, deeply rooted in the truth of the earth, and more overwhelming because of it. The name Homestead made me think of cozy nooks, maybe a communal dining room. This is instead an enormous city that, judging by the sheer quantity of windows, could house many thousands of people. Yet as far as I can tell, the city is empty. Silence lingers with the weight of a thousand absent voices.

Nikki continues forward. The floor is a carpet of blue moss that runs uninterrupted up the pillars. A straight path cuts through it. We follow the path past the pillars, which are so wide that a dozen people my size standing hand-in-hand in a circle would not be able to fully surround them. Another smell besides the pungent odor of earth and moss fills my nostrils. Someone is cooking. My stomach awakens, but another minute passes before I can discern the source. Tucked into the shadow of two pillars is a long table, a large cooking fire, and about a half-dozen people sitting on benches at the end of the table.

As we approach, they break off conversation and turn toward us. The three humans at the table are my age, and all girls. Off to one side sits a severe creature, who I am somehow not surprised to see has tattooed wings folded across her back. The creature across from her is stout and fleshy, with a kind face. Between them, in the middle of the table, sits Wesley. He squeaks and bounds off the table, climbing up my leg and up to my shoulder.

I meant to return before you awoke, he says as he nuzzles my cheek, *but I thought you would need to rest a while longer.*

I'm just glad to be able to wake up at all.

The area strikes me immediately with its emotions. Foremost is fear and confusion—at least we're on the same page there—but there is also comfort, hope, a respite from whatever stormy seas have brought us all together. This reassures me, though I'm too struck by the strangeness of this place to feel it myself yet.

One of the girls smiles and gets up to meet us. Her round cheeks wear the smile easily.

"You must be Jamie. I'm Callie." She wraps me in a hug. "You're safe here."

Something about the way she says it makes me believe her. I don't know whether it has anything to do with how cute I find her bouncy energy and smile.

Nikki acts as a gruff intermediary in introducing me to the others, with Callie chiming in with details. Ora, the winged aileth, seems to find me at best vaguely amusing. Her non-human counterpart is a gnomin named Amby, who has a thick bandage on his shoulder and a gentle grip when I shake his clawed hand. Both creatures are familiar from books, but seeing them in the flesh is still jarring.

Next is Holly, who greets me with a suspicious stare and a bit of reserve. She has strikingly blue eyes.

The other girl, Petra, looks as overwhelmed at her surroundings as I am. She has auburn hair tied into a messy ponytail, and large, quick eyes. Callie invites me to sit next to her, but Nikki takes my arm and leads me toward the one person I haven't met, who tends the pot simmering over the cooking fire.

"Jamie, this is our host, Master Root."

Master Root wears a gray cloak with a hood that covers his head. When he turns, I see deep gray eyes and skin that nearly matches his cloak. He is not human, exactly. Certainly his features could be considered human, but between the completely bald head, the unusual complexion, and the unmistakable feeling of age that emanates from him, he gives the impression of being something else entirely. His thick body makes intentional, powerful movements.

"Jamie Monroe," he says, and his voice carries the deep weight of the entire city of Homestead, the solidity of earth and rock. "I am Master Root."

When I shake his coarse hand his age, his strength, and his wisdom all come to me at once. What's more, by the curl of his lip I can tell that he knows I feel these things.

"Welcome to Homestead. I hope you found your quarters comfortable. It has been a long time since I had visitors."

"They were very comfortable, thank you," I say, trying not to be impolite by bombarding my host with all the questions I want to ask.

"I know you have many wonderings that you would like answered. All of these will be addressed in time. For now, know that I am the custodian of this place, and that you are beyond the reach of those who would harm you. You are very important, Jamie." He doesn't say it the way parents tell their kids they're important, that they matter in the basic but profound way that all humans matter. He says it with an expansiveness that sets my heart racing.

"Important for what?"

Master Root chuckles, making a sound like boulders being rolled playfully around. "That is one of the wonderings that will soon become clear."

Master Root has cooked a stew that, although brown and gelatinous in the most unappetizing way, is exactly what my grumbling stomach wants. From the conversation around the table, it sounds like the others have not been here long. Petra describes her guardian bringing her to the entrance shortly before Nikki and I made a crash landing on the slopes of the mountain.

"Can you imagine having a guardian who would willingly take you anywhere?" Holly says wistfully when she hears this.

"It wasn't really a choice, though," Petra says. "We started getting harassed by the Kelluvas a couple of months ago. My guardian works as an Obscurer, keeping Terraltum business invisible to Earthworlders, so she has the Terraltum government's protection. But those protections didn't fully extend to me."

"Who's your guardian?" Nikki says. "Obscurers have one of the most insane job descriptions—" a quick look tells me she's saying this for my benefit "—surface service, clearing people's memories, cordoning off Intention-infected zones after accidents. There are only a few with the expertise to qualify."

"Trish," Petra replies.

"Tough lady, that one."

"I never saw that side of her," Petra says.

"Must've been nice, my guardian was a gruff old bastard, though he did his best," Callie says, intoning "gruff old bastard" with a gravelly, Southern-inflected accent, and meeting my eyes.

"Gruff old bastard sounds safer, honestly," I say, hoping it's vague enough not to betray how little I know, and gives me time to recover from Callie's glance dropping my stomach into my shoes.

"Not when you don't have the protection of the Terraltum government," Callie says. "When the Kelluvas raided my house, I was barely able to make it out. And if I hadn't run into this one," she points her thumb at Holly, "I never would've made it here."

I try not to think about what would've happened if Nikki hadn't found me. Though all of these newcomers have their own traumatic experiences, I don't get the sense any of them faced anything like a werebeast.

"And now we're all wrapped up in this stupid conflict, whether we like it or not," Holly says.

"Conflict?" I ask.

"You know, between the great houses of Terraltum?" Holly says. She nudges a finger toward Nikki. "Between the princess' family and the rest of the assholes fighting for control."

Nikki's nostrils flare, but Petra cuts in before she can respond.

"I mean, it's all a bit crazy, isn't it? The whole family system is incredibly undemocratic. It's practically medieval."

"Watch who you're calling medieval," Nikki says. Her knuckles wrap around her wooden spoon as if she's preparing to stab Petra with it. "I might just live up to it."

"I didn't mean any offense. My guardian told me all about Terraltum and I'm sure it's a wonderful place. But I absolutely can't wrap my head around allowing government to be determined by a family's name rather than the will of the people."

"It's just a different system," Callie says. "None of us except Nikki have been there, so we don't really know what we're talking about, do we?"

"Thank you, Callie," Nikki says. "Like she said, you're all idiots."

"That's not—"

"I get the sense there is some clarification required," Master Root says from the end of the table. He shoots a look at Nikki's spoon that suggests he's well aware she'd intended to use the remainder of her dinner as a projectile. "If you are done eating, then please follow me."

We slide the benches back from the table and follow the gray figure across the hall.

CHAPTER SIXTEEN: NIKKI

Master Root leads us up a sheer stairway along the wall. His steps are measured and sure, which is more than can be said for the skittish group that follows him. We try to keep our eyes away from the side of the stairs, where the drop is only growing.

The meal was a stew made of mushrooms and earthy vegetables. Ordinarily the mushrooms would've been enough to put me off, but the stew was rich and nourishing.

It still would've looked nice as a decoration on Petra's annoying face, though. I have to remember that the entire point of me being here is to make sure her and the rest of these kids end up on the Laputa side of the conflict. Launching fungus at her probably wouldn't help me get there.

Ora, Amby, and Wesley wander around the cavern below. We reach a break in the stair, and turn off into a passage. Another turn brings us into a large open room, with a semi-circular seating area cut into the earth, and a low rocky stage in front of it. We sit with our backs to a wide, open balcony over the Main Hall, as Master Root calls it. Master Root stands in the middle of the stage, blending into the rock.

He surveys us, letting his eye rest for a second on each person, taking in each presence. When his eye reaches me, something shifts beneath the surface, an almost imperceptible twitch.

"There is no easy way to tell you what I am about to tell you," Master Root says. His voice grabs you by the chin. "Likely some of you know more about the present situation than others, but I suspect none of you know all of it. Therefore, I will start farther back than is perhaps necessary.

"The great families of Terraltum have always been at war, in one form or another. At present three families comprise the core of the government, but this was not always so. Besides House Kelluva, House Laputa, and House Natantis, there were two others, equally as old and regal, equally as warring. House Meluin originated in the northern mountains, while Asavva came from the rich plains so often forgotten by those who dwell in Orella, Terraltum's capital. The alliances between these five houses and the dozens of other minor houses shift more easily and fiercely than the wind before a hurricane. We have a Laputa with us, so don't take my word for it. Nikki, could you describe your feelings toward House Natantis?"

I picture Chancellor Bella Natantis' pitying expression as she spoke my sentence of banishment.

"House Natantis fought on the other side during Barrun's War, thirty-five years ago. But now that they run the government, they're a useful and valued ally, and I would certainly not wish harm on any of them."

Master Root laughs a stony laugh.

"You can see what I mean," he says. "But yes, she is right to bring up Barrun's War. That cuts more quickly to the heart of the struggle we are in. These five houses have been at war for thousands of years, practically since the Skyfolk fled the surface to make their home in the sky."

I watch Jamie's face, seeing how overwhelming this all is for him. It's about to get way worse. My opinion of Paolo doesn't improve, seeing how much he clearly kept from his adopted son.

"While the reasons behind the old conflict may lie behind the murky veil of time, those of Barrun's War do not. Barrun was the last patriarch of House Meluin, which had been struggling for many years. You see, his house, much like Asavva, lived far from the administrative heart of the continent, proud of its separation. But years of strict taxes from Orella and poor crop yields brought on by harsh winters had turned a once proud house into one on the brink. To make matters worse, the Kelluva's had seen their weakness as an opportunity to seize control of the Meluin Caves. These caves are sacred to the Meluin, and house the greatest concentration of Sky, the magical material responsible for Terraltum's very existence, and the source of its people's magic. House Meluin's cultivation of these caves meant that their Intention in the Pure School, particularly as it related to the static variety of Pure Intention, was stronger than any other. But they were still vulnerable.

"At the time, a Kelluvan matriarch sat in the Chancellor's seat. Yura Kelluva was a shrewd and powerful ruler who despised what she saw as the lesser houses. When the Kelluvas struck, all the great houses besides Natantis joined together to defend House Meluin. The cosmopolitan Natantis wanted only to preserve the heart of power in Orella and, not wishing to risk destabilizing the country further, joined the Kelluvas. The battle that followed was the bloodiest in known memory. On the northern mountains, the armies of the five great houses fought through snow and ice, scorching the mountainsides with the ferocity of their assault.

"In the heat of the fighting, House Asavva's army was cut off from their allies. Their patriarch was cut down along with his daughters and sons, his entire house ended in one burst of violence. Meluin and Laputa were driven into the caves under the force of an assault by the well-trained and funded Natantis army."

I picture Grell and her disruptors, the coordination of strikes and counterstrikes. Every time I heard the story of Barrun's War before, it came from someone involved in the fighting. My mother and father were driven into those caves. They remember the shriek of the missiles the Natantis launched from Intention-powered war engines, the cries of their overwhelmed comrades as they fell back into the caves. My mother never speaks of it. But every time my father tells the story, I watch the confidence he's built over the intervening years as our house's patriarch fall away, and I see the scared young man he was, the deep scars that day left. He is also always sure to mention the horrible pain House Asavva experienced at the same time, how House Kelluva stormed through their undefended villages, wiping out or imprisoning everyone in their path, scattering the remnants of the house's nobility to the winds of Terraltum's great plains.

Master Root speaks as someone uninvolved, someone whose family was not shaped by the violence of those days. My hand clenches involuntarily. The Kelluvas, the reason I'm here in the first place. Once again I catch Master Root's eye, but this time I see the pain beneath his placid expression. He's not reacting to one family's suffering. He's reacting to all the human suffering of the war.

"The greatest treachery of that war, though, belongs to Almus Kelluva," Master Root continues. "Not content with winning by conventional means, Almus gathered a force of beasts created by perverse Elemental and Organic magic, twisted creatures mutated from all of Terraltum's animals."

"Werebeasts," Jamie whispers.

"Every great house of Terraltum condemns this sort of magic. To take a creature and pervert it into something so evil is a violation of nature. Both Kelluva and Natantis objected in principle, but during the war, both allowed Almus to lead this force to purge the caves. This was the evil that led to the downfall of House Meluin—the powerful Barrun slew countless werebeasts, but he knew his house couldn't withstand the onslaught.

"Rather than die destroying the evil creatures, he went deep into the caves. At this point his sword had broken and the only weapon left was his dagger, a sharp, Intention-crafted blade that could still have killed many werebeasts. But deep in the caves under the northern mountains, he performed what is perhaps the greatest act of Intention ever conceived."

Master Root pauses, noticing all of us leaning forward. Even Holly, who has been doing her best to look disinterested, stares intently.

"I must admit that here things become murky. Though in the grand scale of the worlds Barrun's War was not that long ago, much of what occurred during its final days has become so contorted by legend that it's difficult to say where reality ends and myth begins. I suspect that the two are never far from each other. We know Barrun Meluin never left the caves, and we can be fairly certain that he was not killed by the Kelluvas—they would've paraded his body through the streets. The story goes like this: Trapped and cornered, realizing there was no escape, he concentrated his entire being, the whole of his power, and poured his life-force into the blade. Some stories hold that he simply vanished, but I think it more likely that he became a mere husk, a body separate from the power that made him who he was.

"That dagger, Barrun's Dagger, as it came to be known, passed to Barrun's daughter, who tried to bring it to House Laputa. It would yet have been a powerful weapon against the Kelluvas. But she was caught and killed, and in the chaos of the fighting, the dagger disappeared. The ferocity with which both houses pursued the dagger suggests that at least part of the story of Barrun's end is true. There could've been a long game of cat and mouse in those caves as the two sides searched for the dagger. The Laputas were well-hidden and the Kelluvas impatient in their search. But House Laputa had its location betrayed by their patriarch's most trusted advisor. A man of one of the minor houses who had earned the patriarch's trust through a shared youth and years of wise counsel."

Anger rises in me once again. My family's betrayal is one of the bitterest parts of the story. Paolo. My father's friend since they were boys gave their position away, turning a battle that could still have been won into a sure defeat.

"You will probably start to see some of the complex web becoming clearer when I tell you that his advisor is very close to someone in this room. His name is Paolo, and he is Jamie's guardian."

Jamie's soft eyes dart around the room. Everyone stares at him, but if they wanted a reaction, they don't get one. I should've left him to be eaten by the werebeast. Holly's eyes burn in Jamie's direction. A deep hush falls over us.

"That betrayal was a ruse, of course," Master Root says. "It brought Paolo fully into the Kelluvas' good graces, which ultimately paid off by giving him carte blanche to raise Jamie as he saw fit. Without that betrayal, Jamie would likely be on the other side of this conflict, as you will soon see.

"After the surrender, House Laputa was begrudgingly brought back into the fold. Despite his usefulness, Almus was exiled to the surface, his crimes unpalatable in the newfound peace. Meluin and Asavva were no more, and Kelluva and Natantis held the power. But things have changed since then. A Natantis now holds the Chancellorship, the Laputans continue to be a thorn in the Kelluvas' side, and the new leader is increasingly resistant to the Kelluvas' dynastic aspirations. She has even considered disbanding the family system. I am in no position to guess what ends House Kelluva now acts toward, but the facts are these: Hiding in secret on the surface, they carried out an experiment more abhorrent than even the werebeasts. Using incredibly complex Intention of the Elemental and Organic Schools, they created eleven..."

He trails off. "I am not sure what to call them. People? Beings? They started in a form that most resembled large eggs. These eggs were entrusted to some of House Kelluva's most loyal agents on the surface. When they hatched, eleven babies emerged."

We can all tell that a terrible truth is coming, the same truth my parents alluded to when they laid out my mission. Clearly none of the rest have quite wrapped their minds around it yet.

"These children were to be weapons in the coming war. They could harness Intention without carrying Pieces of Sky, wielding as much power on the surface as on Terraltum. Instead of relying on the atmosphere around them, their power would come from within. Can you imagine how powerful Intention could be without needing to be first collected from the fabric of the world? Those children would be able to grow into a powerful force for House Kelluva, a force perfect for claiming the surface. Those children, as you may have guessed, are you."

CHAPTER SEVENTEEN: JAMIE

There is no air in the room. Even the light breeze that always seems to blow in the cavern outside has stopped. Paolo, a double agent in the wars for Terraltum? Not the gentle, quiet man who raised me. Though when I think about the stream of strange people who stopped by our house at the oddest hours, the pieces do start falling into place.

But if I don't initially believe the first revelation, I almost laugh at the second. I never knew my parents. I never even saw a picture. It didn't matter, because Paolo was my parent. Master Root has been underground too long, making up wild stories to occupy his time and the surrounding darkness.

Petra must be thinking the same thing because she says, "Are you trying to tell us that we all hatched from eggs? Like some kind of chicken or something?"

No one laughs.

"Hard truths can seem the most ridiculous when they first see the light," he says.

"Or sometimes they're too ridiculous to be true," Petra says.

Nikki frowns, not tipping her hand. Holly stands up. When she speaks, her voice is filled with fire.

"Listen to yourselves. You act like you know what we are. I've lived my entire life in fear. I was raised in a village of banished Skyfolk, all of them loyal to the Kelluvas. The most dangerous among them were not my guardians who, believe me, took any opportunity they could to inflict as much pain as possible. The most dangerous were two others my age, evil bastards with an ungodly amount of Intention. They were named Ren and Lia, but to me they may as well have been named Fear and Pain. I didn't understand how they, like us, could be so powerful, without Pieces of Sky to magnify their Intention. Not until Master Root revealed that they were also Changelings. They never questioned their cause. When power is matched by unquestioning conviction, it can do terrible things."

"I'm not disputing that the Kelluvas are bad," Petra says, "or that we may have been taken away from our parents. But this..."

Holly gives her an almost pitying look. Her eyes focus hard, and suddenly all light leaves the chamber. I spin to look at the torches. They still burn, yet their light doesn't extend beyond the end of the flickering flames. The only light that cuts through the darkness comes from Holly's eyes, which burn with a lapis lazuli blaze. Her presence is as terrible as the werebeast's, although worse because she is so much more powerful, and so much less in control of her strength.

The light returns to the room. Master Root is unfazed by the incident, but the others are shaken.

"This may be theoretical to all of you," Holly says. "But I've been living this nightmare for as long as I've been alive, and I will have revenge on its creators."

"How did you do that?" Callie's voice wavers.

"When you were raised by the people who raised me, you don't have a choice. How do you think I got here?"

When there is no reply, Holly answers her own question. "One day when Ren and Lia were gone, I killed our guardians. The entire village. And it wasn't even hard."

"You can take me at my word or not," Master Root says. "That you are powerful is indisputable. House Kelluva naively thought they could keep you a secret. When House Laputa discovered the project, it was still in the early stages. You cannot comprehend the machinations that have brought all of you here. From well-placed double agents, to a last-minute rescue mission, this road has not been an easy one. But I fear the greatest challenge lies before us.

"I mentioned there were eleven of you in total. If you look around the room you will see four, not counting Nikki of course. That means there are seven others who, despite our best efforts, stayed within the Kelluvas' grasp. They are as powerful as you and, like you, are now coming together. I must ask you, the Changelings that have escaped the Kelluvas, to help us stop their terrible power."

"What are you asking?" Petra says. "It sounds like you mean to use us as weapons just like the Kelluvas."

"That's true. Which is why I will not force you to do anything. If you prefer to go your own way, to risk yourself on your own in the worlds, or even to burrow deep in this mountain and hide safely away, I will not stop you. But listen to me when I say, despite how terrible the war to come will be, we have no hope of averting disaster without you."

Resistance ripples off Petra. She reveals a lot in her unguarded thoughts. Her upbringing has not hardened her as it has the others. She doesn't hide her feelings behind a protective mask. I realize with a pang of embarrassment that her open nature is similar to my own. Perhaps her guardian was like Paolo, trying to shelter her from the truth of what she was. For the first time I wonder if Paolo did me a disservice in raising me so gently.

We all wait for Petra to speak. Nikki continues to watch from the side.

"You tell a hell of a story," Petra says, "but I can't help noticing that you tell it from the perspective of the Laputas. I don't buy that all the Kelluvas and Nantantises are these faceless monsters. I also can't help noticing that there's a high-ranking Laputa among us."

"A banished one," Nikki says.

"Nonetheless. My concern is that there are two sides here, each with their own objectives and reasons for fighting. Who's to say we're not being used for political gain?"

"These are all fair questions," Master Root says. "I do not expect you to believe me when I say that I don't take sides lightly. But this threat is not merely an old story. As we speak, Almus Kelluva, the banished captain who created the werebeasts—and incidentally played a not minor role in your own creation—leads the other Changelings. Our best guess at the moment is that he is slowly building another army on the surface, one that will be led by his prized Changelings, and complemented with a horde of werebeasts. Though whether he wishes to turn this army on Earthworlder or Skyfolk is as yet an open question. There is also the matter of the Sky Engines. Besides providing Terraltum with invisibility, they have a stabilizing effect on the powers that undergird that world. When they were compromised—which we assume was orchestrated by the Kelluvas—all of their functions stopped temporarily. We do not know what may have escaped that containment."

I imagine an army of slavering creatures like the one who cornered me at The Crux, all bearing down on unsuspecting Earthworld towns. Behind them, unbidden to my imagination, I picture a monstrous figure, clad in a silver robe.

"Almus is a zealot by nature," Master Root continues, "and I fear his time on the surface has only made him more radical. He belongs to the cult of Leonis Wingless, whose worshippers embrace the doctrine of *Terramundus*, a cataclysmic joining of Earth and Sky, with only the magical beings retaining power, and the rest being either subjugated or killed. We have to assume that, beyond his familial loyalty, Almus has this goal in mind."

Amid the noncommittal grumbling, I stand up. It feels like the moment calls for it, although I feel a bit silly once I do. "A werebeast tracked me for the past few days. I came face to face with the creature and would've died if it weren't for Nikki. If anyone's building an army of those things, they need to be stopped."

"Jamie, perhaps if the others could see what you saw in that cave," Master Root says. He holds out his hands, and there's a tug of power at my temples. "With your permission, if you could focus on what you saw."

I nod and close my eyes, picturing the gaping jaws, the matted hair, the cold gleam of feral eyes.

A couple gasps escape the others. I keep concentrating, opening my eyes to see that Master Root is projecting the same image in the air before him. My concentration wavers, and the image fades, but it has already had its desired effect.

Petra nods slowly. I sit down, ignoring the stares from the others.

"One small note," Petra says. "Those of us who ended up with the Kelluvas might be Changelings, but I have to believe our existence means more than this plan to take over the surface. We need another name. I'm open to suggestions, but I'm thinking something about where we're from. Skyfolk?"

"Could be confusing," Nikki says. "People from Terraltum often refer to themselves as Skyfolk."

"Skysent," I say.

"Literal," Petra says, "but I like it. Skysent. Like Nikki." Nikki almost smiles as the others nod in agreement.

"In one hour, I will begin leading training for whoever wishes to stay," Master Root says, and as he says it, I can feel by the emotions in the room that we will all be there.

CHAPTER EIGHTEEN: JAMIE

I make my way back to my room for the hour before training. I need time to process. I turn the strange revelations over in my thoughts, but none of them seems real. Despite the fact that the werebeast I encountered is living proof of the story I'm wrapped up in, I can't believe there are ten other people just like me, who hatched from eggs and were created as instruments of destruction.

I wonder what my friend Serra would say if she heard all of this. I've suddenly become like a character in one of her MMORPGs. She seems distant now, and even the never quite defined relationship between us seems irrelevant.

Wesley, knowing not to disturb my thoughts, pretends to nap in the crook of my arm. After an hour, I set him gently on the bed and walk numbly down the long hallway back to the Main Hall.

Master Root takes us down a short corridor to a small room lit by a torch on each wall, wooden stools with cushions on top lined up in a row inside. Instead of taking a place in front of us, he sits at the far end of the row.

We sit and wait for him to speak. The others' echoing thoughts mirror my own. What are we about to be taught? Why are we in this small room? If Master Root is sitting with us, is there another teacher coming?

My eyes keep flicking to the doorway, but no one else enters.

We continue to wait. Master Root gazes straight ahead. His eyes are open, but he doesn't seem to be breathing.

Holly stirs, creaking her stool. The sound dies as if someone threw a blanket over it.

We wait.

Eventually, I realize that Master Root is not going to start speaking any time soon. I settle onto my stool. My thoughts follow the same course they have for the past hour, but being surrounded by my fellow Skysent softens them. Their breathing falls into a rhythm, and my own breaths follow suit. Though my body has settled, in my mind I still bounce between different threads of worry.

Petra's guardian brought her here.

An army of werebeasts.

Is Paolo alright?

A werebeast, who sees itself deep in its mind as a defenseless puppy.

A werebeast, whose jaws swing toward my throat.

Where was Paolo while I was in that cave?

The thoughts chase each other, whipping themselves into a whirlwind.

An egg. From an egg.

Where is Paolo?

A tall, hunched figure, who draws the entire world into itself.

Am I technically a bird?

When Master Root's soft voice finally breaks the silence, it startles me.

"You may be unfamiliar with the term Intention, although doubtless you have experienced its manifestation. Intention is exactly what it sounds like. To accomplish magical acts with Intention is not about believing you *can* do something, or *wanting* to do something. It is about simply *doing* it. Pouring the deepest threads of will toward whatever your goal is, until your goal *is*. These exercises will help you tap into the deeper state of mind where your power lies, which is fundamental no matter which of the Five Schools of Intention you are most adept at. The manifestations may be different, but all the schools and sub-schools ultimately come from the same place. The exercises will in all likelihood be very boring. This is by design. Boredom is an immensely powerful tool."

"You just told us there's a war coming," Holly says. "Now you're telling us to be bored?"

Master Root chuckles. "I didn't tell you to be bored. I am simply telling you that the preparations we are undergoing will likely cause you to be bored. Yes, you will sit here motionless while the Changelings rage on the surface. But what I have found is that boredom is rarely actually boredom. Boredom is the state of mind where you are no longer able to distract yourself from everything you don't want to think about. As such, it is most instructive."

Holly's Intention is getting up and walking out of the room, but she manages to stay put.

"Don't worry, we will start with something a little more interesting," Master Root says. "We will start with a question. What do all of you really want? Not simply want, but want deeply enough to turn the entirety of your being toward reaching it?"

When there is no response, he claps his hands together thunderously.

"That was not a rhetorical question! This is our first concentration exercise. I want you to think about the thing you want most. I want you to see it in front of you, to hold it in your hands if it fits, or wrap your arms around it if it doesn't. I want you to focus all of your attention on it. What does it look like? How does it feel? Does it have a smell?"

I close my eyes and immediately see Paolo. I imagine him standing in front of me, smiling gruffly, his arms crossed over his beat-up olive coat. He is telling me that everything is going to be okay, that he will be back soon to explain my role in all this. Beneath the sadness at his absence is another emotion, one that I hadn't felt fully until now. I feel angry. Angry at him for not properly preparing me for all of this, angry at him for leaving me without really telling me why. It even eclipses the lingering worry that I will never see him again.

"Once you've imagined what you want most, I want you to reflect on the feeling you experience toward it. There is the outward wanting of the thing, that's easy. But investigate one level deeper, toward the underlying sense of what you would do to attain it. That raw sense of moving toward your goal, the way you unconsciously leaned forward at the mere thought of it. Focus on that feeling. Examine it, not as a question of what you would do, but rather as the force behind what you would do."

He lets us sit with this for close to half an hour. It's hard to put into words. Beneath the yearning to see Paolo again, beneath the intensity of wanting to fling myself into his open arms, is the determined resolution that I will see him again.

But I can only keep it going for so long, and soon my mind strays, the pointed focus dissolving into divergent twists of thought.

"Now comes the hard part," Master Root says. "Continue holding onto that strength of will, only forget about the thing you want most. Remove the object, only keep the feeling you have toward the object. Those threads exist regardless of whether they are attached to anything."

I try. I try to make Paolo disappear from in front of me, try to capture that feeling that I would do anything to see him, but the threads seem to be made of cobwebs. Even if I were able to grasp them, they would merely fray under the pressure of my fingers. Either Paolo is there and the threads are clear, or both depart.

"Keep holding onto that," Master Root says. His voice is soft, as if talking too loudly might cause us to lose hold. "Very soon you will put it to work."

What he means by very soon, however, quickly becomes a subject of debate among the group.

After lunch we return to the same room. This time, though, our one instruction is to pay attention to the presence of the other people in the room, to their breathing, the energy they project. It's painfully boring, even for me. Though I can actually identify certain contours of thought, the emotions in the room are so flat and bored that they aren't particularly interesting to read.

Every time I think Master Root will break up the session with another instruction, the silence continues. Boredom morphs into anxiety. Anxiety melts into distraction. At some point I stop following the thoughts bubbling in the room, and allow myself back into my own mind, where things are no more settled.

We keep this up until dinner, at which point Master Root simply gets up. We follow him in silence out to the Main Hall, where somehow a pot of stew already boils on the fire.

I find Callie beside me on the way out.

"My brain was absolutely not designed for that," she says. "I had to imagine I was playing Ping-Pong in order to entertain myself."

"I hope you won at least," I say.

"It was a close match, but I pulled it out in the last set."

"Would've been pretty embarrassing for you to lose your imaginary game of Ping-Pong."

"Trust me," she say. "I'm more than capable."

I like walking with her, I realize, almost as much as I enjoy the fact that I can make her smile.

"Well, I have a feeling there will be more opportunities. I'll take you on next time."

She reaches out a hand for me to shake. I take it before I can think about how clammy my palms probably are.

"Jamie, you are so on."

CHAPTER NINETEEN: NIKKI

After telling us the story of Barrun's War, Master Root gave me the choice of whether I wanted to stay. He only really cares about the Skysent, and he gazes at me a little too intently as he waits for my answer.

The easy answer is that, of course I'll stay. My parents' instructions went beyond merely bringing Jamie over to the cause. Knowing that the Kelluvas plan to make a move on the surface and we have only a handful of true assets to fight down here, the Skysent must remain loyal to our house. Befriending them is crucial to that effort.

But the answer doesn't come as easily as it should. Instead, I find myself thinking about the Conjuring Arena. Not just the grand temple of excellence in Matter Intention that is the arena in Orella, but also the smaller, more aggressive one where banished Skyfolk desperately battle one another on the surface. Now that Jamie is safe, couldn't I return there? Couldn't I begin to tell the story of a banished member of the great houses, who rises through the conjuring circuit on the surface, and eventually returns victorious to Orella?

I've done what my parents asked of me. It should be time for me to follow the path I risked everything to set myself on. I've earned that.

But there is one pretty significant tally in the "stay" column, and that's Master Root himself. He radiates power, and if he's offering to train me, maybe I'll unlock facets of conjuring I never even knew existed. In the end, this thought is tantalizing enough for me to follow my parents' wishes and court the Skysent. For now.

If I'd known what the training actually entailed, though, I would've left immediately.

Rescue missions I can do. Schmoozing my way into a position of power? Not ideal, but a task I can set myself to without dreading each day.

But this is a nightmare.

We continually return to the same tiny room, sit in the same rows, on the same stools. The instructions might be slightly different, or there may be no instructions at all, but every day, the long silence presses down on me in the same way.

My conjuring training with Grell seems like a long time ago, but now I almost yearn for someone to bark orders at us to break this horrid silence.

I have never been able to sit still in the best circumstances, but now thoughts of home fill those long silent hours. My thoughts drift to the flakey butteriness of the biscuits served in my family's kitchens, to the deep timbre of Rian's laugh. The warmth of the fires when winter creeps up on Orella and the wind blows up Hornhill to our estate. Even the rattling of the tram as it winds its way down toward Market Square is a memory strong enough to fill the darkness with pain.

Aside from that, my legs ache. I lead the others through a stretching routine after breakfast, after our morning session, and before bed, but it's hardly enough to counteract the effects of motionlessness.

Though the sessions leave me drained, on the second evening I have such a strong need to move my limbs that I run around the edges of the Main Hall. To my surprise first Holly, then the rest join me.

Each night we sit around the table, eating stew and trying not to think about the next day's "exercises." Master Root always departs at some point, although none of us has yet figured out where he goes. No one is quite sure what to do with this time after dinner, and most of us end up drifting off to our rooms for a demoralized sleep.

While the day's exercises provide little distraction, it's at night, amid the gloom of Homestead's earthen walls, that the unfairness of my situation closes in on me. The life I had planned was banished along with me. A dream, once so close I could've passed my hands through it, is now as far away as it was when I was a little girl who still thought her parents' word meant everything.

On the third sleepless night, I take advantage of the time. I send a squad of conjured goblins to find Ora. After nearly an hour, they locate her in one of the upper rooms looking out over the Main Hall. I follow them up a long staircase, which weaves into the caves set in the wall, and back out to ledges with nothing but the floor of the Main Hall below.

Ora has turned her room into a nest of soft white threads, silky strands covering every inch of the room. Wide windows catch the light from the Main Hall, and Ora has pilfered a half dozen Intention-powered torches from public hallways, which fill her room with a golden glow.

"I really need to get in touch with your interior designer," I say.

Ora holds one of my goblins upside-down, absently tugging at its limbs. I let the poor creature dissolve, and Ora's attention snaps to me.

"Oh yes, he's very good," Ora says.

"I need a favor."

"Not really a favor, since I have to do it." She sits on a hammock that spans the entire side of the room nearest the window. "More like a command. Demand, maybe? I like demand. It makes you sound more childish."

"Not sure you're in any position to call me childish. But okay, we can call it a demand if that suits you better."

"Not that it's anything to me," Ora says, looking tragically out over the Main Hall. I must admit, it's an impressive view. "I spend all day stuck up here with no one to talk to. Master Root has even discouraged me from attending the dinner table. He brings me and Amby food in our rooms."

"Room service doesn't sound so bad."

"Yes, but things are so much more fun when I am the target of unfair treatment."

I resist the urge to flick her perfect ears. "Okay, then you'll love this. I need you to find me a way out of here."

"Leaving already?"

"No, but I don't like not having an exit strategy. I figured you would appreciate finding a way out too."

"Well my fair lady of Laputa, it will please your highness—"

"Shut up."

"—to know that I have already found an exit, and would be happy to lead you to it."

The exit Ora has found is only five minutes and half a dozen turns from her room. We travel up a steep passage, and soon see light ahead. When we crest the rise, stars appear. I have never thought much about stars, but now there is nothing I would rather see. I breathe in the crispness of the air, rejoicing in the way the trees sway with a gentle breeze below.

Ora's tinkling laugh tells me I must be making a ridiculous face. I don't care. I sweep my arms in circles around my head, then run whooping around the entrance. Ora watches in amusement until I sprawl on one of the large rocks nearby. I don't stay out for long, but that brief sweetness of freedom gets me through the next day of concentration.

At dinner the following evening, Master Root is still scouring the stew pot when Holly asks me out of the blue, "Is Intention cool on Terraltum? Like do they use it for things besides living and fighting?"

I smile at the expectant expressions on the others' faces.

"In Orella there's a Conjuring Arena where two conjurers face each other to see whose chimera can overcome the other. It's exactly as awesome as it sounds."

"So they fight?" Holly says.

"Yes, although there's always an objective. One of the most popular is where each side has a flag the other has to capture. There's also a fun event where each side has to get a ball through a net on the opponent's side. Since you can conjure whatever you want, you might imagine that things get real ridiculous real quick."

"If I were playing, I would conjure a giant creature to stand in front of the net," Petra says.

"You wouldn't be the first," I say, excited enough to shake my spoon at her, "which is why that's considered a foul."

"So what, the other person gets a penalty shot or something?"

"Nope, the referee places a Binding Stone on your platform, which weakens your Matter Intention. Depending on the severity of the penalty, it might last the whole game. Get a couple of Binding Stones and your creatures quickly turn into nothing but mist. In some cases people have pushed themselves too hard and ended up with Intention Sickness."

"That sounds bad," Jamie says. He'd been listening intently, his stew forgotten. "Is that bad?"

"Intention Sickness can be fatal if you push yourself too far beyond your abilities. In less severe cases you just need rest and maybe a transfusion of Intention from someone who has some to spare."

"Have you ever been in a conjuring match?" Jamie asks.

It's creepy how this kid reads my mind. "As a contestant? I wish. It's not exactly an occupation befitting my family."

"But you can conjure?" he says.

If it's a show he wants, then it's a show he shall have. I pause to collect myself. The creatures I am about to create are already in the room, their presence waiting to be realized.

"You tell me." I let them come into being, and two-dozen winged creatures about the length of our utensils wink into existence. No sooner do they appear then they begin terrorizing the Skysent, picking up bowls of stew and tossing them at each other and at us. One gets ahold of a spoon, and starts swinging it in an uncontrolled circle, taking out one of the other creatures, and knocking itself over in the process. I spot Jamie frantically pulling on one that has lodged itself in Callie's short hair.

"Enough." The chaos ceases as Master Root extends a hand over the table and the chimera vanish. His eyes blaze at me. With a sweep of his hand, the bowls stack themselves and slide down the table toward him. He picks them up and walks away. Spoilsport.

"I wish I could learn how to do that," Holly says. "Instead I spend twelve hours a day doing nothing. Are we even here to defeat the Kelluvas?"

Master Root stops. Air rushes away from the table, and for a moment I fear he will turn around and confront her. But after another second he continues walking away, carrying both the heavy stew pot and the bowls out of the Main Hall.

There isn't much levity to be found after that.

"I wonder where he goes every night," I say as we get up from the table. Petra gives me a look that tells me she's been wondering the same thing.

The conjuring incident seemingly makes Master Root more resolved than ever to make our training as boring as possible. Our concentration exercises become more abstract, more focused on tiny details in our past or in the room. I find myself getting used to the boredom and can ease into it rather than wanting to fly out of my skin.

On Friday evening—I don't know why, but Callie thinks it's important to keep track of the days of the week—we speculate if there is anything planned for the weekend. We gather in Holly's room, which offers enough space for us to lounge on the bed and desk chair. Jamie sits cross-legged on the desk. Callie insists that we can't do more than a week of these exercises, and that Master Root will give us a rest. I ask her if she's even been here for the past week.

"When I'm in that room I reach a euphoric state," Callie responds, modulating her usually husky voice to a high, dreamy pitch. "I transcend my physical form and become one with the Intention of the room, nay, with the Intention of the worlds."

Petra glances around furtively, but Master Root is nowhere in sight.

"Keep your voice down," she says. "That's literally what he thinks should be happening."

"You must wade into the waters of boredom," Callie continues.

"Then you must intent yourself!" I burst out, causing Petra to jump.

Our chuckles haven't subsided by the time Master Root enters the room. He stands in the doorway for a moment, with an expression that's hard to pin down.

"So Master Root, we've been counting days," Holly says.

"Oh?"

"Yes."

Master Root doesn't respond.

"It's Friday."

Another pause.

"Tomorrow's Saturday."

We all nod encouragingly.

"I see," Master Root says. We wait a few long seconds to find out what exactly Master Root has seen. "You will be wanting a day off, I suppose?"

"Maybe even two." I glare at Petra.

"I don't believe that you can spare a day off. Here's why." Master Root forms a wide circle with his hands, and then spreads them outward, forming a circle. The space between his hands is replaced by a moving image. We crane our necks to see the scene playing out between his fingers, and after a moment it becomes clear that these are our Changeling counterparts.

There are seven of them, and they walk with confidence through the rubble of an enormous building. Where fires burn near them, their leader reaches out a hand and puts them out. One Changeling spits on the crumpled form of an electronic device, barely recognizable from the rubble around it. No noise comes from the image, but the Changelings are laughing. I don't get the sense it is a pleasant sound.

"That building was in Ohio," Master Root says. "Luckily, it was nighttime, so only a few people were hurt."

"Why?" I ask. "Why blow up an Earthworld building?"

"Sheer spite," Holly says. "If they're Kelluvas then they like destruction for the sake of it."

I know the Kelluvas better than that. Though they are indeed vicious bastards, everything they do is calculated. Master Root shakes his head. "They are not so mindless as that. We learned from a Laputan spy that several banished Skyfolk had been hiding in the abandoned upper stories of that building."

"And where are they now?" I ask reflexively. The image still plays, although the Changelings are moving out of view. The perspective makes it look almost like the Changelings are walking into Master Root. The building must have been at least a dozen stories. Its rubble spreads out across an entire city block. The image flickers out.

"Dead," Master Root says. "Their bodies were found the next morning, stripped of their Pieces of Sky."

"Traitors," I say.

"To the laws of Terraltum, certainly." He turns to the confused faces of the others. "Killing even a banished Skyfolk is of course a horrific crime. But taking their Piece of Sky is like taking their very soul."

None of us have the will to respond. Earthworld buildings may not have magical protections, but they are strongly built. The sheer destructive Intention required to bring down a building of that size sends dread through my chest.

"You don't have time for a day off, not if you are going to face those adversaries and prevent further needless deaths. But I can give you a couple hours to sleep in tomorrow morning."

It's good enough.

Despite the fact that to a person we're dead tired, despite the rigor of the past week, and despite even the warnings about the foes we are up against, none of us turn in early. Instead, we act like the stupid kids we are, and stay up deep into the night. Master Root is gone, oblivious to or ignoring the noise we make. We run through the halls of Homestead, weaving deep into its passages, chasing each other along the dim corridors. There is no structure to our romp, no rules to the games we are playing, if they even are games. We run for the sake of running, and hide among stands of glowing fungus in dark caves for the joy of it. By the time the late hours of night have slipped into the early hours of morning, we are exhausted.

Petra disappears down a fork in the corridor, and silence strikes me suddenly after the noise we had been making. I don't know which path she's taken, so I choose at random. The path twists twice, then ends abruptly. A flat wall halts my way forward. It's featureless and disconcertingly smooth. A tiny round hole near the bottom is the only defect. As I approach, light streams from the hole in a deep bluish purple. When I bend to inspect it, the light intensifies, until I have to shield my eyes against it. But I find myself drawn toward it. Its coldness yanks at me, and soon I am mere inches from the opening. This close I can discern sounds coming from the hole. Voices. Whispers. I cannot understand what they say, but I yearn to hear them.

My ear touches the glow's fringe, and I am falling.

I feel uncomplex, fresh, with only a vague sense of the world's weight. I'm in the middle of a room I recognize as our stateroom, but know I'm seeing it for the first time. Workmen move furniture in on dollies, unwrapping their cloth covering with a flick of the hand. The place is shiny, lacking any floor coverings, the floors newly stained.

"Nikki, don't get in the way," mother says behind me.

"They'll work around her," father says. He's standing in the doorway. His hand grasps the freshly painted wooden frame so firmly it's hard to imagine he'll ever release it, like he's formed some form of direct bond with the door. His face is agitated by a tide of emotion. "We're home, Remedia."

"Are you sure we shouldn't have stayed at Swift Hall?" my mother says. "How do we know it's really safe?"

"The war is over, and the peace has held so far. We can't keep leaving our family behind when we have to serve on the Council. This is where I was born. It's where Rian and Nikki should have been born. I would risk everything for them to grow up here."

"The Laputas and their strong wills."

My father lets go of the doorframe and pulls her close. I start untying one of the furniture covers by hand. The workman laughs and lets me do it, despite the fact that with his Intention he could take care of it in a couple seconds.

"You're no exception," father says. I look back at him and cackle as I pull the knot free. "And neither is she."

The tram rumbles above me and the concave underside of Archbridge fills my view. It's large from any angle, but from directly underneath it seems impossible, as if it were the sky itself and not a creation of human hand and mind. On the bridge itself, scores of peacekeeping automatons guard the city's most important artery, but their protection is far away here. My friends Hilde and Bethany have followed me, though Hilde has put up a fight.

"There's nothing to worry about, seriously," I say. I'm not sure I entirely believe my own words. We can already see the tent city, which starts near the exact center of the bridge's span. The late afternoon shadows are deep.

The gnomin colony covers a span of almost a quarter mile between a massive support strut and the bank of the Rhydwel. I lead my companions directly into it. There's no rule that we shouldn't be here, and I've never heard of gnomin, even ones who've dropped out of society like these, hurting anyone. The squalor I'd been expecting doesn't exactly materialize. The tents are made of poor material, patched and re-patched over years of use, but the paths between them are clean and orderly, the entire community arranged on a grid.

We walk down the central thoroughfare. Some older gnomin sit on wood blocks outside their tents, smoking long pipes and talking softly as we pass. The smell of fish wafts over everything—not the pleasant odor of the big river fish from further down the Rhydwel, which are often grilled whole in Market Square, but instead that of the smaller bottom feeders that can be caught from the banks in Orella, and which you can be fined for serving in a restaurant.

We don't meet any resistance, but after a few minutes I notice we've picked up a follower. He's a massive gnomin, almost human height, and with incredibly broad shoulders. Most striking, though, is the crater of mottled flesh in the side of his head, as if he had a third of his skull removed, and the surgeon botched the cleanup.

He stares directly at me with his one beady eye. There is no malice in it. The eye droops, ensnaring me in a dead gaze. Whatever vitality used to be in this gnomin is gone. He follows us, staring blankly, never coming closer than a dozen yards. I try not to turn, but I can't keep my eyes from flicking to the gap where his other eye and half of his forehead should be. The claws on one of his bare feet scrape the cobblestones with each step.

"He scares me, Nikki," Hilde says.

"Just keep walking," I say, pulling courage out of my own display of fearlessness. "He won't hurt us."

He follows us the length of the colony. We pass row upon row of tents, trying to ignore the presence behind us. There's a break in the dwellings at one point, and we slow as much as we dare, sucked in by the sight. A dozen or more gnomin, these with shaved heads and holding long thick ropes that dangle over their outstretched arms, are gathered around a makeshift altar built from what appears to be a riverboat's old paddle wheel. At the wheel's top is a massive object. Though it is horribly charred and disfigured, I can tell from the arching shape that it is a pair of wings. In order to fly with those wings, an aileth would need to be at least thirty feet tall.

I gasp involuntarily when I realize what we're witnessing. The gnomin bend at the waist and kneel, presenting the ropes to the giant burned wings. This is a ceremony to Leonis Wingless. In the old stories about the Winged Ones coming to Terraltum, they always brought plentiful harvests and wise counsel, not to mention the ailethier themselves, who were formed through their union with humans. But there was a Winged One who believed humanity should be subject to the power of the Winged Ones, not merely the beneficiaries of it. When Leonis tried to act on his beliefs, he had his wings brutally removed, thereby destroying his power and casting him out of their order. The stories vary on what happened to him after that, though most say he was unable to live without his power and either threw himself off Terraltum or leapt upwards into the fiery chasm of space. I'd heard rumors of radicals who worship the fable of Leonis, wishing him to return and take up his ruling mantle. I had never thought to see so many at once, though.

Leonis had become merely a whisper, a myth. He was rumored to have been responsible for passing on The Gift of the Ailethier, or in some circles The Gift of the Wingless. This gift, which provided fodder for endless children's stories, gave the ability to lock an area in a stasis, exempt from the rules of time, where an unlucky human could be trapped for hundreds of years, emerging not a day older, only to find their loved ones long dead, and their world changed by the years. Yet it was not an unequivocal gift, for most ailethier who used it died. Or so the stories go. When I did believe in the Gift, I tended to think it was merely innate ailethier Intention.

The gnomin who has been following us draws uncomfortably close, and we are forced to move on before we can see more of the ritual. His feet continue to scrape the ground, and we move as quickly as we dare. As soon as we step beyond the encampment's borders, he disappears into a row of tents at its edge. But even as we leave the gnomin, leave the stench of fish, the eerie sight of charred wings, the flapping of tent flaps in the breeze that always seems to flow under the bridge, his presence still asserts itself behind me, and I know it will be a long time before I forget his one dead eye.

I'm lying in my bed, and my tears have turned my pillowcase into something resembling a map of a single massive continent. For once, I put myself out there and was honest with how I felt. And I lost a friend because of it. I'm too old for the touch of my mother, who is gently massaging my back, to be this comforting.

"I'm not sad, I feel like an idiot," I'm saying, though it's only partially true. I'm sad too. Deeply. But there is also shame, embarrassment, and above it all, a fear that this situation will play out again and again, that I am doomed only to want people who will never want me. That's all experience has shown me so far. "She's never going to talk to me again."

"It'll pass," my mother says. "You don't get to choose who you're attracted to, Nikki, and remember that she doesn't either. It's neither of your fault. It's like a—" she struggles for a word. "It's like a mismatch."

I meet her eyes for the first time, turning over. My face is tight from the tears. I almost smile. My eloquent mother, matriarch of House Laputa, used to speaking before the Council of Families about important affairs of state, and that's all she can come up with? It's endearingly inadequate.

"A mismatch?"

Then I am in Homestead, on my back, staring up at the hole near my head. The purple glow is now a faint shimmer, and whispers no longer emanate from it.

I get up, the weight of dread in my stomach. I sprint back up the tunnel to find Petra. The hole watches innocently as I leave it behind.

When I find her, I chase Petra up a corridor that ends in a room filled with soft moss. We can only see each other's outlines in the darkness. Shortly after I find her, we both slouch onto the moss, too tired to keep up the chase.

Throughout the evening, Petra seemed embarrassed whenever she looked at me, as if she realized how obnoxious she was when we first arrived. Or maybe Callie said something. She has the annoying habit of trying to resolve conflicts.

"You ever notice how it's never really dark down here?" Petra says. Her voice jolts me out of myself. I had been on the edge of a dream.

"Didn't really think about it, to be honest. It's pretty dark in here, though."

Petra whacks me across the shoulder.

"Ow, see? You just proved my point. I couldn't see that coming." For a second, I'm distinctly aware of how close we are. She's still breathing slightly quicker from running here, and I can smell the faint tang of sweat on her skin. I shoot her indistinct outline a furtive glance, and for a second all I can think about is that I'd like to move my hand closer to hers, or reposition myself so I'm on my side, my face right next to hers. I don't move, though.

"Shut up, you know what I mean," Petra says, pulling me back into myself. "Think of everywhere in Homestead you've been. Has even one been what you would describe as pitch-black?"

I give it due thought, though my thoughts quickly turn onto a dreamward tangent about the process of lighting Intention torches. "No, I guess not."

"Don't you find that weird? We're underground."

"Clearly not as weird as you find it." The moss is soft. Petra's steady breathing drifts through the otherwise still air.

"I can't help wondering what it's like. Without the glowing pillars and mushrooms. Without the torches. What it would be like in darkness so true you couldn't even see the tip of your nose."

I squint, blinking to bring the dark outline of my nose into soft focus.

"The torches have been burning continuously since we got here," Petra continues. "But I don't think they're for us. I think they're for Master Root."

We lie in silence. For a long time after Petra's breathing has become shallow and regular, I stare into the darkness of the cave's ceiling, though it's hard to say if my insomnia is more due to what Petra has said, or to the jitters that run through me at Petra's presence.

CHAPTER TWENTY: NIKKI

Master Root's plan for the next day starts with an interminable hike upwards. We walk in silence except for the scraping of our shoes on the rocky path. I know better than to complain, but after the trail has steepened and I have to catch myself for a third time after I've slipped, I'm at my limit. The air, which had been growing increasingly stuffy, finally thins with the movement of a slight breeze, and pretty soon we emerge into blinding sunlight.

"I've officially turned into a vampire," Holly says, shielding her eyes and cowering dramatically. "This light is going to turn me to dust."

"There's no such thing as vampires," I say, though my own eyes are practically shut.

Jamie raises an eyebrow at me, and I nod to reassure him that, no, vampires aren't real. I decide not to mention the giant blood-sucking bats of Terraltum's Western Reach.

Master Root stands a few feet away from us, overlooking a cliff. I step beside him. We have emerged far up on the side of the mountain, well above the tree line. The precipice below is at least three hundred feet. A carpet of green forest stretches for miles in front of us, occasionally cut through by a bald mountain, or undulated by a rolling hill.

"Come, sit down," Master Root says, sitting with his feet over the edge. I sit beside him. The others approach more slowly. Jamie cranes his neck over the drop, and pulls back quickly. I wave a hand to have him sit next to me. If he has a sudden bout of vertigo or something equally as wimpy, I'll at least be able to catch him. Soon six pairs of legs dangle over the rock face.

"Listen."

Wind rises from the ground below, its high-pitched cry mournful like the howl of a lone wolf.

"Today marks your last instruction in concentration. If you can concentrate here, you can concentrate anywhere. We have been in a cave. That was by design, to allow you to tap into the reservoirs of your mind without any distraction. But the purpose of these exercises is not ultimately inward-facing. You strengthen your mind so that you can project outward into the world."

A gale swirls down from the rocks above us, and for a second I feel as though the cold wind will pull me over the cliff.

"To start, I want you to train your eyes on the horizon. Looking at the horizon, it doesn't make a difference whether you're thousands of feet in the air, or down in a low valley. Far enough in the distance, all points converge into one. Now, I want you to slowly bring your eyes down. See every tree between the horizon and the foot of the mountain. Then start working your way up the side of the mountain. Keep going until you have climbed to the bottom of the cliff, until you are staring directly down into the abyss." Master Root snaps his fingers at Jamie. "Don't look away!"

I have spent much of my life riding on the back of a windsteed, soaring at absurd heights. But in this moment I am nearly overwhelmed by fear at the vast emptiness below me.

"Keep staring," Master Root continues, and his voice is as harsh as I've ever heard it. "Know that if you were to fall, your body would become nothing more than a small blotch on those rocks, your Intention reclaimed in an instant by the universe." The wind stings my eyes. I try to stop myself from picturing the image Master Root just described.

"Now, close your eyes."

If the drop was frightening to see, there is something even worse about closing my eyes, knowing what lies before me, but not being able to see it. I focus on the solidity of the stone on the backs of my legs and under my palms, the only sensation telling me that I'm not already falling.

Master Root rises. His bare feet rasp over the rock behind us.

"You are all powerful. I know you have not been able to feel this yet, but you soon will. If you choose to, you could do terrible things with that power. I have often wondered if you are in fact too dangerous to exist."

My stomach clenches. I imagine a hand on my shoulder, a hand as firm as the mountain itself, pushing me over the edge. Is this about to become an execution?

"But I also think of the good you could do," Master Root continues, his voice softening. "I want you to locate that potential within yourselves. In one of our visualization exercises I asked you to imagine what you want most. That is the most basic form of Intention: want, act, get. But there is a much more powerful form, one that you should now be able to understand. It is not what you would do to achieve a goal, but rather what you could achieve that you never even thought possible. True Intention is recognizing this potential inside yourself."

The fear of a moment before is gone. I open my eyes and take in the vastness of the valley, letting its scale creep with a tingle up the base of my spine. The others beside me now have their eyes open as well. I catch Petra's eye. When she sees my face, she gives me a resolute nod.

Master Root speaks again after nearly five minutes. His voice is distant. He's already heading back inside Homestead.

"That concludes today's lesson. We will begin to put what we have learned to work tomorrow." He stalks off, leaving us at the edge of the cliff.

CHAPTER TWENTY-ONE: JAMIE

Master Root designates a new training room, one more spacious than the dark cave where we sat in concentration. A set of wooden bleachers curves around one wall. Though the six of us barely begin to fill them out, they give the room the distinct air of a lecture hall.

Master Root has set a lit candle on a dais in the middle of the room. He calls us up in turn to snuff the candle out.

Petra is first. Master Root says something only she can hear, then steps back. Petra takes a minute to collect herself, closing her eyes. When she opens them, she reaches a hand toward the fire, putting her fingers inches from the flame. Her fingers tense like she's trying to squeeze the flame.

Close to a full breathless minute passes. Petra's expression transforms slowly from concentration to frustration.

"I can't," she says finally. She walks back to us and throws herself onto the back of the bleachers. Master Root doesn't comment. He calls Nikki forward.

"I believe they teach this particular trick to children on Terraltum, regardless of which school they are Natural in," he says. "Let's see what Miss Laputa has retained."

Nikki focuses through a wry smile. She stretches out an arm at a couple paces from the flame. The flame winks out. A trail of smoke rises from the wick's still glowing tip.

"Good. It's still hot, could you light it again for me?"

This time, Nikki concentrates completely. Slowly, the glowing ember on the tip grows, traveling down the exposed length of string, and finally flickering back into flame.

I am last to go. Holly's is the most impressive turn, as she cuts off the flame instantly and without even a puff of smoke, and then re-lights it with a blazing fire that rockets five feet into the air. Callie is able to put the fire out, but does so by transforming the candle around it to enclose the wick and choke it.

"That's cheating!" Holly blurts.

"My only instruction was to put the fire out," Master Root says. "I didn't say how."

"I should've used my hands then," Nikki says, miming licking her palms and clapping them together over the candle. Even Petra, sulking behind us, laughs.

Dread had been growing in me as I watched the others. I've never done anything like this. I try to gather the threads of Intention, but I can't feel even a hint of their presence.

Streams of emotions come off the others: Holly's satisfaction, Petra's brooding frustration. What I have been able to accomplish before has always involved other living beings. I find it natural to read their flows of emotion. But with this, I don't even know where to start.

Master Root stares on impassively. My eyes lock on the flame until everything around it goes dark. I picture it flickering out like it did for Nikki, but the image is fuzzy, separate from reality. I try not to think about my embarrassment, but that only serves to bring it closer to the surface. I sneak a glance over my shoulder at Callie, but her face betrays nothing.

I only realize how long has passed when Master Root says, "Enough. We will try again later." Nikki gives me a reassuring pat on the back and Callie says she thought she saw the flame move and that maybe I'm strong in an area besides Elemental anyway. The encouragement is sweet, but decidedly unhelpful to my ego.

We walk through a couple more tasks. One involves rearranging a set of pebbles on the floor, and the other is to make a thin piece of paper—on its front, an ad for a budget airline taken from some old magazine—float. The others have varying levels of skill depending on the task. Holly has no problem moving the stones or floating the paper. Petra can mainly make the paper float by twisting the material itself, while Callie finds the pebble task easiest.

I manage nothing. I try to use the concentration exercises Master Root taught us, clearing all extraneous thought, and single-pointedly focusing on my goal. But whether the presence of the others is too distracting, or I'm too nervous to concentrate properly, I can't find anything to grasp.

Excitement fills the atmosphere around the dinner table that evening. Despite the day's relatively modest tasks, we're moving forward. The others chatter about what they were able to achieve, who's a PM, or an OE, or any of the other denominations of talent with Intention, half playfully jockeying, half encouraging each other's accomplishments. I join in the congratulations, but I can't help feeling that I'm at a party I wasn't invited to.

We tackle a half dozen exercises each day over the following week. I don't have better luck with any of them. When we have to conjure a small creature, Nikki conjures an entire army of them. When we have to shape a block of metal into a sword, Callie crafts a beautiful, curved scimitar. When Master Root places a block of wood in front of each of us, Petra splits it in half before he can give any instruction, and then has to put it back together. She does this with a creaking sound that reminds me of wood splitting, only somehow in reverse.

But through all of this I can't demonstrate that I'm capable of any Intention. The others all have moments of struggle. Holly, who excels at every other task, can't manage the slightest conjuration. But no one fails as miserably at every single task as I do. I start wondering if this is all a mistake, if there is another Jamie Monroe somewhere, the real one to hatch out of an egg and possess incredible magical powers.

With each passing task, I lose confidence. When Master Root announces new tasks in the morning, I no longer feel anxious. I just feel defeated. No matter what I do, I won't do any better than I did on the task before. The Skysent spend almost all our time together, eating together and hanging out after the tasks, recounting the successes and failures of the day's lessons. They dance clumsily around my inabilities, but even though no one is outwardly mean, they don't have to be. Each day I see them progressing. At first I don't mind that Master Root leaves halfway through dinner each night, only reappearing in the morning, but sometimes I think the others would be a little less enthusiastic if he stuck around.

Things change, though, with our final task of the week. Master Root leads us deep into Homestead. He brings us two at a time into a small room where the only light is a flickering torch on the far wall. Callie, my partner for the activity, gives me a reassuring smile.

"This task is somewhat different than the others," Master Root says. "It is, perhaps, too early for such a difficult task. The Mind School is the least common, and the hardest of all to master. However, it is important for you to develop the ability to work together, to develop bonds that go beyond spoken communication."

Callie raises an intentionally awkward eyebrow at me. I stifle a giggle.

"Not exactly what I'm talking about, but I appreciate the nit-picking."

"Anytime," Callie says.

"I don't have a specific objective for you. In a moment I will extinguish the lights. All I ask is that you move through the space, sensing each other's presence. Please do not speak. The floor in here has been silenced, so you will work without auditory clues." The floor is covered in squishy moss that doesn't so much as rustle when I shift my feet. "Good luck."

As the door closes behind Master Root, the light goes out and we are plunged into darkness.

The only sounds are Callie's breathing a few yards in front of me, and the faint beating of my heart in my ears. I try to slow my own breath. I gather myself for several seconds, then press my thoughts forward into the darkness. I pick up Callie's presence almost immediately. She projects her usual warmth, although it's tempered by concentration. I can place her within a few feet of her exact location. More than that, something draws me toward her.

I begin to move around her. She stands still, trying to pick up my position. Her Intention diffuses in a wild circle around her. She is clearly powerful, but I can tell she has never even thought to use Intention to feel other people's emotions.

I continue to circle, with each moment becoming more certain of her position. I move closer. It takes her longer than I would've thought to realize I'm only a foot away. I slip slightly, and the scraping of my foot on the moss gives me away.

"Are you running around?"

"Not running, exactly," I say.

"You can feel where I am though?"

I nod, realize I'm an idiot, then say, "Yes."

"Wild. I can't feel you at all. Hold on, I'm going to move so you can't remember where I was standing before. Give me a second, then come and find me."

She backs up a few paces, retreating to the right. I follow her Intention easily. When she stops, I walk directly over and tap her gently on the forehead.

"Ow, jeez you weren't kidding." She puts out a blind hand and finds my arm. Her warm hands hold onto me as if I'm an anchor in the dark room. A fluttering sensation vibrates in my chest. "Okay I want to try. Can you back up a bit? I think it would be easier if you weren't moving."

I step backward. Her struggling attempts to find me heighten. She throws more and more Intention out into the room, but as it increases it becomes wilder. Rather than focusing on what I'm giving off, she's flailing around with her own Intention. Frustration builds. As it does, her thoughts become more accessible. There's the blanket annoyance at not being able to perform the task, but there's another layer to it, one that I probably should have figured out before.

She's scared at the idea of failing in front of me. Not in front of anyone, me specifically.

My awareness is pulled forward. Her Mind naturally gravitates toward mine, establishing my location as a goal it wants to reach. Yet she can't identify that draw. It's as if she's cut herself off from it, or maybe has never learned to read it.

As I continue feeling that sensation, more in awe than anything else, the pressure builds on the thread. Before I can do otherwise, I've attached myself to it, and my emotions project outward. I rein them in almost immediately, but not before they strike Callie like a physical force.

Callie stumbles backward. I cut off the connection and run to her, steadying her awkwardly.

"Oh my god Callie, I'm so sorry," I say. Her arm trembles. "I didn't mean to do that. I'm so sorry."

"It's okay." Her voice shakes. "I've never ... what exactly did you do?"

"I'm sorry, I think I projected my emotions to you. I was trying to help you find me."

There's a long pause as Callie gets herself under control. I start losing my sense of her emotions as my own panic takes over.

"It's fine, Jamie," she says.

I don't know how it happened, and I'm worried I've royally screwed up. It's an invasion, even if it was unintentional. But Callie is smiling as the lights begin to come back up.

"You're..." She pauses and shakes her head.

"I'm what?" I laugh through a comically large and unwieldy bundle of anxiety.

"You're sweet," she says. One of her gentle hands is on my upper arm, and before I can respond, she kisses me firmly on the cheek.

As the door opens, Callie lets go of me. Her eyes stay fixed on me as Master Root shuffles in. It's hard to imagine he doesn't notice the gorgeous shade of crimson my face has become.

From the conversation later around the dinner table, no one else had anything as dramatic happen during their task. Petra and Nikki emerged from the room covered in bruises from where they had run into each other a half dozen times, refusing to back down even though they hadn't been able to sense each other. Holly had been paired with Master Root, so it's hard to say if she actually formed a connection, or just sensed the deep strength that emanates from him at all times.

Callie doesn't say anything to the others about what happened, only that I was able to feel her presence, but she wasn't able to feel mine.

When pressed by Holly she says, "We all went through the same thing. Can't we have one night where we don't spend the entire meal rehashing every mundane detail of the day?"

"Alright, alright," Holly says. "If it annoyed you so much you should have said something sooner."

"Well, I'm saying something now."

"Okay, so what should we talk about? You seem to have taken up the role of Conversation Master, so maybe you should tell us."

I catch Nikki and Petra exchanging an eyeroll.

"I want to hear Nikki talk about Terraltum," Callie says. "We're all apparently from there, but she's the only one who's ever been. I want to know what it's like."

"I don't want to bore you guys. I don't think any of it would make sense to you."

"Try us," Holly says, crossing her arms.

When she speaks, Nikki's words flood with love. She starts by describing her family's estate, on the high hill overlooking the capital city. She tells us about the winding staircase she takes to get home, how the steps have been carved directly into the side of the hill, how most carts and people take the long paved road that leads to the front gate. She describes the central courtyard around which the four wings of the manor form a square. The garden in the courtyard is planted by section, with flowers that bloom in different seasons. She swam in the fountain in the center of the courtyard as a child, splashing around with her brother and their cousins, and getting scolded by the house staff when they dripped water onto the parquet floors inside the house.

But her recollection doesn't stop at her home. She describes Orella as well, the overwhelming bustle of Terraltum's capital. She gives a surprisingly detailed account of the system of trams that connects the various neighborhoods within the city and tie vastly different communities together.

From the way she describes the Conjuring Arena, I can tell she admires the conjurers more than any of Terraltum's politicians. She details the most exciting matches she has seen, narrating with the earnest intensity kids at school use when talking about the Yankees' performance in the World Series.

Terraltum doesn't have electricity (they don't need it with Intention lamps available wherever you go) and what vehicles they do have are Intention-powered. Cellphones are not a thing there. I reflect that my own phone, seldom used anyway, is both useless this far underground and ran out of battery after the first few days here.

They have advanced medicine on Terraltum, though. Nikki mentions that it is not uncommon for Skyfolk to live well into their hundreds, some as long as one-hundred thirty years. Apparently a combination of Intention-based medical techniques, magically cultivated herbs, and the thin fresh air keep the population healthy.

Then she delves into the sentient creatures who populate her world. There are those I'm familiar with—like the ailethier and gnomin—but there are also ones I've never heard of, like the vaporous Fantasma and the burrowing Sree. All these beings live in a negotiated harmony and, to hear Nikki tell it, the non-humans often behave more rationally than the humans.

At some point, Nikki stops and looks around.

"How long have I been talking? I was about to fill you in on the mechanism behind Terraltum's invisibility, but I think I've talked long enough that the room is starting to run out of oxygen."

Master Root has long since disappeared to wherever he goes at night, and the fire where the leftover stew had been keeping warm has died almost to embers.

"There's one thing I'm curious about," Holly says.

"I suppose I could take questions now," Nikki says, shifting in her seat with mock importance.

"I was wondering whether everyone on Terraltum has Intention."

"The short answer is yes. It's like anything else, though. People are better and worse at different things. For example, my father could turn the river into a desert if he wanted to, but he can't work with fire to save his life."

"But everyone has something," Holly presses. "Everyone can do some Intention."

"I suppose so. I'd never really thought about it but yeah, it would be really unusual for anyone on Terraltum not to be able to do anything."

"So for example," Holly continues, "someone like Jamie would be really out of the ordinary." She turns toward me. "Not that you're out of the ordinary down here. We're all Earthworlders after all, but you wouldn't exactly fit in on Terraltum."

Nikki frowns. "I mean, I'd never thought about it like that."

Callie can't take it any longer. She shoots to her feet, rocking the table. "Holly, how about you shut your mouth, alright? I already told you that Jamie did better at the task today than any of us."

"He probably just heard your fat ass moving around," she snaps back. It takes all of Callie not to respond to this.

"Anyway, whether or not he did it is irrelevant," she says. "Even if he couldn't do a single task—"

"Which he can't."

"Even if he couldn't, it doesn't give you the license to be such an asshole."

Holly gets up too, and the others back away instinctively. But if it escalates further, I never find out. Wordlessly I get up and walk away from the table, my cheeks hot.

When I get back to my room, I slam the wooden door shut, startling Wesley, who had been napping on the desk.

You look like you've been through a spin cycle, he says when he's recovered.

I close my eyes and tuck my friend into the crook of my arm. I don't feel like talking about what happened at dinner. *Where have you been today?*

I went on somewhat of an exploratory expedition with Ora and Amby. We took one of the deep paths into the catacombs.

And how did you find the company?

Ora is as stuck-up as they come, which shouldn't be surprising given that she's one of the ailethier. Amby is a decent fellow, although one gets the sense that the level of conversation with him is similar to what one might have with a particularly intelligent pigeon.

I manage a chuckle, then say, "You've had a few debates with pigeons in your day, have you?"

Debates? No. Disagreements? Yes. Harsh words exchanged and blows come to? Perhaps. He taps playfully and reassuringly at my arm. He knows I'm unhappy, but he also knows I'm not ready to talk about it. *I suppose Amby is rather large as pigeons go.* Wesley is only ever this silly when he's trying to cheer me up. He doesn't succeed entirely, but I appreciate the effort. I stroke his head.

I don't know how I should be feeling. When Callie stood up for me, the weight behind it was palpable. I understand enough about her to know that she would only behave that protectively if she cared about me. And I still haven't fully processed our last one-on-one interaction, what a kiss on the cheek actually means. It seems like a good thing, but not having the opportunity to stand up for myself makes me feel even smaller than I already did with my Intention deficiencies. If I can't complete any of the tasks, at least I should be able to defend myself.

Holly has undoubtedly shot to the top of my list of least favorite people. At least I'm clear on that.

I try to get some sleep, but my eyes won't close. My thoughts lie like a weight on my chest. Confusion overwhelms everything I do in Homestead. I need to get out of here, at least to get away from the others for a couple days. But I know there is nowhere for me to go. Unless...

Wesley?

He stirs from his shallow sleep. *Something on your mind, Jamie?*

Where does Ora stay?

She has a room off the Main Hall. Why?

I need to speak with her.

Now?

Yes, now. I know it's a conversation that could wait until morning, but I need to be doing something. So much of the last two weeks has been spent in the stasis of not knowing where Paolo is. It's time to act. *Can you show me the way?*

I suppose so, although if she bites my head off for leading you to her, I blame you.

I take full responsibility.

Wesley rides on my shoulder as I pad out to the Main Hall. It's empty at this hour. Most of the torches have extinguished themselves, and a weighty silence covers the huge space. My footsteps seem to echo despite the soft moss.

Wesley points the way up to her room overlooking the Main Hall. I practically run into her as she comes out of her room.

"Well this is unexpected," she says, no surprise in her voice. I don't get the sense that Ora is often taken off guard. "A trilopex and a human come to find an aileth in the dead of night. There's a bad joke that starts that way."

She strokes her smooth chin.

"Oh wait, that wasn't a joke. It was a folk story to keep kids in their beds when they shouldn't be out wandering around. Either way, I recall it ended with the boy's parents finding his remains at the bottom of a gorge somewhere."

"It must've been a joke, then. All good jokes end with a dead body."

"How morbid. I love it."

"I thought you might."

"I assume you need something from me. It's my lot in life to always be needed but never appreciated."

"People would probably appreciate you more if you were less dramatic," I say. Wesley gives the trilopex equivalent of a chuckle.

"Shut up, rat," Ora snaps. I put my hand over Wesley's head to prevent him from leaping at Ora.

"I did come here to ask you for something. I wouldn't ask you if I had any other choice, but I don't think this is exactly a task for Amby."

"Oh?"

"It requires stealth, a bit of cunning, and most importantly, a lot of time away from Homestead. I know this isn't an aileth's idea of an ideal home."

Aileth emotions differ from human or animal ones, but Ora bears hers close to the surface. I've guessed right. Beneath the outward blasé attitude surges a pent-up desire to get out of this boring place. Buttering her up can't hurt, but it's the suggestion that she could leave that gets through to her.

"I need to find out where my guardian Paolo is. I need to know whether he's alive, and more importantly, how I can get a message to him."

"And by what authority are you asking me to do this?"

"I had hoped simply the authority of one good being doing a favor for another."

"Compelling," Holly says with a twist of her lip.

"And if that's not enough, then I'm sure I could make an argument that, as an agent of House Laputa, any order I give would in fact serve as an extension of Nikki's. I'm not making that argument though, because I'm a firm believer that we should help each other not because we have to, but because we can." I turn back down the hallway.

I've almost reached the top of the stairs when Ora says, "Okay Monroe. I'll seek out your guardian. But I expect you to remember that I did this favor for you, should the situation arise where the favor could be returned."

"I won't forget it."

Wesley squeaks at me as we climb down the stairs into the Main Hall.

Jamie, you should have ordered her to do it. It would've been within your right.

You know I don't believe in this weird servitude thing, I say. *Whatever she does for me, I want her to do willingly.*

I don't think you understand, Wesley says. *Ailethier have different rules than we do. They don't consider a favor something one person does for another. They consider a favor a contract. And ailethier are sly creatures.*

As we reach the floor of the Main Hall, I let Wesley run into my hand and stop, meeting his eyes.

I'm choosing to trust her. I can't take being here anymore. If she finds Paolo, I'm going to find him. Owing an aileth a favor is a small price to pay for being able to see him again.

I hope you're right.

As much as I blame Paolo for my inability to do anything other than sense emotions, as much as I'd yell at him for leaving so suddenly if he were in front of me right now, there's a deeper desire within me. He's all the family I have, and I don't feel like myself without him. When I return to my room, I am finally able to sleep.

Peaceful images make their way into my sleeping mind. Bees gnaw on swaths of wild violet. Beyond, boats float on a calm lake, and periodically lift off on silver-white wings. They circle the evergreens that line the lake's shore, touching back down or disappearing into the gentle clouds.

I skim over the top of the lake to the palace on its far shore. Marble columns rise in swoops that suggest the palace is an extension of the lake itself.

I see a glimpse of laughing people behind the palace, most of them wearing flowing robes, a few in tuxedos, and some in sundresses, as they mill about a buffet line. Many have taken off their shoes and lounge with picnics in the grass. Intention lamps burn at odd intervals throughout the space.

The image moves with vertigo-inducing speed, and it takes me a second to register the familiar shape of the Capitol Building in Washington D.C. On the mall are the usual tourists, but many are dressed in those strange flowing robes, not holding paper maps, but instead following phantasmal arrows that appear in the air before them. Among them are ailethier and gnomin. A jojum standing on a shoebox plays a long instrument carved out of bone. The song is staccato and upbeat, and a few people throw odd-looking coins into the hat by his feet.

I speed, still quickly but slowly enough that I can see continuity in my location. We're no more than three miles outside of the city, in a vast open space. I am reminded of the Arlington National Cemetery, but the arrangement of the rows is too wide, and the space is far, far bigger. At the entrance, a fifty-foot statue of Atlas, standing on the world and holding another world of clouds on his back, is crumbling. Its head has already fallen, and its legs are cracked beyond repair. But the way the stones have fallen suggests not true decay with the passage of years, but an intentional design in the original statue. Beyond, through an arch large enough for Atlas to pass through, are rows upon rows of granite blocks. Each has words carved into the sides, and after a second I realize they are names. The granite stones mark mass graves.

I drift, gaining altitude, and try to count the rows, which extend past the horizon in all directions. The granite blocks march away, their lines perfectly straight, the devastation they mark perfectly clear. I turn back to the archway. Above it is marked a single word, the letters glowing a cold blue over the graveyard: **Terramundus**.

CHAPTER TWENTY-TWO: JAMIE

When I make my way back to my room the next day—avoiding the post-dinner Intention-fueled soccer game the others have started playing with a ball improvised out of a vaguely circular mushroom cap we found—I discover Master Root already sitting in the chair in my room. He'd been tending the pot in the Main Hall when I left dinner. I shouldn't be surprised. This mountain is entirely his, and he moves through it with unnatural swiftness. He doesn't react as I come in, as if his presence here is entirely normal. As if any of this is normal.

"Jamie, I've been wanting to speak with you," he says.

"Are you going to tell me that I'm not really special at all and that I don't belong here? Because I can tell you, that would be a relief."

Master Root frowns. "Is that what you think?"

"The others can all do incredible things. I haven't been able to do anything since I've gotten here."

"I suppose you're one of those people who'd like to be able to run before he learns to crawl."

"If I'm surrounded by people who are sprinting, then I'd at least like to be able to walk."

"Nikki filled me in on your encounter with the werebeast."

"Let me guess, she told you how I fainted and was about to get eaten."

"No, she told me how you found your way into the beast's mind sphere without any previous training."

"I definitely didn't mean to," I say. If he's about to compliment me, I'm not having it. "He was lonely. I had to follow his emotions wherever they took me, and they took me in."

"Jamie, there are hundreds of thousands of people who can do the things I'm training all of you to do. Eventually you may do them better than anyone else, but they are, on the whole, entirely normal acts of magic."

Normal acts of magic. I'd have to file that expression away for later use. I sit on the bed with a heavy sigh.

"The truth is," Master Root continues, "I have not been training you properly. I thought if I threw enough tasks in front of you, eventually your power would come through."

"Or it would become apparent that I never had any power to begin with."

"This resignation is precisely what I've been afraid of," he says.

"Excuse me for being frustrated. This is completely humiliating. Everyone can tell I have no business being here."

"You have every right to be frustrated. That's why I want to teach you one-on-one. I think that will be better than letting you try and fail over and over."

I don't miss the implication.

"I know you are tired now. Get some rest. Tomorrow morning I will wake you early to begin. I have told the others to sleep in, so we will have as much time as we need."

"I won't be training with the others?"

"I think it best if you don't. This way I can be a true custodian of your studies." He rises, cutting short any reply I was about to make. "Don't worry, Jamie. We'll pull brilliance out of you yet."

With that, he is gone. I know I should sleep, but instead find myself wandering the halls outside my room. In the passage near the Main Hall, I run into Callie. She asks what I'm doing, and when I tell her I'm just wandering, she says she's down to wander too. Callie walks slowly, keeping one hand against the smooth wall, angling herself so that she doesn't have to break her stride to avoid the torches that stick out every few feet.

"Beyond shitty doesn't begin to describe it," she says. We'd been talking about the "hostilities," as she calls them, her rift with Holly. "If it all went away I'd be so happy, it'd feel ecstatic, probably drug-induced, and definitely illegal."

"You never know what's in those mushrooms Master Root gives us."

She breaks her gaze away from the wall for long enough to shoot me a smile, but not long enough to break her concentration.

"Jamie, are you actually suggesting that Master Root, guardian of the surface and of Homestead—where, mind you, he has kindly offered to house, feed, and protect us—is attempting to drug us? Sir, that is sick."

"I meant no such thing! I envisioned it more as a Master Root as a dealer situation. No drugging involved."

"At least not of the unknowing kind," Callie says, frowning. "Okay I'll buy it."

"How much?"

"As much as it's worth. So, say, seventeen cents?"

"Nineteen and you've got yourself a deal."

"Twenty. Done."

The weight of everything around us seems less heavy with Callie. I wonder if she feels the same way.

"I have a question," I say, forcing the words out before I can think better of it. "When you said I was 'sweet,' back when we were doing the training exercise together, what exactly did you mean?"

"Do you dispute that you are, in fact, sweet?"

"Not necessarily, though I might've preferred charming, charismatic, and possessed of indomitable masculine strength."

"I'm sorry," Callie says. My stomach flips, and not in a good way when I realize she's serious. Nothing beats a bad joke at the wrong time.

"No no no, don't be sorry," I say. "I was just wondering what you meant. That's all."

"I didn't mean anything besides that. Everything you projected to me was really kind and nice. You know, about me. I like that."

I hope that at some point my normal brain function will return, but it definitely hasn't happened yet.

"That's good," I say.

We're at her door and she pulls away from the wall to face me. She does an eyebrow wiggle that is both accusatory and unbelievably cute.

"Sure is, partner," she says. "I would invite you in, but unfortunately I've hit my awkwardness quota for the day. Hit me up tomorrow and we can continue this conversation."

"I'd like that."

"I'm sure you would." Callie disappears inside her room, taking the majority of my remaining dignity with her.

I agonize over this for the rest of the evening, picking over each thing I said, and generally deciding that in each instance, the exact opposite would've been better.

I should go back to my room, but I'm not ready to face my dreams. I have something, at least a flash, almost every night. Their reality tugs at me. They've also been increasing in clarity over time. My world and the vision world are quickly moving toward each other and coming into focus. That collision feels like an impending disaster.

The one thought keeping me going is that soon Ora might find Paolo, and I'll have an excuse to end my humiliation. Whatever is going on between me and Callie is a welcome distraction, but Paolo is still my top priority.

I imagine Paolo's voice repeating one of his favorite phrases when I would get discouraged: *Nothing that happens today determines what happens tomorrow.* But this entire experience has been one long string of depressing todays, and at some point that's a strong indication of what tomorrow will be like. Besides, what advice can a man who's abandoned the closest thing he has to a son really give?

My head is still heavy with deep sleep when Master Root knocks at the door. I find my feet, my eyes half closed. We don't speak as he leads me in the opposite direction from the Main Hall. The torches' murky light suggests the pre-dawn hour. Master Root's feet don't make any sound as they pad down the hallway. My own footsteps echo quietly.

After a few minutes we stop at a wooden door. Master Root takes a key out of his robe and rattles it into the lock. Dust fills the air in the musty room beyond. A large bookshelf covers one wall, stacked with aging, dusty volumes. Mildew and time waft together, the smell somehow pleasant. A large fireplace lies empty on the other wall. A few chairs sit by the fireplace and a ladder is propped against the bookshelf. Neither can have been used within the time I've been alive. The room has a floor of even stone, which a bedraggled rug does its best to soften. A small high table occupies the center of the room, leaving a comfortable space for a dozen people to stand.

"This will be our practice room," Master Root says.

"Is this a library?"

"Of a sort." Master Root holds out a finger indicating I should stay put, and then disappears behind the far edge of the bookshelf. He reemerges holding a groundhog. The animal is placid in his hands. He places it on the table in the center of the room and beckons to me.

I stare into the groundhog's eyes, and immediately fall into the easy rhythm of his feelings. Unlike most creatures out in the forest, he is almost entirely content. As groundhog lives go, his has been a luxurious one. Master Root has cared for him tenderly.

"I am glad you and Chauncey get along," Master Root says.

"Chauncey?" I manage a smile. "Hell of a name for a wood-chuck."

"When you have as many animals to take care of as I do, you find it necessary to entertain yourself when naming them."

"Was Woodchuck Number Seventeen already taken?" I keep my eyes on Chauncey. "What's the point of this? You already know I can read animals' emotions."

Master Root nods. I don't have access to even a sliver of his thoughts.

"I have spent a long while considering what approach would work best for you. How I should best go about drawing out your power. The Meluins had a saying, before they were destroyed: 'when building a house, start with the foundation, not the top floor.'"

"Those Meluins are really known for their sense of humor, I've heard." I am fully aware I'm being an irredeemable ass to my teacher, but I don't care. He started it. Master Root waits for a more substantive response. "Meaning that you can't take a second or a third step in a process until you've taken the first. Like the crawling slash running thing you were talking about earlier. Vis-à-vis walking." Sorry Master Root, I can't help myself.

"Sort of. But remember that the Meluins were a mountain people, who drew their strength from the earth. More than being about completing a task in a sequential order, the saying implies that you should always start from a position of strength. In the Meluin's case, starting with the earth meant anything that came after was stronger because of that base."

"So what you're trying to do with me..."

"Exactly. If you don't mind me being perfectly frank, I've had a hard time teaching you so far. Some students require you to put them in the most difficult circumstances. But not every student responds the same way."

"You're saying I'm weak."

"That's what you hear because that's what you believe. Your attachment to thinking of yourself in this dismissive way is childish and counterproductive. I will do my best to beat this attachment out of you."

"What a great teacher." I contemplate leaving the room, but Chauncey catches my eye. Is the groundhog laughing at me? I take a deep breath.

Master Root produces a lit candle. He sets it on the table by Chauncey, who regards it with indifference.

"The technique I'm about to teach you is far more advanced than those I have been showing your compatriots."

I step forward, placing my hand on the table's coarse wood.

"I want you to spend some time reading Chauncey's emotions," Master Root says. "Enough time that it requires minimal effort to do so."

Once again I strap my attention to the threads of emotion. They rest firmly in my hands, and soon I don't have to think about keeping the connection open. I could even project myself into his mind if I wanted.

"Ready?" Master Root says.

"Sure."

"I want you to continue holding that thread, but instead of bringing it into your own mind, I want you to push it elsewhere."

I never considered that the thread of emotion could do anything other than form a linear connection between the creature's mind and my own.

"I don't know how."

"It will help to visualize it. See if you can direct it toward the candle. I will consider even a flicker progress."

My concentration locks onto the emotions coming off Chauncey. The rest of the room dissolves into irrelevance. I try to picture the thread as a tangible object, one that I could reach out and hold.

It does help. Soon the steady emanation of contentment arranges itself in the air before my eyes in a looping thread.

But I can't quite grasp it yet.

"If I may, one more suggestion," Master Root says. "It may also help if you imagine the thread coming from someone you care about, someone whose Intention you would be invested in more than Chauncey's. All due respect to Chauncey."

I try to picture the thread coming from Paolo. He's the person I know the best, the one who I can most effortlessly read. But thinking about him sends me spiraling into fear and worry over whether he's okay, and that lingering anger at him for leaving. It makes it harder, not easier.

The list of people I can think of is regretfully short, but I try imagining it projecting from Callie.

When I do, the thread takes firmer shape, thin but so apparent that it's almost glowing. I latch onto the wavering string.

The thread isn't connected at my end, I realize. How can I never have seen that in all my years of interacting with animals? I can direct it if I choose to, letting it swing in a breeze, or crack like a whip. I hold it tightly in my mind, directing it with a single purpose toward the candle. My head aches with the concentration. A strange feeling takes over, as if I'm not turning my own will toward the candle, but Chauncey's, as if I'm directing his Intention toward putting the candle out.

That's absurd, groundhogs don't have Intention, I think. The connection breaks.

"Damn it."

Master Root smiles. "You felt it, though."

"Yes, I felt it. Let me try again."

"By all means."

A few tries pass. Each time I find Chauncey's Intention easily, but in the process of turning it toward the candle, it snaps. It's like threading a needle, like the moment when the tip of the thread catches in the eye, but pushing it too quickly causes it to fray and slip to the side.

Then one shred of it catches. Most spins around me, but I hold on to the center. Whirling patterns appear before me. I close my eyes, but the thread's core remains clear. I chance pulling at it, making it sway. It holds, bends. I push it a bit farther, this time not holding back. I aim it toward the candle's light.

As the candle winks out, Master Root claps. Chauncey leaps from the table and disappears under one of the chairs near the fireplace. I lean forward onto the table and rest my head in my hand, exhausted.

"That was magnificent," Master Root says, stepping forward and placing a hand on my shoulder.

"That was—" I break off, stammering. "It wasn't like—it wasn't like I put out the candle. It was like I made him do it."

"You misunderstand. You didn't make him do anything. You simply used the thread of his thoughts—a thread we all put out into the world in some form—to aim your own Intention. You tricked yourself into thinking it wasn't you putting out the candle."

I dig my finger into the space between my eyes to counteract the pain developing there.

"What's the difference?"

"I know that took a lot out of you," Master Root says, "but tricking yourself gets easier the more you do it."

I'm not sure I like the sound of that.

Once he's figured out how I need to learn, Master Root proves to be a capable teacher. He calls the process of using other beings' Intention to my own ends "tethering," and I find the name fits. That first day he only asks me to perform one more act of tethering, making a cup of water bubble. Twenty minutes of valiant effort results in sufficient fizzing, and Master Root concludes the session in good spirits, telling me to rest and return that evening.

CHAPTER TWENTY-THREE: NIKKI

The atmosphere over the next few days could only be described as frigid. During our lessons, Holly and Callie pointedly avoid any interaction, and each seems eager to outdo the other with their Intention. The new sense of competition furthers the gap between those of us who are doing well and those, like Jamie, who are struggling. Holly sits at the opposite end of the table from Callie and the rest of us at dinner.

As unpleasant as the rift is, worse is the nagging thought that I'm moving backward. My parents wanted me to become close with all the Skysent, to bring them over to our side. Having the most powerful split off from the group is not a good sign. Strangely, now that it's not going as well, I am even more committed to my parents' goal. If I'm going to carry out orders, I'm going to do it right, no matter what they are. The conjuring arena can wait.

Jamie leaves immediately after dinner every night, vanishing almost as quickly as Master Root. We stop hanging out together in the evenings. Though I'm inclined to agree with Callie's position, I won't risk taking a firm side by spending my time with her. Instead I return to my room, which grows smaller by the day. It's what I imagine being trapped inside the Gift of the Ailethier would be like. I'm in a stasis where time ceases to exist. My thoughts and the tension around me stretch on forever, never seeming to diminish.

A knock comes at my door after a dinner in which Holly spent the entire meal making snide remarks under her breath, just loud enough so that we could all hear them.

"Who is it?"

"The only sane one," replies the voice from the other side of the door.

I open the creaky door to see Petra standing in the passage outside. At the sight of her cute, angular face, my entire digestive system sends itself into immediate nervous distress, and I struggle to keep my cool.

"Oh it's you. I was expecting Holly." Petra smiles as she walks past me. "What brings you to my humble abode?" She sits at the end of the bed, and only then do I inspect the room. Not only is the bed not made, but what few belongings I have are spread out over every surface, including the floor. I imagine my father's stern voice saying something about the respectability of the Laputa family.

"I need a break."

"I get that."

"Callie and Holly have been visiting me nonstop to talk about their issues." She catches my uncomfortable expression. "Not at the same time, of course. Callie told me she tried to apologize, but when Holly rejected the apology, she used Intention to break the lock on her door so she couldn't get out."

"Hell of an apology."

"Definitely not how I would've done it."

"Holly came to me last night," I say. "She didn't mention that part of it."

"Because it would require acknowledging that Callie actually has a bit of Intention."

I roll my eyes. "Some team we've got here."

"Anyway, that's enough of the drama."

We chat for the next few minutes about unimportant topics, glad to be outside of the claustrophobia of the petty fight. Having an ally who agrees with me lifts the heaviness of the past few days. I notice that even when the conversation falls into silent gaps, they are comfortable rather than awkward. I like how she tips her chin slightly up before she breaks one of these silences.

"I've been thinking more about Master Root," I say. "With how important he finds our training, isn't it weird that he leaves us on our own in the evening? You'd think he'd keep prodding us to make sure we're keeping up."

"Maybe he realizes we need rest."

"He doesn't even stick around for the end of dinner. It's like he has somewhere to be."

I can feel Petra's eyes alight as I give voice to a suspicion that's only been in the background of my mind.

"Okay Nikki," she says, "what are you saying? You don't think he leaves Homestead, do you?"

"I don't. All I'm saying is, what percentage of this place have we explored? How do we know what else could be tucked away?"

"You're on a bit of a Master Root trip, aren't you?"

"I'm sorry I don't have as easy a time accepting all this bizarreness as you do," I say.

"Ironic, since you're the one who grew up on Terraltum."

"Master Root is weird, even for Terraltum."

Petra considers this. I rock back in my chair far enough to test its legs' structural integrity.

"He's not exactly normal," she says after a minute. "But he's helping us. Don't really think I'm in any position to question him."

"That's exactly why I think we should be questioning him," I say, rocking my chair back to a stable position. "Have you noticed anything weird at all? Anything you couldn't explain?"

With all my concentration taken up by Intention and trying to wrangle the Skysent, I haven't had much time to develop this idea. There was the one moment during our meditation on the cliff when I had the sensation that Master Root was about to push me off, but I don't want to push Petra to any conclusions.

"You've given me something to think about." Petra gets up. "I should get some sleep if we have another day of squabbling to endure. I'll tell you if I see anything strange."

"Keep a weather eye out."

"Will do," she says as she opens the door and slips out into the hallway. "We sane people need to stick together."

Watching her go fills me with a faint whiff of melancholy.

I run into Jamie in the passage outside my room the following morning, and we walk to breakfast together. His baggy eyes make him look like a raccoon.

"You ready for today's tasks?" I try.

"You know that feeling of excitement where you can't think about anything else because you know the thing you're waiting for could very well be the best thing you've ever done?"

"Yes?"

"I don't have that."

We say nothing more before we arrive in the Main Hall for our breakfast stew.

As much as I want to keep my attention on the tasks, in the days that follow I pay more attention to Master Root than anything else. He is stern and didactic during our lessons, but always supportive of the Skysent's development. But now that I am watching closely, I realize something I have probably noticed unconsciously for a while. While he celebrates the success of the others and helps them when they fail, he meets everything I do with cold disinterest. Though on average I am the most advanced, Master Root only gruffly acknowledges when I perform a complex conjuration, or when I stop a ball he throws at me in mid-air. While he looks over the others with a protective, almost paternal eye, he never actually meets my gaze.

Now that I've noticed it, it's all I can think about. What had just been musings to Petra have taken root like an invasive weed. Part of me wishes for the simple conclusion. Maybe he leaves dinner early for no better reason than not wanting to be around me. I don't tell Petra any of this when she comes to my room in the evenings. She's begun to speculate wildly—to the point where she's either deductively brilliant or is making fun of me—and I go along with it. It's better than risking not having anyone to talk to. And there's also something about her that makes me not want to say no to her, even if her suggestions turn in a fanciful direction.

I know I should do my best to resolve the conflict between Callie and Holly, but I try to escape it instead. I seek out the entrance Ora found. I never go far, but sitting atop one of the boulders outside the mouth of the cave, the breeze against my cheek, relieves some of the tension.

Another development gnaws at me. The Skysent show obvious signs of growing strength. With each task, their confidence grows, and Master Root meets their confidence with increasingly intricate assignments. Their powers develop in the same two-pronged pattern of any Skyfolk—two stronger schools coming to predominate as Natural and Complementary and the others staying more or less dormant—but for one of the regular Skyfolk these would take years to emerge. While I could already do most of the tasks at the beginning, now I find myself as challenged as anyone else. They may not have known much when they started, but all but Jamie possess a unique knack for Intention and are growing far faster than I would've thought possible. If they keep going at this rate, we might stand a chance against the Kelluvas after all.

To think, I was tasked with rescuing the only one without a lick of Intention. I know at an intellectual level that my parents are intelligent, but this seems like a fantastic mistake of judgment.

Whenever I consider how quickly they're developing, my hand unconsciously finds the Piece of Sky at my chest, the one thing that grounds me in my power. These Skysent don't need Sky. Their Intention is an inherent part of them. During our training, Petra caught me holding the shard a few times, and I quickly dropped my hand to my side.

The training session today is in the Main Hall, and Master Root obviously means to make the most of the space.

"I know that you are all very clever, and you will find creative ways to use your Intention in battle. However, in almost every magical battle throughout history, there is one particular piece of magic that has constituted the majority of attacks. I will allow your foes to demonstrate." He holds his hands out to the sides and an image appears between them. It is brief. The tallest Changeling holds out his hand, his first two fingers and thumb pointed forward. A bolt of white light rockets from between them, connecting with a stocky man in front of him, knocking the man over. Another bolt of light strikes the staggering man in the head. He crumples lifelessly.

"Pure Intention," Master Root says as the images cease. "While certain situations call for bending Intention to a specific purpose, its pure form can be a powerful way to attack your enemies."

"But what does it do?" Petra asks. "It killed that guy somehow."

"Imagine being struck by a hammer. That could be a tap so soft you could hardly feel it, or a strike so powerful it kills you. It all depends upon the intentions—if you'll pardon the expression—and power of the person delivering the attack."

"Is there any way to stop it?" Callie asks.

"That will be a major part of today's lesson," Master Root says.

Holly puts on her best disapproving-of-teacher's-pet expression, but is clearly too interested in impending violence to interject.

While the kinetic branch of the Pure School was part of my schooling, I was always more interested in how Intention allowed trams and barges to move rather than offensive applications. Yet since Pure is my Complementary, it comes naturally. I am paired with Holly, while Callie and Petra work together. Jamie has, probably wisely, bowed out of this particular activity, which Master Root doesn't question. We start by directing gentle Intention at each other, which feels like a soft shove. Spaced over a distance of twenty-five yards, it would be easy to avoid the slow-moving balls of light, but Master Root insists that we experience them hitting us.

Stopping the Intention turns out to be trickier. The secret to casting the bolts of Intention is simply to *do* it, rather than thinking about the mechanics of doing it. Like throwing a ball, if you keep your eyes on your target and trust in the result and muscle memory, the rest simply happens.

But stopping the energy requires you to focus on the very core of the Intention, and to dispel it from within. It's like my conjuring training, reacting to each move your opponent makes rather than planning ahead. But instead of counteracting a lumbering beast or a swarm of sharp-toothed chimera, you have to counter an amorphous, swift ball of pure energy. I'd take the lumbering beast any day.

After my first few feeble attempts, Master Root snaps, "Nikki you are taking the easy way!"

"But I'm blocking them!"

I had indeed been blocking them, projecting a shield of my own Pure Intention that wildly deflects the energy Holly sends at me.

"That works fine for these light attacks, but you're using a brute force method, matching Intention against Intention." I place my hand on the Piece of Sky on my chest. It's warm from the Intention I've been pulling from it.

"You don't think I'm up to it?"

"In theory, if you were to match surges of Intention one against one, then the person possessed of the most Intention would prevail. But when blocking you must take into account the speed of the energy being directed at you. In order to create a solid wall to stop a moving object, it takes a far stronger force than the original casting."

"I had no idea we signed up for a physics lesson," Holly says.

"I am trying to tell you something that may keep you alive." The other group stops and comes to attention at the severity in Master Root's voice. "If you try to match Intention head-on, you will lose every fight that lasts more than a couple seconds. Besides, if you deflect it, you run the risk of hitting one of your allies. Here, send some Intention my way."

Master Root takes a few paces back and faces me in an athletic stance.

"How much?"

"I assure you, you should feel no need to hold back on my account."

This is infuriating enough for me to send a surge of Intention that is larger than necessary, but Master Root projects a shield of pure light that blocks it easily, bouncing the ball of energy toward Holly, who dives out of the way.

"Now send another one my way and watch the difference."

I do as he says. Nothing projects from his outstretched hand, but my attack simply fades into nothingness, disappearing into vapor around him.

"See? At times a well-timed deflection can play to your advantage, but in general it will be more efficient and safer to simply dissolve the attack. Now, try it again."

The lesson is one of our longest, stretching well past three hours. At the two-hour mark I can finally dispel most of Holly's practice attacks. Near the end we stop taking turns, and trade attacks back and forth. The pace quickens, and soon we hurl Intention at each other at a feverish pace. I dispel when I can, block when I can't summon enough concentration to dispel. We circle, closing the distance until only fifteen feet separate us. Holly smiles as she launches attacks from both hands. In response I send a single surge of my own, which splits the space between them, repelling them to the sides and forcing Holly to scramble a defense.

We strike in the natural rhythm of the duel, each attack growing quicker and more powerful, each defense more frantic. I realize out of the small part of my awareness I can spare that the rest are watching us.

We continue, neither wanting to accept defeat. At one point I think I have her when my attack strikes the floor and bounces viciously upward into her forehead. But the blow only causes her to stagger slightly, and her next attack comes within seconds. My limbs and mind begin to tire. Every casting requires more effort than the last.

Finally, one of my defenses goes up too slowly, and Holly's attack hits my ankle. I fall heavily into the moss on the floor, managing to deflect one more attack before Holly rushes forward and hits me hard in the shoulder with another blast. I fall onto my back, stunned. Holly stands over me. For a second I think she will strike again, but instead she holds out a hand to help me off the floor.

Jamie and Petra clap, and when I'm on my feet I pat Holly on the back.

"Well fought, Laputa," she says.

"I want a rematch," I say.

"I think we can arrange that."

Dinner that night is the scene of the worst argument yet between Holly and Callie. Holly lords her superior Intention over the others, which Callie uses as an excuse to hurl more—arguably well-earned—insults at her, noting her lack of humility in less than polite terms. I can't engage anymore. I slip away from the table, leaving my half-eaten stew behind.

I head for the entrance to Homestead to collect my thoughts, but on the way I pass a shadow moving down one of the hallways I haven't explored. I peek my head down, in time to see a large shadow disappearing around the nearest bend.

I follow without thinking, moving as quickly as stealth will allow, keeping the shadow in sight. By the bulky shape I know who the shadow belongs to, but a few more sharp turns pass before Master Root come into view. He carries a large pot, but despite his size and heavy load, no sound echoes in the corridor.

We walk steadily downward. The air grows more pungent down here, like the smell of a house lived in too long without the windows being opened. It is warmer, too, and the moss under my feet is thicker than in most places in Homestead.

Master Root pulls up short at a heavy door, and I scramble to stay out of sight. He sets his burden down and pulls out a brass key to unlock the door. In the split second between the door opening and him disappearing inside, I glimpse a thick mash of stew inside the pot. I try to remember if I saw him making more stew after we started eating, but I honestly can't say.

A few breathless minutes pass. I slip into an adjoining hallway, one that, judging by the lack of a clear wear pattern on the floor's moss, is rarely used. I wait behind the first turn, the closed door just around the bend.

My heart pounds. I think about all of Petra's wildest theories about Master Root's strange behavior. I need to know what lies behind that door.

I wait until I hear the door open and shut again. The lock clangs. I risk enough of a glimpse to see Master Root walking back the way he came, carrying the empty pot in one hand.

I don't know how long I wait, but with every second, nervous energy pulls me toward the door. But if I act too soon and Master Root sees me, the least punishment would be getting kicked out of Homestead and failing my mission.

When I finally judge the coast clear, I pick my way back up the side passage. The corridor beyond is deserted as I tiptoe to the door.

It is far heavier than most of the doors in Homestead. The entrances to our rooms are sturdily built, but this one is reinforced and unornamented, its sole purpose to keep whatever is inside locked away. I place a tense hand against the heavy lock, but even before I push, I know my efforts will be futile. The door is so solid it doesn't even jiggle on its hinges.

I kneel and try to peer through the keyhole, but either darkness completely enfolds the other side, or no direct line-of-sight cuts through.

I place my ear against it. I hear only silence.

Then a muffled sound.

It's almost indistinguishable, and if not for the fact that it repeats several times, I would've thought I imagined it. There's a soft gurgling from behind the door, followed by a faint whine ending in a croak. Though the noise's pitch brings to mind a small creature, its timbre suggests a much larger source. As strange and inhuman as it is, something about it relates an unmistakable sadness. I wait for several more minutes, but hear nothing more.

My stiff back straightens as I rise. This will certainly get Petra's attention. The excitement of that fact dampens as dread descends over me.

What could have made that disturbing noise, and why is Master Root keeping it in a locked room?

CHAPTER TWENTY-FOUR: JAMIE

The tasks with the others over the next few days don't get any better, but every night I work with Master Root, and I can feel my abilities with tethering growing. The others mostly avoid talking about my evident struggles, too afraid it will spark more fighting between Holly and Callie.

A knock comes at my door as I'm dozing off after our afternoon lessons. I mutter a bleary "Come in," and Callie stands in the doorway. I unconsciously smooth my bedhead and sit up.

"Don't get up!" Callie says. "I didn't know I was disturbing a nap. Nap time is sacred."

"It's my time to commune with the divine," I reply.

Callie pulls the desk chair close beside my bed and sits, slightly awkwardly. There's something about the small moments where she's unsure of herself, where she's somewhat of a bumbling idiot like me, that I find enormously endearing.

"I heard there was some extracurricular action going on with Master Root," she says.

"You found out about our Homestead A/V club?"

"More like secret training. Some real MI5 shit."

I snort. "It's definitely not as cool as that. Master Root asked me to keep things quiet, at least until I'm good enough to demonstrate what I can do."

"Of course." When I don't say anything more, I sense a hint of frustration coming off her. "Okay, so how do you feel about this? It's good news, right?"

"Yeah I guess."

"Jamie will you just tell me what's on your mind? We both know full well that you could tap into my fricken' brain at any time. It's not fair that you're holding this back. Especially when we're trying to help you."

"You know I would never tap into your brain. At least not intentionally."

Callie waves this off. "That's not the point."

"What is the point?" For a second I fear she's about to stand up and walk out of the room.

"The point is that I thought we had a connection," Callie says. "Was I wrong about that? Because that doesn't mean anything if you're not willing to share how you're feeling with me."

"No, you're not wrong. At least... I don't know. I'm not good at this type of stuff."

"What type of stuff?"

Dammit, she's going to make me say it.

"This girl/boy stuff."

"Heteronormative, but continue."

"Dammit, you know what I mean! This relationship-y stuff. Dating and things like that."

Callie smiles. "Far from eloquent. But good. Glad we're on the same page."

"We are?"

"Look dude, you may be a steel trap made out of deflecting jokes when it comes to your own emotions, and your ability to do literal mindreading has me more than concerned, but despite it all I genuinely enjoy spending time with you. Like a lot. I would even consider thinking about pondering the concept of maybe potentially dating you."

"I've never felt more flattered," I say, trying to keep my heart rate under three-hundred beats per minute.

"So what do you think?"

What I think is that I want to jump out of bed and kiss her right on her beautiful face, but the mere thought of the physical movements required for that paralyzes me.

"I'm thinking that, if you're asking a question, then my answer is yes."

She stands up—she's short but still towers over me on the low bed.

"I wasn't," she says, bending toward me. "But good."

She plants a kiss on my lips before I can react. A single kiss, soft but firm. She straightens, smiles at me, and makes for the door.

"Bye Jamie, I've got pondering to do."

My entire body vibrates with the remnants of the kiss. I feel nauseous. Maybe in a good way, I can't tell. Only then do I realize Wesley had been watching the whole thing as he pretended to sleep.

"Come on, Wes. Spit it out."

"I have observed that in human relationships, awkwardness and the complete inability to communicate in any remotely meaningful way often symbolizes mutual attraction."

"I feel judged," I reply.

"You should. You are judged. But you are also liked by someone who happens to like you. That's not nothing."

"No, it's not." I didn't think panic would be my response to this sort of thing. I'd often imagined what it would be like if Serra, my friend from school, had told me she had feelings for me, and I'd always thought that I would be able to collect myself and speak frankly. But my brain doesn't seem to have the program for that installed at the moment.

CHAPTER TWENTY-FIVE: NIKKI

In the past few days, Petra and I have scouted Master Root's comings and goings. She was somehow even more excited than I expected about the door. In several visits we still haven't been able to unlock it, but we have timed down to the minute when Master Root will bring his delivery of food. Petra and I positioned ourselves in the passage nearby, and Petra created a mirror in the air to see when Master Root opened the door. But the quick glimpse beyond revealed only a torch-lit wall covered in moss. Petra and I stayed up late into the night on several occasions, throwing out ever more fantastical ideas for what could be behind the door.

With the door standing in the way of our investigation, I decide to talk to Master Root one-on-one. Maybe he'll reveal something if I steer the conversation in that direction.

Master Root is not in the Main Hall. The stew for the night's dinner already waits over the fire, untended. I head for a passage I've never been down before, one I've seen Master Root use a few times after his feeding sessions. Once in the passages leading off the Main Hall, I am instantly hopelessly lost. Three separate corridors shoot off the central one, and each of those branches off at least half a dozen times. I try to keep track of the twists and turns, but before long the earliest turns become hazy in my memory.

Just when I am considering turning around to find my way back, I come to an open cavern about twice the size of my room at home. No door separates the passage from the space beyond. A trickle of water works its way down the rocks in one corner. I pass an earthen alcove with a smooth shape resembling a bed, and find Master Root in the far corner, reaching into a shelf high on the wall.

"Ms. Laputa," he says without turning around. "What can I do for you?"

I stop at an awkward distance. Master Root turns toward me, holding a heavy glass jar. Inside appear to be a dozen glowing earthworms. He opens the lid and pulls one of the worms out.

"What are those?" I ask, giving my thoughts a second to re-form.

"The mountain around us is a living thing, in its own way. My little glowing friends will make sure it remains healthy. It is getting to be time for a checkup."

My eyes rest on the glowing creatures, which inch around the edge of the glass, frosting its surface with slime.

"I assume you are here for other reasons. Speak." His eyes don't quite meet mine.

"I was curious about Jamie's training," I say. "I don't like secrets."

He surprises me by answering without hesitation: "I am teaching him complex Mind Intention. Hopefully it will be enough to aid your cause in battle, as he's shown himself incapable of any other kind of Intention."

"Is this because of what I told you about him accessing the were-beast's inner mind sphere when I rescued him? Is it that level of creepy Mind Intention?"

"He's lucky he survived that encounter," Master Root says. "If the creature had known how, it could have trapped Jamie in there."

"Is that possible?"

"There are few fates worse than being trapped in the deepest sanctum of someone else's mind. Not too pleasant for the one doing the trapping, having someone constantly rattling around your brain, but some have thought it worth the hassle to permanently incapacitate a persistent enemy."

I try to imagine being stuck inside the brain of another person, but as I can hardly imagine being there in the first place, I don't have much luck.

"I've been thinking something, although I don't want to sound dramatic." My spine chills as I think through what I'm about to say. "Do you think maybe Jamie might be Singular?"

"You think he's Mind, and Mind only?"

I can't respond, because there's no way to know for sure. But the thought had crossed my mind more than once. Singulars possess Intention from only one school, but that Intention has the potential to rise to profound and terrible heights.

"There have been no documented Mind Singulars since Barrun Meluin," Master Root says.

"Then maybe he's just a Natural Mi, with a late-emerging Complementary."

"It would be exceedingly late for a Complementary to emerge. Especially for a Changeling."

"Skysent," I correct automatically, before I can fully think through what Master Root is implying. "You're actually banking on him being a Singular? Isn't that risky?"

"This whole enterprise has been risky."

Master Root turns back to his worms, but I don't move.

"Master Root," I say, trying to keep my voice level, "why don't you like me?"

If the question surprises him, he doesn't show it.

"I don't dislike you. Certainly you are more of a bother than most of my other pupils, but you have a quick mind and a natural cleverness that is a great quality in a student."

"Then why do you barely acknowledge my presence?" I press. "Don't think I haven't noticed how you barely even make eye contact with me. I'm a student here, the same as anyone else, even if I'm not really Skysent."

"I am not of Terraltum," he says. "I am not truly of the Earthworld either. I am one of the guardians who long ago decided it best not to take sides in the battles between earth and sky. I took such a vow. In order to stay within my role, I am only to interfere if I see a perversion of Intention. The existence of the Changeling is a perversion, and their use for the gain of the Kelluvas threatens the natural order of the worlds."

"More than the Kelluvas setting werebeasts on Laputan soldiers, or the Natantis blowing up the side of the mountain and half an army with their war machines during Barrun's War?"

"You'll remember that Almus Kelluva was banished after the war for creating the werebeasts."

"Only after the Kelluvas had used his creations to win the war," I say.

"But the Changelings are far more upsetting to the balance of nature. A werebeast is more powerful and cruel than the creature it came from, but not excessively so. These Changelings have far more potential to disrupt the order, particularly if they take one side or another in the ongoing conflicts of Terraltum."

"But you are placing the Skysent on a side," I say. "You're setting the Changelings of the two houses against each other to ... what? Hope they all kill each other?"

"To maintain the balance of power."

"This is completely insane. And it doesn't explain why you treat me like I'm transparent."

"It is a lot harder to maintain a position of neutrality when a potential heir of one of the houses of Terraltum is benefiting from my training."

I open my mouth, but don't find any words. He's still been training me, though. He's taking a side, by his definition, and breaking his vow. Every time he sees me it must be a reminder of this.

"If it helps, you can think of me as an outcast of Terraltum. Because guess what? That's exactly what I am."

"Do you really think you will never return?"

The question catches me off guard. I've spent so much time wishing I could return home, but always because I wanted to go home *now*, not because I had any sense of *never*.

"I am certain you will return at some point," Master Root continues. "The reason for your banishment sounds questionable at best, and these sorts of crimes have a way of seeming less relevant over time."

"Don't give me false hope." I cannot allow myself to follow this line of thinking. If I let myself believe that my parents' appeal could work, or that in a year and a half I could petition to come home, then that would be all I could think about. It would crush me.

"Trust me Laputa, Terraltum isn't done with you."

It's only after I return to the Main Hall that I realize I've completely forgotten to probe about the locked door. It seems like every conversation I have with Master Root is a rope sliding through my grip, and the more I try to catch hold of it, the faster it slips away.

CHAPTER TWENTY-SIX: NIKKI

Master Root trains Jamie every evening after finishing with us, cutting off our tasks early to stop by the locked room before disappearing for the rest of the evening with Jamie. The rest of us hang out in Callie's room. Holly and Callie have obviously decided that being in the same room as their enemy is better than spending the evening alone. Despite the occasional awkward moments, I prefer having everyone together again. As it often does, the conversation turns to the subject of Jamie's mysterious training, which has been going on for the better part of a week.

"I don't think he's actually training," Holly says. "I think Master Root is being nice and not wanting him to be embarrassed. They're probably playing double solitaire."

"When've you ever known Master Root to do something to protect our feelings?" Petra says.

"I agree," Callie says. "I for one think it's got something to do with the Mind School."

"Why do you say that?" I ask, surprised how easily she's guessed it. I had been letting them keep their secret.

"Remember when we had that assignment where we had to sense each other? Jamie could genuinely sense my presence. It was like he could read my emotions, or Intention, or something." She shivers. "It freaked me out, to be honest."

"How does that work?" Holly asks.

All eyes turn to me by default. Representative of Terraltum and all that.

"Well, as you know, different schools of Intention come naturally to different people. For example, Holly is particularly good at a sub-school of Elemental that may be better classified as the pyromaniac variety."

"And proud of it," she and Callie say in unison. They laugh, though they meant it in very different ways.

"Most forms of Intention are outward facing. Like my conjuring. I project energy into the world in a particular form. It's large scale. You intend something, and it happens. Mind is more intricate than Matter or Elemental. Reading emotions requires a greater level of complexity. You can't just project. You have to let them come to you."

"It's pretty impressive, I think," Callie says. "To hear him talk about it, it's like it comes naturally to him."

"Do you think it helps him recognize the massive boner you've had for him since day one?" Holly says.

"Holly, rude!" I say reactively.

"So rude," Callie says, but then grins. "But yes. Yes it does."

The room erupts. Callie's crush on Jamie had been an only somewhat kept secret, and putting it out in the open feels like a big deal.

"Continue with your lecture, Nikki," Callie says. "I'll try to keep my boner out of it."

"By Sky itself you're a tough crowd," I say. "Jeez, where was I? Oh right. Letting things come to you." I avoid eye contact with anyone, knowing it could break my rhythm if I burst out laughing again. "That's the theory, anyway. I've never really tried it. Terraltum looks down on mind magic, despite the fact that some of our most influential politicians use it. Bella Natantis, the Chancellor of Terraltum, is rumored to be the most powerful practitioner of the Mind School in recent memory."

"How powerful is it, though?" Holly asks. "What could someone have access to?"

"You mean the ability to read emotions versus the ability to read actual thoughts?"

Holly gives me a noncommittal nod, like she means more than that.

"There's not really a known limit to the Intention of the Mind School. The ability to experience others' emotions is the most common, but I've heard rumors of abilities far beyond that. Barrun Meluin, the last patriarch of House Meluin before it fell in Barrun's War, is rumored to have been able to implant ideas in others' minds, or to make them experience whatever emotion he pleased. My mother and father were trapped with him in the Meluin Caves during the last days of the war, and they said that whenever he was around, they never felt despair. It was like he constantly filled them with hope, even during the direst times."

"Always nice when powerful people have benevolent intentions," Petra says.

"I don't know if the Kelluvan army would see it that way," I continue. "The other rumor is that he filled enemy soldiers who didn't have the ability to shield themselves with a sense of abject terror so powerful that they collapsed, unable to fight. Imagine that, an entire almost victorious army of Kelluvan warriors and werebeasts behind you, and you're so distraught you can't even hold your weapon."

I never know how much of this part of the story to believe. Maybe I don't want to believe that anyone could wield such power. Your thoughts and emotions should be your own.

"Do you think that's the sort of thing Jamie's learning?" Holly sounds jealous.

"Barrun Meluin was an outlier," I say. "He was a Singular, meaning he only had proficiency in one school. Singulars develop very differently from the rest of us."

"Jamie's only shown any power in the Mind School," Callie says quietly.

Silence builds between us.

Petra breaks the silence with a sigh. "Whatever it is, knowing Master Root, we're not likely to find out anytime soon."

"I just hope it can help us when the fight comes," Callie says as I give Petra a pointed look.

"I doubt it," Holly says. "Not that I care what it is, as long as it helps keep us alive."

"What would Mind Intention do in the kind of fight we're going into?" Callie asks, though not unkindly.

"We have to trust Master Root on this," I say. Petra returns my gaze, and I'm speaking directly to her, not sure whether I believe my own words. "He's doing everything he can to ensure that we're as prepared as we can possibly be. He wouldn't send us out without everything we need. Any secrets he's keeping, I'm sure he has a good reason for."

Petra's mouth twists up in a wry smile, but before anyone can respond, Jamie's head pokes in the open door. He can't quite hide the excitement brimming behind his flushed cheeks.

"Hey guys, what'd I miss?" he says as he bounces into the room.

"We were discussing Terraltum trade disputes," Holly quips.

"Oh cool," Jamie says. "Any interesting ones I should know about? I do love a good bilateral negotiation."

"There's no such thing as an interesting trade dispute you insufferable moron," I say.

"What were you doing with Master Root?" Callie asks, trying and failing to keep her tone casual.

All she gets in return is a gleeful smile. "I've been told that's privileged information."

"Nikki's a princess," Petra points out. "She's got loads of privilege, so it'd be chill to give her the information." Too bad I already have it.

"Not helpful." The more time I spend with Petra, the more her calling me a princess has become a running gag. And the more I like any time she points these light jabs at me.

"Sorry, should've been more specific. The information has the privilege of not being shared with anyone besides me and Master Root."

"And you have the privilege of being an infuriating and very squashable twerp," Holly says. It's on the border of what only a few days ago might have hurt his feelings, but something's changed. He grins.

"Squashable twerpiness aside," I reply. "Let's all agree that you and your privileged information can take a flying leap off the edge of Terraltum."

Jamie settles at the foot of Callie's bed. There's amusement on her face as she pulls her feet out of the way, and she looks less awkward than I would've thought given the most recent conversation. I note that their feet touch—not enough to be obvious, but definitely enough that it catches my eye. He leans his head against the wall, and I realize that his excitement is mingled with exhaustion.

Callie gives him a light jab in the ribs with her foot and says, "Come on guys, we're not getting anything out of him. I propose instead we set up a betting pool on what we're having for breakfast tomorrow morning."

A collective groan fills the room. Her hand brushes Jamie's knee as he groans loudest.

"If it's stew again, I'll take that flying leap with Jamie and his privileged information," I say.

The next morning, when Master Root places a steaming bowl of stew in front of each of us, it takes several minutes for the giggles to subside.

CHAPTER
TWENTY-SEVEN: JAMIE

B etween my training and having Callie to focus my attention on, my days in Homestead quickly change for the better. At night I work with Master Root in the library, and he teaches me how to use Intention based on the emotional threads of other beings. Though the entire process makes me uncomfortable, the results are dramatic. Within a week I have cut through a block of wood, made another groundhog run away in fear, and turned a pile of sticks into a roaring fire. Tethering is incredibly draining, so between tasks Master Root and I sit in the chairs in the library, either conversing quietly or sitting in silence as I recover.

"But why are there so many rooms here?" I ask when our conversation veers to Homestead itself. "It could probably hold hundreds of people."

"A couple thousand, actually, at its peak. Homestead was once a thriving underground city, home not only to my fellow custodians of the surface, but also to all manner of magical creatures. Banished Skyfolk, a large population of gnomin, even a few ailethier came and went. It was a community of misfits. Not always a perfect one, but we had a life here that wouldn't have been possible anywhere else."

"So what happened?"

"A combination of factors. It started when the rest of my people dispersed, in the last two hundred years or so, responding to the great assault humanity had been waging on the Earth's natural resources. Time was when we could orchestrate everything from here, preserving earth, water, and air through our unified strength." His voice fills with sadness whenever he talks about the others. How lonely his silent vigil must be. "Once my people left, there was no one truly in charge, and factions began to form. You'd be surprised how thoroughly the politics of Terraltum can transfer down here, though twisted without a true reference point."

"But weren't many of them banished? Why would they care about Terraltum politics?"

"Those are the right questions to ask. Differing viewpoints on how this place should be run emerged, and once people took sides, differing viewpoints became differing ideologies. Disagreements formed between people who previously agreed with each other. All because they felt the need to take a side. Humans will do that. And a house divided against itself cannot stand, as the expression goes."

Master Root barely contains the bitterness in his voice.

"It sounds more like entropy in a closed system always increases."

Master Root chuckles darkly. "Perhaps. But in the case of Homestead, it wasn't a closed system. When things got too contentious, people just left."

"Better than the alternative, I guess. But everyone?"

"All that remained were a group of fanatics, the disciples of Leonis Wingless. And me, of course. I am bound to this place, regardless of who else is here with me."

"I've heard that name—Leonis—a couple times," I say. "People say it like you would imagine medieval monks saying the name Lucifer."

"The religious myths of Terraltum—especially those of the cosmogonic variety—tend to take a different tack then surface ones, primarily because the origin of Terraltum is on a time-scale of only a few thousand years. There is no need for all-powerful deities requiring faith to commune with, when the Winged Ones have been gone for mere centuries."

"Leonis was a Winged One?"

"Yes. The Lucifer analogy is more apt than you might think, at least in the Miltonian reading. Terraltum in its newness was a sort of Eden, though with far more people and more of the challenges of a fledgling society. Leonis did not believe in the separatism of Earth and Sky, of non-magic and magic. He believed in *Terramundus*, a final moment in which Earth and Sky would be joined once more, and those with Intention would rule those without. Though 'rule' is not quite the right word. A better phrasing would be 'submit to genocide,' I think. He gained many followers, and his own power far exceeded any human capacity to stop him. There are valleys on both Terraltum and the surface that can attribute their origins to moments when Leonis released his wrath upon the land."

I shiver. A grid of granite blocks stretches in all directions in my mind's eye. Behind them is an archway, bearing a single glowing word.

"But he was stopped," I say.

"Yes, he was powerful, but not powerful enough to overthrow his own kind. His wings were cut from his body, and his power was reduced to a mere fraction of its potential. The myths diverge from there, though. Some sects believe he was killed entirely, while others say he was only contained, that the Winged Ones could not bring themselves to kill even a fallen member of their own kind, and therefore devised a system of bondage whereby humans could keep him from reaping further havoc."

"Which of the two do you believe?"

When Master Root does not respond, I say instead, "And his followers in Homestead, what happened to them?"

"They became too radical, too narrow-minded in their thinking. I had to ... arrange for their departure."

"I hope you're only referring to departure from Homestead."

"In most cases, yes. Too much talk! I have another task prepared for you."

I sigh. My entire body aches with the effort of the last two hours of tethering, but I suppose I have energy for one more task.

My relationships with my fellow students have improved. Every time I walk into a room with the others, a haze of inquisitiveness rises around me, a wall of misty unanswered questions. It's still isolating, but in a much more fun way than the pity I had previously inspired.

I realize, too, how difficult I must've been to be around. I spent so much time feeling bad about myself that I forgot to enjoy the good others had to offer. Now that I have a purpose here, I can appreciate Callie's unfailing upbeatness, Nikki's flair with any act of Intention, and even Holly's tendency to say the most outrageous thing possible. Maybe the secret to being happy is to be happy already, and let the rose-colored glasses that follow do the rest.

Holly continually tries to extract an explanation for my disappearances, but with Master Root's clear instructions not to tell anyone what we're doing, I simply tell her that I'm taking a more theoretical approach. As a result, I get to enjoy her increasingly flailing attempts to wheedle the information out of me.

"Will you just tell me? What, is it something weird where you have to like balance upside-down for an hour? I promise I won't judge."

"It actually involves focusing on an image of the most annoying person you know, then using that annoyance to crush your enemies." I stare at her very intently.

"Does it ever get old, being a wise-ass?"

"Never."

"For you, maybe."

Her expression suggests she's about to put me through the nearest pillar. I don't know why I enjoy the ripples of aggravation she projects. Maybe because now I'm worth aggravation.

I decide not to push it any further.

"If it makes you feel better, it's as challenging as your training, only tailored to my particular inadequacies."

Holly rolls her eyes. "Well I'm glad we could put your inadequacies to good use."

But my nightly sessions with Master Root instill the real excitement. For the first time in my life, I face a task that is not only difficult, but also worth the challenge.

"What are you smiling about?" Callie asks one morning. I had been thinking about how, the night before, I managed to conjure a smaller imitation of Chauncey, which proceeded to chase his forbear around the table.

"Nothing," I say, trying to turn my face stern. I almost pull it off.

"Smiling again. Tsk-tsk." I can tell she's happy I have something to smile about.

"You're right, me and Master Root have been working on my scowl. Don't want to spoil it for all of you by bringing it back too early."

"You've been working on being an idiot too, I see," Callie says.

"I don't have to work on that," I say.

"Don't bother trying to take that smile off his face," Petra butts in, tearing into one of the breakfast rolls Master Root started baking after overhearing Holly's slightly too loud remarks about the repetitiveness of the menu. "You need your energy for the trials today."

"How bad can it be?" Callie asks.

"Really damn bad," Petra replies. "Remember when we had to climb the tree that kept trying to throw us off?"

Callie rubs her wrist reflexively. She just got off the brace that resulted from that particular adventure.

"Master Root told me it's gonna be ten times worse than that."

"Why not twenty times?" Nikki pipes in cheerfully. "Not like we can't handle it."

"Point me in the direction of one of the Changelings," Holly says. "That'll be all the challenge I need."

"Personally I sort of like not having to fight to the death," Callie says.

"How boring of you," Nikki says.

I laugh. "It is kind of the point of our existence, remember."

"And don't you forget it," Holly says.

I find myself thinking this idea over during my late morning sleep. Turning it into a joke doesn't really soften it. I don't feel like

I was purpose-built for anything, other than the generic human experience of living, breathing, eventually dying, or so I'm told. I could see there being something comforting about having a singular reason for existing. But not this one. I can't believe anyone can truly exist to destroy. Especially not someone like Callie.

Since I began my tethering practice, my vivid dreams have become more frequent. I've come to the conclusion that the persona I inhabit in my dreams is consistent—though its emotions change, the underlying heft of them does not—and it is definitely not me. This persona is always on the move, always a step away from a fight, powerful but exhausted most of the time. He works in a pack, but his thoughts are subdued by the lonely weight of leadership. Why would my mind show me a consistent dream persona? Surely in the vast web of possibilities, my imagination could come up with more than one mind to inhabit.

The thought almost calls it into being:

My muscles ache. We can't even have a fire this close to our goal, and the others are taking it out on me. That's fine, let them sulk. As long as they're ready to fight tomorrow. I don't even believe it will be a challenging fight. We've made such quick work of everyone we've encountered so far. Still, the road has been grueling, and even an easy fight can leave you bruised, your Intention tapped out. We've been fighting for so long already.

"Evey," I call in a whisper to the girl next to me, whose head had been nodding.

"If the next words out of your mouth aren't 'here's an extra blanket and pillow, enjoy your sleep,' you may as well keep your mouth shut," *she replies.*

I hate her, though it's in the same way I hate all of them—we share a bond none can understand, a loyalty that I will take with me to my grave. She's still a pain in the ass.

"Can you conjure something to entertain me? My brain is restless."

"I can," Evey says, before closing her eyes again. "But I really won't. Go to sleep dude."

Every rebuttal, every small act of aggression or resistance is a sign that I'm losing them. This didn't happen at the beginning. If we don't find our goal soon, I run the risk of my authority lapsing. And I know that ultimately I am accountable for our success. Losing my authority won't change that, or the consequences.

"You're right," I say. "Goodnight."

CHAPTER TWENTY-EIGHT: JAMIE

At the end of that week, long after it has become clear to all of us that Holly and Callie are not making up anytime soon, Master Root schedules a task in the Main Hall. He calls the two of them forward, and they begrudgingly join him next to one of the spiraling pillars.

Nikki nudges me and says, "About time he gave them a talking to."

"I think this is more than a talking to," I reply as the two girls step to either side, leaving about ten yards between them. Master Root provides a few more muttered instructions, then turns to us.

"I have noticed some tension between these two." Nikki and Petra actually laugh out loud. I've noticed them spending more time together, and their laugh has the synced up feeling of friends who've discussed a subject long enough for it to become a private joke. "I can't make you like each other, but it is nonetheless crucial that you are able to work together. That is why only Holly and Callie will perform this task. The rest of you have proven competent enough when it comes to working with each other."

Relief. If I can sit out this lesson, that means a reprieve from failing at it.

"Their task is to cast a protective aura around each other. This is one of the fundamentals of the Pure School. While the basics of the spell aren't difficult, it requires that the person receiving the spell doesn't resist." We practiced protective auras a couple days ago, shielding mannequins from each other's attacks. Everyone except me got the hang of it in less than half an hour. We still haven't found my mannequin's head. "I have mentioned a few times the difficulty of using Intention on a person. Some have such a naturally Intention-resistant disposition—Background Intentionality, to use the technical phrase—that it is very hard to hurt them using Intention at all. These two have only the resistance created by their mutual antipathy for each other. Not a particularly effective form of protection, but certainly one that can interfere where protective auras are concerned. Ready?"

What happens next is perhaps the most spectacular failure I have witnessed at Homestead, including my own.

"Ow!" Callie shouts. "I thought you were supposed to be protecting me!"

"I would if you would stop resisting! You're fighting me."

"Forgive me for not letting you do whatever you want to me, you psycho." I can't say I blame Callie on this one.

Holly doubles down, and the resulting flow of Intention knocks Callie backward. Callie has no better results, although she at least manages not to actively harm Holly. Warm frustration rises off them. As it does, their task becomes harder and harder, the resistance to each other growing with each passing minute.

Master Root's eyes continue to narrow, until he finally says, "While I'm sure we are all enjoying this fine display, I'm going to give you some incentive. In one minute, I will send an attack your way. If your protective auras are in place, it will not harm you."

I lean forward. The frustration quickly turns into panic as they make a last flailing attempt.

True to his word, after a minute Master Root unleashes a blast of energy. It catches Callie and Holly in the chest, sending them sprawling. They don't have time to get up before Master Root's voice tears through the hall.

"How can you expect to fight without an ounce of teamwork? I have never seen something so atrocious, even from children like you. If the threat of an attack isn't enough to put your pettiness aside, I must have gravely underestimated your capacity for stupidity! If not for yourselves, then at least do this for the sake of the others."

Holly shoots to her feet. "You're one to talk. Do you get some kind of sick pleasure out of attacking kids?" She steps toward him with a fighter's posture.

"You have no idea what I would do to ensure your survival."

"You would happily beat us up, we've learned that already."

"I suppose it is time to show you." He holds his arms wide, and suddenly a red mist fills the hall, so thick that I can't even see Nikki next to me. The mist resolves into a three-dimensional, life-sized image all around us. Terrible cries fill the air. Shapes run in all directions. In the center, near where Master Root stands, are the now-familiar Changelings. This is the best look we've gotten at them, but there is too much happening to identify them individually. They fling Intention about, striking down the fleeing people. One boy has a bow, and fires an arrow that moves impossibly fast, riding a wave of Intention through two of his enemies, who collapse amid wracking spasms on the ground. A girl conjures a hellish feline beast, which cuts brutally through flesh.

An older man doesn't flee. He attempts to ward off the Changelings' attack. He stands tall, directing a few of his own attacks at them as the gap between them shrinks. The world around us silences as the tallest of the Changelings steps forward, easily sending one of the man's attacks bounding away.

"We told you all we could," the man says. "We haven't seen Sampson for months. We withheld nothing, why do you continue to kill my people?"

"I thought that was pretty obvious," the boy says. "We're killing you because you don't have any more information left. It would be pretty stupid to kill you before that."

The man hurls a solid bolt of Intention at the Changeling. It disperses seemingly of its own accord in the air before him. The Changeling takes two steps forward, holding out both hands. With a wrenching twist, the man's neck snaps, and he crumples to the ground. The Changeling walks over to his body and crouches beside it. He reaches for the string hanging around the man's neck, and the blue shard that dangles from it.

The scene resolves. The air in the Main Hall is silent once again.

Holly and Callie are on their feet, Holly rubbing her shoulder and obviously holding back fury.

For the first time, Master Root tells us the names of the Changelings, presenting each of their faces in turn. There's Khelum, the leader who just killed the man in the vision. Evey's spritely face has an almost mocking playfulness to it. Apparently she's the best at conjuring, while Ren is a sandy-haired Changeling with a strong ability with metal. There are also Lia, Anna, Jason, and Collin, though past the first few, the other Changelings all blur together into a mass of fearful power. They range in size from the burly Collin, to the tall and strikingly attractive Khelum and Lia, to the smaller but compact Ren. Yet all somehow feel larger than any of us. I remember that Lia and Ren grew up in the same Skyfolk village as Holly. She referred to them as Fear and Pain, though I can't remember which was which.

Master Root's voice chills me. "You are not fighting me. You are not fighting each other. You are fighting the Kelluvas and their Changelings. Their plan to take the surface is now beginning to become clear. They seek one of the exiled Skyfolk named Sampson."

"Who's Sampson?" I ask.

"A smuggler who was caught stealing Sky from the Caves of Meluin."

Only Nikki registers that this could be of note.

Master Root continues, "Sky is incredibly difficult and dangerous to transport. Even powerful Pure School acolytes struggle to keep the substance's volatility under control. Sampson is one of the few to master the technique to move the material."

Nikki puts her hand unconsciously to the Piece of Sky on her chest. She says, "But if they're on the surface, how much Sky is there to transport? Why find Sampson?"

"That is the most important question. But we've seen a clue already. Did you notice what the Changeling did once he killed that man?"

I hadn't registered it before, but the ornament hanging from the man's neck matched Nikki's. And Paolo's. A Piece of Sky.

"There are several hundred banished Skyfolk on the surface, most of whom have been allowed Pieces of Sky. A few of these shards put together would have little effect, but the Changelings have wrought such a trail of death and destruction that they now have several dozen Pieces of Sky. Sky is a powerful source of raw strength. Imagine what Almus Kelluva, who already has the skill and experience to create vast numbers of werebeasts, could do with such extra power."

"Do you know where Sampson is?" Petra asks.

"I have an idea. However, your first entry into this fight is a card we can only play once. It is unclear to me that this is the correct moment. We don't know yet how important Sampson will be, or whether the Changelings have located him. The simple fact remains that the amount of Sky on the surface is finite. Even if Almus were to attain all of it, we could still probably contain him."

"What in the name of Earth and Sky does all of that mean?" I'm surprised that this question comes again from Petra. Nikki gives her a warning glance. "You can somehow see whenever the Changelings are destroying things, but you can't find this one guy?"

A long silence follows. I brace for another angry outburst, maybe another scene of destruction. Those always drive the point home.

Instead, Master Root's eyes fill with sadness, and the weight of thousands of years, usually hidden, comes to his face.

"I have the gift of Sight, as do all my people. This comes from our deep connection with the earth, which absorbs everything happening on its surface. Time was that I could sit in a room in Homestead and observe the entire world, every twist of fate, every love, every loss.

"But as time went on, humans began interfering with the natural systems governing the earth's balance. Over the last couple hundred years the earth has become an increasingly poor conduit. Now only the strongest emotions, felt by the most people, allow me to tap in. Joy, yes, but mostly pain nowadays. Terrible deaths, it turns out, still make a deep impression on our Earth."

Whatever response Petra had dies on her tongue.

"Come on Holly," Callie says. "We can do this."

Holly still seems unconvinced. "Fine, let's try again."

They stand apart again, focusing intently, but this time with more urgency. Something shifts on Holly's face as she levels her hand at Callie. Callie's eyes widen, and she smiles.

Master Root directs a ball of Intention at Callie. It disperses in a cloud of white smoke. Callie laughs as Holly pumps a fist. The onlookers cheer. This victory is, we finally understand, for all of us.

Callie's turn. Holly stands with relaxed shoulders, doing her best to embody trust. We shout encouragement. Callie's face is as intense as I've ever seen it. Holly shakes involuntarily.

"Come on, Holly," Callie says. Sweat collects on her upper lip. Both girls vibrate, struggling against the force growing between them.

"It's not happening," Nikki whispers to me.

"Callie can do it," I say.

"It's not Callie. Holly can't give in."

She's right. Holly can't submit herself fully.

Maybe it's the fact that I want so badly for them to succeed, that I know they need to resolve their differences for the good of all of us. Or maybe it's the fact that I've only completed one task successfully and need to do *something*. I reach out to Holly, wading through the diffuse emotions billowing off her. I gather them into a single thread. I grab it, and yank myself forward, out of myself.

Frustration of the usual variety pours off her, but it is far deeper than I anticipated. She wants to allow Callie to cast the protective aura, wants it so badly that she is on the verge of tears. The weight of her past locks down her frustration. It is a weight made of locked shed doors, hunger, the stink of gasoline and the rush of cold air.

Fires burn near my cheeks—Holly's cheeks—creeping closer as a shrill voice cackles. The backs of my hands are raw and bleeding. You're nothing. You're worthless. You'll never be anything. An abomination. Someone whimpers in the darkness, and I can't comfort them.

Somehow, I stand up to all of this, all the pain and doubt, all the mistrust and deception. I roll it all back, and in doing so, roll it into myself. I take all of it in.

Destruction unfurls before me. A town burns. Fire springs from my hands, indiscriminate, torching whatever it touches. Flesh melts off bone. My friend lies on the ground behind me, a deep cut along the knotted muscle of his chest. The bastards will pay.

I step toward a crumpled shape lying in the road. It's a body with charred clothes. The body moves, still clinging to life.

"My daughter," it says in a shattered voice.

"Julian."

"Have mercy, please. This can all be set right, my daughter."

"I'm not your daughter." I bend, place a soft hand on his shoulder. I make my expression reassuring, considering his pleas.

"We can make everything okay again, I promise."

My touch remains soft, but I turn all of my Intention outward, along with the rage. This man has been my hell. His eyes plead.

It is the last expression he makes before he dies.

Blank space. Nothingness. Blackness. Screams.

A shout of joy rises as the protective aura finally surrounds Holly. When Master Root casts his Intention attack and it winks out of existence, the others rush to congratulate Holly.

But I don't join in. I am sitting on the floor, absolutely exhausted. They hug each other, laughing, and I cannot pick myself up.

Nothing but pain fills my mind. It's so consuming that it takes a second for me to realize that Holly is standing above me.

"That was the spookiest thing I've ever experienced," she says, her face serious.

"What are you talking about, Holly?" Callie says. Her face is flushed in triumph.

"I wasn't the one who let you cast the protective aura," Holly says. "At least I don't think so. I felt something coming from pipsqueak here. He ... I don't know ... *made me* do it."

The others stare down at me. I can feel their emotions stuck between their automatic disbelief of anything Holly says, and concern that what she's saying might be true. Obviously I've crossed a line, at least in Holly's mind.

"Come on," Nikki says, helping me up. Callie offers me a hand as well. "You're pretty spooky too."

"It's not the same," Holly says.

"Of course it's not the same," Nikki snaps. "But you can't choose your powers. You wanted Jamie to be powerful, so here you are. Now we know exactly the type of training he's been doing with Master Root."

Holly and Callie exchange a look. I can tell that something has shifted between them since the successful aura, regardless of my role in making it happen. I hope that they're not now united in their disgust with my powers. Nikki claps me on the shoulder and gives me a reassuring nod, before turning to continue congratulating Holly and Callie.

Holly and Callie's dispute softens dramatically over the next few days. The hostile silences and caustic remarks are replaced by tentative jokes, and the entire group soon hangs out together again without any issues. But I can feel my distance from the rest of the group—already present due to my training and lack of non-Mind Intention—continue to grow. When the time comes, will they still want me on their side as they fight the Changelings?

CHAPTER TWENTY-NINE: NIKKI

Holly's reconciliation with Callie is in some ways also a reconciliation with the rest of the group. Because none of us wanted to be involved, Petra and I had obviously isolated her—perhaps more than we should have, especially given that I'm supposed to be making sure she's on our side.

A couple days later, I find myself filling her in on our investigation of Master Root's comings and goings. I don't know why it surprises me that she was harboring her own suspicions, although she hadn't acted on them as Petra and I had. She insists we stay up deep into the night and show her the door. So, late that night, the three of us wind our circuitous way through the warren of Homestead.

We pull up short outside the strong wooden door with a heavy lock.

"And you haven't been able to get in?" Holly asks.

"Not without forcing the door," Petra says. "We didn't want to do anything Master Root could find out about later."

"I don't know about you, but I'm not really concerned what Master Root thinks," Holly says. "He's put us through hell. The least he can do is stop with the secrets."

"We could ask him," I say, the doubt in my voice making it obvious it's not a real suggestion.

"We could also just break down the door and find out for ourselves," Holly says.

Nods of agreement make their way around our loose circle. I see the fire in Petra's eyes. She needs to know what lies beyond. However unpleasant Holly may be at times, there's something about her that spurs everyone toward action when inaction had seemed easier. It's a quality I deeply respect.

She lifts a mischievous eyebrow at us, then reaches toward the hinges on the door. Her hands project pure heat. I add my own less powerful effort, and soon all three of us pour heat on the hinges.

With no warning, the hinge dissolves into a flowing stream of liquid metal, and the door falls forward into the room with a deafening sound. We step in, uncertain.

The air is rank. Low ceilings hang above, and soft moss covers the walls and floor. An odor of decay, of rotting food and worse, stings my nostrils. Dim light from Intention lamps flickers shadows across the walls, but provides more than enough illumination to see the creatures sheltering along the far wall.

They are monstrous, deformed shapes. Though similar in size to humans, they lack discernible human features. They have long faces, with skin that hangs loosely over twisted necks. The skin over the rest of their bodies is loose too, splotchy, as if prematurely aged. But the most disturbing part of the creatures is their eyes: pure black, filled with confusion and fear.

Despite their horrifying appearances, the croaking noises they make portray no threat, only terror. Seven creatures in all cower under soiled blankets on beds that have been arranged in two long rows. They watch us with those frightened eyes.

I should be scared. I've never seen anything so disturbing before, but a strange recognition awakens in me. A high shelf along one wall contains three thick leather volumes. I take one down, opening it in the middle. It takes some time to identify what I'm reading. The words arranged across the page in a flowing scrawl are observations, detached and scientific, about feeding habits, sleep patterns, and other behaviors. Seeing that the creatures pose us no threat and are too scared even to make for the open door, Holly and Petra gather around me.

I find an earlier page, scanning for a decisive starting point, right below a heading that says, "Observations conducted by Master Root, 2nd. January, 6823 SCT," and then begin to read:

"The first iteration has been a clear failure. While every indication during gestation suggested the eggs were healthy, upon hatching the creatures revealed themselves to be inhuman. Indeed, the donors would've been unable to recognize their descendants. Rather than children with strong abilities in Intention, we instead created mere shadows, without a shred of magical ability or even human intelligence.

"But what in the process could have gone wrong? Almus assured me the proportions for the nutrient bath were correct, and the instructions were followed to the letter. Perhaps the samples obtained from the donors were not viable. Perhaps their Intention alone is not enough, and more invasive means of harvesting are necessary. I have severe misgivings about the implications of this fact, though I know the reward will be great. The sickness of the surface requires a magical presence to cure, and how could the answer not lie in creatures purpose-made for that duty?"

"What does all of this mean?" Petra says.

I reach for the final volume on the shelf, and this time head straight for the beginning:

"There can be no doubt of success this time. I have been assured that the donors have been willingly obtained, and that their families have received generous compensation. We have eleven healthy eggs in six tanks."

I stop. Eleven eggs. Eleven Changelings. I close the book.

"I'm so sorry," I say.

"I always wondered why Master Root felt so strongly that he needed to protect us," Petra says. "I guess in a way we're his children." I'm astounded at how level she's able to keep her voice.

"So are they," Holly says, pointing to the frightened creatures that still crouch in the corner of the room. My stomach turns. I can't imagine what my Skysent friends feel, to know that the precursors to their own existence are the hideous creatures in this room. I put an arm around Petra's shoulder, and she buries her face in my tunic.

"We should go," I say finally. We do our best to close the door and create a new hinge, but with any investigation Master Root will find it altered.

It doesn't matter. After this, he can't maintain the illusion of the benevolent teacher. Master Root said the Changelings were upsetting to the balance of nature, yet in his own words he had hoped they could cure the disease of the surface. Not for the first time I wonder if the solitude of his home has pushed his mind beyond the breaking point.

OF EARTH AND SKY

We march in silence down the twisting corridors. I ruminate on the terrible existence of the Skysent. They were created as tools, scientific inventions designed for a single purpose and with no regard for their inherent humanity. It makes me hate the Kelluvas even more to know they're behind this.

But how is my goal of turning the Skysent to the Laputan cause any better? Rather than releasing them from their role in the conflict, I'm simply steering them to a different side of it. Did my parents know the extent of the Kelluvas' treachery? Could they imagine the cost of existing for a single, destructive purpose?

But the Kelluvas are not here. Master Root is. We've decided without needing to consult each other—we're on our way to confront him, here and now.

CHAPTER THIRTY: JAMIE

I'm sitting with my back to a tree trunk, watching rain drip from the branches around me. My spot is more or less dry, but occasionally some of the misty spray will reach my face. The blood on my ripped jeans is fully dried, and I consider wetting my hands to scrub it off.

My phone buzzes in my pocket. I put my hand to the device. Intention pours out of it, and the voice on the other end feeds directly into my language-processing center without me having to accept the call. It's the call I've been waiting for, and I already know that Almus will be on the other end.

"Khelum, I trust you are in a safe position to talk?" the voice says. Strong, clear, projected through the Intention-buffered satellites of K-Corp's telecom network.

"Yes sir. I'm in Rock Creek Park. Seems I'm only ever in the woods nowadays."

"Better to stay off the grid. Your most recent mission was proof of that."

My heart races. Do we finally have a lead?

"The trace you placed on the Laputan agent's device worked to perfection," Almus continues.

"We can't go after the agent themselves, though."

"No, too risky. The Laputan network is too tight. But with the metadata from the agent's communications, we tracked several calls to an *address in Brooklyn, an apartment owned by a lobbyist named Molly Richards. There's a money trail, but mostly it winds back on itself—she's kept a low profile, even for K Street. But go back fifteen years and there's no trail at all. Job experience at a couple companies that never existed, a college diploma but not even so much as a yearbook photo. It's like she fell out of the sky."*

"I take it that's literally what happened," I say.

"We think Ms. Richards was part of the Laputas' inner circle, but she's definitely not part of the spy network now. If she was at one time working on their behalf, it's a good bet that she was high up enough to have the information we're looking for."

I stand, keeping my hand on the phone but crouching to prevent my head from hitting the wet branches.

"I'll gather the others. We'll move on the Brooklyn address immediately."

"Good," Almus says. "Keep me updated. The portal will be open to us soon enough. The joining can proceed as planned."

A surge of excitement shoots through me, and I am on my feet in my room before my eyes are even open. I know I've learned something real. There were too many specifics for this to be a mental fabrication. The rain was too real, the flow of Intention through my body too strong—and unlike anything I've felt in waking life. I know now with absolute certainty that all the times I've had these visions, I've been seeing through Khelum's eyes, the eyes of the leader of the Changelings.

For the first time the reference points are clear. Even the name Molly Richards is familiar, and after a second I realize it matches the description of the woman who I overheard having a conversation with Paolo all those years ago. The one who had wanted to disappear.

I find Master Root in the library, and quickly recount my dream. My vision.

"So it seems the Changelings have turned their attention from one banished Skyfolk to another. There has been no word of them searching for Sampson for some time. If this means they have found him already is still unclear. But if they've surmised the location of a former Laputan agent on the surface, one who used to be the main liaison between House Laputa and the governments of the surface..." Master Root stares at me, gears turning.

At that moment Nikki, Holly, and Petra burst into the room. I don't need to be able to sense their emotions to know that they are collectively *pissed*. Callie follows behind, still rubbing the sleep out of her eyes.

"So what does this mean?" I say, instinctively wanting to give a few seconds of breathing room before the conversation turns to whatever they're so angry about.

"It appears the Changelings only want one piece of information out of the Laputan. An alternate route to travel to Terraltum."

A snowy mountainside high in the sky. A river running through the bed of a long valley. On the far side of the valley, the ground disappearing, and miles below a second layer of terrain barely visible through the clouds.

"A portal," I say involuntarily.

"There are no surface portals anymore," Nikki says through her gritted teeth. "They were all destroyed after Barrun's War. House Laputa led that initiative."

"And the final portal has been in the family ever since," Master Root says through a smile.

What I at first mistake for surprise on Nikki's face, I quickly realize is hope. This portal might allow her to go home. I briefly fill the others in on what I saw in the vision, before Master Root continues:

"With this move the Kelluvas have tipped their hand. If they want both the location of the portal and an expert at transporting Sky, their goal has become obvious. The Terraltum end of the portal is in the Mountains of Meluin, where the Meluin Caves house vast quantities of Sky. The simplest explanation is that they mean to transport Sky to the surface. If this is the case, our timeline has accelerated. If they succeed, they could put such power to terribly destructive ends, particularly on the surface where such activities would go undetected, and where Earthworld authorities would be powerless to intervene."

"So we solve the Earthworlders' problems for them," Nikki says. "Why does it somehow seem *more* appealing when I put it like that?"

"This is more than a mere Earthworld problem," Master Root says. "I have laid out the facts as best I can, and yet I cannot help but feel that we are missing something important. Portals, as gifts of the Winged Ones, represent a level of Intention beyond human understanding. The power to manipulate space and time can be used to simply transport someone from one place or another. But we rarely think about how else it might be used. Or for what purpose"

"I'm gonna go ahead and stop you right there," Holly says.

Master Root turns to her. "You all seem agitated. Is there something you want to tell me?"

"We should be asking you that," Nikki says. "This whole conversation became moot the minute we found out what was behind that locked door."

We all watch Master Root intently, but as usual I'm one step behind. "What the hell are you guys talking about?"

"Master Root created the Changelings," Petra says. "Created all of us. In collaboration with the Kelluvas."

For a second I think my heart has stopped beating. And then it's racing.

"We found his failed previous experiments behind that door," Nikki says.

"Please, allow me to explain," Master Root says. There's no surprise in his voice, but I think I catch a hint of sadness there.

"I'm beyond excited to hear this," Holly says.

"The earth is sick. You know this, you've seen the impact a polluted world is already having. The earth depends on balance, thousands of cycles that have to be perfectly aligned in order for the earth to thrive. My job as guardian of one of the Earth Centers is to keep this balance, but to be honest it has not been possible for some time. When Almus first came to me, he knew what a struggle this had become. He offered me a way of addressing this imbalance, of curing this sickness. Beings with magical abilities strong enough to set the earth's systems aright."

"No being could be that strong," Nikki says.

"I am," Master Root replies. "Or was. Almus gave me a path forward, a reason to hope. Over time I became so wrapped up in the work that I began to miss the signs—the signs that these beings would be powerful but not necessarily as powerful as I needed them to be, and the more important signs that Almus was going to use them for his own gain. He deceived me."

"You knew what Almus was," Petra says. "You should've seen what he was building."

"The union of hope and fear can blind a person to all else," Master Root says. "I am deeply sorry for this."

There's a long pause as we exchange looks between each other.

"This is royally screwed up," Callie says.

"Agreed," I say. I feel my skin crawling. The expression on Petra's face tells me I should be glad I didn't have to see what was behind that door. The previous "experiments." All of our attention turns toward Nikki.

"We've benefited from his training," Nikki says, turning toward us and away from Master Root, as if he's no longer a participant in this conversation. "He even trained me when he wasn't technically supposed to. He's kept us safe, and prepared us for the fight ahead. We have to acknowledge what he's given us."

"He's given us deception," Holly says.

"He has," Nikki says. "I buy that he believed Almus' lies. I buy that he thought he was doing the right thing. But how in the name of Earth and Sky can we trust him after this? What else do you think he's lying about?"

"Where do we go from here?" Petra asks.

"If Jamie's visions are right, then we know exactly what the Changelings are about to do," Nikki says. "I say we go face them. Now. No more hiding, no more finding out their movements in fits and starts. We take them on."

"Yes," Holly says. Callie is wide-eyed.

"You're not ready," Master Root says. The words are quiet but devastating.

Nikki turns to face him. "Maybe not. But you lost the right to make that call a long time ago."

"What are you going to do, keep us hostage here?" Holly says.

"I won't keep you," Master Root replies. "If you decide to go, that's your decision."

"I think that's our decision," Callie says quietly. The emotions flowing through the room are perfectly clear. Callie speaks for all of us.

I follow the rest out, but before the entrance to the Main Hall, Ora materializes beside me, and pulls me roughly into a side passage.

"What's up, Ora?" I say.

"I found him."

Paolo.

CHAPTER THIRTY-ONE: NIKKI

After the day's revelations, I am too exhausted to sleep. There is a point of mental exertion beyond which sleep is impossible, where any attempt to rest only sets the mind spinning again. I am at that point.

At least I have company. Petra lies on her bed, staring up at the ceiling as if it's personally offended her. We leave tomorrow.

"My brain hurts," she says. I sit on the desk by the foot of the bed, spinning a flat stone I found earlier that day.

"Have you tried clearing your mind and looking beyond the pain?" The platitude comes out entirely reflexively at this point, but any mention of Master Root feels like a blow.

"Yes, but it's not working. Entertain me, woman."

"I wish I had prepared a song."

"If you start singing, I'll find the one window in this place and jump out of it."

I sweep the rock onto the floor and slide off the desk. "The stage is set," I say, motioning broadly at the desk. Petra wraps her arms around her knees and watches the empty space.

I haven't told a story with conjuring since I left Terraltum. It'll be harder without Rian to provide the narrative, but I trust Petra not to make fun of me if it's cliché or stupid. I like when she makes fun of me, anyway.

A dragon the size of my fist roars to life. It startles Petra as it lurches into the air and buzzes over her head.

"Behold, the mighty dragon Yureg!"

"Aw, look how cute he is."

"Silence! This is the most fearsome and loathsome dragon who ever lived." I have Yureg spout a fireball at Petra for good measure. It burns a tiny hole in her sleeve. My audience tamed, I am off on the story of Yureg. It's a tale similar to one I've told on other occasions, but I make up variations as I go along. All the villagers, about the size of pebbles, run in fear from Yureg. But the adorable monster only wants people to talk to. One of the girls from the village wanders into his lair one day on a dare from her brother. When the dragon wakes, he finds the girl, Clara, crawling on his tail. Friendship ensues.

"You didn't have the guts to have him eat her, did you?" Petra says.

I ignore her. Even the fact that sharing this feels deeply personal, as vulnerable as I feel I can be in front of Petra, I'm in my element, and it will take more than a beautiful girl busting my metaphorical balls to throw me off track.

The plot thickens when Clara's brother tells their parents that the dragon has kidnapped his sister. The people of the town spend their entire savings from the previous year's harvest to hire a freelance ice dragon, hoping to rescue Clara and rid themselves of the beast once and for all. A massive battle follows, with the two dragons flying around Petra's bedroom, shooting fire and ice at each other, eventually crashing into a tangled oblivion on the floor.

"Clara watched them fall, knowing that Yureg was no more. Her friend, the only being who had ever understood her, was gone."

I pause for effect.

"And then she returned home, to the people responsible for her friend's death. There was nowhere else to go."

Petra watches me patiently, but the next sentence sticks in my throat. I want to say that she eventually forgave her family for what they'd done, that she understood they'd only wanted to protect her.

Instead my thoughts are drawn back to Terraltum. I imagine riding one of the hovercraft up to the landing platform, seeing my mother, father, and brother waiting for me there. It's an image that's been present in one form or another since I left. For the first time I consider that when I go back, things might not be the same. My city, my family, might be different than the ones I left behind.

I need Rian here to pick up the pieces of my story, to help me push through when I stumble. I let the conjured creatures dissolve.

"I'm sorry," I say, and leave the room.

I follow the familiar path to the rocky area outside the mountain. This quiet place has been my sanctuary over the past month. The air is cool tonight, though it bears the first hint of approaching summer as it stirs the trees whose highest branches sway twenty feet below me down the mountainside. The fresh air fills my lungs satisfyingly, like a guzzled glass of water after a hot day of flying. I sit on a boulder near the door.

A few squirrels chase each other through the rocky scrub, though it takes me a second to recognize the surface creatures. I had half assumed them to be Sree, the burrowing creatures who pop up out of the ground nearly everywhere on Terraltum.

"Can I join you?" Petra stands in the entry.

"I don't see why not," I say, though I would prefer solitude. She sits on a rock a respectful distance away.

She doesn't mention the story. She must understand, at least somewhat.

"I can't believe we're leaving this place," she says.

"I know. It feels like we've been here forever. Or maybe that we just got here. I honestly can't tell."

"Funny how we've been so wrapped up in what Master Root's been up to. I never thought when we actually found it, it would mean the end of our time here."

"You find one brood of accidental surface demons, and all of a sudden everything changes, huh?"

"Don't be crass. I'm one of those surface demons." Petra chuckles and flicks a pebble off the rock she's sitting on, speeding it up with Intention so it hits my arm with enough force to sting.

"Hey!"

"Heir to House Laputa and you can't even deflect a pebble?"

"I'm not the heir, my brother is."

"Oh, my apologies, your highness."

"And besides, you caught me off guard."

Petra's smile stands out in the moonlight. She has a beautiful smile. The stars here are much clearer than they are in Orella, scattering themselves like the freckles on Petra's face.

"In a funny way, Homestead was starting to feel like home," I say.

"Not home, exactly. More like a second home. My mom—my guardian, I mean—sent me to boarding school for a year. I worked my butt off there and was homesick a lot, but by the end I had a similar feeling about the place. Like it was somewhere I'd worked hard to be, like it was somewhere I belonged. But there's nothing like returning to the place where you grew up." She sighs. "You know, you all might be the closest things to friends I've ever had? I know. Holly's kind of an irascible jerk and you're royalty or whatever." This time I flick a pebble in her direction. "But it's incredible to know there are people like me out there, people who understand what it's like to live inside my head."

"It's pretty cluttered in there," I say. "Why only a year?"

"You have a knack for picking the biggest can of worms to dive into, huh? Well, I guess I did bring it up. The thing you have to understand about my upbringing was that my guardian did everything she could to give me a normal surface life. We never talked about anything having to do with Terraltum unless it was absolutely necessary. Even though she worked for the Terraltum government as an Obscurer, she never discussed what she was working on. I think sending me to boarding school was in this same vein—surrounded by kids my age, normal surface adults instead of her, you know? It's what I wanted too, and for a while it worked perfectly. I really did feel like an ordinary kid."

She pauses, and I say, "What happened?" to fill the space.

"I played lacrosse during my spring semester—it's a surface game where you throw a ball with a stick—it's not important—but I noticed the same man was coming to all the games. There was something off about him. He didn't react to the game like any of the other spectators, and I thought he was spending too much of his energy focusing on me. He also dressed oddly, sort of old-fashioned. He always wore a scarf and pea coat, which he never unbuttoned, even when it was warm. I asked around to see if he was someone's parent or relative, but no one knew anything. Eventually I told my coach, and she went and gave him a talking-to.

"But then things got weirder. When my coach came back, she said he was a nice man, and that he hadn't done anything wrong. He was just watching, after all. I remember the look in her eyes. She was usually an intense person, but her expression was completely vacant. It looked like she had been brainwashed, and in hindsight I suspect that was exactly what happened.

"From that point, the man got bolder. I'd see him walking around campus on my way home from the library. He never came close, but that pea coat was a constant presence. I never went anywhere alone, though in reality, what could a bunch of middle school students do against someone who more than likely had powerful abilities with Intention? I waited longer than I should have to tell my guardian. I didn't want to believe any of it was happening.

"Then one night he was waiting outside of my dorm when I walked out. Middle of the day, on the way to class. Should be safe, right? But there he was, a gray scarf poking out of his coat. He spoke to me, asking if we could talk. He said I was in danger, and he had urgent matters to tell me about. Matters concerning Terraltum. I wonder what would've happened if I went with him. I might be one of the Changelings right now, for all I know. Whatever spiel they'd been using to convince them had clearly been working, and I'm not quite full of myself enough to think it wouldn't have worked on me.

"I barricaded myself in my room and called my guardian. As an Obscurer, she knows how to travel fast, and she was there in under an hour. As far as my school was concerned, I came down with mono and had to finish up the semester at home. But the truth was, it wasn't safe for me to be away from my guardian anymore."

"God Petra, I'm so sorry," I say.

She shrugs, and I notice how good a shrug looks on her shoulders.

"Could've been worse. Anyway, recent events have made it clear that I'm not destined for a normal surface life." She pauses, and for the first time worry creases her brow. "You'd think knowing that we'll all be together would make it easier, the thought of going out there to face the Changelings. But it doesn't. I don't want any of you to get hurt."

"We're not going to," I retort, although the thought has more than crossed my mind.

"So you are going?"

"Of course I'm going."

"Sorry, I thought—you're not really one of us, you know. You don't have to go. It's not your fight if you don't want it to be."

"I am perfectly aware that I'm not one of you egg people. That said, your mission and what benefits House Laputa are one and the same. You need one reasonably intelligent person to make sure you don't make a mess of things."

"That's why Holly's going, I guess." Our laughter turns into a long silence that stretches comfortably between us.

"I'm scared, Nikki," Petra says after I've faded back into my own thoughts. "We've been training hard, but I don't know if we're up to this."

"What are you talking about, of course we are."

"You and Holly, maybe. Maybe even Callie. You're all so strong. But me and Jamie? If the Changelings are as strong as we think they are..."

This takes me aback. While Petra hasn't shown the frightening abilities of Holly, and has clearly not spent as much time with her Intention as I have, I've never felt she was anything less than capable. She actually outpaced me in several trials.

"What in the name of Earth and Sky are you talking about? You've been up to every task we've had to do, and your Organic work with wood is second to none. You could take them on single-handedly."

"I've never really hurt anyone before," she says quietly.

"Ah." My mouth twitches to one side as it attempts to find the right words. "Hopefully we won't have to hurt anyone too badly."

"Some of the things we've done here could have killed someone, and Master Root won't be there to stop it."

"If a teacher's students can't function when he's not there anymore, then the teacher hasn't done a good job."

"But how do you teach someone how to hurt? Kill?"

"You can't. Or you shouldn't. Only the moment when it's absolutely necessary will tell you if you have what it takes. There's nothing you can do to prepare. But I know that when the time comes, you'll do exactly what you need to."

I don't know if that's the right thing to say. I watch Petra's face for a reaction. Under the light of a clear moonlit night, freckles dust her pointed face, and she wears her light brown hair up in a messy ponytail. She has the kind of face that probably couldn't hide a lie if it tried, and this earnestness is precisely what I find so attractive about her. It's not like the beautiful masked faces of the other members of the great houses. My stomach does a little flip at the thought, and I try not to dwell on her perfectly formed ears, the almond shape of her eyes.

Pull yourself together, Laputa, I almost say aloud. This is not the time for my weakness for pretty, earnest girls to get in the way of the fight ahead. Petra is more than that, though, and it terrifies me.

"Nikki, I need to speak with you," says a voice behind me. I turn, and this time Ora floats at the mouth of the cave, luminous and terrible in her beauty.

"What is it?"

"Not here." She eyes Petra, who stares at her in awe. They've seen each other often during the past month, but the effect of the moonlight on her silver tattooed wings is striking.

"Fine." I climb down off my rock, give Petra my best nonchalant shrug, and follow Ora inside. We find a private alcove along a side passage.

"To start off, you know I was so terribly bored underground," she says. "We ailethier are people of the sky. We need to be out flying, exploring, doing."

"Laputans are people of the sky as well. So out with it, being underground is making me impatient."

Ora's expression is sheepish.

"I want to establish that I was very bored, because it will make you understand why I'm not completely responsible for what I've been doing."

"Whatever, preemptively forgiven."

"Jamie asked me to find his guardian. And I found him."

"You what?" I hiss.

"I found him."

"Paolo. The double agent who disappeared instead of protecting Jamie?"

"I knew he seemed familiar," Ora says with insincere innocence.

"If the next words out of your mouth aren't, 'and then I stabbed him and decided to keep the whole thing to myself and not tell anyone but you because I thought you would like to confirm he was deceased,' I am going to be very unpleasant to deal with."

"Seeing you get so worked up is almost worth it."

I expect my anger to explode, but instead I crumple.

"He sounded like he was torn, for what it's worth," Ora continues. "He really considered staying to help you." I dash off down the passage, leaving Ora behind.

CHAPTER THIRTY-TWO: JAMIE

Ora's information wasn't much. She'd spotted Paolo in a small seaside town in Maine. She could give a reasonable estimate of where he was staying and the fact that he'd been there for some time, but other than that I didn't have anything to go on.

It didn't matter. I haven't seen a trace of him since the remnants of the skirmish at The Crux, and this is the first confirmation that he's alive.

Alive. I never allowed myself to believe that he was dead, but a lingering voice in the back of my mind chimed at odd moments that the most likely explanation, more likely than him abandoning me, was that he had been killed.

I sit on my bed after hearing the news, turning over the options. The other Skysent are depending on me. We need all the help they can get against our more organized, more numerous counterparts, and I know that with my tethering abilities I am no longer irrelevant. I am supposed to fulfill a destiny, to play a part in a war for which I was created.

But my thoughts keep returning to Paolo. I need to know why he left, what could have made him abandon me. My heart pounds at the thought of seeing him again, of letting him wrap me up in a broad hug, his beard prickling warmly against the top of my head.

The others are afraid of my new power. If I leave, they'll probably be relieved. That's better than the alternative.

Then there's Callie. Do I know what exists between us? Is it something I can even put a name to? There seems to be the potential for a real relationship, given time, but am I willing to throw away my chance of seeing Paolo, my chance of having my whole family together again after nearly losing it, over that potential?

I realize then that I'm not. Whatever anger I have toward Paolo and his decision to leave, being with him is most important.

I begin packing my belongings. There aren't many—just the small backpack I took from home, with a change of clothes that sat in the corner for the past month while I wore the simple cloth pants and tunic of Homestead. I'm pulling the last zipper shut when the door flies open.

"Jamie," Nikki says, breathing heavily. "Please tell me you haven't seen Ora."

"I just talked to her," I reply, before seeing her expression. "Oh."

"You can't leave. If we split up, the Changelings are going to crush us all. And your guardian won't be able to keep you safe."

"Do you really think I'm going to be any good to you?"

Nikki closes the door behind her and stands in the entrance, willing me to fight my way out. "I don't know what Master Root has been teaching you, but I do know that what you did to Holly with the protective aura was ridiculously powerful. With our luck, you'll end up getting caught and turned into one of them, and we'll have to fight that ridiculous power."

"I have to find him." The words barely make it through my clenched teeth.

"He abandoned you. He left you to die in the worst way possible."

"You don't know him," I snarl. Wesley watches from the desk, stone-faced. "You grew up with every privilege. You couldn't possibly understand what it's like to depend entirely on someone."

"Careful, Jamie," Nikki says. "You're dangerously close to insulting my family."

"And you've already insulted mine."

"Paolo deserves to be insulted. A coward who turns his back on the people he cares about is no better than—"

I don't mean to. But with all my training, the pattern comes naturally. I pull the threads of Intention off Wesley and direct them at Nikki. Buoyed by my anger and fear, the Intention shoots out much more strongly than I intend, and flings Nikki sideways ten feet. She strikes the top of the desk and rolls off it onto the slate floor.

I don't stop to see if she's okay. One glance at Wesley tells me all I need to know about what I've done. But he follows me nonetheless, as I open the door and sprint down the passage, following the directions Ora gave me for the exit.

CHAPTER THIRTY-THREE: NIKKI

T he floor presses heavily on my body. No, that's not right. I can't remember why, though, and the floor continues to press upward on me in a rather rude and uncharacteristic fashion.

I groan. My confusion begins to wear off, replaced by whirling dizziness. If I weren't here on the floor, I wouldn't believe what just happened. Jamie, the kid who mere weeks ago couldn't make a candle flicker, threw me headlong across the room.

That might not seem like a big deal. Though I'm not aileth-skinny, I'm not as heavy as some objects Holly and I have moved recently. But performing Intention on a person is different. Their Intention offsets your own. It's a natural law. Without any action on your part, your Intention will move to defend you however it can.

Which means that Jamie has serious power if he was able to throw me like a person-shaped bocce ball.

I struggle to a sitting position, deciding whether I'm more angry at Jamie for leaving, or more in awe of his newfound abilities. In the end the latter only amplifies the former.

Before I can get up, Master Root is kneeling over me, placing a hand on my temple.

"Are you hurt?"

"I think I'm alright. Jamie just ran out of here. He's trying to leave."

"I know."

"Aren't you going to stop him? Change the passages, or close the exit or something?"

He smiles sadly. He could. But he won't. "I will not keep Jamie here against his will. If I force him, I'm no better than the Kelluvas."

"I'd rather be like them if it meant I got to go on being alive."

"I wouldn't."

Master Root's fingers are cool against my forehead, and I instinctively recoil. But some of the pain subsides instantly with their touch.

"It must be his choice." His eyes cloud and become distant. "And I do not think his leaving means he will no longer be part of the battle to come." A thought strikes me, and I catch my breath.

Despite my desire to turn away from him in disgust, I can't help asking, "Master Root, can you see the future?"

"Seeing is such a strange word we use when referring to the ability to feel oneself at a point in the stream of events other than the position that one currently occupies."

"Fine, can you—ah—feel the future?"

A shake of the head. "The future is like a fly. Reach out your hand to grab it and it closes around nothing but air. Does that mean the fly wasn't there?"

"No, it just moved to get out of the way."

"Now you're getting it." Master Root stands, offering a hand to help me up. "You should be alright. The others are in the Main Hall preparing for your departure."

Master Root leads me down the narrow passage to the Main Hall. My head throbs, but I am more okay than could be reasonably expected from someone who recently did a convincing imitation of a sack of potatoes. Dread, which had been slowly creeping up since we decided to leave Homestead, now rips with full force through my chest. The way Jamie threw me aside. He's the least powerful Skysent, as far as I know, and I was powerless against him. I can't imagine facing his more powerful brothers and sisters.

When I see the others already gathered in the Main Hall, I can tell I'm not the only one whose thoughts move in this direction. They all sit, their expressions ashen. Callie's finger scratches nervously at the table. I sit beside Holly.

This should be the breaking point. If there was ever a time to say screw it to my family's wishes and go make a name for myself in the banished conjuring arena, it's now. I don't owe anything to my parents or these powerful teenagers.

But as I meet Petra's eyes, I realize that's beside the point. I don't owe her, or the rest of the Skysent, anything. Yet I want to help them just the same. I want them to win, and when they do, I want to be by their side.

"It looks like we lost one already," I say as Master Root fades into the background, clearly understanding he's not wanted. "Are we still going through with it? Facing the Changelings?"

A moment of tension follows. Holly nods her head. No matter what, she's going to fight. Callie and Petra study the floor.

This feels like the moment when I need to step up. Being the leader my parents wanted me to be has felt so obscure so far, but here is a clear opportunity, something concrete.

"I understand why Jamie left," I begin. "This looks bad no matter how you slice it. But the way I see it, we're a family—or the closest thing any of us has really got. I for one can't turn my back on family. If what Jamie saw in his visions is true, there isn't much choice. I'm facing the Changelings, and you can either stick with me, like family, or you can leave."

Holly's grasps my shoulder as she says, "I'm with you, Nikki."

"She's not even a Skysent and she's going," Petra says. "I'm not going to be the one to back out."

Callie nods her agreement. I can't imagine the betrayal she must feel with Jamie disappearing. Even if they weren't officially together, it's hard not to see his decision as clearly stating his priorities. In her situation, I don't think I could avoid either chasing the asshole down, or never speaking with him again.

"Thank all the gods of Earth and Sky," I say. "Not sure if I ever liked our odds, but at the very least they haven't gotten any worse."

CHAPTER THIRTY-FOUR: NIKKI

Master Root bid us farewell at the doors of Homestead. None of us actually said goodbye. Ora and Amby stayed behind, as they would only draw attention on our journey. Before we left, I couldn't stop myself from chewing out Ora for what she'd done. All the rage and frustration of the past few months poured out in such a blur of anger that I don't remember half of what I said. I do recall telling her she'd better come up with something pretty goddamned helpful if she wanted any shot at her letter of recommendation. She left in a huff, and as soon as the anger fizzled out, I felt horrible for using her return home as leverage.

I still would've been glad for her company. The Changelings have been moving quickly, leaving destruction in their wake. I see a newspaper at the bus station, the destroyed office building on the front page. A gas leak, the explanation goes, but it's still unusual enough to catch Earthworld attention. I wonder how long it will be until we find ourselves on the front page of the newspaper.

The Changelings don't know we have come together, so hopefully we can collect Molly before they do, and get her into hiding willingly.

Rain droplets dot the window of the bus, nearly blocking out the gray sky. I wish I could fly to our destination. Even in the rain, it would beat sitting in this scratchy, cramped seat, waiting for the cars in front of us to inch forward.

At the very least everything has been arranged in advance. The bus makes its way through what I gather is essentially the entirety of Manhattan. I keep my face pressed against the window. The number and variety of people is not so different from Orella, though the shops and restaurants lining the streets strike my eyes as garish, aggressively advertising whatever they're selling in a way almost unheard of on Terraltum.

What really gets me, though, are the cars. I could understand driving a car in the country near Homestead, where you can move at fantastic speeds along rural roads. But here they seem pointless. They stop every block, and I wonder why the people don't get out and walk. Certainly it would make our bus ride quicker, since we spend close to an hour driving, even after we've made it into the city.

When the bus finally pulls over to the side of a busy avenue, I breathe deep the smell of the city. I've missed this. There are the predictable scents of people crammed too close together, and the wafting scent rising from the nearest food vendor. Onions, garlic, and what is that? Paprika? Over it all hangs an unfamiliar acrid odor, which I guess comes from the cars.

Callie guides us down to the subway, which at first seems similar enough to the tram on Terraltum, only underground. People pack close together as they do on the tram, ranging from men and women in suits and formal dresses to people dressed mostly in what appear to be garbage bags. The moneyed of Terraltum may dress in fitted robes rather than suits, and the poor may be more likely to carry around trinkets to sell than carts filled with plastic bottles, but the experience is recognizable. Here, two worlds are brought together in close quarters, the barrier between them becoming hazier, if never quite breaking. We all rattle along through the dark, keeping our eyes to ourselves.

I catch a glimpse of the subway map. The tram in Orella is intricate enough to make switching lines necessary for many trips, but it's nothing compared to this twisting, convoluted mess of interweaving colors passing over multiple bodies of water. This city is too big, too complex, too intricate to understand, or even to exist.

By the time we leave the subway and make our way down a block of uniform brownstones, I have begun to feel somewhat small.

Our accommodations are in a first-floor apartment in a brownstone on a tree-lined block. We find the key under a pot on the front porch. The apartment consists of a single long room, with several beds clumped awkwardly in the front, and the approximation of a kitchen in the back. It's stiflingly hot. Summer has come early and insistently. We open the back door and front windows to let the breeze run through, and with a little trouble, get the ancient window fan to start. We buy burritos at a restaurant a block away, and eat them on the plastic chairs on the patio in the back.

Petra laughs when I take my first bite.

"What, they don't have burritos on Terraltum?" she asks. A smudge of guacamole adorns her cheek.

"Not exactly. Most of the food in Orella is sweeter—pastries, sweet meat buns, things like that. You have to go to Asavva to get spicy food like this."

"I could go for a croissant right now," Callie says, halfway through her burrito, which is quickly escaping its wrap into the foil on her lap.

Petra gives an appreciative sigh.

"Master Root's cooking didn't do it for you?" Holly says.

"I love stew as much as the next girl," Callie says, "but if you think about it, everything we ate in Homestead did have the distinct taste of dirt."

I say, "Tonight's stew is mushroom and barley served in our artisanal wooden bowls. You'll notice overtones of earth, and crisp fungal notes." Somehow being out of the claustrophobia of Homestead has made Master Root, despite the secret he kept from us, just a little less threatening.

"Mushrooms are in fact fungus," Callie points out.

"I don't mind mushrooms, but I generally prefer to avoid eating anything that could be described as fungal," Holly says.

Petra is mid-bite, but says, "Are you kidding? Whether or not something can be considered fungal is my primary criteria for if I'll like a food."

"Criterion," I say.

"Huh?"

"Criteria is plural." I can hear my mother's voice in my ear and inwardly cringe.

"Oh my god, shut up," Holly groans.

"Apologies that my grammar doth offend, Lady Laputa," Petra says.

"Wait, is that grammar or syntax?" Callie is clearly on my obnoxious side.

"Not you too!" Holly says. Petra has started giggling. When she discovers the guacamole on her face, her laughter only intensifies.

As responses to fear go, I suppose silliness isn't such a bad option. When there's a break, after the burritos have disappeared and the foil wrappers have been crumpled up and used as missiles, Callie says what I guess was on her mind all day.

"I'm sad Jamie's not with us. I know we didn't know what he could do, but..."

"I know," I say, sensing that completing that sentence will not end well. "It doesn't feel right without him here. He might be a mopey little bastard, but there's something reassuring about him."

Callie nods, jaw pulsing as she holds herself back from crying.

"I know he's not out of this yet," I say. "My gut tells me we'll see him again soon. And my gut is rarely wrong."

That does push Callie back from the edge, but I still think it would be better to change the subject completely.

"Should we go over it all again so we're clear?"

The others agree, and I put on my best impression of a military commander.

"According to the Laputan spy, Molly is on a late-night flight from Washington D.C., which arrives around 3 o'clock this morning. Her apartment is only a fifteen-minute walk from here. There are too many variables to intercepting her at the airport, and we can't risk her running. We don't know exactly when the Changelings will arrive, but we know they're coming. Hopefully we can convince Molly to come with us quickly, and avoid any confrontation. That said, there's no guarantee they won't arrive before we do."

"I'm ready to see exactly how intimidating our siblings are," Holly says, playing with a flickering fire at the tip of her fingers.

"We do have to be ready for a fight, but if we can get out of there without one, that's what we do. Remember, Molly has information the Kelluvas need, the location of the portal. If they have Sampson already, that means they would be able to start moving Sky down here. Should that happen, we've already lost the battle for the surface."

"But she can't be the only one who knows the location," Petra says.

"Of course not. But she's the only one outside of the Laputan spy network. She's been living as an ordinary Earthworlder, cut off from the conflict. The Laputan spies are all much better protected than a woman who's been trying to hide. You'll notice Master Root didn't even tell us where the portal is."

Holly says what everyone else won't. "You mean, in case we get captured, they don't want the location to be brutally tortured out of us with a combination of Mind Intention and werebeast teeth. Got it."

"You're not wrong," I say. "And if the Kelluvas have the location of the portal, it'll be difficult to stop them from reaching it. This is our best shot to keep them contained on the surface."

"Also, getting tortured sucks," Petra adds.

"Also not wrong." The shadows that had been falling on the edges of the patio as we ate have now stretched themselves into full darkness. "Finally, remember Master Root's warning. We don't know all the factors at play here, or what the Kelluvas' final objective is. We have to be on our guard. Now, I think we should all try to get some rest."

As I lie between the prickly sheets on the bed I'm sharing with Callie—Holly is in the twin bed next to ours, while Petra sleeps on a cot in the corner—I try to find calm. I know I should sleep, but all I can think about is the image of the office building between Master Root's hands, the rubble of an ordinary building, with seven shapes moving disdainfully through it.

Even when I do find sleep, my dreams have me walking the halls of the building, only to have it sway beneath my feet, collapsing in the moments before I wake in a cold sweat.

I plunge back in, but this time I'm in a potion shop. I put money down on the counter, but the clerk—who has a gnomin's face but aileth wings—points to the sign that reads EARTHWORLD DOLLARS ONLY!!! Before I can explain that I don't have any Earthworld money, a hand grabs my shoulder and I know that the Changelings have come for me.

Callie stirs, and I know her dreams can't be much better than mine. Across the moonlit room, Petra breathes steadily and shallowly. Her lips part slightly, and one hand hangs from the edge of the bed. For a second I consider going over to her, holding her hand in mine, maybe even planting a kiss on her cheek. I let the sensation resolve, trying not to think how scared I am that one of us won't make it through the next day.

Early in the morning, we ready ourselves as best we can, fighting through our grogginess. Based on the baggy eyes around me, none of us have slept well. I wish we had some kind of common uniform to make us look like a legitimate fighting force. Instead we wear uncomfortable Earthworld jeans and loose-fitting sweatshirts. We look for all the worlds like a band of Earthworld teenagers on a suspiciously timed vacation. Back what feels like a million years ago, I had hoped that bonds through the Conjuring Arena would bring me strong friendships, people I could trust in the most trying circumstances. Looking around at the scared but determined faces, I realize that hope has become a reality.

The walk to Molly's apartment is maybe half a mile. Her apartment overlooks a wide traffic circle with a massive arch in the middle. After the regularity of the brownstones nearby, it appears out of place, more the kind of structure we'd have on Terraltum, with its triumphant statues of charging soldiers and rearing horses.

Nearby, a fountain sends jets of water into the early morning air. We skirt around the edge of the traffic circle, past the front of the Brooklyn Public Library and the entrance to a park. A few people still wander around the edges of the traffic circle at this hour, and a steady stream of cars rushes past. At the locked front door of the apartment building, we exchange nervous glances.

"Ready?" I ask.

Holly nods. "Callie, you're up."

Most locks on Terraltum have protections to avoid Intention interference. Here, though, Callie simply winds her Elemental Intention into the metal pins inside the lock. She focuses for close to a minute, her eyes closed. We listen closely to the faint ticking sound of the lock falling into place.

Then comes a louder click, and Callie pulls the door open.

"Welcome!" she says, slightly breathless.

We take the elevator to the tenth floor. Elevators exist on Terraltum too, but I'm not used to ones that can only move vertically.

"Down here," Petra says, pointing toward the stairwell at the end of the hall. We pass apartment 1008, where Molly will soon be returning, and shelter on the landing, propping the heavy door to the hall open an inch.

"We good?" I ask, sitting on the windowsill. My heart beats fast, and my thoughts have sped up to match it.

"Me and Callie are on hallway duty," Petra says.

"You know it," Callie says.

"Glad we're clear," I say. "We want to make this as quick as possible."

We don't have to wait long before the elevator bell rings. Footsteps echo down the hallway, accompanied by the sound of rolling wheels. Keys click together. A door opens and closes.

"Give her a minute," Petra says.

When the minute is up, we tread silently down the hallway, clustering around the door. I take a deep breath and rap on the door. A breathless silence. Then movement from inside.

Footsteps approach the door and Molly says, "Noreen, it's too early for this. Go back to sleep."

"It's not Noreen," I say. A shadow crosses in front of the peephole. I might be too short for her to see me through it, but Holly and Petra are definitely visible over my shoulders.

The door opens a few inches, and a severe face peers out. Molly is in her late fifties or early sixties. Her expression is more annoyed than fearful.

"Kids, I don't know what you're doing, but I'm not making any donations. Get out of here before I call the super. Or the police, depending on what kind of mood I decide I'm in."

"We're not after a donation," I say, trying to keep the nerves out of my voice. Everything rests on our ability to convince her quickly. "Molly, my name is Nikki Laputa."

The annoyance on her face disappears in an instant. She is a tall woman, but she seems to shrink several inches, her posture slumping, the confidence of normality broken with these few words. When she speaks next, her voice has become a hiss.

"I don't work for House Laputa anymore. I've left Terraltum politics behind for good."

"Please, can I come inside?"

"No. Tell your parents to keep their business on Terraltum where it belongs."

She makes to close the door.

"Please, Molly, your life is in danger."

"My life's always in danger." The door slams. The corner of my mouth twitches. I listen closely, but can't hear any indication of Molly moving away from the door.

"Molly," I continue, "believe me, we wouldn't pull you back into this if we didn't have to. But the Kelluvas have found your location. They're on their way as we speak."

"I have a few choice words for Almus Kelluva when I see him."

"It's not Almus you have to worry about. It's his Changelings."

A pause. Holly seems like she might be preparing to break down the door.

The door opens again, wider this time. Molly scours us with fearful eyes.

"Can we come inside?"

Molly opens the door wide, turning and leading us into a well-furnished living room. Petra and Callie stay behind, making their way to opposite ends of the hallway. Holly and I shuffle in awkwardly. Molly points us to a white couch and leather armchair, and sits at the forward edge of a reclining chair.

"Are they..." She indicates the whole group of teenagers with a nervous hand.

"The Kelluvas didn't manage to hold onto all the Changelings. Four of them escaped. They call themselves the Skysent now."

"I only saw three."

"One left," Holly says, bitterness seeping through the words.

"I met Jamie once," Molly says, "back when I was still working for the Laputas and meeting with Paolo. Is he the one who left?"

I nod. It's an indictment, but also confirmation that Paolo was successful in keeping him out of the Kelluvas' grasp.

A small bulge under Molly's sweater shows where she wears her Piece of Sky. She may try to be an Earthworlder, but the Sky still ties her to another world.

"And the others, they know where I am?"

"Yes. They know you have the whereabouts of the portal to Terraltum."

"The portal?" There's genuine confusion on Molly's face. "I haven't even thought about the portal in years. Why do the Kelluvas care where it is? Doesn't Almus have enough to do with pillaging the surface for his own profit? I thought K-Corp's shares were doing well."

"He means to transport Sky to the surface. Beyond that, surface domination. That's the theory, anyway."

A crystallizing silence falls.

"Looks like I'm not the only outcast who's resurfaced," Molly says. "Do the Kelluvas have Sampson already?"

"Not as far as we know."

"Only a matter of time, though. If Sampson gets his price, he'll come willingly."

Molly stands and walks into the tidy kitchen across the room. She runs water and starts washing dishes that appear to be clean already. After a minute of silence, I shuffle over to her.

"I know this is bad news," I say, low so only she can hear. "You obviously have a life here. I know what it's like to be pulled out of one life and thrown into another."

"It wouldn't be the first time," Molly replies, examining the suds on her hands. "A lot of us went our separate ways after the war. It's nice on the surface, if you can forget what it's like to be around your own people."

"I was banished."

"No kidding."

"I may have inadvertently caused a minor political crisis with the Sky Engines. In the current tense climate, people are sensitive to the possibility that Terraltum might not always remain a secret."

"So Terraltum knows how I feel."

It takes me a second to realize that she's joking.

"Please, Molly, you need to come with us. The Changelings could be here any minute."

Molly nods vacantly.

"I suppose I always knew this was temporary."

A loud thump sounds in the hallway outside, followed by a shout.

"They're here!" Petra's voice rings out against the cracking of plaster.

I am already bounding out into the hallway.

"Holly, protect Molly!"

I emerge from Molly's apartment into chaos.

Out of the corner of my eye, I catch movement and react just in time to roll aside as a metal chain springs from the hand of a Changeling at the elevator's door. He is short and sandy-haired. From Master Root's description, I remember his name is Ren.

The chain snaps back toward my legs to trip me, but I fling enough Intention to make it clank, limp and harmless, off my shoes. Callie whips the chain back toward the boy, and suddenly they are dueling, the chain swinging back and forth through the air, thrashing in time with the injections of Intention from the two combatants.

Three other Changelings join him. One, who must be the conjurer Evey, has summoned a swarm of angry, scaly creatures Petra does her best to fight off. Without thinking, I launch two goblins with pickaxes at the creatures, who disappear when the sharp metal buries itself in their bodies. The conjurer whirls. She's taller than the boy, with dark hair and eyes.

I dispel a ball of Intention hurled by the boy nearest me. A second blast comes from the tall, strikingly handsome boy next to him, and I find myself lifted off the ground, barely landing on my feet as my hip crashes against the wall.

The two boys disappear inside Molly's apartment. Callie is still occupied with the dancing chain above her. Creatures leap up to bite at Petra's face. She collapses a portion of the ceiling to ward them off, but in doing so inadvertently takes out my goblins, leaving her unprotected against the three remaining creatures. From her shouts of pain, I guess the conjurer has given the creatures venom.

I gather my Intention and send a full-sized wolf at the conjurer. She leaps to the side, narrowly avoiding its snapping jaws. A scrabble of pebbles appears beneath the wolf's feet, and he loses his footing. It's enough time for the conjurer to whip up her own beast, a white tiger almost twice the size of my wolf. My wolf charges forward, but one swipe of the tiger's massive paw sends him against the wall with a sickening crunch.

A crash sounds inside the apartment. Breaking glass, and a noise too loud not to be a wall being taken out.

"Nikki, watch out!" I duck instinctively at Callie's warning, but not before a chain wraps around my arm. It sharpens on my wrist, digging into the skin and pulling me off balance.

The chain snaps away under Callie's effort. She has cuts all over her arms and legs, where pieces of metal have flown off the chain between her and the sandy-haired boy.

I hear a growl, and the tiger's jaws are almost on me. Two darting birds are all I can muster with short notice, but it's the right move. They dive at the beast's eyes, and for a moment I am spared.

Petra has beaten back the lizards, and directs a few bursts of Intention toward Evey, who proves nearly as adept at dueling as conjuring. Flashes of light streak across the hallway as more explosions come from inside the apartment, and the door opens. I duck under another blast of Intention.

The tall boy comes out first. Khelum, the leader of the Changelings. Time slows as we lock eyes. He's aggressively handsome, with dark hair and eyebrows and a hint of stubble on his chiseled cheeks. His eyes burn intensely, and I am reminded of portraits of old patriarchs of the great houses, of the power evident in a single gaze. He looks back at me in surprise, and I know he recognizes me as a daughter of House Laputa. As his enemy.

The other boy—I think his name is Jason, though it might be Collin—follows him, bleeding from a head wound but carrying a senseless Molly.

"Let's go!" Khelum yells, sending Intention in all directions, knocking back me and Callie long enough for the sandy-haired boy to disengage. They rush down the hallway toward where Petra still duels the conjurer. I see the attack coming toward her, and send out the strongest protective aura I can. She's still knocked back into the doorway of an apartment next to her.

"Out of the way!" comes Holly's voice from behind me. Fury fills Holly's eyes. The Changelings have almost reached the door to the stairs, past where Petra crouches with the wind knocked out of her. I see fire growing first in Holly's palms, then up her arms and across her chest.

"Holly, don't!" I shout. Too late.

Her eyes blaze red, and she presses her palms together, pouring Elemental Intention into a concentrated ball of pure blazing fire. It consumes her entire body.

She unleashes a blast of fire more powerful than anything I have ever seen. It ripples in a solid wave from her chest toward the retreating Changelings. Accompanying it roars a sound like an entire forest being consumed by a blazing wildfire.

Khelum turns as the wave of flame reaches him, and stands his ground in front of his followers. He crosses his arms, his face screwed up in concentration. The wave strikes him, and for the briefest beat all sound ceases.

Then the world is thrown into a single monotone red as the energy disperses in all directions, blasting everyone to the ground, except for the leader, who stands triumphantly. Flames catch on the walls of the hallway. Then Khelum drops to one knee, and all is silent.

The other Changelings scramble to help their leader up. They're quickly on the stairs. I find my way to my knees. Holly lies limp nearby. I crawl to her.

I have no thought of following the Changelings. I only care about my companions.

Holly is alive. Barely. Her chest rises heavily, but I can't wake her. My heart lurches as I turn toward Petra, but she's on her feet, breathless but okay. Callie stands as well. The walls burn around us.

"We've got to get out of here," Petra says. Already, panicked voices come from inside the other apartments. As if on cue, the fire alarm in the building goes off, and the sprinklers turn on, dousing the fire on the walls. Petra has the good sense, even as we drag Holly inside Molly's apartment, to pull some of the water off the floor with Intention and douse the rest of the fires. No need for us to do more damage than we have already.

I am numb as I pull Holly across the threshold. The pristine apartment we had been in a few minutes ago is completely destroyed. The central wall dividing the living room from the bedroom has been reduced to rubble.

Holly's head lolls at a sickening angle. I can't wrap my head around it. I don't know what to do next. I freeze in the middle of the upheaval, staring silently ahead at her body.

I've seen destruction on Terraltum, like when I visited an area outside of the capital that had been hit by a tornado to help with the rescue efforts. But I've never stood directly in its aftermath. There is shouting around me, but I can't comprehend it.

"We can't help her here," Petra says. "We have to get out of here."

Her voice calls me back with its clarity, its pure leadership. The leadership I should be demonstrating as a Laputa, but can't seem to conjure with Holly lying there, with the ruins around me, and our mission to rescue Molly failed.

"Nikki?" Petra says, her voice soft but firm as she puts a hand on my shoulder. Her touch electrifies me. I meet the intensity of her eyes.

"We need a ride out of here," I say.

"Do it."

Though I find it nearly impossible, I force my Matter into this one action, blocking out everything else. I have to do this. Failing is not an option. Before long, Hediad and Droellaf, my windsteeds, crouch in the center of the floor.

Somehow we lift Holly onto one windsteed's back. The windows were blown out in the fighting. We streak through the opening, off into the night, giving no thought to the possibility that we'll be seen as we fly back to the apartment. Leave the cleanup to the Obscurers. Holly lies in front of me on Hediad, while Callie and Petra hold onto Droellaf's back.

There is no sign of the Changelings. Sirens sound in the distance as emergency vehicles streak toward the charred apartment building.

We land on the patio outside our safehouse, crashing through the bushes at the edge of the tiny backyard. We lay Holly out on the patio's cold stone. I thank Hediad and Droellaf, and let them fade into nothingness.

"Holly is really bad," Callie says, little inflection in her usually cheerful voice. She sits across from Petra, and both have their hands over Holly. With intense concentration, they do what they can for her.

One of our training exercises in the Organic School with Master Root involved healing wounds. Of course, it was difficult to practice, since most of the time there wasn't anyone seriously injured in Homestead. Master Root used dummies and other proxies to simulate the experience, but I can tell, watching Callie and Petra work, that those simulations fell far short.

Holly breathes unsteadily. I do my best to reach into her weak Intention, then pour my own Intention into her. She obviously contracted Intention Sickness from the fire blast. Stupid, stupid Holly. I am drained after a few minutes. Giving away Intention is not something that comes naturally, and soon I can barely keep my head up.

I know that even in my parents' worst nightmares they wouldn't have pictured me next to a dying friend in a strange Earthworld backyard. But they did nothing to prepare me for anything close to this. Master Root even said we weren't prepared. Yet I pushed us to face the Changelings anyway. Holly might not know her limits, but I'm responsible for her even being in this situation.

The next two hours pass in a haze. Callie and Petra spend all of it hovering over Holly, trying to buffer her flickering Intention. They manage to keep her breathing, but there is barely any Intention coming from her. Holly moans quietly at points, but never regains consciousness. I keep pouring as much Intention as I can into her, knowing that I risk Intention Sickness of my own if I give too much.

After two hours, though, her pulse is a little stronger. I can sense that much.

Petra still wears resolve on her tired face. Callie had to stop a few minutes ago. She's broken down completely.

"Got anything left?" Petra asks me. "I could use some help here."

"No," I say, putting my hands on Holly's heaving chest. My eyes meet Petra's. I've never seen her like this. Brief flashes of fire when we were investigating Master Root, sure, but her expression now scares me with its intensity.

And it's the most beautiful thing I've ever seen.

Together we pour ourselves into Holly's cold body, finding any place where we can bolster her life force with our own. Petra's Organic Intention is so pronounced I can feel it through Holly's body. Mine feels like a mere dying ember beside it. Morning begins to grow around us.

CHAPTER THIRTY-FIVE: JAMIE

The bus ride from the town nearest Homestead gives me no problems, although it makes stops at every small town on the way, and I have to change buses somewhere in central Massachusetts. Ordinarily I would nod off to make the trip go quicker, but my thoughts spin too rapidly. I let my gaze fall softly out the window, trying to slow my thoughts, to catch my breath and bring my heart rate down from its current hammering tempo, but nothing works. I think about Nikki, about Callie and the rest of the Skysent. I'm abandoning them when they need me most. But I can't pass up this opportunity to find my family again.

Wesley hasn't mentioned it, but I can tell he is deeply troubled that I used his Intention to hurt Nikki. I honestly didn't mean to. It came so easily. But I won't tether with him again, as easy and powerful as it was.

The town Paolo is staying in has found its purpose at the water's edge, with shops and restaurants catering to summer tourists. A few dozen people crack lobsters on the deck jutting out from the edge of a restaurant over the water.

I could hang out in the center of town, hoping to catch a glimpse of Paolo when he happens to walk through. Or I could wander around aimlessly, praying that I stumble across him. I sure am a planner.

The days are long, but the sun already falls low in the sky. I'm not sure what I'll do if I don't find him tonight.

There's another possibility, though I'm not particularly confident in it. Before arriving at The Crux, I remember being able to discern the presence of a concentration of Intention. I didn't realize its significance until Nikki explained it to me, but the necklace Paolo wears is a Piece of Sky, the substance that gives Skyfolk the ability to harness their power on the surface. It's no wonder I've never seen him without it. The way Nikki described it, they wouldn't remain fully human without their Pieces of Sky.

But most importantly, Pieces of Sky act as powerful draws of Intention, like magnets that pull magical energy from the area around them. If I have any skill at all, I should be able to detect that. Like I said, I'm not confident in this plan.

I head down onto the beach, taking my shoes off to feel the sand's grittiness between my toes, picking my way between shells and seaweed. I sit down and try to project an aura of calm and gentleness so the seagulls that dot the beach will come near me. To this end, I also employ the remainder of the meatball sub I ate most of earlier, removing the tinfoil and breaking off pieces of the now soggy bread. Before long three seagulls swoop down to snap up the meal. As stupid as they are, the gulls do have easily recognizable Intention flows.

I close my eyes and try to turn the animals' Intention toward the town, paying attention to any point where it catches, or where a vortex of energy draws it inward. The task is amorphous, frustrating. One minute I think I've found something, the next I realize my own Intention has merely circled back on itself.

I absently break off more pieces of bread as my sensations heighten. I'm not doing anything differently, but the swells become easier to read. I lose track of my purpose when I begin to feel the whole mass of emotion emanating from the people on the pier, the people further out into town, even those in their living rooms watching TV. All project a certain degree of energy, some positive, some negative, some anxious. This energy gathers together in a single soup flavored by the emotions of each contributor. For a full ten minutes I find myself lost, almost intoxicated with the inherent Intention of humanity.

Then I feel it. A presence too unmistakably magical to be entirely human burns somewhere in the distance. All the energy is sucked toward it as it consumes and fashions it into its own power. It's stronger than I'm expecting. Could a single Piece of Sky do this?

I cut off the connection with the seagulls, feeling slightly light-headed. The gulls disperse as soon as the sandwich disappears and my usefulness has been exhausted. I now have a waypoint. Even without the gulls to assist me, I can still identify the presence, so strong as to make me wonder why I couldn't recognize it before.

The presence leads me not toward any of the dozen houses spread aimlessly near the center of town, but instead down the main road out of town. The traffic doesn't lighten, but the houses quickly fade as I walk on the sidewalk alongside the road. It's the sort of sidewalk that seems to be placed there arbitrarily, with no real hopes that anyone would ever use it, as it doesn't lead to anything. Weeds shoot up between the cracks, threatening to turn the sidewalk into an extension of the grassy verge.

Within twenty minutes, the vortex of energy grows stronger, until it becomes so overwhelming that I couldn't have failed to recognize it. The sun has begun to set, but I sense the flow of energy almost visually, like a shining beacon leading me to Paolo.

The sidewalk ends and I walk in the overgrown grass, which is choked with sand and asphalt from the roadway. The source of energy turns to the side as it nears, off into the thick trees.

"Ready, Wes?" I say, reassuring myself by patting Wesley on the head. He perches tensely on my shoulder.

"I don't like this, Jamie."

"I know you're disappointed in me for leaving."

"Not that. Something isn't right here. There's no way one Piece of Sky could produce this much energy."

"You think this place is like The Crux?"

"I don't know." Wesley's concern doesn't help my own anxiety. But I'm not about to turn back now.

The untamed forest slows our progress, but gives me something to focus on besides the growing dread in my chest. We have to stop a few times and backtrack when we come up against a thorny bush or fallen tree blocking our way.

A sharp cry cuts through the forest, and I instinctively crouch down. It's feral, inhuman. It also comes directly from our destination. I continue toward it, careful not to break too many branches or step too heavily in the dead leaves scattered over the ground. Though the sun set minutes ago, here in the forest night has already descended.

We pull up short outside a clearing. I realize the wooden structures jumbled in front of me are cabins, the kind typical of New England summer camps, although they don't house campers now.

Angry growls and groans emanate from the cabins. I can't see inside. I'm not sure I want to. The cabins form a circle around a central campfire. Its blaze throws jittering shadows into the trees. Several people sit in camp chairs by the fire. I sneak closer, staying to the shadows at the edge of the clearing. I consider stepping out and announcing myself, but none of the half dozen people look like Paolo. And those noises.

The people are dressed not in ordinary Earthworlder clothes, but in long dark cloaks. One figure stands out in particular, a tall, powerfully built man with black hair slicked back and hanging in strings at his wide shoulders. I realize with a lurch that I recognize this man, even at a distance. His dark hair and burned face are unmistakable. He's the same one I saw on the newscast right after Paolo left, the CEO who ran a company called K-Corp. He looks different without a suit on, but it's definitely him.

I'm not close enough to make out their conversation, but it's obvious that the black-haired man is in charge. I turn my attention once again to the Intention vortex, which is now almost overpowering and comes from not far behind the people. I continue silently along the edge of the camp so I can see beyond the edge of one of the cabins. A large metal cabinet comes into view. A potent blue glow originates from between the open vertical doors, a glow the same color as Paolo's necklace, though much more intense.

As if able to feel the attention I'm paying to the cabinet, the black-haired man steps toward it. He stretches his hands out, at a distance of about six feet. His face fills with terrible pleasure, and his arms shake with the sheer energy coming out of the container. The motion unsettles me. He steps back, his expression changing from elated to quizzical. His eyes scan the perimeter of the clearing, passing over the top of my head. I duck down, sure he has felt my presence.

But instead, he returns to his companions at the fire. A sharp laugh breaks through the evening air, followed by more snarls from the cabin closest to them. A woman, also dressed in a cloak and probably in her fifties, walks to the cabin. She disappears inside for close to a minute, and returns with a huge creature behind her. I recognize the grizzled face of a werebeast, but this is not the lanky body of the wolf-like beast that chased me. This creature is huge and bulky, with black matted fur. I guess that it used to be a bear.

The woman holds a chain attached to a collar around the creature's neck. It follows obediently behind her, but she gives the chain a few unnecessary yanks all the same. The black-haired man steps forward. He runs his hand appraisingly along the strong jaw and forelegs, totally unafraid. His hands still pulsate with blue light. He places them on either side of the beast's head. He closes his eyes, and his arms bulge as he squeezes. Blue light flashes, and the creature gives a pained cry. The man steps away as the creature howls. Before our eyes, the already huge creature grows still larger, muscles rippling out from under its matted fur, its eyes bulging and crazed.

The black-haired man sits again, satisfied, as the woman pulls the still reeling creature back into the cabin. The black-haired man continues to let his eyes wander around the edge of the clearing, although his gaze doesn't near me again.

A hand grabs my shoulder, and before I can cry out, another covers my mouth. They've found me.

But it is not one of the dark-robed people from the camp who crouches beside me. It is Paolo. His presence has an ethereal quality, his outline hazy as it always gets when he's shielding himself from unfriendly eyes in the forest. But it's unmistakably him. New lines streak his face above his unusually thick beard, and his eyes are wide as he slowly removes the hand from my mouth and holds a single finger to his own.

His gaze portrays a degree of mania, as if he hasn't slept for a long while, and finding me here is another stumbling block in an already spectacularly inconvenient series of events. He indicates that I should follow him, and we slink away from the camp, staying low.

Neither of us speak until we have left the forest and are at the side of the road.

"Jamie, I don't know what to say," Paolo says.

"I wanted to find you. I thought you might be in danger."

"I am in danger. And now you are too." Paolo studies me with a concerned expression. "Are you alright?"

"I'm fine. It's good to see you."

Paolo's eyes well and he wraps me in a hug. "It's good to see you too, Jamie. I was just surprised to find you here, that's all. Come on. We can't stay here."

Anger stews inside me. I'm happy to see Paolo, but I can't forget that he left me on my own with a werebeast on my tail, that when I most needed him, he wasn't there.

We walk mostly in silence back into town, and then to one of the cottages on a quiet cul-de-sac. The house is white, with a crisply manicured front lawn, and arbors along one side where vines weave their way upward.

"This your vacation house?" I say. Paolo manages a rough smile.

"If this were a vacation, I would demand a refund."

The interior is as disheveled as Paolo, with dirty dishes and a few beer bottles cluttering the kitchen counter, and the pillows that should be on the living room couch strewn across the floor. Paolo, unfazed, moves a half-finished carton of lo mein off the couch to clear a spot for me.

"You will not believe the month I've had," Paolo begins.

"I'm gonna stop you right there. You do know that after you left, a werebeast came after me and almost killed me, right?" I never speak to Paolo like this, but something about stepping over this boundary feels extremely satisfying. "You do know that I've spent the last month training with people who are apparently my brothers and sisters, that I am supposed to be some sort of weapon, hatched from a god-damned egg for the purposes of a war I've never heard of?"

"I do know all that," Paolo says softly.

"Then what the hell were you doing? I needed you. I would've been killed if it wasn't for the Laputa they sent after me."

"Nikki's grown into quite a conjurer from what I hear. Her parents must be proud." I know he's trying to deflect my anger by changing the subject, but my curiosity is piqued, and I fall into the trap.

"She hates you," I say. "I might too. I haven't decided yet."

"I suppose she has every reason to. I'm very sorry Jamie. I should've been there. But know that Master Root had informed me of your safe arrival in Homestead, that I knew you were okay."

So Master Root knew Paolo's whereabouts this whole time, had even been in communication with him. I suppose it made sense that he'd withhold his location, since I ran off as soon as I found it out. It still stings.

"Allow me to explain what I've been doing here, and maybe you'll find some small measure of forgiveness."

"Don't hold your breath."

"I saw that you identified the leader of the group I've been following."

This feels like a diversion tactic, but I bite. "Big guy? Black hair?"

"Almus Kelluva." He sees my reaction to the name. "Yes, that's right. The banished brother of the Kelluvan patriarch, Holmund. His crimes were deemed so foul that, after the war, he was expelled without a Piece of Sky. His existence should've been a shadow one. Without the ability to channel Intention, one of the Skyfolk quickly loses any sense of meaning in their life. It is a serious punishment, but one that Almus seems to have overcome."

"That big box in the camp."

"Almus has managed to collect several dozen Pieces of Sky by killing or robbing banished Skyfolk. That much Sky in one place gives him access to even greater power than he'd have on Terraltum."

"But isn't there a ton of Sky in the Caves of Meluin? Wouldn't it be easier to mine it from there rather than taking it piece by piece?"

Paolo's face twitches with what I take to be pride at my knowledge of Terraltum.

"That's likely what they'd prefer to do. But the Kelluvas on Terraltum can't risk the consequences if they're found removing Sky from the caves. If it's Almus, they can claim it's a rogue element. Our main concern, though, is what Almus will do with the Sky he does have. Already he has been busy raising another army of werebeasts."

I envision Almus placing his hands on the bear's head, how the creature grew and twisted before my eyes.

"Why here?" I ask. "This isn't the most inconspicuous place to build an army."

"That's one of our few advantages. You may have noticed that Almus could only get so close to the Sky. It's notoriously tricky to move the stuff. Most people can't even touch a concentrated amount of it. Almus wants to expand his operation, but he's stuck here."

"So why not break it up? It's in pieces anyway. You could have different people carry the chunks."

Paolo smiles again, but shakes his head. "It's not so easy. Once you've put it together, Sky binds to itself. Only the advanced Pure Intention techniques from the static sub-school, pioneered by the Meluin, can break it apart."

A banging sound comes from upstairs. My heart jumps, but Paolo's expression doesn't change.

"Speaking of which, I have someone I need you to meet." Paolo rises and leads me up the stairs.

This is a lot to take in.

At the top of the stairs, Paolo removes a key from his pocket and unlocks the door to his right. He peers in through the crack, then opens it fully and steps inside.

I follow him into an ordinary bedroom. The sight of the man on the bed, though, is far from ordinary. Strong ropes bind him to the sturdy bedposts. An uneven beard grows from his face, which, like the rest of his body, is dangerously thin. An uneaten plate of chicken and mashed potatoes lies on the bed beside him, gravy splashed over the edge of the plate onto the comforter. He snaps his arm away from the bedpost as we enter, banging the wood against the wall.

"Sampson, cut it out," Paolo says.

I look up at Paolo in horror. "Did you kidnap that guy?"

Before Paolo can answer, Sampson spouts, "I'm a prisoner against my will! Save me! Save me!"

"Shut up," Paolo says. "Jamie doesn't need to hear your whining."

"Paolo..." I know I don't fully understand what I'm seeing, but it still doesn't look good. I try to remember what Master Root said about Sampson, but the explanation seems abstract against the reality of this man.

"Sampson was one of the best Sky technicians on Terraltum. Very talented, although with an unfortunate tendency to take bribes from the wrong people. When he finally got caught, well, Sky is too precious a resource to allow people of his dubious character to mess around with."

"Banished?" I check his neck. "I don't see a Piece of Sky."

"He had one when he left," Paolo says. "Life on the surface has not been kind to this man."

Sampson's eyes are wild. "I need my Sky back."

"I've told you," Paolo says. "There are other ways besides making deals with the Kelluvas."

"You have piles of Sky lying around too? Do me a favor and spare me a piece, will you?" He stares longingly at the necklace around Paolo's neck.

"Very talented," Paolo says, "but the poor devil's been driven a little insane by being without his Sky."

"That's awful," I say. Animal fear ripples off Sampson. Spit coats his stubble.

"It is," Paolo admits. He steps toward Sampson, who aims a weak kick that Paolo bats away easily. Paolo places his hand on his clammy forehead. After a moment, Sampson's eyes close and he dozes off. "I suppose you've filled in the gaps by this point?" We turn to leave the room. Paolo locks the door gently behind us.

"More or less," I reply as we climb down the stairs. "Almus needs Sampson to ... what? Separate the Pieces of Sky?"

"To contain them. Turns out it's easier to box them up than to break them apart. Go on."

"So Almus needs Sampson to contain the Sky, making it portable, in return for his own Piece of Sky back. And, if I had to guess, Almus was involved in the Piece of Sky being stolen in the first place."

"Precisely. Sampson was actually one of the first Almus visited. Lucky for us, he didn't realize the extent of the problem that moving Sky would become. By the time he did, Sampson had dropped off the map."

"That's why you left," I continue. "You were going to head Sampson off before he could reach Almus. And the potion maker?"

"He was my contact. Sampson tended to stay close to The Crux to maintain some connection to concentrations of Intention, so Hermus kept an eye on him."

"There was a fight at The Crux. The whole area was scorched."

"The potion maker told me that two Changelings had persuaded Sampson to come with them, and had made camp at The Crux."

Regret creeps into his voice. I try to imagine what our life was like before all this, how oblivious I must've been not to notice all that was on his mind. The gulf separating me from the person I was just a month ago stretches like a chasm, while for Paolo it is merely a difference of a few moves, already laid out but now brought to their natural resolution.

"You found the Changelings at The Crux."

"Yes, I found them. If I hadn't surprised them, I don't know that I would've been able to beat them. I've never seen that kind of Intention in such young people before."

"But you did beat them."

"Sort of. I created enough of a commotion that Sampson ran off. With my Organic skill, I tracked him down before they could."

He looks up at the ceiling as the bed creaks upstairs. In the ensuing silence I consider asking about how he captured Sampson, or about the wider ramifications of these machinations. But a thought nags at me.

"Why'd you have me look for the book about werebeasts? Did you think one might be after me?"

Paolo doesn't respond right away.

"I was disturbed by the jojums' reports of werebeasts. When I received word that Sampson had resurfaced as well, I had to move quickly, and I knew I didn't have time to tell you everything you needed to know."

But that's not true, I almost say. There was time before all of this started, when I naively thought I lived in a world where magical beings were only benign curiosities. I need to tell him his decision to shelter me almost killed me, or at least that he could've taught me a little bit of defensive Intention.

"You set me up to fail," I say. "I wasn't remotely trained to fight a werebeast, much less the Changelings."

"I trained you the best I knew how," he says.

"How to read the emotions of the forest? I'm sorry, but the other Skysent, you haven't seen what they can do. None of my abilities would be remotely useful in a fight. It doesn't exactly matter if I can feel that the person hurling pure Intention at me is trying to kill me. Pretty sure I could figure that out without Mind Intention."

"Jamie, I wanted to keep you out of this conflict. I wanted a life for you that was more than just being used as a weapon."

"You can't fight what I am," I say. I see his face grow dark at the idea that I believe this about myself.

"What you are is my son."

"If you were my father, you would've wanted me to be prepared for what was ahead."

Paolo pauses, hurt clear on his face. I can also feel him considering how much to tell me, like he's always done. It didn't used to bother me, but now this consideration sickens me.

"Have you heard the term 'Singular' before?" Paolo asks. He doesn't wait for me to respond: "In reference to Intention, a Singular is someone who shows evident power in only one school of Intention. Most people have two—me for example, I'm an OE. I'm Natural in Organic and Complementary in Elemental."

"I know I'm useless at anything else, I don't need to be reminded." But as I say this I think over my training, the power of the tethering I was able to do with Master Root, and remember that I'm *not* useless. I'm just used to thinking of myself this way.

"Singulars can only manage one school. But what they can accomplish in that school is often far beyond what others even consider possible. Jamie, I tried to train you in every other form of

Intention. Don't you remember all the little tasks I tried to give you when you were young?"

I try to remember, but he hasn't given me anything other than Mind Intention tasks for such a long time. "Like when I was seven?"

"In Intention users, the schools usually emerge by the age of eight or ten at the latest. Jamie, I've known for a while that you were a Singular."

"This feels like an excuse for a shitty training."

"Maybe it is," Paolo says. "But think about it, have you ever done things with Mind Intention that feel far beyond what you should be able to?"

Yes, I think to myself, *and it scares the crap out of me.* I bite back my rage for a minute. It hasn't lessened with Paolo's confessions. If anything, I'm now even angrier that he didn't tell me I was a Singular, that I could be so powerful. Paolo suggests we order a pizza. Ordering a pizza has always been Paolo's way of apologizing—whether for something he's guilty about, or some misfortune the world has thrown at me. But I don't think pizza is going to cut it this time.

"Would you mind making the order?" Paolo asks. "I can't chance my voice being picked up over the phone."

Though he doesn't explain further, an explanation clicks in my mind. He wanted to call me, to hear from me that I was okay. But the Kelluva's reach extends even to something as basic as a phone.

I pick up the phone.

Telling Paolo about my journey proves a welcome distraction from my anger. I tell him everything, about finding the cave underneath our house, about enlisting the jojum for help, and my journey to the potion maker. I relate the nearly disastrous events at

The Crux. He stares in amazement as I tell him about entering the creature's inner mind sphere. At this I can see him nodding, and I know he feels vindicated in treating me as a Singular. I almost wish I didn't tell him so he wouldn't get the satisfaction.

The only interruption is the pizza's arrival. Paolo pays with cash from a ridiculous wad of bills.

I skirt around Callie for the most part, but I can tell Paolo suspects something the third time I mention her abilities with metal and Elemental Intention. It's embarrassing that I can't talk about her without gushing, and I do my best to rein it in, but Paolo knows me too well. Thankfully we're in too tenuous a spot for him to bust my chops.

By the time I reach the complex tethering lessons, I bow to the fact that he was right about my being a Singular. Not about keeping me out of the conflict and concealing what I was. But on this one thing, he was right. Is it enough for me to trust him again?

"I still don't get why the Kelluvas didn't come for me sooner," I say. "They knew I was a Changeling, and yet they let me stay with you, who's clearly been working against them."

"There's some clarity I need to provide about my exact role here," he responds, picking a slice of pepperoni off his pizza and popping it into his mouth. He often eats his foods deconstructed like this, but before now it had never made me want to shove the whole piece of pizza into his mouth and yell at him to just eat it like a normal human. "You've probably guessed, based on the portal and the visitors we've had, that I've served as a conduit for Laputan spies to the surface. Well, that is a role I've kept hidden. In the open, I've professed my loyalties to the Kelluvas, even betraying the Laputas at strategic times to keep up the fiction. This allowed me to be your guardian and train you on my own, with minimal interference. Almus thought he could just claim you when the time came. As he became increasingly more aggressive with using the Changelings to bring about his ends, it became clear that he wouldn't stop bothering us until you joined him. That was the moment, combined with the possibility of them getting Sampson, that I had to let my true loyalties show. Turns out, the werebeast was a ruse to draw me out—Almus had suspected me of being a double agent for some time, and had sent the beast as a sort of emissary, knowing that if I was truly on his side, he would have no problem with me submitting you to its care."

"Wait, what?" I almost spit out a sip of soda. "Its care?"

Paolo sighs. "Jamie, the werebeast wasn't coming to kill you, at least at first. It was coming to collect you, and take you back to Almus. Only when it became clear that you weren't coming did it turn hostile. This is how Almus works. If you'd successfully defeated the beast at that point, then he'd have known you were worth pursuing, and he'd have sent the Changelings to collect you personally. If not, then he'd have been just fine with you dying. He wins either way."

"If it wasn't for Nikki, the werebeast would've killed me without much problem."

"If it wasn't for your training in Mind Intention, you wouldn't have survived either."

Though this is true, I can't admit it. The fact is, he set me up to fail. I want another slice of pizza, but suddenly can't imagine indulging in anything Paolo bought for me.

"I think it's time for bed," I say, getting up.

I sleep that night on a real bed for the first time in over a month. Strange how accustomed I've become to Homestead's hard wooden plank covered in a firm mattress of what I could only assume was a mixture of earth and moss. I toss and turn on the comfortable bed Paolo made up for me in the bedroom on the ground floor. Paolo has cast protective wards around the property to hide our unique Intention signatures. Even knowing we're protected, that Paolo is snoring upstairs and would do anything to protect me, I still feel exposed being aboveground.

I can't stop returning to one thought. However important Sampson is, Paolo still decided he was more important than protecting me. Maybe he thought I would be safe in our home, that whatever protections he had placed on it would be enough to keep me from harm. But the fact remains that I faced a werebeast on my own, and if not for Nikki I would've been an unwilling participant in the beast's digestive cycle.

He was doing what he thought was right. He wanted to keep me out of it.

He should have known that wasn't realistic. You were part of this from the beginning.

But he hoped...

He hoped blindly.

Aren't we all guilty of that? He tried to create a world for me.

He created a fantasy and locked you inside.

Did Paolo really believe he could prevent me from becoming what he knew I was? Was there ever a real hope that I could have a normal life?

With those thoughts running against each other, I slouch into powerful shoulders.

They're so tired, glad of a chance to rest. But it's a temporary respite, and already the clock is ticking on needing to rise again, needing to fight again.

When does it end? With one goal achieved, as far away as even that seems, will we be able to stop?

But my heart tells me there's no stopping. The divine crusade we're on does not have an end. The sleeping bag wrapped around me provides warmth but no comfort, because I know that soon I will have to rise again.

But rise I will. And when I rise, I will do my duty. My duty is greater than any of us, greater than Kelluva or Laputa, Natantis, or even Terraltum itself. My duty is to the fate of both worlds, and their natural order. Their oneness.

I wake from half sleep to a terrible moaning coming from Sampson's room. I listen carefully, but don't hear any indication that Paolo has woken. The sound continues, fading into soft whimpers.

Moving carefully on the squeaky bed and hoping not to wake Wesley, I rise and pad up the stairs to Sampson's door. It's locked, but the key hangs from a peg on the far wall. I unlock the door as soundlessly as I can, shutting it behind me before turning to the dark shape on the bed. If there were an animal to tether off of in the room, I could conjure an Intention light to fill the darkness, but instead I let my eyes adjust to the room.

Sampson squirms. I approach slowly, and am almost at the bed before he notices my presence.

"The boy. Where is the guardian? Downstairs sharpening pegs to slide under my fingernails, or perhaps preparing a fire to burn me alive?"

"You're not in the hands of the Kelluvas. Things could be a lot worse."

"Things could be a lot better too," he says, sitting up as straight as his bonds allow.

"You're safe for now. That's all you can ask for."

"None of us are safe."

"Safe as you can be, then."

Sampson considers me. His emotions project outward, unguarded. He's enjoying having someone to spar with besides Paolo. Any contact besides his captor is a breath of humanity.

"Why are you so important?" I ask. "You can move pieces of Sky around, sure, but if you're such a threat, why are you still alive? I don't imagine the Laputas would ever think of moving Sky to the surface."

"This fickle war has always been one of contingency."

"Explain."

Sampson smiles sickeningly. "The Kelluvas need Sky now. It must be obvious that they mean to create a machine of war that can operate on the surface. A figure of speech, of course. Almus has always favored the intimidation of werebeasts over the Intention Engines the rest of Terraltum's inbred royalty is so in love with."

"But who does Almus mean to fight with this werebeast army? There isn't exactly an army of Laputas down here."

"Foolish boy. You're thinking in too narrow terms."

"Enlighten me, then." His dismissive tone annoys me. I wonder how much he knows about my birth, about what I am. Surely he's noticed the lack of a Piece of Sky on my chest.

"Why do you think the Laputans keep open a portal to the surface? They're not sending soldiers through."

"Information?" I guess.

"No, more than that. The surface is the next battleground. Already House Laputa has installed pawns—aware of their status to greater and lesser extents—in governments around the world. The United States has of course been a primary target, being historically the greatest power, and one of the most susceptible to political gamesmanship."

"But they're not the only ones."

"True. House Laputa has always been somewhat restricted in its view of political influence. Aside from his company, K-Corp, Almus already has an army of lobbyists who can exert his political will much quicker than the 'elected' Laputan stooges."

"And an army of werebeasts, if all else fails."

"No one creates an army of those things as a backup. Almus will use all his pieces in concert when the moment comes."

"How?"

Sampson shrugs, and I still can't read any deceit in him. "That's beyond what I've been concerned to think about."

My mouth twitches. There's a lot to consider here, but its source bothers me.

"The Kelluvas wouldn't be happy with you revealing so much to me."

"I'm not one of them." Genuine vehemence fills his voice. "I don't want any part of this. I said this was a battle of contingencies. I meant that. Both sides will use me however they can."

His eyes, which reflected a quiet confidence as he explained, are now filled with pain. I sense nothing guarded in his emotions, nothing that indicates this is anything but the truth.

"All I want is to be outside of this conflict. Paolo thinks I'm some kind of agent for the Kelluvas, but I want nothing to do with them. I'm stuck here because Paolo doubts my intentions." Sampson's eyes blaze into mine. "He believes the worst of me." His desire to leave radiates desperately. In it I can read that he wants to run away *from*, not run away *to*. The gaunt face is now pleading. "If I were free, I would disappear. I have connections, a network of banished that is more than capable of erasing my existence. Please." The pent-up fear pours out. "I can't be part of this anymore. You can set an innocent person free from this pointless conflict."

What he's asking is ludicrous. Paolo gave up so much to capture him, to keep him here. I don't believe that he could disappear completely. But what I do believe is the pure emotion coming off him. Nothing in the fear, the pain, or even the anger indicates anything besides the desire to escape. If I set him free, could I trust his connections to shield him? Paolo must've doubted it, but then again Paolo works for the Laputas. Surely there's something to Sampson's description of contingencies. The Laputas likely have as much desire to use Sampson's abilities as their enemies.

"Please." Sampson holds his hands out, and I can see the deep grooves the ropes have dug into his wrists, the raw skin almost melding with the cord. His humiliation at being reduced to such pathetic pleas is almost as pitiful as his efforts to loosen the knots.

He is like me, an unwilling participant in a war he doesn't understand. He is like me, contained by Paolo's skewed sense of who and what needs to be protected. The war's outcome means nothing to him, as long as he can emerge on the other side of it unharmed. He owes nothing to anyone. There is one thing I can trust in this man, because it is precisely what I can trust in myself: He will follow his own path to survive, rather than doing what others want.

I step forward. I will not follow what is expected of me. This man needs help, and I am in a position to give it.

As my fingers untie the knots on the bedposts, Sampson's body relaxes. Immeasurable gratitude shines from his eyes.

He flexes his sore limbs as he sits up amidst the soiled covers.

"Thank you," he mouths, getting to his feet.

"There's a fire escape off the back window."

Standing, he is at least a foot taller than me. He takes a step toward me. Then there's an almost imperceptible shift. His thankful expression changes to one of triumph as, with a second step, he darts in my direction and swings his arm with unforgiving force.

I don't have time to process the blow, which knocks me against the dresser. All air leaves my lungs, and Sampson stands over me, any pitifulness gone from his face.

"Boy, I knew you were of the Mind School the minute you walked in the room. You're good at reading emotions, I give you that. Especially fake ones."

What's coming off him now must be his true emotions: victorious elation. I struggle to get to my feet or cry out, but my head spins. I can't comprehend the dance he just took me through, filling his words with enough truth that his real emotions would remain hidden.

"There's a lot to be gained in this war," Sampson says. "I hope you'll remember when the time comes that I'm only doing what's best for me now. You'll think differently about that if you last to the end of it."

With that he exits. I find my feet, but before I can alert Paolo, I hear the sound of the back window opening, and the fire escape descending. I gain enough wind to yell "Paolo!"

He runs up the stairs seconds later. He hurls a ball of Intention through the open window, but Sampson's figure has already faded into the surrounding trees.

Paolo's gruff voice betrays no emotions. I know him well enough to know that means he's trying to contain his rage. "Come on. We have to stop him before he gets to Almus."

Paolo's gray pickup truck waits in the driveway. He guns the motor as soon as we get in, backing onto the road and spinning the tires before the car lurches forward. As we wind through the twisting roads of the sleeping town, Paolo doesn't speak. He doesn't tell me off, doesn't ask why I let Sampson go. Instead, he keeps his eyes focused on the road ahead of us. Wesley has retreated into the back seat of the car.

"When we get there, can you stop him on your own?" Paolo says finally. "We'll have better luck if we're able to spread out." It feels like an olive branch, an acknowledgement that I can actually help. But it's an olive branch I'm not ready to accept.

"Look who suddenly trusts my abilities," I respond before I can fully consider what exactly that entails. There may be a chance of finding a creature to tether with in the woods, but finding one at a moment's notice is no guarantee.

"Now isn't the time for this."

"If I'm as weak as you made me, maybe I'll get trampled so quickly there won't be another time."

Paolo bites his tongue, his face set under his grizzled beard.

We pull up along the side of the road near the Kelluvas' camp. We pick carefully through the underbrush, and then Paolo breaks off, leaving me alone. I approach the clearing, trying to keep my attention on the woods behind me. But as before, the scene in front of me pulls me in. I have come out much closer than before, close enough to clearly hear the fire's crackling.

Almus still sits by the fire. His lackeys must be sleeping, as they are nowhere in sight and the fire is dying down. He stares pensively into the flames, which cast shadows over his scarred face. After a couple minutes someone appears at the far side of the clearing, but it isn't Sampson. In fact, it isn't one figure, but seven, and I know immediately that they must be the Changelings. Comparing them to my Skysent friends, I have to admit I don't like our chances. They give off a battle-hardened air, and they walk into the clearing in near military formation. The leader is tall and chisel-jawed, but I see the tired slope of his shoulders even at this distance.

"Father," the leader says, bowing to Almus.

"You have returned, my children," Almus says. "Khelum, what have you brought me?"

"Exactly what you seek, father," Khelum says. "Molly had the information we wanted. But it wasn't easy. We were ambushed by the other Changelings. It appears they have come together, as we suspected."

Almus scans the ragged group. I fidget, and have to remind myself to be quiet and keep my lookout for Sampson. Nikki. Callie. Petra. Holly. If any of them are hurt I'll never be able to forgive myself for leaving them.

"You're all here. Our great cause has brought you back to me once again, as I knew it would. Did you inflict any casualties?"

At that word I can almost taste bile in my throat. If anything happened to Callie and I wasn't there...

"Difficult to say. We left when we had what we needed."

"And what of Molly?"

"Dead, sir."

A tight smile flashes on Almus' face. "Good." He puts his arm around Khelum, and turns away from the others. "And are you alright? Not hurt too badly it seems?"

"No," Khelum says. "One of them was powerful. She blasted us with fire, and it took all of my energy to shield us from it. It nearly gave me Intention Sickness."

"Yet here you are," Almus says proudly.

"Here I am." His simpering smile makes me want to run into the clearing and rip his teeth out. They've begun walking around the near edge of the camp, leaving the other Changelings to brood in the shadows. Even one who appears to be injured stands still, waiting for the council to be over. "We know where the portal is. Assuming Molly told us the truth."

"If she thought there was a chance it would save her skin, she would have."

"Looks like she miscalculated."

Almus laughs coldly and claps Khelum on the shoulder. He pulls him into a hug. Though sound travels well through the clearing, I can't hear what Almus says next.

"What's next, father?" Khelum says, stepping back.

"Next comes the joining. When it is complete, nothing will contain the power we are about to unleash. Terramundus is imminent."

"I can feel it," Khelum says. If what Khelum is describing is dread, then I can feel it too.

Intention comes off Khelum, stronger and easier to read than any words. I follow the threads, but before I can name the emotions, they pull me in. I resist, but the current is too strong. Suddenly I am outside of myself, and the sensations around me are not my own. *There is obvious affection here, a level of gratitude to the man who raised him. There's fear too, at zealotry he can't understand. But what Khelum feels most of all is weariness, both at the most recent fight, and a deeper fatigue at the long trail of destruction behind him. I feel the length of his road, how many places he's been, how much death he's caused.*

As suddenly as it started, the link breaks, and I am back in my own mind, collapsed to my knees. Though I knew my visions had been from Khelum's perspective, I'm still unprepared to experience one so directly in waking life.

"I would ask your leave to rest for a couple days," Khelum says. "The others are tired, and we don't think that our adversaries will be much trouble now. We left one with Intention Sickness, and the rest with minor injuries."

"Very well. I can't have you going out into the field injured."

"Thank you."

"But be ready to leave the day after tomorrow," Almus snaps. "That should be more than enough time to rest."

"Thank you, father. I am sure we will find the portal open to us."

"I hope so." The arm around the shoulder, the way they pull each other aside to talk, all suggest that Almus and Khelum are close. Yet I can't imagine looking at someone I cared about, seeing how exhausted they were after a fight, and immediately putting them back out again. If Almus cares about Khelum, it's in the same way a wealthy breeder cares for his prize horse.

Khelum turns from Almus and marches back toward the other Changelings, who pace back and forth by the dying coals of the fire. Khelum speaks to them, and they disperse to whatever corner of a cabin is not already occupied by a werebeast.

For the briefest second there's another flash of Khelum's thoughts, a whip of disgust at having to share quarters with the loathsome creatures. But the connection quickly breaks again as a shadow darts from the edge of the clearing nearest the Changelings. As Sampson comes into view, a bolt of Intention flies from the woods behind him, knocking him to the ground. The Changelings' response is instantaneous, any hint of lethargy falling away as they strafe the woods with Intention. I hear crashing that must be Paolo sprinting away, and several disappear into the trees after him. Two Changelings stand over Sampson, who has fallen to the ground, shielding his head with his hands.

I stumble through the dark forest. Roots snarl at my ankles as I spring back to the road. I make it to the truck first, covered in scratches from the whipping branches. The key is still in the ignition. I hop into the driver's seat and start the engine.

I drive to the point where I think Paolo will emerge from the woods, positioning the open passenger door closest to the side of the road. Lights blaze in the trees, both the blinding white of pure Intention and the crackling red of fire.

A breathless minute passes. Have they caught him? But then Paolo barrels out of the trees, indiscriminately hurling Intention behind him as he stumbles up the slope toward the road. An Intention-driven arrow whistles out of the woods behind him, missing him by inches and skimming over the top of the truck. He vaults into the passenger seat, and I stomp my foot on the gas pedal. Paolo hangs out the side of the truck, holding onto the roof and protecting us from the barrage of Intention still coming our way, dispersing what he can and deflecting what he has to. I keep my attention ahead, ignoring my heart's anxious pulsing. A quick check in the rearview shows Khelum standing in the middle of the road, arm outstretched. No attacks volley in our direction, but I see intense focus on Paolo's face, which he directs toward the rear tires, and realize that Khelum is trying to seize the tires to stop us. Sweat beads on Paolo's face with the effort, and no matter how much pressure I place on the gas, the truck fights me.

There is a lurch. The tires shriek, and the entire frame of the truck shimmies as the rear rises four feet in the air. We toss from side to side, Paolo's face grimacing, my grasp on the wheel locked tight.

Paolo releases a wild shout of effort, which materializes in a blue flash of light.

With a sudden burst of motion, the tires catch, and we rocket forward, veering wildly. I let instinct take over, and my hands scramble to straighten us. Somehow Paolo has held on.

Then we are driving straight like any other car on the dark road. Paolo relaxes into his seat and closes the door.

"Do you want me to drive?" Paolo asks after a while.

I shake my head. The headlights blare into the darkness ahead of us. I've slowed to a few miles per hour over the speed limit, though every part of me wants to take the speedometer over a hundred. I don't need to ask where we're going.

If the Kelluvas have Sampson and know where the portal to Terraltum is, they are going there immediately. And if we're going to defend the portal, that means we're going home.

CHAPTER THIRTY-SIX: NIKKI

T he entire apartment has become a makeshift infirmary. Over the course of two days, Holly has shown slight changes, enough so that she can open her eyes and speak softly. The only true cure for Intention Sickness—given that we don't have a tub of jojum feet handy—is rest. But the recovery is far from linear. At times her fever spikes and she moans incoherently, and it requires a constant watch and the help of the tepid water in the bathtub in the apartment's tiny bathroom to keep the heat from overcoming her. An old Terraltum trick says that putting a Piece of Sky in the water conducts healing Intention into a person's body. I immediately notice its absence when I set mine by her feet, and it's hard to tell if it helps since she's in so much pain. But we have to try anything we can. We stagger watches. Despite my exhaustion, I insist on tending her as much as possible, and spend the rest of the time either sleeping or sitting quietly with Callie and Petra.

Callie is reserved, shaken by the pain around her, lacking the will even for short conversations.

Petra is the only reason I don't fall into a similar state. She orders us around like she's been the leader this whole time, offering words of encouragement and optimism even as she drags Holly's feverish body into the bathtub. As much as I try to help, I have to admit that Petra is the one keeping the group from falling apart. Her intensity is magnetic. I find myself trying to find any excuse to spend time with her, even foregoing an hour or two of sleep to sit with her while she tends Holly.

I can't escape the feeling that I've brought the Skysent into this. This is my war. The entire purpose of my mission was to bring them into the Laputan fold. Hell, I was the one who talked them into leaving Homestead. We could've had months more training with Master Root, despite his creepiness. Instead, I talked them into jumping off a bridge when I had no idea how far the drop was.

"There's something bothering me," Petra says unprompted when we're sitting together with Holly. Petra sits with her feet in the bathtub, using only part of her concentration to keep the water cool and fight the fever that still rages in Holly, who shifts restlessly. I note Petra eyeing her bare, strong—though scarred—torso when she thinks I'm not looking. Is that interest, or mere curiosity?

"Aside from the obvious?" I reply, from where I sit cross-legged on the ratty bathmat a few feet away.

"Well yes. But also about all of this shit we've found ourselves wrapped up in."

"That sounds like the obvious."

"Shut up, I'm building to a point."

"Fine, I'll let the professor speak," I say.

"Thank you. That's exactly the kind of respect I deserve." She takes a second to wriggle into as important looking a position as she can muster on the edge of the tub. "What I mean to say is, if the surface is so important to the Kelluvas, to your family, to everyone, why all this secrecy? They should be sending soldiers and armies, not fighting through proxies like the Changelings."

"You don't understand Terraltum politics," I say, immediately wishing it hadn't come out like that. "Sorry. What I mean is, there are all of these unspoken rules in the circles these families operate in. Everyone knows everyone else wants whatever leg up they can get, but nobody would be careless enough to be caught doing anything directly. The balance of power is that fragile—the difference between a banished Kelluva like Almus and his brother the patriarch showing up on the surface could be the line between peace and The Assembly calling for the entire Council to be dismantled."

"Then at the end of the day all of this violence is about propriety?"

So much of my upbringing concerned how to conduct myself within the complex social structure of Terraltum's politics. How to speak in lengthy soliloquies without saying anything of true substance, how to avoid suggesting a rival's motives were anything but pure, while adding enough bite to your words to convey that you weren't naïve enough to be taken advantage of. Every dinner guest at our house tested our manners and ability to represent our house, which Rian always did so much better than me.

The instinctive ferocity with which I've missed my parents hasn't afforded me much energy to miss Rian, but when I think about all he did for me, all the laughter and conversation we shared over the course of our childhoods, my heart aches to be back with him.

Despite my sadness—or maybe because of it—I have an overwhelming urge to pull Petra towards me, to brush my lips against hers, to take her in. But I pause. We've grown so close recently, so much closer than I usually become with people I've known for a relatively short period of time. Her face is beautiful in its familiarity, but also because it always has a smile for me, her friend. Can I risk losing this friendship, especially now when we all need each other? I've sensed a charge in the air between us. How deep this goes, though, or if Petra will be willing to acknowledge it, is the exact quantity I need to put at the center of this risk/reward scale. How good it would feel to let my honest instincts take over, to abandon all mental calculation and embrace whatever this feeling means.

"Are you okay, Nikki?" Petra asks.

"Yeah, fine," I say, turning my eyes from Petra down to the floor. I reach up and put an awkward arm around her back, and we hold each other close. She's a fire burning beneath the thin layer of her shirt. It might not be everything I want, but this closeness is enough for now.

The next day Holly has recovered enough to sit propped up on one of the beds, although when we try to take her out onto one of the patio chairs, the sun hurts her eyes and she has to return inside.

By that afternoon, Holly even manages to crack a smile or two through her otherwise worried and exhausted face. Normalcy of a certain kind has settled over our accommodations, but that's broken when a crash comes from the back patio. Petra and I are already on our feet, rushing to the back of the apartment. Something moves outside. I peer out the window, the others craning their necks around me. My chest hammers. Did the Changelings find us?

More movement on the patio, a smaller crash. But when the intruder comes into view, I burst out laughing.

"What the hell?" Petra says. "What is it?"

I unlock and pull open the back door.

"Hi Amby!"

On the back patio, Amby attempts to put back together a flowerpot he's inadvertently smashed.

"Oh, hello Ms. Laputa," he says, abandoning his hopeless project with a regretful look. He wears an unconvincing disguise of human clothing on his stumpy body.

"Don't worry about that," I say. "Come on inside."

Amby follows us into the apartment. He gives Holly a concerned look as we pull up a chair for him.

"Amby, what are you doing here?" Petra asks.

"Master Root sent me."

We wait, breathless.

"Whoever is willing, you are needed now."

Not an hour later, after Amby has explained the location of the portal and the impending fight to protect it, I conjure my chimeras on the patio. As we climb on their backs, I wave to Holly, who watches us depart from inside the back door. Holly, always the most gung-ho to enter the fight, won't be part of the defense of the portal. She's much too weak to participate, and everyone knows we have even less of a chance without Holly by our side.

We are heading for the home of a traitor—or at least someone I thought was a traitor—and a boy I saved from a werebeast.

The flight is uneventful, the beating wings of my windsteeds strong and consistent. We move through a hot night with a clear sky, perfect for flying. Staring out over the winking lights below, I almost forget the trials of the past few days. Hediad is happy to be flying too. I steer him in playful, swerving patterns, despite protests from Amby, who sits behind me.

The gnomin proves a surprisingly capable navigator, and only once do we have to circle back so he can try to spot a landmark.

"Amby, I don't think I ever asked you why you're on the surface, how you came to be bound to House Laputa," I say once I have tired of swooping back and forth and have steadied onto a straight course.

"It isn't a happy story."

"A happy story wouldn't exactly fit the mood of where we're headed."

Amby pauses, then says: "How well do you know the terms of the Coexistence Pact?"

"Enough." I had practically memorized the Coexistence Pact—often referred to as The Compact—during my inter-species affairs focus in school. It's one of the cornerstone documents of Terraltum, a treaty set down five hundred years ago, and includes laws that bind gnomin to humans for crimes against their own kind, the presumption being that working for humans is a nearly intolerable punishment.

"Well the important thing is that The Compact isn't like most human laws. It's enforced with a powerful combination of human and gnomin Intention. This Intention is absolute—it doesn't know mercy, or change with a change in fashion. It remains in place until the end of the sentence. Period."

"So you're stuck with us until the span of the sentence comes to an end."

"But my sentence doesn't have a timespan. We gnomin are objective-oriented creatures, so we define the length of service in terms of a goal completed. The more unattainable the goal, the more serious the punishment. Minor offenses get sentences like helping a child do well on their end-of-term examinations, or making sure eighty-five percent of the plants in a family's gardens bloom."

"You make it sound almost pleasant," I say.

"Most humans treat us well. That's also part of The Compact." A long pause fills the space behind me. Hediad clears his throat with a growl, and the sound vibrates beneath us.

"What is your goal, Amby?"

"I will serve House Laputa until the Kelluvas are defeated and a Laputa assumes the Chancellorship."

His tone is so flat and matter-of-fact, his recitation of his sentence so calm, that it takes me a second to register how serious it is. The likelihood of a Laputa sitting in the Chancellor's chair in either of our lifetimes is staggeringly small. His sentence is for life.

"Amby, I'm so sorry. Why were you given that sentence?"

"You know about our social hierarchy, don't you?"

"Of course." Gnomin are known for their tri-tiered system. Only by luck of birth or exceptional talent can a gnomin become part of the top level.

"I was part of the middle tier, fit to work in the cities of Terraltum. I was a keeper of accounts for Tarmund's."

Swanky stuff. Tarmund's is the shop on Riverwalk where my parents would buy me dresses for the most formal occasions. A single article of clothing there could cost six months of even a well-off citizen's salary. I always felt sickened when I put on the gorgeous, shimmering dresses.

The name rekindles the embers of longing within me. Riverwalk starts to the east of Archbridge, the great archway that serves as the central artery between the north and south sides of Orella. The walk itself is a promenade stretching for about half a mile, lined with the most expensive shops. Not coincidentally, Riverwalk lies directly next to Banker's Row. Unlike the cramped shops in Market Square across the river, the shops here often encompass a whole block, enough space for room upon room of luxury goods, and on-site workshops where Orella's master craftsmen do their work. Elegant people strolling along Riverwalk can look across the river to the hulking Conjuring Arena, whose rowdy crowd can be heard even among the flowering trees of the promenade. I miss my city.

"I was good at my work," the gnomin continues, "and paid handsomely for it. I daresay I lived better than most humans in the city. Ten years in that shop, and I'd be inducted into the top tier, serving on an advisory council among diplomats and dignitaries. I wore a silk suit while greeting our eminent customers during the day, and straightened the books at night."

I would not have thought him capable of the longing in his voice.

"But then I went with Tarmund to negotiate a shipment of wool from the shepherds out on the Plains of Asavva. Tarmund always kept me by his side for these negotiations. I had a knack for it back then. The shipment went off like a charm, and I secured us a good price for the wool of the fine sheep of Asavva. But Tarmund fell ill and couldn't travel.

"I had heard that a local tribe of low tier gnomin lived nearby. I had never seen the lowest order of my own race before, and truthfully I was curious. As a fairly open-minded gnomin, I always had my suspicions that the tier system was a load of nonsense designed to keep the powerful in charge by allowing them to decide whose life has value."

"Sounds about right." My mother has gone on a rant or two to that effect.

"It's not that different from your system of great houses," Amby replies, voice flat. "I went to see these gnomin. They welcomed me with open arms. At first they were mainly curious at my fine suit and the cologne I wore. They sat around me, several dozen of them on the porch of the ramshackle building where they all slept, their meager work completely forgotten.

"I told them of life in the city, but I also learned a great deal about their lives. Life on the plains isn't easy. The soil is practically unfit for growing, and frequent storms boil up in the autumn and knock down crops and buildings alike. They showed me the shelter they had to dig to protect themselves from the worst of the weather. They invited me to their table, willing to give up their portion of food even for a rich guest. I brought gifts of cured meats from Orella, as well as sweets from the best shops on Baker's Lane. They accepted them only begrudgingly, though I could see how the delicacies transfixed them.

"One of them caught my attention from the beginning. Her name was Melanie, a gnomin perhaps a few years younger than I was, but with the hardened sensibility of someone forced to grow up quickly. She had a smile like lightning and a laugh like thunder. Had I only stayed there a night or two, things might've been different. Melanie might've remained a pleasant memory among the many I made during my time among her people. But I stayed for two full weeks while my master recovered.

"And two weeks is more than enough time to fall in love and do something stupid."

I gasp. I know it's rude that I never thought of Amby as capable of falling in love, but the thought of the squat, bumbling gnomin falling foolishly in love with a gnomin girl is not where I expected this story to go.

Love shimmers beneath the surface of Amby's weary voice. "I spent every day with her, out in the fields, and sat by her at the table or around the fire at night. She was fiercely intelligent, questioning everything I told her, challenging my most basic assumptions about my life in Orella. The specifics of our courtship are probably uninteresting to you, and besides, those are not wounds I want to reopen. But after my two weeks there, I couldn't leave her behind. She agreed to travel under the guise of extra help for Tarmund. She came back to Orella, and I found her lodgings near mine, fine but simple enough to avoid attention.

"Those next three months were the best of my life. We went together to every corner of the city, and through her eyes I discovered it anew. From the great silver fountains of Memorial Square, to even the smallest hole-in-the-wall restaurant in the back alleys of the ailethier quarter. We were in love with each other, in love with the city, in love with discovery and newness and life.

"It couldn't last. We were probably seen by a dozen other middle and high tier gnomin on any given day, and they soon began to ask questions about this beautiful but obviously common gnomin. Maybe I didn't recognize the danger. Maybe I chose to ignore it. But in any case, when we married in secret in the caverns beneath the city, I didn't realize it would be the last night I spent with her. You see, speaking with a low tier gnomin for someone of my station is not considered a crime. But marrying one? I was befouling the reputation of our entire race. When they pulled me in front of a trial, the Gnomish Authority judged me as if I were the high tier gnomin I had aspired to be."

"What happened to her?" I ask, my voice barely audible over the rushing wind.

"I never found out. But the gnomin in charge have few qualms about murdering those in the low tier. It's possible she was banished to the surface, though I've never seen a hint of her. I've been too busy working under my sentence to House Laputa to really investigate."

Fear strikes me. "Your sentence, who came up with it?"

"I think you already know." He places a soothing, although admittedly claw-like, hand on my shoulder. "Don't be disappointed in your parents. It was the Gnomish Authority who stipulated the severity of the sentence. Your parents were only tasked with the specifics. It took weeks of negotiation to reach a sentence deemed severe enough for my crimes."

My own parents sentenced this gnomin to a lifetime of servitude, a lifetime of exile and separation from the woman he loved. All for the crime of loving someone he wasn't supposed to.

They've got some explaining to do, this matriarch and patriarch of House Laputa.

"Can I do anything to help you? Can I change your sentence? I am a Laputa after all."

"No. Gnomin sentences are non-negotiable once they've been set down—the Gnomish Authority is strict in that regard. There's only one thing you can do."

"What's that?"

I can hear the smile creeping into his voice behind me. "Defeat the Kelluvas and bring the Chancellorship to your family."

I reach back and take his hand in my own.

"I promise you, I will do everything I can to ensure that becomes a reality. And if Melanie is alive, I swear to you on the name of my house and all the great houses of Terraltum, I will find her and bring you together again."

CHAPTER THIRTY-SEVEN: JAMIE

W e arrive home to find it looking like a werebeast tore through it. When we find the claw marks that confirm that is exactly what happened, Paolo and I set to work cleaning up the mess and covering the most obvious damage. There's more serious preparation that needs to be done, but neither of us can stomach leaving our house ripped apart like this. My room in particular bore the brunt of the beast's anger, and as I try to clean it, every rip through my mattress or claw mark on my dresser brings me back to the night in the cave at The Crux, the way the moonlight glinted off the creature's claws and teeth.

When the defensive preparations begin in earnest, I see the full extent of the secrets the house held from me. It already has a wealth of defensive measures built in. Dozens of oddly placed windows provide vantage points on the yard and driveway below, and the small balcony on the second floor, with sturdy walls high enough to shield it from the ground, provides an optimal position from which to defend the front door. The front porch has already been rigged with pressure plates that, when activated, open a trapdoor over a pit ten feet below. The trees behind the back door have hooks drilled into them to support thin, nearly invisible wires between them that can wrap themselves nastily around the legs of anyone who comes in contact with them. The house itself already has protective wards to prevent any minor Intention from damaging it, and Paolo spends many hours outside, muttering under his breath and focusing on strengthening the Organic enchantments.

Then there is the greenhouse. The plants are all familiar, but I never realized they're actually extremely poisonous when activated with the right bit of magic, powerful enough to kill an intruder with their noxious gasses. That's where I used to lie on the couch reading graphic novels, taking in the fresh air I thought the plants produced.

Sometimes I think my entire childhood consisted of one elaborate pastoral lie, a fake idyllic experience masking dark forces that stormed around me. I guess Paolo could've done worse.

Ora arrives a few hours before the others do, and Paolo puts her immediately—and indignantly—to work.

When Nikki's windsteeds swoop down onto the front lawn, I have to run out to direct the Skysent around the traps hidden in the tall grass. Nikki and Amby climb down off one of the chimeras, while Callie and Petra drop off the other, stretching cramped limbs. Nikki speaks softly to her two chimeras, nuzzling their heads with hers before allowing them to fade away.

I stand a few feet away, my heart racing. I haven't forgotten how I left Homestead. I've been preparing for their collective wrath for the last two days. Nikki leads the group toward me.

"Jamie, I'm happy to see you," she says, wrapping her arms around me in a hug that is so sudden and forceful that I stumble. "Don't worry, I'm still mad at you."

"Hi Nikki," I manage.

"I know family means more than anything, and we need each other for this fight. Just promise you'll stick around this time."

"This is my home," I say in answer.

Callie is next. My face and neck burn, and I imagine I vaguely resemble an overripe tomato. But if she was trying to hold me in suspense over her reaction, she doesn't do a good job of it. That's not her. The smile on her face is, though.

She wraps me in a bone-shaking hug that lasts what must to the others be an awkwardly long time. But it's not nearly enough time to hold her against me, to feel her breath flowing in and out, to match the pounding of her heart, apparent even through our shirts, to my own. When we pull away and she tips her head slightly up to catch my eyes, my grasp of reality departs temporarily.

Petra puts a firm hand on my shoulder.

"This is really adorable, but can you please tell us where the traps are, so we don't die before we get to the house?"

"Oh sorry," I stammer. "If you cut straight across at a diagonal from here you should be fine."

She and Nikki start toward the house. Paolo waits on the front porch.

Callie gives me another squeeze, but neither of us have come up with any words yet. There will be time for that later. Hopefully.

They've left Holly behind, but they assure me she's okay. I'm the last to come up to the house, and I feel my position at the back of the pack is probably a suitable metaphor. From their faces I can tell they've been through a lot, much more than I have, and have grown both stronger and closer because of it. It reminds me of the friends at school who'd spent three months together at summer camp and entered the school year with so many inside jokes that it was impossible to have a conversation without them bursting into incomprehensible laughter. Only a much deadlier, more serious version of that.

The happy moment of reunion is short-lived. As soon as Nikki steps foot on the front porch and sees Paolo, her eyes darken.

"Ms. Laputa, welcome," Paolo says with a slight bow.

She pulls up short as he holds the door open for her. She stares past him for what seems like a long time, considering. It's enough time for all of us to crowd onto the porch.

"If I had any sense at all, I'd take advantage of this opportunity to slice you to pieces for what you did to Jamie," Nikki says, her voice soft.

"I understand," Paolo says. "But it would be a shame to have to fight the daughter of a man I love as dearly as your father." Paolo has always been gentle in his words and actions, but I see a faint glimmer in his bearded face, a fierceness that speaks of a more fiery past.

"It would be an awkward situation for you, I'm sure. But keep your wits about you, Paolo, you might just need to fend me off before this is all over."

"Your father is a great man. I'm glad his daughter inherited his stubbornness."

"I'm not sure he would have anything so positive to say about you."

Paolo laughs, and the sound breaks some of the tension. "Likely not. Ebben Laputa is never one to dole out compliments, is he?"

Nikki's cheeks tip slightly toward a smile. She walks through the front door, and for a moment I feel like I've stepped outside my body, seeing this collision of worlds. But I know now that my home and the wars of Nikki's family have never really been separate.

CHAPTER THIRTY-EIGHT: NIKKI

"Here's the situation," Paolo says. We're in the greenhouse living room, scattered on the faded couch and in chairs pulled in from the kitchen, sipping on homemade chai lattes. It's my first one, and it reminds me strongly of the teas we would drink back home, made from the sweet but slightly astringent seed pods of the *poliver* tree. "For now, we're the only thing standing between the Kelluvas and control of the portal. I've been in contact with several members of my house, who are loyal to House Laputa and will make their way to the portal from the other side to help us."

"House Swift?" I ask.

"That's right. But it's a long journey from Swift Hall to the portal, and it may be a matter of a day or more before they arrive. If the Kelluvas act now, we are on our own. My guess is that if they control the portal, they will begin harvesting Sky immediately and transporting it to the surface, establishing an entrenched defense in the Meluin Caves as Almus continues to build his army."

"There's the other element to this, the Leonis factor," Jamie says. "Everything that I've seen in my visions has turned out to be true, and in them I've seen Leonis Wingless in his stunted form."

"Almus belongs to the cult that worships Leonis," Paolo says. "My assumption is that they're searching for a way to bring him back to his full strength, but we don't know how—the use of pure Sky might bolster him somewhat, but it's unlikely to do the whole job. Whatever they're doing, though, it involves the portal. That is why we simply cannot let them control it. If we do, they will soon control the surface. Any questions?"

Something nibbles at me, beyond simple fear at the idea that this powerful being, one who we all thought was a distant memory, is back. But I can't quite place it.

"Is there any way to, like, destroy the portal?" Callie asks. "What makes us think fending them off once will stop them from coming again?"

"It's theoretically possible," Paolo says.

"I won't hear of it," I say, wiping chai from my lip. I glance over at Ora. I don't think appreciation is an emotion she's capable of displaying, but her thin smile is close enough.

Paolo notes the others' confusion.

"The manipulation of space and time falls outside of any of the five schools," he says. "In fact, it is often described as requiring all five schools at once. A portal is the most obvious manipulation. Another is The Gift of the Ailethier, which creates a stasis immune to the rules of time. When magic like this comes into contact with other magic of its kind, the typical outcome is a temporal disruption powerful enough to destroy one or both acts."

"But we're not going to make Ora blow herself up just to collapse the portal," I say.

"I agree," Paolo says. "The Gift is half power and half curse. To the one who uses it, the effects are almost always fatal."

357

"What a way to go out, though," Ora says. "I don't fully believe in this Wingless business. There's no one more evil to my kind than that traitor. He turned on our ancestors, on the Winged Ones. The Winged Ones wouldn't have left him in a state where he could come back."

She catches the expression on my face, which must display my skepticism. I'm not as willing as she is to ignore Jamie's visions.

"If he *was* alive," Ora concedes, "and I thought I could do even the tiniest amount of damage to him, I'd take that opportunity no matter the cost."

"Well let's hope it doesn't come to that," I say. "We succeed together, or we fail together."

Murmurs of assent rise from the rest of the group. Even Ora nods along.

We set to preparations over the next few hours with grim determination. We reinforce the house in a dozen places, and continue to build the traps Paolo had already been preparing.

Jamie and I tie up a pulley system controlling an Intention-strengthened net that, when the appropriate pressure point is triggered, will scoop up whoever is on the ground below.

"I need to know something," I say to Jamie as we pull on the rope.

"What's that?" He meets my eyes for a second, then turns back to the rope. The gesture is slightly clipped, nervous. He's obviously still ashamed of what happened when he left Homestead.

"You were having a hard time in Homestead. With Intention, I mean." His cheeks turn the color of a particularly striking sunset. "But the night you left, you threw me on the ground like it was nothing."

"I'm sorry about that, I was really angry. I shouldn't have…"

"So that's all it was?" The rope catches on a tree branch, and we struggle to untangle it.

"Well, no. Even if I was angry, I couldn't have done that on my own. I had some help."

"What do you mean?"

Jamie's words gush out, as if they'd been collecting behind a dam. He tells me all about his training in the Mind School with Master Root, about the complex tethering, about how that night he tethered with Wesley's Intention.

I've never even heard of tethering. It's not a technique that comes up anywhere in the standard magical training on Terraltum. Something about it unsettles me, and Jamie's tone suggests he feels similarly.

"So in order to fight, you'll have to tether with Wesley," I say. Wesley is apparently off assisting Paolo with some task, or more likely driving him crazy.

Jamie shakes his head vigorously. "No. I don't think everyone notices when it happens—at least not animals—but trilopex are much more intelligent than most animals. It really upset him. I couldn't make him do that again."

"What will you do then?"

"Me and Paolo caught a few birds. We put them in a cage I can carry with me, so I always have an animal to tether with."

Before I can control it, a laugh ripples through me. I don't know why exactly, but the image of Jamie running around a battlefield holding a cage full of canaries strikes me as funny in a way nothing has in a while.

"I'm just imagining you fighting with a giant birdcage on your shoulder," I say through giggles. "It's a rather heroic image."

I hold my arm up, miming holding a bulky cage, flexing for effect. It's enough to get Jamie laughing.

"Being heroic's your thing," he says. "I have to muddle my way through it."

"Glad somebody noticed my calling."

"You make it pretty obvious that's how you think of yourself."

"I should be offended," I say.

"Are you?"

A breath passes before I can answer. How does this kid always know the words that cut straight to my insecurities, and manage to say them with a smile on his face?

"Let's finish setting up this trap," I say. "I'll get back to you."

"I wait with bated breath."

We finish tying off the last of the ropes. Afternoon warmth has descended, but a cool breeze stirs the evergreens around the clearing. There's no indication of what's about to happen. I try to enjoy these last hours, to fold myself into the softness of the wind, but the tightness in my chest won't let me.

As night approaches, a hush falls over the house. We're sprawled on the couches in the living room, doing our best to relax. It doesn't last long. The front door swings open and Ora bursts in. She's ruffled—although her version of ruffled would still beat me on my best day—and panting.

"I've spotted them not a mile from here," she says. "They're coming fast."

"We'd better get ready then," I say, shooting to my feet.

"And Almus has brought a pack of werebeasts with him."

CHAPTER THIRTY-NINE: JAMIE

I grew up between these walls, in this forest, on this slice of land that belonged to only Paolo, Wesley, and me. Now a pack of werebeasts and murderous Changelings marches toward us. I don't know how strong the defenses are. Dammit, until a couple days ago I didn't even know they were there in the first place. And I don't know how strong my friends are. There's been no sign that defeat is a possibility, from Paolo or anyone else. Is it confidence or denial?

The minute I can, I pull Callie aside and ask if we can talk. She follows me upstairs to my room. It's so small when I'm seeing it from her perspective. We had to throw out the old mattress because it was too torn by the werebeast, and the room feels oddly bare without it. Callie surveys the pictures on the wall. Most are missing after the werebeast slashed them.

"What's up?" she says. She leans against the bookshelf and directs her attention out the window.

"I wanted to tell you something."

"Oh?" She crosses her arms.

"Yeah. Sorry. That's what I wanted to say. I'm sorry for leaving. I know things got rough out there and I don't know if I could've made a difference. But it wasn't right not to be there."

"Is that all?"

I take a hard breath. "No. I'm sorry I left you. You specifically."

She turns toward me, and beside sadness, I register a faint spark of anger.

"I was furious with you. I couldn't believe you would do this to me. To us."

"I'm sorry."

"Stop apologizing. It's so goddamn easy to forgive you. It must be nice to go through life that way, always saying sorry and having everything be better."

"I don't think everything's better," I say, panic rising. "And I wouldn't apologize if I didn't mean it."

"That's what's so annoying. I know you can trace every emotion coming off me."

"With you I can't." That hangs in the air for a long time.

"What do you mean?"

"I mean that if I really try, yeah, like what happened during training in Homestead. But if I try to casually pick up your emotions, it gets sort of confused. It's like they wrap around my own emotions so tightly that at a certain point I can't tell one from the other. It's like I can't tell where I end..."

"... and I begin."

Callie watches me intently.

"This has never happened before," I continue, "and it scares me."

She steps forward, and before I can react, her hand is against my chest. "I don't think I'm a particularly scary person. But it's nice to have that effect."

When we kiss this time it's not a short peck. It's long, so long, our tongues darting out at each other, never a hesitation before it takes us further into each other. Her body is warm against me and my hand runs down her side, down the broad curve of her butt. She shivers slightly as she pulls me even closer. Without meaning to, I've pressed her against the bookshelf. Her arms wrap around my neck as my hands creep up under her shirt, against her soft stomach.

Then a knock comes at the door. We pull away, the surge of energy turning into embarrassment as we see Petra in the doorway, making a show of covering her eyes.

"Damn so this is where the action is," she says.

I haven't let go of Callie's hand.

"They're close, it's time to get ready," she says.

We follow Petra out of the room. The heat between our palms is all that remains of the moment. But it's enough for now.

Paolo catches me as I make my way across the living room. I try to stand with soldier straightness, but Paolo wraps me in a hug, almost lifting my shoes off the floor. I never used to wear shoes inside, but I can't exactly go into battle barefoot.

"Are you ready?" he asks. He keeps his voice low. The four birds in the cage I'm holding chirp frantically.

"We've prepared everything we could."

He taps my forehead. "But are *you* ready."

Part of me wants to say yes, to tell him I forgive him for not preparing me for this. But I won't lie now.

"You probably should've asked that question a lot sooner," I say.

Paolo's eyes are desperate as he waits for me to elaborate. But instead I turn away. I can feel his pain behind me, still feel it as he disappears up the stairs, and I am left alone with Wesley in the corner of the living room. I pet him behind one floppy ear as I check on my birds.

"Let's hope these bird brains can muster up some Intention."

Jamie I've been thinking, Wesley thinks to me. The transition to thought-speak tells me he's about to say something serious.

I thought we agreed you'd stop doing that.

If you need to, you can use me to tether.

No Wesley, I won't do it. It's different using an animal who doesn't have the kind of consciousness you do. They don't recognize what's happening. I pause, thinking Wesley might protest. When he doesn't for a second, I think, *I never asked you what it felt like.*

Wesley's silence is cut only by Paolo's footsteps on the roof above me.

And don't lie and tell me it was fine, I say. *We're past protecting each other's feelings.*

Wesley nods, and I know he will tell me the truth, even if it means I won't be willing to do what I need to do.

It was like standing at the top of a high precipice, looking out over a far drop below, and having that sudden thought: "What if I stepped off the edge?" But rather than being a question or a rogue urge, that thought was an overwhelming physical need, and I jumped without a second thought.

I meet his gaze, and the terror there is worse than any physical wound I could have caused.

"Wesley, I'm sorry." Amid all the destruction and death I know is coming, this revelation stings the worst.

Jamie, I would gladly throw myself off any cliff if it meant you might be safe.

I don't doubt the truth of this, either, but I resolve that no matter what happens, I will never again tether with Wesley.

I'm serious, Wesley says. *If the moment comes when there is no other choice, you have to use me.*

Okay, I say. Now I'm the one who's lying.

CHAPTER FORTY: NIKKI

We spread throughout the house. I take a spot on the staircase where an open window provides a vantage on the front lawn. We have every corner covered, although not as thoroughly as we'd like. We've received no word of the reinforcements from House Swift. If my parents were going to send some secret force to aid us, it hasn't come. We're on our own.

Petra pulled me aside as I climbed the stairs, on her way to the opposite corner of the house.

"Conjure something crazy for us, okay?" she said.

"How does a giant white flag sound?"

"Dear lord, a princess of a floating continent, and you can't dream any bigger than sarcastic surrender?"

I smiled, and we hugged. When we stepped back, there was resolution on her face.

"We're going to get through this," she said. "One way or another."

I made a silent resolution that if we came out the other side, I would tell her how I felt. It seemed such a small thing, knowing the danger we were about to face. Though an army of Kelluvan werebeast somehow seems simpler.

The wait is excruciating. In order to comfort myself, I imagine my parents beside me, urging me on, telling me I can do this.

I keep my eyes on the start of the forest on the far side of the lawn. Paolo has planted burning torches outside, illuminating everything in front of the trees. Their light can't quite cut into the woods, though. The dancing shadows beyond look like nothing so much as enemy figures.

"Everyone alright?" Paolo stands on the balcony overlooking the yard, but has amplified his voice with Organic Intention so all of us can hear. We respond with dull murmurs of "fine," or "we're okay."

"Everyone gets a nice vacation after this, how does that sound? You can all sit on a beach somewhere and sip mango juice out of a coconut."

"I'll do you one better," I say, throwing enough Intention behind my voice that I hope everyone can hear. "You can all come and stay on my family's estate. We can start up the fountains and everything, and you can have food brought to you anywhere and anytime."

"Sounds pleasantly fattening," Paolo says. "How about this, let's beat up on these Kelluvan jerks, and then hammer out the details later. Sound good?"

Not two minutes later, a shape appears at the edge of the clearing. At first I think it's a large man, but I soon see by the way it lopes along the ground that it can't be human. Two more shapes run behind it, and as the first shape catches the light of the torches on the lawn, I see that they're werebeasts.

The three beasts rush toward the house, and the yard becomes chaos.

Intention rains down from the watchers in the house, while balls of flame and metal rocket from the trees toward us. A few of the better aimed blasts of energy strike the werebeasts. One stumbles, and with a crunching noise falls straight into one of the spike-filled pits on the lawn. The cacophony around it almost drowns out its cries of pain.

The house is well protected, but even so, the force of the assault shakes its frame. I send out a small flock of conjured birds with sharp beaks and talons, which dive off into the trees in pursuit of the hidden Changelings. From the raised voices in the trees, as well as the slight twinge of pain that means one of my conjured creatures has died, I know they had no trouble finding them.

Two of the werebeasts make it to the steps leading up to porch, where Ora waits for them. Ora blasts one in the chest with a ray of pure white light, and it falls to the ground in a giant lupine heap. The other lunges around her, slashing with a ferocious claw. Ora sidesteps, but not quickly enough to avoid a nasty scratch on her arm. She cries out, flapping her wings to get out of the creature's reach. It leaps, impossibly high, and latches onto Ora's feet, trying to drag her down. They struggle, but it is obviously too heavy for Ora to stay airborne.

Through the noise of battle, I hear a choked, inhuman voice, that nonetheless says one very clear word: "*Die.*"

I hope I never again hear a werebeast speak. It opens its jaws to bite her, but before it can strike, Ora unleashes another blast of Intention. At that close range, the creature's head dissolves. Its headless body crashes into the porch, sending splinters in all directions.

I see three more werebeasts, these more bear-like than wolf-like, run out of the trees, carefully skirting the traps. I throw a couple bears of my own out of the open window to meet them. They roar as they crash into each other, but I don't have time to watch their fight. The shower of energy continues. One spell shatters the window next to me completely, sending me reeling back out of the way of the glass shards.

Suddenly the torches on the lawn go out, and the only light comes from flashes of Intention.

I can't see what's going on down below, but I do my best to divert some of the heavy fire now being directed toward Ora on the porch. Fierce growls match the sound of rending claws as the werebeasts and chimeras battle it out.

But any thought leaves my mind as a steel object from the trees screams through the window, catching me on the leg. I stumble, trying to catch myself, but my injured leg can't hold my weight. I fall down the steps, scrabbling with my hands for purchase. I thump all the way down the stairs, coming to rest in a painful pile at the bottom.

My pants are torn, and a deep gash is visible through the gap in the fabric. I can tell the rest of me will soon be bruised. I try to get to my feet. A wave of nausea courses up from my wounded leg, and I have to close my eyes to avoid vomiting on the bottom step. I force myself to inspect the wound. While it is wide, the object that struck me must have been hot because I'm barely bleeding at all—the wound cauterized instantly, and the projectile passed along the side of my leg. A small comfort as my entire thigh pulses in pain.

An explosion rocks the second floor, and I hear wood and shingles tumbling out onto the roof of the porch. The protections must be wearing off under the heavy attack. There's another flash of pure white light on the porch. I can see Ora's figure through the slats in the banister and the living room window. As I watch, one of the werebeasts leaps from the ground below, and knocks her to the ground. I cry out, but I can't get up. The creature stands over her, rearing back to deal a killing blow.

But before it can, the front door swings open, and Amby rushes forward, holding a massive axe. He raided Paolo's small armory before the fight, but I never thought he could look so terrifying carrying the weapon. The gnomin swings in an upward slice, which carves clean through the creature's shoulder. It bellows in pain, and aims a retaliatory swipe toward Amby. He's quick, though, and wards off the blow with the flat of the blade. Ora blinds the creature with a burst of light, and Amby spins to deal a crushing blow to the back of its neck. It dies before it can howl again. Amby roughly pulls Ora off the porch, closing the door as a hail of Intention strikes the porch.

"I'm fine, let me go," Ora growls.

"You are now, begging your pardon," Amby says. He's panting from the exertion of wielding an axe twice his height.

The assault has slowed, and with the relative quiet I find the ability to direct my Intention to my leg. I can't heal it fully now, but I can at least dull the pain. Amby runs over to me as Ora gets to her feet, brushing herself off.

"You're hurt, Miss Laputa."

"I'll be fine." I struggle into a crouch, pushing any thought of pain away with sheer force.

"Your injury looks very bad."

"No time to worry about that now." I use his shoulder to leverage myself to my feet, an indignity he accepts without comment. "I'm glad you and that axe are on our side."

He smiles, but then realizes that he is dripping viscous werebeast blood on the carpet, and quickly hurries to wipe it off on his pant leg.

"Amby, you take the front door. Ora, could you provide some cover from above with me?"

"Nothing would make me happier," she says. Besides her shoulder, she is largely unhurt.

Together we climb the stairs back to my spot overlooking the yard. What had once been an open window is now a four-foot round gap which, although offering less protection, at the very least gives a better view of the battlefield below.

The torches flicker back on as all attacks stop. My eyes scan the corpses of the werebeasts. Six large beasts, all lying dead at various points on or in front of the porch. For a moment there is complete silence, a silence so deep after the noise of the attack that it tricks my brain into thinking that it's over, that we've warded off the enemies and are now safe.

A figure appears in the shadows. This time it's a man. As he steps into the light, I recognize Almus Kelluva. I'd recognize the large shoulders and jet-black hair of a Kelluva anywhere, and even if I've only ever seen a portrait of him, the distinctive burns that mar his skin as a result of some evil Intention gone awry stand out in the torches' glow.

He strides confidently forward into the circle of light. I half expect a dozen magical missiles to rifle down toward him, but we restrain ourselves. He weaves contemptuously around the traps that haven't yet been sprung on the lawn.

"What a night!" he says. "We have lit up the sky in a display not seen since Barrun's War. It is truly beautiful to fight at night, isn't it, Paolo, my dear friend?"

I can't quite see Paolo in his position on the balcony, but his voice quivers with anger.

"I've never called you a friend, Almus, and I don't intend to start now."

Almus' laugh has no joy. "Come, come, one who served my family so well couldn't be anything but a friend. We took cordial council not two months ago. Have you changed so much since then?"

"I haven't changed at all."

"I can only assume you are jealous of what I've created, the greatest warriors our house has ever seen."

At these words, seven teenagers step out of the shadows. They linger at the edge of the torchlight. I identify Khelum and Evey at the front of the pack.

"They're not warriors, they're children," Paolo barks. "Even a Kelluva should know better than to mistake children for soldiers."

"You think these are children? Do you know what we created them for, the power they wield?"

"The reason they exist and the life they are allowed to live don't have to be one and the same."

"You ignorant traitor! If not for you and your Laputan friends, all of them would be living their full purpose, the one purpose they've ever had, to win us this war."

Paolo's voice remains steady. "There's no war yet, and there doesn't have to be. Leave the portal and Sky alone. Let the

Changelings and Skysent live as normal a life as they can. Do you really think, once the Chancellor and the rest of House Laputa hear of this, there won't be consequences?"

"Consequences? You speak as if to a child who doesn't understand that when he pushes the first domino the rest will fall. This is merely the beginning. The reemergence has begun, and when it passes through you, it will impose its divine will on both surface and sky. Our worlds will take their natural—and just—order." He steps forward lazily, his eyes scanning the faces that peer down from the house. "Your numbers seem a bit thin."

"You're talking about killing children, Almus."

"You want to talk about killing? What about the creatures you have so brutally murdered?" He points to the bodies of werebeasts strewn across the yard. "These are all my children, all my creations. You've shown no remorse at killing them. At least they died for a greater purpose."

"You keep them in cages," a small voice says. It's Jamie, and a moment passes before I realize he's out on the lawn by the far corner of the house. He was stationed by the door there, but from the rubble he picks his way through, I guess there's not much wall left on that side. "You don't create new life, you torture animals until they become unrecognizable abominations who can't even recognize themselves." He walks forward, holding a small cage with four large birds inside. They vary in size and color, but all watch peacefully. The image is not as humorous as I'd found it earlier. Somehow, the way he holds the cage makes it seem a powerful weapon.

"Speaking of cages," Almus snaps.

"Oh, sorry," Jamie says. He sets the cage down. Almus watches ferociously as Jamie tries to get it open. It takes a few seconds as he fumbles with the latch, jiggling it unnecessarily back and forth. Almus' anger, so raw and brutal a moment before, seems almost comical in the face of Jamie's feigned struggle. "It's always a bit sticky—yep, there we go." With a creak, the door opens, and the birds fly out. Instead of flying off, they spin in a spiral above his head, before arranging themselves in a line behind him. Jamie tosses the cage aside.

Almus keeps his attention on Jamie, but speaks so we all can hear. "I must say, you're even less impressive than I'd imagined. My Changelings told me you abandoned your friends when you realized you were too weak to help them. I would've run the Changeling program through another iteration if I knew it would produce such a runt."

"Enough, say your piece and be done with it," Paolo snaps.

"My offer is full amnesty for all of you. Even you, Paolo. If you step aside and allow us to reach the portal, you won't face the same fate as Molly. She was a brave soldier, back in her day, but she didn't put up much of a fight."

My eyes barely have time to catch up with what happens next. A blaze of white light erupts from Paolo's hand, straight down at Almus. Almus braces himself, redirecting the flashing light toward Jamie. I put my hand over my mouth as the haze of white cyclones around Jamie, seeming to swallow him. But as quickly as it came, the light is gone, darkness seeming for a second to cut the entire area from existence. When light returns, Jamie stands unhurt and defiant, with his birds squawking above his head.

That's the coolest thing he's ever done, and by the expression on his face, I can tell he knows it.

Almus yells in anger, and the Changelings rush forward. As they do, another half dozen werebeasts follow them out of the trees. From the branches above, four or five deathcrows shoot forward.

I don't think. There isn't time. Hediad appears in the air before me, and I leap out the second story window onto his back. The last time we were attacked by deathcrows we were carrying an injured boy and being pursued. This time the fire of battle radiates from the stabbing pain in my leg.

Hediad wings forward under the force of my blazing Intention. He meets the first deathcrow with his sharp talons, practically ripping the bird in half.

Below us the assault has quickened. Jamie retreats into the rubble of the first floor, trading surges of Intention with two of the Changelings, while Paolo and Almus are engaged in what appears to be a long-range fist fight, as they hurl solid streams of energy toward one another.

I spot Petra on the third floor, using Intention to hurl splintery boards at her enemies. The Changeling Anna is launching gusts of wind her way, whipping the boards into a spiral so violent I can't tell who is controlling it. Amby charges forward with his axe. Even as he runs, I see him get hit by a blast of energy and fall to the floor of the porch. I'm not sure where Callie is, but I do see two of the Changelings focusing all of their efforts on the opposite corner of the first floor, near the kitchen.

I know Petra is as strong as any of the others, but I can't help watching every movement made in her direction. It's irrational, but I feel that simply by keeping a close watch I can ward off any danger she might face.

Hediad spins to avoid a deathcrow that shrieks toward us. It swings back around as two others make passes. We're too quick, though, too in tune, rolling to avoid them almost before they can attack. We swoop down to the battlefield. Hediad snatches a lynx-like werebeast in his claws, then soars straight upward. The creature screams, trying to claw at Hediad's hide. When we're high enough, Hediad simply lets go, and the creature plummets to the earth, barely missing Almus as it dies.

"Atta boy," I say, patting the back of Hediad's head. We don't have long to celebrate, though, as another deathcrow barrels toward us. This time Hediad puts his head down and charges, driving his bony head through the creature's chest.

I duck, barely avoiding a ball of green Intention that whistles past me. I turn toward its source, and see the conjurer, Evey, floating on a windsteed of her own. She looks uncomfortable in the air. Reddish hair billows around her head.

"You're good, Laputa," she says. "I'd hoped to have another round with you."

"I'm flattered you've spent so much time thinking about me. Seriously, it means a lot."

"Shut up."

"But to me, you're just another rookie conjurer who doesn't realize when the match is already over."

As I say the last words, Hediad is already springing forward, diving straight at Evey's steed. They streak upward before Hediad's claws can reach them, and we follow hot on their tail. We gain quickly, and for a second I think this will be an easy victory. But a swarm of angry bees flows out behind Evey, forcing us to spin off and level out. The swarm disappears almost instantly behind us, but it had the desired effect. Evey circles back around, this time sending a stream of crows toward us. I respond with a hawk, who tears most of the crows apart, enough that I can dodge the others. My leg wound twinges, but I cannot feel pain through the brutal ecstasy of the fight.

Is there something genetic in me, some tragically advantageous Laputan trait, which makes me enjoy this proximity to death so much?

I see the faintest hint of a smile on Evey's face. She's enjoying this too. It's like a conjuring match in the arena. Only with potentially deadly results.

But Evey clearly isn't playing by arena rules, because she sends a ball of Intention at me while the birds are still fighting. I spin out of the way. The heat of pure energy passes by, and I turn the momentum into a forward swoop. Evey swings her steed to the side, narrowly avoiding a direct impact. This time, though, Hediad's claws catch the back of her steed. It gives a rasping cry. Evey tries to pull away, but the claws have found a hold, and each attempt to pull away drives Hediad's claws deeper. She urges her steed to spin, to dive, anything to get away, but it's resisting her, in too much pain to respond to her pleas. I've bested her here. Hediad would do anything for me, no matter the cost to himself.

It's possible we could shake her off her windsteed, but I don't risk Evey sending any more Matter my way. I leap from Hediad's back, leading with my feet. My shoe catches Evey on the shoulder, unseating her and sending her tumbling off its back.

I struggle to right myself on her thrashing windsteed. Evey's shriek ends abruptly when the ground fifteen feet below meets her. As soon as she hits the earth, her steed disappears, but Hediad has positioned himself beneath me, and I fall easily onto his back.

With a twinge of discomfort, I pick out Evey's shape in the yard. She is alive, although her leg is obviously broken. Her moans barely register over the noise of fighting.

On the far side of the lawn, I see a deathcrow advancing on Jamie. He is keeping it at bay with some kind of shield, but as he does, the Changeling named Lia lobs balls of fire at him. I spur Hediad forward.

The deathcrow is ready for us. It feints to one side, and we miss and have to curl back. But that gives Jamie enough time to focus his attention on dispersing Lia's Intention rather than dodging it. He pulls strength from the birds above him, turning the fireballs into puffs of smoke. He steps forward and kneels.

I corkscrew, and the deathcrow follows me, but I keep my eyes on Jamie. Tremors ripple through the scorched earth on the lawn. Lia pauses in the middle of conjuring another ball of fire, and reels as her feet suddenly sink into the earth. She doesn't stop sinking until she's up to her waist. When she tries to pull herself out, the ground has become solid again.

Turning my attention back to the deathcrow, I decide to get a little fancy. Maybe it's the mania of battle, or maybe the gash on my leg has caused more blood loss than I thought, but I picture in my mind's eye the sparkling shape of massive flowering fireworks.

What I get instead are slightly disappointing sparks of white light.

It's enough though. The deathcrow's beady eyes fill with fear, and it shrieks as it turns away from the flashing light. In the split second of distraction, Hediad descends, plunging his sharp beak through the creature's chest. I have a much closer seat than I would like to the creature's mid-air execution.

Hediad roars in triumph, filling the already noisy battlefield with the sound of his victory.

CHAPTER FORTY-ONE: JAMIE

E nergy surges through me. The force of what I've been able to do—blocking Almus' assault, trapping Lia waist deep in the ground—ripples around me, swooping up to the birds and through every fiber of my arms and legs. Is this what it's like to feel your own Intention? Is this what it's like to be powerful? It's almost enough to make me believe I could perform acts of magic on my own, but every time I follow the flow of Intention, I confirm that it's a trick.

From above on the third floor, Petra sends fragments of my house flying at the two Changelings rushing Amby in front of the porch. Ora does her best to keep them away as well, and for the moment the area near the front door is locked in a stalemate.

I drop to the ground as a row of jagged disks flies toward me. The sandy-haired Changeling, Ren, sends half a dozen disks at me, most disappearing into the trees overhead. His final one is perfectly aimed, and only a blast of air at the last moment sends the blades into the dirt. I rise as he prepares to throw again, then I see Callie, arm outstretched. The blades veer off course as soon as Ren throws them, twisting into a vortex around him. He screams in rage as the air becomes a riot of metal. Callie pushes harder, but the disks spiral upward, narrowly missing Nikki as she passes on her wind-steed.

In the moment of distraction, I see Collin and Jason passing into the rubble of the living room, making for the back stairs. Petra is alone up there.

"Callie!" I shout. I wave and she sees the two Changelings moving to corner Petra. She sprints toward me and releases the disks. They spin out of control, shredding roof shingles and smashing one of the last intact windows.

Hediad shrieks overhead as Callie reaches me, and I read Nikki's intentions a second before she makes her move. A shroud of purple dust rises from our feet. The illusion is ten feet tall and at least fifty wide. It cuts us off completely from Ren and the rest of the battle. We dash to follow Collin and Jason, looking like we've teleported as the illusion falls and we're no longer there.

"You alright?" I say as we climb the stairs.

"Somewhat, yeah," Callie says. A cut stripes one cheek, and the ends of her black hair cling to it, but otherwise she is unhurt. "How are your birds doing?"

"They're holding up," I say with more confidence than I feel. Everything I do drains them.

"It would've been fun to visit you here. You know, back when it was actually a house."

"What, I can't invite you back to my rubble pile?"

"So romantic."

We stop as we come to the top of the stairs. The back staircase comes out on a narrow bedroom Paolo and I never quite knew what to do with. It's currently mostly boxes surrounding an ancient LCD TV and a mildewy futon.

A ball of Intention streaks our way. It smashes into the door-frame with a bang as we deflect it. Jason stands in the center of the room. He's shorter than I am, and has his hair cropped close over muscular temples.

"The boy with the birds," he says. He shows no fear at being outnumbered as he picks his way around a box of old PlayStation controllers. "My hunch is that the birds are for show. Nothing like pretending your Intention's more complex than it actually is."

His hands glow green, but other than that he doesn't strike. I catch Callie's eyes darting around the room for something to launch at him.

"I wish it didn't have to be so complex," I say. "I'm spending a fortune on birdseed."

There's a crack from the next room. Whether it's more of my childhood furniture, or an entire wall coming down, I can't say. Jason glances over his shoulder, and I strike.

My ball of Intention is powerful, but all it does is tear apart boxes as Jason vaults on top of the futon next to him. His Organic-augmented motions are unfathomably quick as he leaps from the futon directly in front of us, and puts out his hands, two fingers on each hand pointed.

Vines burst from the doorframe beside us, ensnaring our legs and arms. I gasp as the vines pull at me, any thought of defending myself forgotten as I struggle not to be ripped limb from limb.

Callie screams. Jason walks calmly forward. The vines continue to curl tighter and tighter. My shin feels like it's about to crack in half.

"Not much Organic between you, huh?" he says.

Tighter and tighter.

I try to pull anything off my birds, but they're crashing around the room in a haywire swarm.

A vine shoots down from my arm to wrap around my neck. I can feel resistance—Callie must be doing something at least—but the vines continue to grow, chafing the razor burn on my neck.

Breathing is becoming a terrible effort. I cough, but it's airless. Jason's temple throbs as he winds his vines even tighter. We are now fully suspended in the doorframe, arms outstretched. The vines have become so thick there is no differentiation between those that hold me and those that hold Callie.

I'm helpless. I groan, but the words are insensible.

One Changeling, one missed step, and we're trapped. I feel consciousness beginning to slip away. As I do, I can sense Callie's presence beside me. She radiates panic, pain, but also a deep solace in being by my side in what could be our final moments.

For a second, I don't recognize the figure behind Jason. The freckles scattering her pointed face are clearly visible, though, as she approaches silently.

Petra winds up and kicks the back of Jason's knee as hard as she can. He's a stocky guy, but he goes down fast. The vines loosen. No sooner do they release us than they stream toward Jason. Petra puts all of her Organic into directing them straight at their creator. She doesn't bother with precision. The vines strike Jason with the force of a charging bull, crashing so hard that they break the floorboards, and send him tumbling into the living room below. He doesn't even cry out.

We're on our hands and knees, coughing and fighting for breath. Petra kneels beside us.

"Sorry I couldn't get here sooner, guys," she says. "Had to take care of Collin first."

If I were to picture a warrior, it would not be this slight girl wearing a sweatshirt three sizes too big. But by her expression, the ferociousness behind her eyes, Petra is every bit the fighter.

She fusses over us for a minute, but before we're even on our feet, there's a *BOOM* outside. I realize with nauseous guilt that in my struggle to pull any Intention out of them and save myself, two of my birds have collapsed. The last of their life twitches out of them on the floor. I corral the remaining two, willing them to continue flying, and we're on our way back downstairs.

There's another *BOOM* as we emerge. Ora staggers. Amby is locked in a brutal sparring match with a werebeast in the body of a mountain lion. Its claws move with blinding speed, and every motion Amby makes to ward it off comes only a fraction before it finds his flesh.

The source of the noise reveals itself to be Khelum and a powerfully built Changeling whose name I remember being Anna, each firing a ball of pure Intention toward Ora. They bring the two powerful pulses of energy together next to Ora. The sound of her dispelling two attacks at once rattles both my eardrums and the clapboard on the porch.

We swell toward Khelum and Anna like a tide. We may not have had their training in destructive magic, but we are Skysent, and power is in our blood. With Ora beside us, we hurl Intention in a strafing line. Anna is hit but only staggers, while Khelum beats a hasty retreat toward Almus. We pass Evey's unconscious form, and blast our way through two werebeasts foolish enough to get in our way.

Wesley tugs on my ear. *Paolo needs help.* I follow his pointing paw to where Paolo and Almus are dueling at the edge of the trees.

They circle at a distance of about ten yards, their stances low, athletic, stepping without so much as a glance over dead werebeasts. Each man waits an unthinkably long time, then unleashes a blast of pure energy, which the other deflects, or turns into a counterattack. Paolo is aiming his efforts along the ground, trying to knock Almus off balance. But Almus' feet dance over Paolo's attacks, using the fraction of a second when Paolo is concentrating on attacking to aim a surge of energy at his head.

A werebeast harassing Paolo complicates things. Twice as I run toward them, warding off Khelum's counterattacks, I see Almus almost land blows when Paolo is distracted by the beast.

I summon everything I can from my birds, not individually but from their collective will, find the wooden stakes from a nearby trap, and wrench them out of the earth. Three stakes drive into the werebeast's leg, pinning it to the ground. A deflected attack from Paolo knocks it senseless.

My legs shake. As I near, I feel the drained energy of my two remaining birds. I pull whatever strength I can from them, and find the weakest spot I can in the tree behind Almus.

The sharp *crack* is too loud for the falling tree to catch Almus off guard. He somersaults backward, and the tree spreads itself across the hard ground between the two fighters. I aim a few bolts of Intention at Almus, but he turns them easily aside, sheltering behind the tree's corpse.

I absently think how the tree I just pulled down was the same one I broke my arm falling out of several years ago. Some sort of justice, I suppose.

Paolo steps aside, seeing the change in momentum. It is now Khelum, Anna, and Almus sheltering within the branches of the fallen tree. Intention turns to sparks that catch the leaves, and are quickly doused by sprays of earth or smoke.

We fan out. Callie and Petra are on either side of me, while Paolo, Ora, and Amby form into a semi-circle boxing our enemies against the tree line. Can it be that the werebeast army has been exhausted? Are there more snarling presences in the shadows? Nikki circles overhead.

Khelum eyes me. He appears to be counting his fallen comrades. His gaze tugs at me.

"Well, well, well," Almus says through a gap in the fighting. "This certainly tips things."

"You're outnumbered, Almus," Paolo growls. A chunk of his right ear is missing, and the blood is caked over the entire side of his face. "Leave this place. This is my home, and I will see you dead before I allow you anywhere near it."

Almus leans against the tree. His hair is still slicked flat against his scalp, so perfect it looks like he took a breather from the fight to comb it and add another dab of mousse.

"And while you're at it, give up Sampson," Paolo says. "I know he's waiting for the portal to be clear so you can start moving Sky."

Almus' laugh is so shrill I fear the birds above me will fly off.

"We didn't bring that useless idiot with us, I'm afraid," Almus says. "He will be employed in his own way, in time, but tonight is not the night for that."

Paolo frowns. There's something wrong. The portal was always the goal, wasn't it?

"This was a test of the destructive force of the Changelings," he says, indicating the house—which now looks even more off-kilter than before—and the pits in the yard. "All that's been confirmed is that those Changelings not loyal to our cause must be eradicated."

"Tonight is not the night for that, either," Paolo says. But I can tell he's unsettled. "Come on, Almus, what do you really hope to gain here?"

Before he can answer, a voice rips through the clearing. Its guttural tone reverberates as if amplified a hundred times over.

ENOUGH WITH THIS.

CHAPTER FORTY-TWO: NIKKI

The air shakes with the new arrival. A tremor pulses through Hediad, and for the briefest instant I imagine he has become incorporeal. But he's still solidly beneath me.

The figure does not step out from between the torches where the werebeast first charged. It walks instead up the gravel driveway. As it crosses onto the lawn, I catch a hint of blue framing its eyes, and realize that it's nearly half as tall as the trees around it, fifteen, twenty feet or more. Its cloak shines silver in the light of the torches. It moves at a glide, making no sound other than the roar it instantiates in my ears with its words.

I CAN HIDE NO LONGER.

The Skysent have taken a step back, while Paolo stands with his mouth agape, as if confronted with pure impossibility. Almus and the two Changelings who are still standing are actually kneeling.

I HAVE NO MORE TIME FOR YOUR GAMES.

"My lord, I'm glad you have chosen to reveal yourself now," Almus says. His voice sounds terribly small. "The truth is now in the open."

THE TRUTH IS MY PRESENCE. THE TRUTH IS MY RULE.

I will Hediad to be quiet as we circle above. I marvel at how steadily Petra stands. She looks so tiny when faced with a creature out of legend.

YOU WILL ALL KNOW ME. I AM LEONIS WINGLESS. I HAVE COME TO ABANDON THIS STUNTED FORM.

I wish I could imagine anything more imposing than this twenty-five-foot monster, but I can't. He carries a shroud of fear around him. I have to force myself not to turn and fly away. Panic doesn't stop my brain from churning, though. Something about his presence here reminds me of an old lesson in school. When Leonis was first contained, the Winged Ones trapped him and brutally removed his wings, severing much of his power as well. I can make out the outline of the stumps beneath his silvery cloak.

YOU HAVE BUT TWO CHOICES. SURRENDER AND JOIN MY RIGHTEOUS CAUSE, OR HAVE YOUR BODIES TORN FROM THE FABRIC OF THE EARTH.

Think, Nikki, think. Leonis here in his stunted form. The defense of the portal.

As if conjured with Matter Intention, Master Root's face appears in my mind. The way he hesitated when explaining the Kelluvas' intentions. The power of the Winged Ones, put to a purpose a human could not understand.

Clarity arrives with only more fear.

The portals were one of the last vestiges of the Winged Ones' power, as they alone could manipulate the space between two points. Leonis used to be a Winged One. The portal's power is his also. Surely merely drawing power from the portal wouldn't be enough to return him to his former power?

But everything the Changelings have done has driven toward this point. They must believe it will work.

Understanding spurs me into action. I streak down, knowing I'm about to draw Leonis' attention.

"The portal!" I shout to my friends. "We have to stop him from getting to the portal!"

A sort of trance breaks. They seem to understand, or at least Paolo does.

I regain altitude and turn back toward the house.

NIKKI LAPUTA. COME DOWN FROM THERE.

"Hediad, move!"

Too late. I feel a terrible gnawing beneath me.

Agony grips me as Hediad's pain transfers directly to me. He hisses and shudders. We cruise toward the house, but he isn't flapping his wings. He is absent, a mere shell of conjured flesh beneath me. This shouldn't be possible. A chimera's consciousness is tied to their embodied form. But Hediad's consciousness is gone. I struggle to stay on his back as he rockets earthward. I try to conjure something to slow my fall, but the pain in my heart is too deep. It leaves me useless as we plummet towards the house, and through the wide kitchen windows.

CHAPTER FORTY-THREE: JAMIE

I cry out as I watch Nikki crash into the house on her dying chimera. The house shakes as they plunge through the windows. In the pause following the horrible sound, I lock eyes with Khelum. Contempt and pity ripple off him, unshielded. Despite the chaos around me, I wonder why I can always sense Khelum's emotions so strongly. Is he just worse at hiding them than everyone else?

As if spurred by my question, my mind is sucked forward. Vertigo overwhelms me, and for a moment I have changed positions on the battlefield. I see a frightened-looking boy, with two small sparrows barely aloft behind him. These thoughts are familiar, like I've already lived them myself. Then it's like being bucked on the deck of a ship in a storm. I stagger back, returning to my own eyes, my own mind. Khelum takes a faulty step as well. Whatever he felt before, it is now overwhelmed by confusion, accompanied by a delicious touch of fear. I try to keep my own fear at bay.

He follows the fear with a blast of Intention, and the fighting begins anew.

With the massive figure of Leonis marching beside them, our enemies are possessed with a frenzied energy. I deflect several attacks, not even able to dispel as my two remaining birds' will slips. Then, following Nikki's command, Callie and I are off across the yard at a run, Ora close behind us.

Paolo and Almus have renewed their battle, while Petra struggles to control the flailing branches that she uses to keep Anna in place. As they fight, Khelum breaks free.

Khelum's Intention thrums toward us. We spin, and only with Callie and my joint strength do we stop it. We sprint a few paces, before ducking out of the way of another projectile. I stumble, knee scraping against the prone claws of a dead werebeast. Callie yanks me to my feet, and Ora steps into the path of the next missile. The air sizzles as she turns the pure Intention into a mass of popping sparks, which undulate back toward Khelum.

They drop to the lawn like used fireworks.

In the confusion I only now see Amby, who is even closer to the house than we are. Leonis continues his unhurried progress down the driveway, but as he notices Amby, he stands totally still for a second. A premonition of dread comes over me.

"Amby!" I call out. The word is cut short as Intention—more a dart than a bolt—savagely rips the air above my head, cutting short the life of one of my birds. The last one barely flies.

Then Leonis unleashes his force, and half the yard churns into the air. We tumble into the dirt.

The concussion clears my ears of all except a low throb. I wipe grit out of my eyes to see Callie already springing to her feet beside me. Amby is wedged between the gutter and the eaves on the roof above the porch—or what's left of the porch. His arm moves vaguely. Dirt and sod coat every inch of the house, and is piled so high in the kitchen that I almost can't see where the window used to be.

A furrow twenty yards wide and at least half as deep cleaves the yard. Leonis slides down into it as if it were a ramp built for his personal transportation.

I don't know where this strength comes from. Maybe it's Callie beside me. Her eyes meet mine. Behind the fear, and the blood and mud that coats her face, there is the warmth that was the first thing I noticed when I met her in Homestead. Even through the heat of battle and the smoky air, I catch the trace of a smile on Callie's face.

As Leonis dips out of view, we run like we've never run before.

"I need to get to the portal," Ora calls through gritted teeth as she deflects Khelum's ever more desperate attacks.

"Obviously, we have to keep him from getting there," I say.

"No, I need to destroy it," Ora says.

"That'll kill you," Callie says.

"The Gift came from Leonis himself," Ora says. "Only fitting that it should stop him from ascending to his full power."

"There has to be another option," I say.

But there isn't. Leonis rises from the trench as my feet hit the shredded wood that used to be the porch steps. He is a force of inevitability, and we don't stand a chance against him.

"That thing is an insult to my ancestors, to The Winged Ones," Ora says. "I'll do what I have to."

An angry roar comes from behind us, and I watch in awe as Khelum leaps from twenty feet away, his muscles contracting with an unmistakable blue flash of Intention. He streaks toward us. I brace myself as he barrels directly into me, and together we roll through the open front door, carom off the coat rack—which falls behind us—and settle with him on top of me, holding my arms against the floor.

For the second time I feel the wind leaving my body. Khelum is far larger than me, and could probably choke the life out of me without much difficulty. Instead, his hand closes over the last of my birds. It chirps weakly. Khelum squeezes.

"I guess that's that," he says. I stare up into hollow brown eyes. His curly black hair is almost gray because of all the debris, but even a thick smear of mud can't hide his stark, handsome features. "Come on Jamie, just wait it out here with me. It'll be over soon. You don't need to get hurt more than you already are."

I squirm, but I feel like a mouse trapped under a cat's paw. If I wriggle even one limb free, it will only be for Khelum's amusement.

A blur propels through the doorway, and in the second before it strikes, I catch the outline of tattooed wings and resolute aileth eyes.

Ora tackles Khelum, and much like we tumbled moments ago, they tumble down the hallway. They come to their feet directly in front of the cellar door.

Then Ora launches herself forward with her wings, and kicks Khelum through it.

He screams in bursts as he careens down the stairs.

Whatever his state, Ora will have to go past him to get to the portal. I see Callie standing in the doorway, facing the yard. Framed over her shoulder is the silver mass of Leonis.

"Go," Callie says. "I'll give you time."

"Callie," I say, taking a first step toward her.

"No, Ora needs your help. She was right, we have to blow it up."

I know she's right. Ora will need Khelum distracted if she's going to use The Gift, and powerless as I am, I can at the very least provide that distraction.

"See you on the other side, Callie," I say as I turn toward the cellar door.

I catch one last glimpse over my shoulder of Callie standing with feet apart, facing down Terraltum's most powerful being. I almost think I see a smile on Leonis' hardened features. Then all becomes light, and the only thing I can see is Callie's silhouette, being plunged into a veritable ocean of brilliant white.

And I plunge into darkness. I run down the stairs and pass through Paolo's study without a sign of Khelum. There are no animals down here to tether off of. There's only me and my lack of Intention. The secret passage is open, the shelf that serves as a door standing at a crooked angle. Beyond I hear echoes of fighting.

Khelum is shockingly agile for someone who just got kicked through a door and fell down a flight of stairs. His attacks smash urns and send pieces of armor and weapons flying as Ora dodges along one wall. I run down the central walkway, almost slipping a couple of times over the wet stones. I pick up the nearest projectile to hand, the helmet from Paolo's battle armor, which has a scorch mark in the center of the breastplate. At fifteen yards, I hurl it at Khelum's head with all my force, feeling something unpleasantly like a pop in my shoulder.

He's so surprised by my presence that he barely ducks in time, and the metal catches his shoulder on the way by. He staggers.

"Gotta watch out for the flying objects, my dude," I say.

"Immediately before I rip your throat out doesn't seem like the best time to be making jokes," he snarls.

A pure current of thought comes from him. *I can't believe this tiny piece of shit is still breathing.* Beneath that I can feel unbridled frustration. He should be more powerful than this. He *is* more powerful than this.

I wink at him.

"Guess you'll have to catch me first."

I barely avoid a circular fury of Intention as I drop to the floor. I run down the opposite side from Ora, sheltering behind cases filled with glass jars that shatter as Khelum's attacks strike them, skidding to my scraped knees, and then sprinting again, weaving back and forth but moving toward the portal.

Khelum is becoming more and more visibly frustrated, and I let his rage build as I dodge attack after attack. He swats Ora's attacks aside with contempt, but all of his attention has turned toward me.

With every moment I fear we'll hear the sound of feet on the stairs and see the shape of the Wingless. Ora needs time if she's going to use The Gift. And time is running out.

An urn shatters around me, sending a spray of jagged ceramic across my chest. Yet all I can think of is Callie, standing in the doorway, surrounded by pure white. I'm in the rearmost corner of the chamber.

"You couldn't catch me on the surface," I say. "Think you'll have better luck on Terraltum?"

I duck behind the waterfall at the back of the cavern and sprint down the smooth passage, seeing the dim light of the portal ahead. Khelum curses in rage. I plunge through the portal and am swallowed by the cold.

When I exit the shallow cave beyond the portal, I stand once again on a mountainside on Terraltum, high above a river valley.

It's still a few minutes before sunset here, and I wonder absently as I run, where geographically the invisible world is hovering.

I wade through deep snow. In my jeans and sneakers, it doesn't take long before my legs are completely soaked. Khelum runs behind me, but he must have been thrown off by the portal, because the distance between us has widened. I look back in time to dodge a ray of light aimed at my head.

I have never been a great runner, but everything inside me gives me strength. I don't know where I'm going, only that I have to escape.

Snow, as far as the eye can see.

Khelum's Intention whistling over my head, burying itself with a hiss in the snow. His anger is a blazing fire behind me.

Two conjured birds, smaller than deathcrows but with similarly evil features and sharp talons, swoop toward me.

Can he have made such a mistake? I stop in my tracks and search the air in front of the birds, trying to find their threads of Intention. There. I pull it from the one on my right, directing it toward Khelum...

The bird stops and shrieks. A splitting pain rips through my skull. My mind loses shape, falling momentarily into desperate confusion as the bird explodes in a shower of sparks.

I am running again, but now the other bird bears down. Its wings cut the air, not slowed by the snow like I am.

Wesley makes a noise on my shoulder, and points with his paw toward a dark hole in the side of the slope, where a gap in the snow reveals the entrance to a cave. A magnetic pull of Intention comes from the opening.

The Caves of Meluin.

Icicles collect like fangs at the crest of the narrow entrance. A faint glow comes from the stone inside. Taking a deep breath as if preparing to plunge into cold water, I enter the cave.

The walls of the tight passage are perfectly smooth, and glow a dull blue. It's warmer in here, both because it's out of the wind, and because the stones give off their own heat. Intention crackles in the air. The power of this place is unmistakable.

I spin in time to see the bird rocket inside. It dissolves into nothingness in the air with a sound like shattering glass, rent into pieces by the cave's Intention.

Khelum is not a conjured creature, though, and he's not far behind.

I follow the narrow passage for about a hundred feet before reaching the first fork. I take a left into a tunnel that plunges steeply downward. I make a mental note of the turn.

At the bottom of the slope, I hear a voice. My stomach flips.

"Jamie, my brother, where are you?" He speaks from the fork in the passage, out of sight but too near for comfort.

I slow my footsteps to make as little noise as possible. Another dim light suddenly fills the passage. I hear the crunching footfalls of heavy boots coming downward, and my heart sinks. He's guessed right. I quicken my pace, but as I do, my feet scuff the floor.

Khelum's pace quickens.

Abandoning all hope of stealth, I run. Over a flat area, past two turns and to another fork.

I follow an instinct, turning left instead of right.

I hear Khelum pull up short at the divergence. Hearing my racing footsteps, he plunges into the passage after me, his flickering light sending shadows down the blue walls.

"Lead on!" Khelum shouts. "I've always wanted to play hide-and-seek with my brother."

"Glad I could be part of your emotionally stunted fantasy," I shout back.

"I forgot to mention that the loser ends up with their head smashed in."

"Dude, why couldn't you just be normal? I always thought it would be nice to have a brother too, but you're seriously making me reconsider."

"There's another option."

I whirl to the right, and then take a left. I'm completely turned around. Khelum is gaining. A million thoughts race within me, and for the first time I really think about how little I want to die.

"The other option is that you join the side that's going to win," Khelum says. "That tethering trick is pretty cool. I'll let you live if you teach it to me."

"I'm really not into the idea of helping a murderous bunch of assholes get power. So, while I completely respect your decision to be one of said murderous assholes, I have to politely decline. What do you think is gonna happen if you win? Do you think Leonis actually cares about you or the Kelluvas?"

"We could be real brothers," he continues, his voice close. I pull up short. The passage has suddenly become a solid wall. I backtrack, but before I can reach the previous turn, Khelum's imposing figure stands in my way. His hands glow with conjured light, but he lets it die out, leaving us in the cave's natural blue dimness.

"Got you." He smiles broadly and steps forward, with enough caution to suggest he still doesn't believe I'm completely powerless. "I was serious about my offer." He stops ten feet away. "We could be brothers, united in the common cause of *Terramundus*. I'd really prefer not to kill you."

"Can I ask you something, Khelum?"

He seems taken aback that I know his name.

"I was raised by Paolo. I spent my childhood searching for magical creatures in the woods, learning the best parts of the magical world. What was childhood with the Kelluvas like?"

"Your childhood sounds pleasant," he says, "but also explains why you're so weak. While you were wandering the forest, I was learning to unleash this gift we've been given."

Fire springs from his hands. He swings his arm in a dazzling arc, creating a ring of fire around the edges of the passage. It winks out, and all heat is sucked out of the air. I find myself shivering until the cave's warmth slowly returns.

"If Leonis hadn't gotten to them, I would have killed your friends myself," Khelum says.

I don't hesitate before charging forward. There's no Intention in what I want to do to him. I want to bash his skull against a rock, to pummel his throat with my fist until his breath comes in a wheeze.

But with an easy wave of his hand, I stumble backwards, almost locked in place.

"I could help you unlock the same power. The potential is there. I've seen what you can do through tethering. Imagine if you could wield the same power unaided? You could become as powerful as I am. Maybe more so."

He's stepping forward slowly, and there's a current I didn't expect in his voice. He's pleading with me. Khelum doesn't want to kill me. He believes he's making me a fair offer, and there's a good chance that if I said yes, he would honor it fully.

But he's made the wrong assumption, the assumption that I'm motivated by the same things he is. For him, power is an end in itself. I have never desired power, other than what I could use to defend myself and those around me.

Use me, Wesley says. *It's our only chance.*

Run, Wesley, find your way out. Tell Paolo what happened.

I will not let you die.

One of us can make it out of here. Return to your people.

I block out his complaints and step toward Khelum. Wesley doesn't leave my side.

"So, what, you want me to work for the Kelluvas? I've seen enough werebeasts to know that's not the team I want to be playing for."

Frustration grows in Khelum, vibrating into my consciousness.

"This isn't about Kelluvas or Laputas. The houses of Terraltum are mere pieces in a wider game. One house rises to power, another falls, and the cycle begins again. There are forces beyond the petty families, which the arrogant lords of Terraltum have forgotten. When all this is over, there won't even *be* a Terraltum and a surface. All will be one."

"That's some means-to-an-end horseshit."

Khelum's eyes travel to the roof, likely wishing there was a saner version of me up there.

"Our war is already won."

"If you win this war, I hope you remember the price you've paid in the blood of your brothers and sisters, all for people who've never even seen you as a person."

His frustration spills over. The flow of his emotions nearly overwhelms me. He is furious at me for rebuffing him. Hatred and love mingle unsettlingly in his thoughts about the Kelluvas, and the powers they fight for. There is hatred and love in his thoughts toward me as well, and I can tell that, although he is fully prepared to kill me, he doesn't want to if he can avoid it.

As I dig deeper into his thoughts, I fall out of my own consciousness. The passage becomes a blue blur. I stumble, but before I fall, I lose all sensation.

For a split second I am nothing, a formless entity without mind.

And then I am staring at myself through Khelum's eyes. With some satisfaction, I note that my face looks less scared than I felt. But it quickly changes and my own voice, so alien to me when not filtered through my own ears and the bones in my face, comes out of my body on the other side of the tunnel in a whisper.

"What did you do?"

The hands of the body I am occupying tremble. I note the rough calluses on Khelum's palms.

"This is unexpected," I say in Khelum's voice. He quivers in my body. Wesley dashes madly back and forth between us.

But I am not scared. As strange as this sensation is, I feel at home in this body, in this mind. It's as if I was meant to inhabit it. The residual thoughts are oddly comprehensible, as if they were thoughts I could've had myself, but never did.

I know this won't last, though. Already I sense how tenuous my hold is. My own face is stricken with pure panic, but so far Khelum hasn't been able to do anything in my body.

"Khelum, you said I could be powerful," I say, enjoying the strong, low tone that comes from my throat. I notice the muscles of my chest. It'll be a bit of a letdown returning to my own scrawny body.

"I already am powerful, and like it or not there is some bond between us. I can't explain it. It's more powerful than the simple bond between all the Changelings—we call ourselves Skysent, but we're all the same in the end, all Changelings. From the point when I saw you in the forest, I could feel your thoughts stronger than anyone else's."

"This is beyond the worst magic the Kelluvas could ever dream up."

"I agree. Want to know the scariest part?"

My scared face tells me that no, Khelum doesn't want to hear the scariest part. I supply it anyway.

"I don't even have to try to do this. It just happens."

"All that time in your little forest, Paolo was really creating a monster in the woods."

"That might be the only thing he and Almus have in common."

I step forward and place a hand on Khelum's bony shoulder. Is my body really this fragile? He flinches away.

"I'm going to leave now. I don't think you'll be able to stop me. In any case, I don't advise trying. I might accidentally do something like this again, and I can tell your mind isn't up to another go-around."

I rub my hand over my occupied body's strong forearm.

"Goodbye, Khelum. I'm sure we'll see each other again before *Terramundus* comes."

I walk forward to where the passage stops. He backs away from me, toward the exit. I grab onto the thoughts coming from my own mind, and with a force and sound like a thunderclap I return to my own body.

It's like being hit with a defibrillator. For a second I fear I will lose consciousness, but some last reserve gives me strength. The same cannot be said for Khelum. He doubles over, retching onto the wall of the cave and slumping to his knees, unable even to turn his head. His moans of agony follow me as I run back up the passage.

Wesley scampers up my leg and onto my shoulder. Khelum's cries tell me that he's in no state to follow.

To my surprise, I remember every turn I took, every twist burned into my memory by fear. My spine tingles, and a laugh comes unbidden to my lips. Pure animal elation roars over me. Nothing about my situation should be making me this happy, but the rush of what I just did strikes me in a manic wave.

A half dozen more turns fly by, and I emerge from the cave. The wind blows more strongly. Night has fallen over the mountain, but the snow reflects the light of the moon. I still feel Khelum's anguish through the rocks of the cave.

No, Khelum's pain isn't coming from the cave. It's coming directly from his mind. I've widened the connection between us, and it will be a long time before it closes again.

I run as fast as I can toward the portal, following the deep tracks of Khelum's pursuit. If Ora was successful, it won't be there anymore. But I have to know. Part of me hopes she failed, that we somehow won the fight anyway.

But if she did fail, the more likely outcome is that I will return to a destroyed home where Paolo and all my friends have been slaughtered. I wish I hadn't been so harsh with him the last time we spoke.

No light illuminates the cave. Before, the portal cast a shimmering haze over the rough-hewn rock a few feet in front of it.

The portal is gone.

Does this mean Leonis successfully merged with it, and grew even more powerful? Or did Ora sacrifice herself with the Gift of the Ailethier and destroy it?

My entire life lies behind that wall. Paolo, my home, the only human friends I've ever really had. I can't even confirm whether Callie is alive. What did that blinding light around her mean? My shoulders ache.

I step back, my eyes searching every inch of the cave for another portal, another way out of this world. But the cave is as ordinary as any other, its stone as solid and impenetrable as stone ought to be.

At that moment the cold truly strikes me. Now the wind carves straight through my chest, an icy reminder of how very far from home I am. I may have survived, but no magic I'm capable of will allow me to reopen the portal.

I walk back into the snow, and direct my gaze down the mountainside. For the first time I notice a path that carves along the edge of the cliffs. I can also see that, because of the steepness of the descent, the snow peters out before long, replaced by scruffy vegetation with only a dusting of frost over it.

I exchange a glance with Wesley. He gazes down into the valley below, and I sense his excitement. Whatever the circumstances that have brought us here, this is still his home.

I make my way through the deep snow to the head of the trail. I slip a few times, but catch myself before plunging fully into the snow. I hope it will not be so cold once the snow thins. That thought keeps me going.

Half sliding, half walking, I reach the grooved path. The snow is still deep here, but along the trail the lower layers of snow have been packed down slightly, so that rather than coming up to my waist, it only reaches my knees.

As I trudge, I keep glancing back up the slope to the mouth of the cave where I left Khelum, my eyes tuned to his outline against the gray of the snow. A couple times I think I see movement that turns out to be nothing more than the wind tossing a drift.

Wesley pats me reassuringly on the shoulder, and I run a finger over his gray-blue head. I'm glad he's with me, at least. I plunge forward.

"Wesley, do you think they'll be alright?" I say through already labored breaths.

"We have to hope that the Ora's stasis will prevent them from killing each other," Wesley says. The unspoken fact is, even if the portal breaks down, we don't know that there will be any stasis to save them.

"We're just kids, Wesley." I should be angry. But the deepest part of me feels sadness, sadness at the ability of people to hurt and kill one another. Those killing and dying in the rubble of my childhood home are all human, capable of love and empathy.

That's the heart of my sadness, that all of them should know better, that no cause is worth harming anyone. My tears freeze almost instantly on my cheeks.

"You're not a kid anymore after today," Wesley says.

It's true, and it sucks.

After a few minutes, I fall into a rhythm, looking over my shoulder less frequently, allowing my numb feet to find their own way forward. My gaze rests instead on the valley beyond. Its beauty serves only as another reminder that I am a stranger here, and I must face whatever lies ahead with no knowledge and only the assistance of a trilopex and my own meager Intention.

I plunge onward, trying to ignore a prickling that I now worry is frostbite on my hands and face.

Then I make out shapes and hear voices coming from a couple hundred yards downhill on the path. I stop and look for a hiding place, but there's no shelter here, other than perhaps the snow itself. The voices grow nearer. It's a party of ten or more people, moving swiftly. They've already seen me, and rush up toward me with excited shouts.

I don't try to hide. I don't have the energy. I stop and wait for them, up to my shins in snow, my nose frozen, not knowing whether they are friend or foe, but hoping that all my struggles weren't for nothing.

CHAPTER FORTY-FOUR: NIKKI

T he last thing I saw before time itself ceased to have any meaning was a demon out of the scariest folk stories. The height of four ordinary people, with blazing blue eyes. His feet had just crossed the threshold, past where Callie lay motionless, falling only moments before as all the light in the world was sucked into her. When The Gift struck Leonis, I thought I could see his large shoulders sag ever so slightly, in something like a sigh, before his silver-clad body dissolved into mist.

For exactly three seconds, I allowed myself to believe that he was dead. Those three seconds were some of the most wonderful, and most naïve, of my life.

There is nothing to do in stasis but think. The Gift of the Ailethi-er is tremendous fodder for folk stories, where a young prince or princess gets snared in the pocket of timelessness for years, and during that time works out the solution to every problem their kingdom faces, emerging ready to overthrow the aileth queen who trapped them and save the society that had been in decline during their years away.

The reality is far more painful. A couple minutes after Jamie charged down the stairs into the basement, a sphere of light burst through the floor below me. I didn't have time to get up before freezing in place, a chunk of the wooden cabinet in my hand, and my shoulder still gaping where it had been lodged. My eyes are locked in a sidelong stare, catching my head at an awkward angle.

Perhaps the strangest part of stasis is how free it feels. While I can't move, my limbs are no burden. My neck, which would've cricked after only a few seconds at this angle, doesn't pain me at all. I realize the only pain is what I felt at the moment when the stasis kicked in.

And that is substantial. Gashes and bruises cover my head from where I crashed through the kitchen window, and my shoulder insists that it's had enough, and I should put it out of its misery. My leg feels as if it's made of wood. The pain burns consistently, though, not pulsing in the way wounds typically do.

Some of the nastier folk stories tell how an evil aileth would leave an unlucky human in anguish, seconds before death, creating a stasis to trap them in endless pain. Such a fate is supposed to be the worst possible result of meddling with ailethier, and tends to be reserved for the most lecherous, conniving, or obnoxiously wholesome folk heroes.

But my pain quickly fades into the background. No, it doesn't fade exactly. It simply becomes the background, the backdrop for all my other thoughts, rather than the sole point of focus.

I think of Ora. She owed us nothing. All she needed was a piece of paper with my name on it, and she could have returned home. Yet she sacrificed herself. She knew what Leonis' rise would mean. The very being who had given her race The Gift, thwarted by its unintended power.

If I had wings, I would tattoo them in her honor.

Time stretches on. I do not move, I do not blink, but this is strange only because I am used to moving and blinking, not because my body has any need for such things. Even as hours pass, I don't need food, or to use the bathroom. That's the strangest part of it, the irrelevance of the basic human maintenance that consumes such a large portion of one's day. Sitting completely still without even having to fidget is as disquieting as the fly caught in mid-air in front of me, its wings fully visible between flaps.

I spend most of the time worrying about what comes next. Did Jamie get away from Khelum? Are Callie and Amby okay?

How stupid we'd been to think we could stand against the Changelings. How blind we were not to see the force that was using them. Even without the army of werebeasts, they would probably have gotten the best of us. We should've retreated onto Terraltum and closed the portal behind us. Or blown the damn thing up and run anywhere on the surface. Maybe then we would be safe. Maybe then Hediad...

Hediad. The greatest torture of this stasis is that I can't attempt to conjure him again. I have a horrible feeling that I won't be able to, that he is gone for good. Even so, I wish I could try. I have to know whether my friend is truly dead, or if he waits in the ether wherever conjured creatures dwell, ready to come when I call him next.

Crying without tears strikes me as the strangest sensation so far. My emotions overrun, but my eyes stay dry, and I miss the release tears provide. Sadness flows through me, but it does so on a closed circuit, with no outflow to ease the tension. It builds and builds.

A wall of sadness. A wave. A damned hurricane of pure sorrow.

But then it becomes clear. There is no way out, no external force that can make the sadness go away and soothe this pain. My only path is forward, straight through the core of my grief. I allow it in, and when it rushes into the undammed reservoir of my mind, it brings not only the flood of Hediad's death, of worry for my friends, of the uncertainty of the future, but also unbidden tagalongs. The unfairness of how Master Root treated me. The fear that Petra will reject me.

And then there's the anger, the seething underbelly of all I've done since leaving Terraltum. Anger at my parents' dismissal of my path—even if they were right about the dangers it presented. Anger at their failure to save me from this fate. More than anything else, anger at the circumstances that took me from the life I wanted, the life I fought so hard for. That these circumstances have nearly killed me, and maybe still might, is merely an addendum to everything else that rages inside me.

I'm committed to this new path now. I know that. Not for my family, or even stopping Leonis from achieving his horrible ends. No, I must protect the Skysent, who've been brought into this against their will, and I must help Amby, whose love is now wrapped up in the success of our cause.

Smaller thoughts come too. Rian making fun of my conjuring when I was nine and proudly showed him the army of ants I had created. My aunt saying the Conjuring Arena is for the uneducated rabble and a real Laputa wouldn't go within a mile of it. The bewilderment I felt the first time my parents were railed against in the press, and I realized the world didn't see them how I did. All things I had managed to push away, writing them off as trivial, never examining why they hurt so much.

All of these things mattered, I realize. Not in themselves necessarily, but in the reasons behind them. They mattered because of what they said about who I was. Who I am.

I don't know how long it takes me to reach this conclusion. But eventually I see all of these emotions in their full clarity and, to my surprise, I start to laugh. Admittedly it's not the most natural laugh because I can't move, but that doesn't make it any less real. I laugh, not because my frustration at Rian disregarding my conjuring, or my anger at my parents allowing me to be banished are funny, but because they make so much sense. Because they are fully understandable and human and real.

In this moment of laughter, the stasis breaks and I laugh aloud, my voice filling the entire kitchen.

Pain pulses through my body, and the dull constant sting of my wounds becomes a roaring wave. I still hold a chunk of cabinet in my hand.

"Can you walk?" says a voice. A woman with a kind face and auburn hair streaked with silver is framed by the doorway.

"Who are you?" My vocal cords are covered in a thick layer of rust.

"Time for that later," she says, coming toward me. She pulls me gently to my feet, eyeing my wounds with concern. "You've been brave, Nikki. I need you to be brave a little longer."

She leads me out what's left of the side door to the gravel driveway. A gray pickup truck waits there, its doors open. Petra already stands on the truck's bed.

"Come on, come on!" She waves her arms at me, then helps me up.

"Petra, what's going on?"

"We're getting out. Here comes Paolo."

Paolo runs across the lawn, holding something in his strong arms. Blasts of Intention rip the air behind him. Two people I don't recognize, a man and a woman, are deflecting the attacks, which come from Almus and the remaining Changelings out in the yard. Amby runs beside Paolo, who is supporting most of his weight even as he carries his obviously heavy burden. Ora is nowhere to be seen.

Paolo staggers closer. With a flinch of dread I realize what he's holding. It's Callie, who hangs limply over his arms.

When Paolo reaches the truck, he hefts Callie's body onto the bed next to us. He climbs up beside us, followed quickly by Amby. The woman who found me in the kitchen starts the engine as the two unfamiliar adults retreat toward us.

"Stop messing around! We've gotta go!"

The unfamiliar man is short and can't be much older than twenty.

"Doing our best, Trish." The other woman is tall and thin, and a bit older. She takes measured, confident strides despite the chaos around her. They slide into the passenger side. The woman leaves the door open, hanging out the side of the truck to deflect another attack as the engine roars, gravel flies, and the truck speeds down the driveway.

A few attacks follow us until we turn onto the road. Paolo has positioned himself between Callie and the rest of us, blocking her from our view. Dirt and ash cover the cheeks above his rough beard, matching the cold gray of his usually bright eyes. His ear is a ragged mess of skin and cartilage.

Once we turn onto the main road and the attacks have subsided, Trish continues to gun the motor. The other woman keeps her position hanging out the door, her eyes aimed high, expecting an attack from above. Minutes pass and still no attacks come. For now, we are safe.

The back window of the cab slides open and the man sticks his head out.

"Everyone alright back there?" he asks.

No one answers.

Paolo says, "Thank you for coming to get us, Eli. How long were we in stasis for?"

"Only a couple days," Eli answers. "The Gift triggered all of our alarms and we thought we might have to do some obscuring. If we'd had longer we might've been able to get a better rescue party, but the stasis was unstable."

"Well thank you," Paolo says. "We wouldn't have lasted much longer." His expression has a wild urgency behind it. "And the portal?"

"I checked," Eli says. "The same temporal conflict that caused the stasis to be unstable knocked out the portal. It's gone."

Paolo eyes bore into the grooves of the truck's bed. It takes me a second to realize what Eli's words mean.

"Jamie was on the other side of the portal," Petra says.

Paolo's eyes don't leave the truck bed. Amby kneels beside Callie, searching for a pulse. He turns away.

"I checked," Paolo whispers.

As hurt as I am, I only have two thoughts: the first, that Jamie is stranded alone on Terraltum; the second, that Callie is dead.

Because I cannot bear to approach the second thought, I focus on the first. Surely there must be other portals. But no, I know that's a desperate hope. The government of Terraltum carefully monitors all movement to and from the surface. Even banished Skyfolk like me receive an official escort on our way down. Only one portal bridged the gap, and it's closed. I wonder what pain Paolo is experiencing right now. He and Jamie didn't end things on the best terms.

With the portal gone, are we any better off? The Laputan plans depended on it for communication with their contacts on the surface, but surely this is better than what Leonis had planned. Even if he is still out there.

I lean my head against the hard plastic on the side of the truck. The rumbling movement of the wheels sends vibrations through my skull, but I have no energy to direct toward being comfortable.

Petra sits beside me, shoulders slumped. She takes my hand in hers. I do my best to convey the lie that I'm totally fine with my eyes. She squeezes my hand tightly and doesn't let go.

I close my eyes, feeling myself drifting on a pulsating wave. Petra's hand is my only anchor.

The conversation around me becomes unimportant. Only pain is real, so much harder to ward off now with the flow of time reintroduced.

I don't recognize the roads we drive down, but I can guess our destination. Paolo kneels in front of me.

"Are you alright, Nikki?"

"I always thought scars were cool." My shoulder still drips blood. Paolo places a gentle hand over the wound and closes his eyes. Subtle movements of Intention course beneath the surface. When his hand lifts, the flow has stopped as the wound knits itself roughly together.

"That should hold for now. When we arrive at Homestead, Master Root can do his work. You may be disappointed in the scar department."

"Tell him to leave it," I say. "I need to be reminded."

Paolo doesn't ask me to clarify as he studies my face.

"The way you grit your teeth, pretending you're not in pain. It's exactly like your father used to do."

"I got my mother's brains though, thank the Winged Ones."

"A blessing at that," Paolo says, managing a smile. "But you have the heart of both. I never thanked you, for what you did for Jamie."

"He needed rather a lot of rescuing, didn't he?"

"He always has." The regret on his face rends my heart.

"I know he'll be okay. I've never seen Mind Intention like his before."

"That's the only thing that gives me hope." I can tell it scares the hell out of him, too.

Our eyes return to Callie's body, now half hidden under a cloak Paolo has draped over it.

When we finally reach our destination, I fall asleep in a familiar room, on a firm mattress. Master Root enters at some point during the night, but I fall back asleep with barely an acknowledgement.

When I awake, soft bandages cover my head, and dressings cling to my tender shoulder and leg under a clean brown tunic and pants. If it weren't for those reminders, I could almost believe I had dreamt everything that happened since we left Homestead, that I am still training and simply dreading what lies ahead rather than having already lived through it. I peel the bandage off my shoulder. The wound appears to be fully healed, but Master Root did indeed leave a scar, a lighter stripe against brown.

Dread haunted my entire training in Homestead, but the reality is far worse than I could have feared.

I am well-rested, and judging by the fact that my injuries now feel more like bruises, I guess I must've slept for some time. The packed earth in the hall outside is cool on my bare feet as I wind my familiar way to the Main Hall.

I hear voices before I reach it, far more of them than I expect. A half dozen people sit around the table in the center of the room. Master Root, as ever, tends the cooking pot nearby. The occupants of the table turn toward me. Paolo is there, as are Petra and Amby. Our three rescuers sit around one end, while at the opposite side is Holly. She springs from her chair and wraps me in a bone-crushing hug.

"I missed you, Laputa," she says. "Sorry I couldn't be part of the fighting."

"We could've used you."

Petra is out of her seat as well. The relief on Petra's face fills me with indescribable warmth.

"Holly, you're okay?" I say.

"Of course," Holly says. "Much better once I was able to take care of myself rather than suffering through your botched attempts to play doctor."

This ease is nice, but two absences haunt the space between us like specters.

"I heard you had the bright idea to fly your chimera through a window," Holly says.

"It wasn't exactly a controlled landing," Petra says. "Although it did provide the whole situation with some much-needed drama."

"Always happy to oblige in the drama department."

"I've had about as much drama as I can handle for a while," Petra says.

"Are you kidding?" Holly says. "One fight without me and that's the end of the dramatics?"

"If I complained about you being too dramatic that might be more accurate," Petra says.

The insulted expression on Holly's face quickly turns into a grin.

"I think we can all agree, with the possible exception of our bloodthirsty friend, that a little relaxation might be in order," I say.

Master Root appears beside us. His gravelly voice is as calm as ever, but he meets my eyes much more directly than I'm used to.

"Nikki, welcome back. I am happy that your wounds have healed." Master Root's expression conveys nothing. "You must be hungry. There is food here. Although it's not really the right time for any meal in particular, I find a hungry stomach doesn't care what the clock has to say."

Over the next few minutes I am introduced to our three rescuers in between gulps of hearty stew. There is Trish, the woman who came to get me in the kitchen; Eli, the short younger man; and Heather, the tall woman. As we trade introductions, Petra sits next to Trish, and I am reminded that Trish is Petra's adopted mother. Though her official title is Obscurer, like Paolo she was working on behalf of the Laputas to ensure that one of the Changelings ended up on the right side. The other two were banished to the surface, but remain sympathetic to my house's cause.

Quickly the conversation turns to a more somber subject.

"We'll hold the funeral tonight," Paolo says when Callie first comes up.

"She doesn't have any parents we could have invited?" Heather asks. "I mean, parents in the person who raised you sense."

"Callie's adopted father has not been seen in months," Paolo replies. "We haven't been able to find him—or even confirm he's still alive."

"Callie's family is already here," I say.

The rest nod, and a deep silence falls over the table.

I spend the day with Holly and Petra, wandering aimlessly through the mazelike corridors of Homestead. We spend much of the time in silence, each of us understanding that, though it is good to have company, what we've been through is still too fresh to discuss. We are soon lost, but it doesn't seem a problem to be lost in these corridors, where any turn could reveal a flowing stream, an impressive cave, or a pungent collection of fungus. One aspect of Homestead has changed, though. There have always been many rooms, but before now they've been empty, giving the impression of a once thriving but now uninhabited underground city. Now furniture fills many of them.

We come across a cluster of several dozen rooms, all of them with fresh bedding.

"There are enough to house a small army," Petra says. Her auburn hair is tied back as usual, and wisps fall lazily around the base of her neck.

"I didn't see anyone else here," I say.

"Do you think maybe they're going to make this some kind of headquarters?" Petra asks. "I mean for the Laputas. Now that the portal is closed, well…"

We walk out of one of the rooms, emerging into a circular central area large enough to fit a couple hundred people. A full kitchen lines one wall, along with a semi-circular table that joins neatly with the columns supporting the room's ceiling.

"Master Root can't help the Laputas, at least not explicitly," I say.

"Like he hasn't been helping them already," Holly snorts.

"I'm content to allow him his own definition of that. As long as he defines neutrality in a way that works against those monsters."

"Do you think maybe Master Root is bringing others like him here?" Holly asks.

Petra shakes her head. "There are too many beds. If I understand right, there are only a half dozen or so of his kind, and anyway, they're bound to protect the different Earth Centers."

Holly gives her a disbelieving look.

"What, you never thought to ask him about his people?"

"Honestly no," I respond. "I was too busy being creeped out by his experiments."

"I was more focused on getting through his ridiculous training," Holly says.

Petra sits on the edge of the table, letting her long legs swing. "You know I hated him for all that. Everything he put us through. I understand it all, though. He knew exactly what was waiting for us out there, the challenges we would face."

"And he still let us go out there," I say.

"He did," Petra agrees. "But he did genuinely try to prepare us. He told us we weren't ready, and he was obviously right. He clearly cares about us. When he heard the news about Callie ... You weren't there, Nikki, but he put a three-foot dent in one of the pillars in the Main Hall."

"Really?"

"Yeah, it was impressive," Holly says.

"What I'm trying to say, though," Petra continues, "is that Master Root is doing what he thinks is necessary, even if it tears him up inside to do it."

A long silence ensues. The room is completely noiseless this far underground, away from the Main Hall and even the sound of flowing water that finds its way into the deepest corners of Homestead. I can't help filling the silence with thoughts of a figure in a silver robe, a figure whose wings end abruptly in cruel stumps.

Petra must be thinking the same thing because she says, "I don't think I understand how Leonis ended up on the surface. Wasn't he supposed to be trapped somewhere? According to the stories?"

"I don't know..." I start to say. But then something clicks. Before I left, my parents told me that the Kelluvas had orchestrated the failure of the Sky Engines. I also remember something Willem had said: *To tell the truth, we don't exactly know everything that the engines are responsible for. There are areas beneath the auxiliary machines that don't appear to have any relevance at all to invisibility.*

Winged Ones bless me. The Kelluvas didn't stop the engines to expose Terraltum. They stopped the engines to release Leonis. I explain my theory to genuine shock from everyone in the room. No one seems to know how to respond.

"I don't know what's going to happen next," I say after a while. "But I want to promise you that no matter what happens, we are together. I may not be Skysent, but—"

"You absolutely are Skysent," Petra interrupts, "and you're one of us." She points to the Piece of Sky poking out from underneath my shirt. "Being born on another world and not being hatched from an egg doesn't mean you're any less our friend. It just means you're a little less strange to start off with, which isn't the worst thing."

I laugh, but am genuinely touched.

"It's okay Nikki," Holly adds. "I think you're plenty strange."

"Thanks, Holly. I am a stuck-up princess, after all."

"Stuck up or not, if we ever get to Terraltum, I'm staying at your estate," Petra says. She hops down off the table, and we start back toward the Main Hall.

We gather in one of the small rooms off the Main Hall for Callie and Ora's funeral. At the request of Master Root only he, the three teenagers, and Amby attend. Flowers cover the walls and a polished coffin rests on the table. Candles encircle the coffin, providing the only light in the dim room. We all stand, pulling into a tight circle around the coffin. The wood is clearly fresh, but unlike most of the woodwork in Homestead, there is nothing rough or purely functional about the work. Bronze clasps wind with an ornate, spiraling pattern down the side, while the top crisscrosses in a subtle parquet. I guess that Master Root made the coffin after we arrived, although I imagine that for most woodworkers it would've taken weeks or months to create.

Ora's body disappeared along with the portal, but her sacrifice stays with us.

I think about Jamie, stuck on the other side of the portal. Does he know, as he likely makes his way toward my home, that Callie is dead? Is he even alive to have that thought?

Everything about Master Root's demeanor speaks of love and sorrow. Rarely have I seen him so human, like a parent who has lost a child. I can't help thinking of his other creations. Petra's eyes don't leave Master Root's face. I wonder if she's thinking the same thing, wondering if he saw Callie as another experiment, another culmination of a recipe. Or did what started out as an experiment grow into something more? I still don't think I can ever trust him.

We rest our hands on the soft wood, letting silence build for several minutes. The warmth of the candles rises over us. When Master Root speaks, his voice matches the quiet of the room. He speaks of Callie's goodness, her kindness, and all the outward things that made her uniquely who she was. He speaks also of her ability with Intention, the fierceness beneath the soft surface.

I can't find anything malicious in his words, no hint of an ulterior motive, no suggestion that Callie was less than a human being who he cared for deeply. When he finishes, each of us takes up the thread in turn, doing our best to put our feelings toward her into words.

Nothing we say seems like enough, but we plow ahead anyway, finding new ways to express the same basic fact: Callie was our friend, and she is gone.

Then we go around the room again, eulogizing an aileth who all of us were at one time insulted by, who seemed to think she was superior. Yet who, in the final moment, sacrificed herself that we might live. I don't think any of us get the words for this reckoning quite right.

When we finish speaking, silence once again falls. We meet each other's eyes in the soft light of the candles. Sadness fills all of them, but beneath burns something else. Only when I catch Petra's gaze

423

do I fully grasp that the emotion under this sadness is a resolute-ness, an insistence that whatever happens, those of us remaining will take care of each other.

Then I feel it. Between us grows a crackling, beautiful energy. It fills the air, as tangible as the candlelight. It blooms from the hands that rest on Callie's coffin, flowing through each body, and out into the room. Tomorrow we will question, tomorrow we will fight. But now we need each other. Surveying the swaying shadows on the faces around me, I am reassured as I let the first tear fall.

EPILOGUE: JAMIE

I am not underground. After my time in Homestead, that fact
asserts itself more immediately and instinctively than even the
lingering cold, the burn on my cheeks and fingers. The bed is far
more comfortable than the one in Homestead. It's draped with
three layers of soft wool blankets, the one on top sporting intricate
embroidery of a jungle cat in mid-sprint.

I feel out for Wesley, but I can neither see him nor sense his
emotions in the room. Maybe the trilopex guest room is down the
hall.

I sit up. The room has a warmth to it, its walls hung with ta-
pestries, and embers burning low in a grated hearth. The lamps in
the far corners are clearly not electric. They bathe the room in soft
light with the faintest blue Intention undertone. There's no one
else here. The chair on the other side of the room is empty save for
what appears to be a bathrobe and a towel. I'm a guest, then. Or at
the very least a comfortable prisoner, which honestly, at this point,
I'll take.

Jamie?

Though there's no one physically in the room, there is a presence
here.

I hope I'm doing better than "presence."

Khelum? I think. But I know instantly that's not right. I can feel him, and I know that I will always feel him to some extent. That connection remains open. But Khelum is far away right now. This presence doesn't have the fire of the lead Changeling. This presence is kind, gentle, and achingly familiar.

Callie? I think. It's unmistakable, though I don't dare consider why her voice is coming from inside my own head.

That feels right, Callie says.

What happened? At the portal—are you alright.

Hate to be the bearer of bad news, but I'm like 287% sure I'm actively dead.

There's not an area of my brain that's able to process this. A flash of light from Leonis, the most powerful being of earth and sky. Callie's silhouette framed in the doorway of my home. But why can I hear her?

There's a pause. Way too long of a pause.

Sorry Jamie, my conception of time is pretty messed up in here. Sometimes I feel like I just sort of ... fade out. Her voice is far away.

Callie, I'm so so sorry.

I can feel her struggling to hear me. It's like we're on the phone but each going through a tunnel simultaneously.

I wish I knew more about Mind Intention. Every time I've begun to think I understand my abilities, something I've done, or something Master Root has taught me, has found a way to unsettle me.

Have you considered the possibility that I'm just a manifestation of your burgeoning psychosis? Callie says, and though it doesn't come with the same physicality, the way she snorts at her own joke is terribly, unfairly real. She sighs airlessly, and then gives off a warm sound that I interpret as a yawn. *I'm going to rest now. It's tired in here.*

Callie—

I'll be here if you need me.

With that, she is gone, and I am alone again.

Acknowledgments

A big thank you to my beta readers: Lauren, Brian, and Christina, for invaluable insights that helped me bring this book to its present form. I am also grateful for early page reads from Tyler and Peter, who put the tone and setting in perspective and laid the groundwork for the eventual shape the story would take.

I am immensely grateful to the Brooklyn Speculative Fiction Writers group for providing a welcoming environment where imaginative minds can meet.

Thank you to my parents (in all their various formats)—your love and support continue to mean so much to me.

And to Lauren, my fiercest supporter, without whom I doubt I'd have the resolve to see this through to the end. Thank you for everything.

About the Author

Ethan Peterson-New (writing as E.M. Peterson) is originally from Western Massachusetts. He is a graduate of Middlebury College with a degree in English and Film, and lives in Brooklyn.

For more info, head to em-peterson.com. Keep up with all his new releases and take a deeper dive into the world of Terraltum at newsletter.em-peterson.com.